Sea of Hearts

C.R. Sturgill

Second Edition Copyright © 2022 C.R. Sturgill
Original Copyright © 2016 C. R. Sturgill
All rights reserved.
ISBN: 0-9885653-6-6
ISBN 13: 978-0-9885653-6-4
DreamHeart Books
Marion, Virginia

Other Books by C.R. Sturgill:

Fantasy World

Dreams from the Heart: Tales
of Hope & Love

For More Information
& Updates:

Follow on Facebook
https://www.facebook.com/crsturgillauthor/

Visit Website
http://www.crsturgill.com/

This book is dedicated to the best and most supportive parents and grandparents I could have asked for: James & Janet Sturgill, Clifford & Dean Wilcox, and June Sturgill. I stand on the shoulders of giants.

TABLE OF CONTENTS

CHAPTER I

"Pirates ho!" a shrill voice cried from high overhead in the crow's nest.

Eight-year-old Henry Wellington stopped chasing his older brother, James, with his wooden sword and stared at Timmy.

"Are you sure, lad?" Captain Fitzgerald called back, walking quickly to the port rail on the main deck. He shielded weathered eyes from the brilliant sun and squinted at the faint speck on the horizon. "What kind of ship?"

Timmy, the skinny young sailor perched in the crow's nest, stared breathlessly through the long spyglass. "Frigate...fully gunned."

"What flag are they flyin'?"

"Black, white skull...red eyes."

"By thunder!" the captain shouted. "All hands on deck! Hard to starboard! Man the braces and lift every scrap of canvas!"

Henry watched sailors appear from all parts of the ship—some grabbing the braces and sheets and others scurrying up the ratlines—to ensure all the sails on all three masts were raised, trimmed, and filled with wind. Slowly the ship turned and gained speed, angling away from the distant frigate. He rushed to join his father, who now stood with the captain.

"Pirates?" Peter Wellington asked, staring at the approaching ship.

"Aye, sir. That's the *Bloody Seas*, captained by Captain Bloodstone—one of the fiercest pirates in the Caribbean. He's a little far north of his normal range."

Henry strained to peer over the rail at the black dot in the distance. "That's a pirate ship?" He had heard stories from the other crewmembers about pirates during their journey from England. He didn't know exactly what they were like, but they sounded like very bad men.

"Not now, Henry," Mr. Wellington said, extending his hand. "Can we outrun him?"

"Doubtful," the captain responded soberly. "That ship is built for speed."

"I'll kill that mean old pirate and all his crew!" Henry shouted, striking his sword against the rail. "James, come help me!" Ten-year-old James rushed over to stand next to Henry.

"Can we fight?" Mr. Wellington asked, ignoring Henry.

"I only have twenty men and six guns. Bloodstone keeps ninety-nine men at all times and has thirty-six guns."

"So, what do we do?"

"Pray, Mr. Wellington. Pray."

Henry and James followed their father up the ladder to the quarterdeck. From there, they watched the infamous pirate ship steadily grow larger. The *Bloody Seas* was a massive, three-masted ship painted pitch black. Henry could now see the black flag flying high above its decks. Although he couldn't discern the details of the skull yet, with its glowing red eyes, he felt an ominous chill nonetheless.

This had been an exciting journey for Henry and his family. They were moving from England to the New World. His mother had passed away from the fever the past winter, and his father thought their family needed a change. His father owned a very profitable textile business in England and felt confident it would do as well in North Carolina. After a long journey, they were only a day away from their destination. All three had been in such good spirits for the entire voyage. But now...

"By thunder, that's a fast ship!"

Henry turned to look up at Captain Fitzgerald, who had joined them at the rail. The Captain's face was pale and gleamed with a thin layer of sweat. He appeared tired—or sick.

"Tell me about this Bloodstone," Mr. Wellington said.

Captain Fitzgerald, dressed more like a British naval officer than a merchant captain, studied the wealthy man's face and then glanced at Henry and James. He mopped his brow with the sleeve of his long blue coat and sighed. "Dreadful scourge, he is. Some say the devil himself. Supposedly started off just attacking the Spanish—for some kind of wrong they done him. Now he targets anyone and anything. He's a very sick and twisted man and very unpredictable. He's bent on becoming the most infamous and feared pirate ever."

"What's your plan?" Mr. Wellington also wiped the sweat from his forehead with the wide sleeves of his white silk shirt.

"If we resist, we'll all definitely die. I'll have to surrender and offer Bloodstone our cargo. Maybe he'll be in a kind mood and spare most of us. But you and your boys need to hide in my cabin. Lock the door. If someone tries to get in, hide beneath the bed. Maybe they won't search my quarters."

"Boys, we are going to the captain's cabin for a bit," Henry's father said as he turned and walked toward the ladder leading to the main deck.

"No! I want to fight the pirates!" Henry said, stomping his foot in anger. He just had a wooden sword, but he knew they could defeat the mean men with his brother and father beside him.

"Henry, come now!" his father commanded.

James grabbed Henry's bare shoulder and helped guide him behind their father. Henry tried to shake free, but his brother was bigger and stronger. Soon they were all three inside the modest captain's quarters, beneath the quarterdeck. Henry's father left the door ajar six inches or so, and then the three rushed over to the back windows of the cabin and stared at the rapidly approaching ship.

Henry could now make out the pirates rushing about the deck of the *Bloody Seas*. It was evident even from this distance that they were readying weapons and guns for a battle. They were even scarier than he had imagined from the stories. His heart pounded in his chest, and his hand squeezed the hilt of his wooden sword. The cabin was silent except for their ragged breathing.

A flash of light from the front of the pirate ship preceded a loud roar. Henry spotted black objects sailing through the air and disappearing overhead. He then heard the sickening sounds of ripping sails and splintering wood outside the cabin door. Two more light flashes, booms, and flying objects followed the first. Now, several screams mixed with the crashing sounds.

"They're attacking!" James stated the obvious.

The sound of destruction from the deck—joined by shouting voices, screams, and moans—continued for another minute, even though the pirates fired no more shots.

Then the ship fell eerily silent, except for an occasional moan. The pirate ship drew steadily closer until Henry could see the wicked grins and smiles on the evil pirate faces. The *Bloody Seas* veered slightly and slid alongside their much smaller ship. Henry saw the many cannons lining the upper deck as well as the ones protruding from the open cannon ports on the deck below. The pirates lined the starboard rail of the upper decks, all brandishing guns or swords.

The stern of the ship soon passed out of sight of their window. Henry scurried behind his father and brother back to the cabin door and wedged between their legs to press his face up to the open crack. He was horrified to see that the top half of the main mast, along with the crow's nest Timmy had stood in moments before, had fallen to the deck, landing just before the forecastle. The other masts had sustained significant damage, and the remaining sails were shredded, the tatters dancing in the wind. Debris and pieces of canvas littered the deck.

Henry watched as the large frigate sailed parallel to their ship and slowed its speed to match it. The pirate ship was a truly ghastly sight. It was painted black from bowsprit to rudder and to the top of the masts, and "Bloody Seas" was painted on the hull in bright blood-red paint. Above the white sails, the large black flag flapped in the wind—the white skull, with glowing red eyes, sneering.

Nearly half the crew of ninety-nine lined the starboard side of the ship. The pirates brandished various weapons: cutlasses, axes, blunderbusses, and pistols. They growled, cursed, and grinned wicked grins at the unarmed sailors. Although not visible, Henry guessed the remainder manned the cannons below deck.

Captain Fitzgerald and his young first mate, Richard, stood conferring on the main deck in the middle of the ship, with most of the remainder of the crew surrounding them. On the other boat, the mob of pirates parted, allowing an imposing figure to approach the rail.

"Captain Bloodstone..." Henry's father whispered.

Captain Bloodstone was a large man, well over six feet tall and weighing at least 250 pounds. He was dressed in a long black coat with brass buttons, a red silk shirt, and loose black breeches tucked into knee-high black leather boots. At least four pistols, a cutlass, and a dagger hung from a large black belt with a brass buckle. A black tricorne hat completed the ensemble, with black curly hair flowing from beneath it. His face, brown and leathered from years of weathering, bore a coarse black beard. Two other pirates followed close behind, probably the quartermaster and boatswain.

"Arrr! Who be the cap'n of this here ship?" Bloodstone called out in a deep, booming voice.

Their ship was so quiet that Henry and his family could hear every word.

Captain Fitzgerald stepped forward. "It is I. Captain David Fitzgerald." His voice only trembled a little.

"And what be ye haulin'?"

"Cloth—linen, cotton, a little silk. And some rum and provisions."

"Open your gangway and extend a plank. Get some hands haulin' your cargo up on deck," Bloodstone ordered as if it were his crew.

Captain Fitzgerald shouted out the orders. Most of his men rushed below deck through the open hatches and returned carrying crates of clothing, stacking them near the rail. A couple more removed the gangway and extended the gangplank from their ship to Bloodstones. Several pirates lashed the two ships together with ropes, and at least a score rushed across the narrow plank and began grabbing crates and carrying them back to their boat. Several pirates stayed aboard the merchant ship, keeping an eye on the captain, his first mate, and crew. All had flintlocks or cutlasses drawn.

Captain Bloodstone, accompanied by another pirate, walked across the plank when the cargo had all been transferred. The other pirate was dark-skinned and wore a black leather waistcoat with no shirt underneath and black leather pants. He wore a wide black slash around his waist, hung with pistols, and a black scarf on his head. A black patch covered his left eye, and a scar extended above and below it. Although not as physically imposing and much younger, he was almost as intimidating. The other pirates moved aside, allowing the two to reach the captain and his first mate.

"Ye been right helpful, Cap'n," Bloodstone said. He then drew one of the pistols from his belt. "I'd like to let ye go free to sail your empty ship back to the motherland. But that might hurt me reputation. Nothin' personal, ye see." He raised his pistol to the captain's head. Another pirate grabbed Richard as he started to move forward.

"Halt, you mean pirate!" Henry was shocked that the shout issued from his mouth. His fear of the pirates was replaced by concern for his captain. He surprised himself further by squeezing through the door and charging onto the deck. His father's hand brushed his shoulder but couldn't grasp it in time to stop him. Henry brandished his wooden sword and scurried past the surprised pirates and sailors.

Henry saw Captain Fitzgerald take advantage of the pirates watching him and strike Bloodstone's arm with his hand, knocking the pistol away. Bloodstone stepped back just as Fitzgerald swung at his head with the other fist. The punch missed, but not that of Bloodstone's tanned companion. His fist crashed into Captain Fitzgerald's jaw, dropping him to the deck. Bloodstone leveled the pistol at the fallen captain's head and squeezed the trigger. The ball struck Fitzgerald in the top of the head, spraying blood and brains onto the deck and the boots of those closest to him.

"No!" Henry shouted, continuing his charge toward the massive pirate captain.

"Frigate ahoy, bearin' hard from port!" a voice called out from the *Bloody Seas'* crow's nest. "'Pears to be navy."

"Blast it to Hades!" Bloodstone roared.

Henry met Bloodstone's evil gaze as he drew another pistol, dropping the empty one to dangle from his belt. The one-eyed pirate was closer to Henry and drew a long dagger and took a step to intercept him.

"Hold, Diablo," Captain Bloodstone commanded. "Let's have a lookey at the swab."

"You killed the captain!" Henry shouted, stopping before the giant pirate and pointing his sword at his stomach. His heart pounded, and his sweaty, shaking hand threatened to drop his weapon. He couldn't retreat now, but he realized how big of a mistake he had just made. His brains would soon be spread all over the deck, mixed with his captain's.

"He attacked me, swab. Just 'fendin' meself. But I like your spirit. Ye 'minds me of me at your age," Bloodstone said, grinning.

"Henry!" Henry's father's voice cried from the captain's cabin. Henry risked a glance over his shoulder and saw his father rush out of the cabin. Then a tall, wiry pirate grabbed his father just before he could reach him.

"Do not harm my son! You have the cargo. Please just leave us be!"

"The frigate's closin' fast," the pirate called out from the *Bloody Seas'* crow's nest.

"All this ruckus be ruinin' a good day! Hold him tight. Let me have a better look at this Henry." Bloodstone scanned Henry up and down.

Henry looked back and forth between his father and the pirate captain. "Let my daddy go, or I'll run you through!" Henry yelled.

The pirates laughed heartily.

"Well, blimey! Look at this. The boy be marked by the gods!" Bloodstone pointed to the dark birthmark on Henry's left chest. "Hmmm…looks like a bird. Maybe a hawk."

The brown mark had been on Henry's chest since birth, but he had never considered it to resemble anything. Most people just thought he had dirt on his chest.

"Captain, we need to be leavin'," Diablo said with a slight Spanish accent.

"Aye. We be takin' this one with us, though. The lad be marked and will be good luck. He's now the Hawk. Turner, take the boy to Wesley."

A gangly pirate emerged from the throng and scooped Henry up. He threw him over his shoulder like a grain sack before Henry could even move. Henry yelled, screamed, kicked his legs, and tried to hit the pirate with his sword, but Turner ignored the protests and quickly transported him over the plank and onto the other ship.

As they reached the pirate ship, Henry managed to steal a glance back at the merchant ship and briefly met his father's eyes. They were wide, and his mouth was open—his face a mixture of horror and shock. Henry looked at the captain's cabin and saw that the door was only cracked again. He thought he saw James's white face in the gap. "No!" he yelled as loud as he could.

CHAPTER II

"Well, what the devil you be doin' here, little boy?"

Henry had been carried down to a small cabin on the gun deck of the pirate ship. The cabin was dimly lit from the light spilling through a couple of small windows and an oil lamp burning on a table. It was sparsely furnished, with only the table, several chairs, a bed, and some book-filled shelves built into the walls. Clothing was strewn carelessly about the floor.

The heavyset speaker had a chubby red face, gray hair poking out from beneath a red scarf, a scruffy gray beard, and a pair of small round eyeglasses resting halfway down his red nose. He sat in a chair on the far side of the table. He wore an old, stained, long-sleeved white shirt, unbuttoned halfway down to reveal curly gray hair on his chest, and a pair of baggy blue breeches. He wore a brown leather knee-high boot on his right foot. His left leg was a wooden peg extending from the pant leg.

As Henry stared at the old pirate, the gravity of the events of the past two hours crashed down on him. He was aboard a real pirate ship with a pirate captain that had just shot and killed Captain Fitzgerald. Another pirate held his father; his brother was still in the captain's cabin aboard the other ship. Now, an old man with a peg leg was addressing him. He dropped his sword, ran past the seated pirate, and dove onto the hard bed. He cried into the dirty pillow as hard as he had ever cried.

Henry heard the chair slide on the wooden floor, and the old pirate stood up and walked toward him. The clacking of the peg was slow and loud. He had no more bravado or fight left in him. If the pirate wanted to kill him, then so be it. He continued to cry and waited for a bullet or blade to enter him.

"What's that crazy pirate thinkin' now?" the old man asked as he settled heavily into the large blue-cloth chair on the other side of the bed. "What's your name, boy?"

Henry snuck a peak at him from underneath his hand, which covered the side of his face. He still sobbed, but the tears had mostly quit flowing. "Henry," he said quietly.

"Well, I'm Wesley, the cook on this heap o' boards. Don't s'ppose the cap'n told you what I'm to do with you, did he?"

"No. I hope he's dead by now!"

Wesley chuckled. "Don't reckon you'd be the only one. Maybe someday, lad, but I doubt today's that day."

"He killed our captain! And another pirate is holding my daddy. And my brother is hiding all scared in the captain's cabin." Henry turned over on his side, so he could look at Wesley. Wesley didn't seem as mean as the other pirates. He wiped the remaining tears from the corners of his eyes. "He won't kill them all, will he?"

"Hmmm. Cap'n Bloodstone's a hard 'un to figure, son. I've been sailin' with him for nigh ten years now and still can't make him. Maybe not…maybe not."

"What's he going to do with me?" Henry asked, now staring in fascination at the wooden leg.

"I reckon you'll be our swab. Cap'n must be fond of you, though. Never took on one this young before."

"What's a swab?"

"A swab cleans the decks and other such dirty chores about the ship. Hard work, but not too bad for a healthy lad such as yourself."

Suddenly, loud booms erupted above them, rocking the ship backward and forward from the force. Henry recognized the sounds instantly. He rolled back over and buried his face in the pillow. He heard Wesley stand up and return to his chair at the table.

A short while later, the cabin door opened and shut again. "Mr. Wesley, I assume ye met the Hawk?" Bloodstone walked over and collapsed into the big chair.

Henry shivered at the captain's rough voice. He kept his head buried and didn't even sneak a peek at Bloodstone.

"The Hawk, Cap'n?" Wesley said.

"Hawk! Stop your blubberin' and turn 'round here so Wesley can have a look at ye."

Henry slowly rolled over and sat up in the bed. He glanced briefly through wet, reddened eyes at Bloodstone and then at Wesley.

"Now, don't that mark on his chest look right smart like a hawk?" Bloodstone asked.

Wesley leaned toward the small boy and peered over his gold-rimmed glasses. "Well, I reckon it do, Cap'n."

"What did you do to my father and brother?" Henry demanded.

Bloodstone stared at Henry, his face lined with a heavy scowl. "It's a right woeful tale indeed."

Henry's bottom lip rolled down, and his red eyes moistened again.

"Now, there'll be no more of your blasted cryin', Hawk! Wipe your eyes and listen up."

Henry wiped his eyes and did his best to not cry.

"Well, me, your father, and the first mate were parleyin' right civilized like when to me surprise, we were set upon. A Spanish frigate had sailed right upon us and opened fire. Evil devils those Spaniards are! Me crew and I managed to get back aboard the *Seas.* But I'm afraid your daddy and brother and all the other matey's on your ship didn't fare so well. We'd saved 'em all if we could, I swear to ye, but the scurvy dogs had us all dead to rights. We fired our cannons at the mangy curs and sent 'em runnin' like bilge rats, we did. But your ship was up in flames by then."

Henry's lip quivered again, and he quickly wiped at his eyes. "But I saw you kill my captain!"

"Be respectful, lad," Wesley interjected before Bloodstone could respond.

"Ye also seen him attack me. Punched me sorely in me jaw, he did. I never wanted to harm the man. Seemed like a right solid cap'n. But I had no idea if he had a pistol stashed or a dagger meant for me belly. Had to shoot him, lad. It be him or me at that point. Just a sorrowful day all the way 'round, it is."

Henry stared at Bloodstone. The captain seemed like he was telling the truth. But Henry's mind was reeling. His father and brother were dead, and he was now all alone aboard a pirate ship in the New World. He was tired, sad, and scared. He couldn't speak.

"Keep your chin up, lad. Got ye a home right here, ye do. As we say, t'morrow be a new day. It'll be some right hard work, but there's lots of adventures and excitement on the open sea. Ain't that right, Wesley?"

"That definitely *ain't* a lie."

Bloodstone glared at Wesley. Henry looked back and forth between the two men, not understanding the gaze they exchanged. Finally, Bloodstone's face softened a little. "Mr. Wesley's gonna fix us all some supper directly now. Ye can eat and then get some sleep."

Wesley brought Henry a plate of food a short while later. "Here you go, lad. It's some rough fare, to be sure. We've been at sea for a while now, and the cupboards are 'bout bare. It'll stick to your ribs, though. You can sleep in my bed tonight, and I'll sleep in the chair." Wesley set the plate and a glass of water on the table and quickly exited the cabin.

Henry crawled out of bed and sat down at the table. The meal consisted of brown beans, salted pork, and hardtack biscuits. Wesley had told the truth about the food, but Henry was starving. He gobbled down the meal and washed it down with the dingy, warm water. He then climbed back into the big bed, covered up under the foul-smelling blankets, and quickly fell asleep.

***

Shafts of light from the small windows illuminated the room the next morning. Henry quickly sat up, blinked hard, and looked around. He was instantly disappointed to see that the previous day and night weren't a dream, and he was indeed on a pirate ship. The cabin door opened, and Wesley limped in, carrying a plate of food and a glass of water.

While Henry ate breakfast—boiled eggs, salted beef, and hardtack—Wesley moved busily about the cabin, searching through piles of clothing on the floor. He finally pulled up a stained white shirt and began cutting it with his dagger. "Once you finish eatin', try this on."

Henry ate quickly and donned the shirt. Wesley had cut a foot off the bottom and several inches off the sleeves. It was still large, but not too much so. Henry only buttoned it halfway up, leaving his chest, and birthmark, visible. Wesley then tied a red scarf around Henry's waist, picked up Henry's wooden sword off the floor, and slid it underneath the scarf to the hilt.

"Not a bad lookin' swab at all. Now, let's find you some work to do."

Henry's thoughts turned briefly to his brother and father and all the other people on the other ship—but only briefly. Wesley led him up the ladder to the main deck. It was much larger than the merchant ship but designed similarly. The ship had a forecastle, a quarterdeck, and three tall masts hung with lots of square sails. A number of pirates were scampering up and down the ratlines, and one pirate, the topman, stood in the crow's nest, high above the mainmast. One difference between the ships was the weapon racks and many cannons that lined the rails of the upper decks. Wesley said he would show him the lower decks once all the pirates were awake and moving about.

Wesley found Henry an old mop and a bucket of water and set him to mopping all the upper decks. Quite a mess was left over from the celebration the night before. Some pirates milled about the deck, and some tended the sails, but most were sleeping off the celebration. Everyone seemed much friendlier than they had when they had attacked his ship the day before, but they were mostly quiet and subdued.

Henry examined the weapon racks closer as he worked. They held many different types of guns, swords, spears, axes, and boarding pikes. He wondered what it was like to shoot all the guns. He also wondered if he could have a real sword or dagger to replace his wooden sword. He was really captivated by the big iron cannons—six on each side of the main deck, four on the stern, and four on the bow—along with the different types of ammunition stacked around them.

To the starboard side of the ship, and at the limits of sight, he could see land. He thought it must be the New World. The sky was almost cloudless and deep blue, and the sun soon grew hot, with not much of a breeze stirring. He quickly grew bored with mopping and was already hot, tired, and sweaty. When he realized no one was paying attention, he quickened his pace and barely brushed over large sections. When he reached the forecastle, his bucket was empty, so he mopped with a dry mop. Luckily, no pirates were close by to witness it. When he finished, he went searching for Wesley.

He found him cooking lunch in the galley—the large kitchen and dining area on the gun deck beside his cabin. "I'm done, Mr. Wesley," he said proudly.

"Done, eh?" Wesley turned to look at Henry. His face was red and shining with perspiration. "Guess it's time to show you the rest of the ship, huh?"

Henry frowned. "More cleaning?"

"It's a big job, lad, and dirty." Wesley took the bucket from Henry and filled it with water from a spout extending from a water barrel. He handed the heavy bucket back and led him onto the gun deck.

This deck was full of more cannons and cannon balls. Wesley described the cannons and their various components as they walked. The cannons were chained to the walls and floor, with the balls stacked behind them in shot garlands. Rammers and swabbing sponger rods were fastened overhead. Buckets of water sat nearby, with linstocks propped against them. The air was comfortable here, and the lighting good since most of the gunports were open and allowed air and light to enter. At the far end of the ship, doors led to the officers' cabins. Some of the pirates sat in the corners on the floor eating.

Another hatch and ladder led to the orlop deck. Most of the pirate crew was found here. Some were still sleeping in hammocks hanging from the ceiling, spaced only inches apart, but most were moving about rolling up their hammocks and storing them in the racks on the ceiling and walls. Others were climbing the ladders to the upper decks. A couple of metal frames with handles on each side were set into the floor. Wesley explained they were pumps used to clear the hold if they were taking on water. The stern side of the deck had doors leading into the infirmary. Nothing else was on this deck besides a few open dining and gaming areas. The air was hot and stale, with no windows or gunports, and smelled of sweat, unwashed bodies, and urine. Several lamps hanging from the ceiling provided the only light.

The last deck was the hold, in the very bottom of the ship. The hold was almost completely filled with casks and crates of food, water, rum, and loot they had taken, including the trunks of clothing from Henry's merchant ship. He thought of his father and brother again, and his eyes glazed over. He saw a few empty pens with straw on the floor inside, appearing like they had housed animals. The air was thick, hot, humid, and difficult to breathe. It reeked of rotten meat and mold. Wesley had to duck to walk beneath the low ceiling. At the far end of the stern side of the deck was the magazine—full of casks of powder, fuses, and ammunition. Wesley warned Henry to stay away from that area. A spark or flame could blow up the entire ship.

Wesley glanced down at Henry. "Watch out for the bilge rats down here. Big as cats! Once you finish, get some more water from that cask over yonder, and then swab the deck above. The crew should be out of your way by then."

Henry was a little scared after Wesley left him alone. The only light was from a couple of oil lamps, creating large darting shadows. He hoped Wesley was joking about the size of the rats, but he did hear a lot of scurrying and gnawing. He quickly mopped what floor was exposed, refilled the bucket, and climbed up to the next deck.

Once he had finished mopping all the decks, Henry wearily returned to Wesley's cabin. Wesley fixed him hardtack and a bowl of what he called pirate stew—a watery broth with chunks of several types of meat—and let him eat in his cabin at the table. Afterward, Henry climbed into the bed and napped for several hours.

***

"Time to meet the crew." The sun was low on the starboard side when Wesley woke him.

Most of the pirates were scattered about the upper decks. One large group was gathered in a circle, watching a pair throw dice in the middle. The crowd was loud and boisterous. Another large group sang crude songs as an older pirate played a stringed instrument. Several smaller groups gathered here and there, playing cards and other games of chance or telling stories. Wesley led him up the ladder to the forecastle. Captain Bloodstone and five other pirates stood there surveying the scene below.

"There be little Hawk! How's your first day a piratin'?"

"Fine, sir. Hard work, though."

The pirates, including Bloodstone, chuckled. "I s'ppose it is. Lots o' good times too. I'd like ye to meet me officers. This here is Diablo, me quartermaster. He's mean as a snake, he is, but a good hand. All the pirates answer to him."

Henry looked at Diablo. He was the one-eyed, dark-skinned pirate that had punched Captain Fitzgerald and almost stabbed him on the merchant ship. Diablo glared coldly at him with his one good eye, barely nodding his head. He was much younger than Henry had thought when he first saw him. Henry didn't like Diablo.

"And Spider here is me bosun. He can climb like a spider and handles the sails and riggin' and such. Makes sure we have as much or little sail as we need."

Spider was a short, wiry man. He stood a little hunched over, and his arms appeared too long for his body. Several daggers hung from the sash around his waist. He grinned at Henry, a grin missing a couple of teeth. He seemed nice enough.

"Next be me gunner, Andre. He be a Frenchman, and you're likely as not to understand him, but he can sure as the blazes make some bombs."

Andre was dressed in fine, colorful clothes and wore a blue tricorne hat with a feather sticking out. He had shoulder-length black hair and a thin black mustache and exuded an air of royalty. He removed his hat and bowed low. "My pleasure, Mr. Hawk," he said in a thick French accent.

"Next, we have Mr. Bones. Bones is me surgeon and carpenter. If it needs a fixin', Mr. Bones is the man to fix it. Just ask Wesley and Diablo." Bloodstone chuckled.

Mr. Bones was tall, maybe as tall as Bloodstone. He was very skinny, but not in the strong, wiry way that Spider was. His red doublet glowed brightly in the fading daylight. He wore a black tricorne hat similar to Andre's, minus the feather. He smiled at Henry and gave a little bow. "A pleasure to make your acquaintance, Mr. Hawk." He spoke with a British accent. Henry liked Mr. Bones.

"Me navigator, Hobbs. He handles the charts and steers the ship. Never been lost a day in his life." Bloodstone clapped the navigator hard on the shoulder.

Hobbs was a short, heavyset man, probably not much younger than Wesley. His cheeks were puffy and red, and he wore small round glasses. His balding head was uncovered, the setting sun reflecting off the top. He looked out of place aboard the pirate ship. "Well met, young Hawk."

"Ye'll be workin' closely with me crew here. They're gonna teach ye all about piratin'. You're a swab for now, lad, but ye'll be a pirate one day—a good one too, I'll wager. Ye'll bunk with Wesley, and he'll teach you readin' and writin'."

Bloodstone detached a sheathed dagger from his belt. "Now, take this here dagger. Even a swab needs a blade for his chores. Just don't go cuttin' yourself or anyone else." The sheath was shiny black leather, and the dagger's hilt appeared ivory with a red gem in the middle. "Go ahead. Take it, boy."

Henry reverently reached out his little hands and grasped the dagger. It was almost a foot long and very heavy. He slowly withdrew it from the sheath, the silver blade shining brightly in the sun's rays. It appeared that the knife had never been used. Bloodstone, Bones, Spider, Hobbs, and Wesley all laughed at his amazement.

"Arrr!" Bloodstone shouted as he turned from Henry and faced the pirates below. "Listen up, ye bunch of bilge rats!" This time his booming voice stopped all the noise. All eyes were upon the captain.

"This here lad is our new swab. Henry be his God-given name. But he be marked by the gods. Show 'em your mark, lad."

Henry looked at the imposing captain, sheathed his dagger and handed it to Wesley, and then unbuttoned his shirt and spread it open. He retrieved his blade and stared at the pirates below.

"That be a hawk, or I swear I've never seen one. From this day forward, he is the Hawk. He be a swab for now, but he also be learnin' to be a pirate. I gave him me prized dagger, I did, and I'm gonna treat him as good as if he were me own boy. And if anyone harms a hair on his head, they just as soon be harmin' me. Now, let's hear it for the Hawk!"

The pirate crew below started cheering and chanting, "Hawk, Hawk, Hawk." Some fired their pistols into the air; others drew their swords and waived them about. Henry was amazed. He looked up at Wesley, who reached down and rubbed his head. Henry then looked at Bloodstone, who grinned and winked. Bones and Spider both nodded in approval. Diablo met his gaze briefly and then turned away, a heavy scowl still on his face.

Henry turned to the pirates, drew his dagger out of its sheath, and thrust it in the air. The roar grew even louder.

CHAPTER III

The last week of the voyage passed quickly for Henry, or Hawk, as everyone now called him. Wesley made sure he stayed busy with plenty of chores. By the time supper was over and Wesley had read him some verses out of a big book called the Holy Bible, Hawk would fall fast asleep in a hammock that Wesley had hung in the corner of his cabin.

Hawk learned much more than just swabbing decks that week. He spent time with each of the officers, other than Diablo. Spider taught him how to climb the ratlines, rigging, and ropes and also showed him the basic workings of the sails and how to use the wind to move the huge ship. Mr. Bones taught him how to repair the damage to the hull and the sails. He didn't seem to fit in with the rest of the rude and crude pirates and kept to himself most of the time, but he was friendly enough when engaged.

Andre showed him the workings of cannons and the variety of cannon balls he could make as well as powder cartridges for the cannons and other guns. He also made the grenadoes and tended to all the muskets, blunderbusses, and pistols. Hobbs mainly stayed on the quarterdeck, steering the ship with the large wheel, which turned the rudder under the stern. He also used a large compass housed in a binnacle, a ring sundial, an astrolabe, sounding leads, and a backstaff. His job included maintaining charts on the Caribbean and Atlantic coastal waters and islands.

Hawk didn't see Captain Bloodstone very much. He stayed in his cabin beneath the quarterdeck most of the time. He would come out and make a round about the ship, talk to most of the men, and then disappear again. Occasionally, he would poke his head into Wesley's cabin to speak to them both.

The pirates were a strange collection from all parts of the world, with many different accents. Much of their clothing came from the ships they seized, so they wore a wide variety of mismatched pieces of all colors and materials. Some even dressed like naval officers from various countries. Most wore hats or scarves on their heads, and almost all wore a sash around the waist or a belt. Earrings were a common adornment. Most went barefoot aboard the ship or wore rope sandals, and Hawk was told that boots were mainly for fighting. Weapons were plentiful, and most of the men had several pistols and daggers on their persons at all times.

The pirates worked hard about the ship during the day. Then, after a steadily declining fare for supper in the evenings, they enjoyed themselves on the top decks. They rolled dice and played cards and backgammon, sang and danced to the musicians playing fiddles, penny whistles, and lyres, and swapped stories. Most drank a foul-smelling drink called rum. Hawk knew it must be good, though, because they seemed very happy when drinking it and grew happier the more they drank. The ones that consumed the most usually slept the latest in the mornings.

All the pirates treated him well. Diablo was the only one who actually frightened him. The quartermaster hardly spoke to him, and when he did, it was to command him to move out of the way or fetch something. Hawk tried his best to avoid him. He thought about his father and brother some, but he stayed so busy that he didn't have much free time to think. Hawk followed the captain's orders and didn't cry again. All in all, he was growing content with his new life.

***

As the days passed, the pirates talked more and more about a place they called the Rock, an island they considered their home. On the morning of the sixth day, Billy Hawkins—at about fourteen, the youngest pirate after Hawk—cried out from the crow's nest, "Rock ho!"

The bustling about the ship quickly grew louder and busier, and pirates began to rush onto the main deck from down below. Hawk ran to the forecastle railing to see the source of the excitement. On the ship's starboard side was a long, raised strip of land covered with thick brush and trees. They rounded the strip's tip and steered into a hidden inlet's mouth.

Most of the canvas was reefed, and they sailed cautiously into the cove. Ahead of them, large trees blocked off the water, stretching across from each side, and it appeared that the ship would crash into them. Suddenly, Diablo, who had walked up close to him, blew two quick bursts out of a curved brass horn. Hawk heard rustling from both landmasses, followed by a loud creaking. To his amazement, the two large trees began to rise out of the water. Foot by foot, they slowly raised until soon they stood on their respective beaches. At first, Hawk thought green leaves covered the trees. On closer inspection, he realized it was green scraps and strips of canvas resembling vegetation and thick enough to prevent anyone from seeing what was on the other side.

The *Bloody Seas* sailed past the trees, which Henry heard being lowered back into the water behind them. A sheltered cove lay beyond, surrounded by land on three sides. A smaller, two-masted schooner was anchored close to the beach on the port side. Their ship sailed beside it, an anchor was dropped off the stern, and the sails fully lowered. Another group of pirates, probably fifty-strong, was on the beach in front of them, waving and cheering enthusiastically.

Hawk tried to stay out of the way as the longboats were lowered into the water, and the pirates transferred the cargo up through the hatches, down to the boats, and rowed the boats to the shore and unloaded. The process was repeated until all the cargo and pirates, including him, were on the island's shore.

The pirates then picked up the remaining cargo and headed into the thick vegetation past the sandy beach. Hawk grabbed a sack of grain and fell into line. A trail wound its way through thick bushes and growth taller than him. A sword would have been needed if someone wanted to leave the trail and explore. Gradually, the dense undergrowth gave way to a pine forest. Hawk was instantly fascinated by this stretch of land. The pine limbs above were thick and blocked out most of the sun's light. On the ground, the forest was mainly open.

"There's ol' Razortooth," Wesley said, huffing behind Hawk.

Hawk followed Wesley's gaze to a large pond. After a moment, he saw the enormous alligator submerged just below the surface, about ten feet from the closest bank. Only its head was above the water, its large, evil, unblinking eyes watching the pirates pass. "Does it ever bite anyone?"

"Aye, we've lost a mate or two over the years. They got a little too drunk and wandered too close," Wesley said.

"Why don't you shoot it?" Hawk asked, still staring back at Razortooth even though he was well past.

"The cap'n likes him. Calls him his pet." Wesley chuckled, but Hawk didn't find the humor.

The land began to rise, and the soft, sandy ground transitioned to firmer dirt. Soon the pine trees gave away to older, taller oaks. The forest wasn't as open here, but it still begged to be explored. They passed another couple of ponds, but Hawk didn't see any alligators. As the land rose, it became rockier, with large boulders strewn about. Then, suddenly, the trees were gone. Straight ahead was a large clearing of tall grass, with tree stumps scattered about.

In the middle of the clearing stood a wooden palisade, almost ten feet tall and made of the rough-hewn lumber from the trees that used to fill the clearing. Square gunports were cut out of the bottom half of the wall every ten feet; a cannon barrel poked out of each. Other smaller round holes were cut about halfway up the walls and spaced between the cannons.

The palisade was three-sided. The fourth side was a rock wall —the base of a large, mostly barren, rocky mountain. The top of the mountain was flat, with only a few small bushes visible. Hawk realized that it must be the Rock. The trail led up to an open wooden gate, and he followed the pirates in, his mouth hanging open in amazement.

Six small, thatched-roof huts stood in the right half of the enclosure and two large wooden buildings on the left. Straight back were two wooden doors set into the rock, their hinges bolted into the stone. Cannons lined the three palisade walls, and muskets and blunderbusses leaned against the wall in between.

The pirates split up and carried their spoils to various places. The barrels and casks went through the right door and into a cave in the mountain. Some of the crates went into the smaller of the two buildings on the left and the remainder in the cave behind the other door in the rock.

One of the large buildings contained the galley, dining area, and food storage, where Wesley kept an abundance of dry food, fruits, vegetables, and spices. Extra fruits and vegetables were stored in one of the cool caves. A freshwater spring in that cave also supplied all the clean, cold water they needed. The island was a paradise for the pirates, and the great meals and nutrition helped them through the rough days on the sea.

One of the six huts was assigned to Wesley, and Hawk continued to stay with him, still sleeping in a hammock. Bloodstone and his other officers occupied the other huts, with Andre and Hobbs sharing one. The remainder of the pirates slept in hammocks in the other large building.

The next day, Bloodstone and about half the pirates took the schooner and sailed to a city called New Orleans to sell the loot they didn't need and buy some items they did. They were gone for a couple of days. Hawk was glad that Diablo went with them. Mr. Bones and several helpers worked on careening the *Bloody Seas* in the harbor. They laid it on its side, using the giant anchor and ropes tied to tree stumps and stakes to hold it in place. Then the pirates scraped off barnacles—which slowed its speed—repaired and replaced damaged boards and sails, and applied a mixture of tallow, oil, and brimstone. Then the hull was repainted black.

***

Hawk loved life at the Rock. He didn't have nearly as much work, and the food was fresher and tastier. A group of designated hunters, fishermen, and gatherers went out almost daily. The hunters returned with deer, wild goats, boar, rabbits, squirrels, turtles, pheasants, and doves. The fisherman caught flounder, sea bass, perch, and crabs. The gatherers knew where to find figs, limes, dates, papaya, grapes, and wild onions.

Hawk learned a lot more about pirate life at the Rock. The pirates had a list of rules, called articles, that governed every part of being a pirate, including how to divide up treasure: Captain Bloodstone received two shares; Diablo, Wesley, Spider, Andre, and Mr. Bones received one and a half, and the remainder of the pirates received one share each. Bloodstone also gave Hawk a share for his first voyage. He received one gold coin, called a doubloon, and two silver pieces, called pieces of eight. He was fascinated by the treasure and kept the coins in a small leather pouch, which Wesley had given him, tied inside the sash around his waist.

The pirates also came together and voted on their next adventure. Usually, Bloodstone made his suggestion, and everyone else eagerly approved. They kept a record of which pirates would make up the ninety-nine and which ones had to stay behind. The ninety-nine was just a superstition that Bloodstone had. He said it was his lucky number. However, a number of pirates no longer sailed at all. Some stayed behind due to amputations and permanent injuries, others because they were too old. Some stayed behind only until their wounds healed sufficiently. Bloodstone, Wesley, Spider, Hobbs, Andre, and Mr. Bones always went. The crew also periodically voted for captain, but Bloodstone always ran unopposed and was always reelected unanimously.

Hawk liked to go out with the hunters and gatherers and explore the island. The pirates were the only people living on it, and the alligators were the only things that scared him. Several more of the freshwater ponds contained the beasts, but none were as big as Razortooth. If the pirates were hungry enough, they would kill a gator, but that was a last resort. Sometimes, Hawk would wander off by himself, brandishing his dagger in place of his wooden sword, attacking any tree or bush that stood in his way. He also flung it at any animal within throwing distance.

He didn't totally forget about his father and brother. Still, their images, and the prior eight years of his life, quickly faded into distant memories—almost dreams. His new life was good and exciting. He had chores to do, but he also had much free time to use as he pleased. Bloodstone was stern and strict but didn't care about little details, such as bedtime and whether he was in sight at all times or not. He also knew that life would only improve when he was old enough to learn how to shoot guns and cannons, fight with swords and daggers, and capture Spanish ships.

In the evenings, Wesley taught him how to read and write—most of the pirates could do neither. Hawk already knew how to read a little, but only from a few children's books his father had brought from England. Now he had to learn to read adult books. A lot of the reading came from the Bible. Wesley read passages to Hawk until Hawk was old enough to read them to Wesley. He also had many other books, including the *Iliad*, the *Odyssey*, the *Aeneid, Robinson Crusoe, Don Quixote*, and countless others. Any time they captured a ship, the pirates would give any books found to Wesley and any charts and maps to Hobbs. Hawk loved the stories of adventure and great battles most of all. But he didn't realize then that he was embarking on an adventurous life just as exciting as any of the books they read.

CHAPTER IV

"Now, take the shot," Andre whispered into Hawk's ear.

Hawk slowly exhaled his breath and squeezed the musket trigger. The gun roared and kicked hard into his shoulder, but he managed to keep it from flying out of his hands. A second later, the deer standing fifty yards away collapsed.

"Great shot!" Andre clapped him hard on the back.

Hawk grinned and rushed to his fallen quarry. Andre had been teaching him to shoot firearms since he turned ten. Andre not only made and maintained the weapons. He was also the best shot. Hawk learned how to load and shoot muskets, blunderbusses, and flintlocks. Until now, Hawk had only shot targets. Now, he was a hunter.

Most pirates were proficient with guns, but they didn't really practice. Many battles ended up being fought with swords after the first rifle volley or two, so shooting wasn't a skill they honed. But Hawk wasn't allowed to fight in battles yet, so he practiced shooting. He was quickly becoming one of the best marksmen.

***

"Arrr, well, attack me if you're goin' to," Bloodstone roared.

Hawk gritted his teeth, grasped the hilt of the short cutlass tightly, and charged the towering captain, much as he had two years ago with his wooden sword. The captain just stood there, his own blade hanging by his side. Hawk was suddenly worried that he would actually kill Bloodstone. What would the crew do to him, then?

Bloodstone suddenly leaped to the side, a stunning move for someone so large. Before Hawk could slow or change the direction of his charge, Bloodstone kicked his left leg out and struck just beneath Hawk's blade and into his stomach. All momentum was halted, and he collapsed onto the ground, desperately trying to breathe again.

"Sorry 'bout that, Hawk. Two lessons. One, ye can't just charge in all reckless like. Two, ye have to be ready for more than just your opponent's blade."

Hawk eventually managed to suck in some gulps of air and refill his lungs and slowly climbed to his feet. Bloodstone stood a few feet away, grinning through his matted beard. Hawk leaned over, placing both elbows on his knees, his right hand still gripping his cutlass.

Bloodstone walked a couple of steps closer and leaned forward to look at him. "Ye alright, boy?"

Still bent over, Hawk suddenly raised and thrust his cutlass upward. The point stopped at the bottom of Bloodstone's ribcage, pressing slightly into his thick tunic. "And mighty captain Bloodstone is dead by the hand of the Hawk," he said.

Bloodstone looked down at the point of Hawk's sword and then at Hawk's smiling face. For a moment, Hawk thought he would receive the full wrath of the unpredictable captain. Finally, the big man shook his head and laughed his deep booming laugh. "Well played, Hawk. One day ye'll be too much for me to handle, I'll wager." Then Bloodstone swept Hawk's blade away with a frightening quick swipe of his cutlass. "But that day won't be today."

Bloodstone and Hawk sparred at least weekly. The big captain was considered the best swordfighter on the crew. He was surprisingly quick and agile to be so large and knew every fighting trick. But Hawk was a fast learner and pushed Bloodstone a little more each session. He also trained with other pirates who weren't as skilled as Bloodstone. He couldn't outduel anyone with a sword yet, but he soon surprised most of his sparring partners with his quickness and cunning.

***

Over the next couple of years, Hawk went on most of

Bloodstone's voyages. He still swabbed the decks but also quickly became a helpful hand about the ship. He bounced around from Wesley to Spider to Andre to Mr. Bones to Hobbs. Diablo was the only officer who didn't want his help.

He spent most of his time assisting Spider with the sails and rigging. Spider was a kind, easygoing man who liked to joke, laugh, sing, and entertain Hawk and anyone nearby. Hawk soon became the best ratline climber on the ship and was usually the one that manned the crow's nest—the topman—to spot enemy sails.

With Hawk's intelligence and reading skills, he also became a skilled chart reader and navigator under the tutelage of Hobbs. Bloodstone and Wesley told him that was an invaluable skill; not even Bloodstone or Diablo could navigate. If a navigator made a mistake and didn't know the bearings of the ship or its heading, the results could be disastrous. A reef below the surface could slice the hull open and sink a ship. Or a ship could ground on a sandbar or become lost at sea, resulting in starvation and dehydration when supplies ran out.

After the battles, Hawk usually helped Mr. Bones patch up wounded pirates. Occasionally, they had to amputate an arm or leg, which consisted of giving the pirate some rum to drink, sawing off the injured limb with an old rusty saw, and sewing the stump closed with catgut. Afterward, the injured pirate received a sum of money from Bloodstone, depending on which limb was removed, as per the articles. Mr. Bones was also constantly stitching up minor cuts and bullet holes. The infirmary also housed a good supply of ointments, tinctures, teas, and salves for any other sickness or disease. Medicine was something else taken from their "prizes".

***

They were sailing the schooner, not the *Bloody Seas*, on one particular voyage and had a much smaller crew than usual. "Hawk! Get your lazy bones out of your blasted hammock and onto the deck!" Bloodstone roared.

Hawk nearly fell onto the floor, trying to wake up and

extricate himself from the hammock. "Sorry, Captain," Hawk said, standing before the imposing man. Hawk was large for twelve years old, already showing broad shoulders and some definition to the muscles on his naked upper body. But he was still dwarfed by Bloodstone.

"Can ye feel it, boy?" Bloodstone asked, ignoring the apology.

"Feel what, sir?"

"Feels like it be a good day for some killin'!"

"Killing? Do I get to fight today?" Hawk asked, his heart suddenly racing wildly.

"Aye. Least some shootin'. Now get dressed and meet me on the deck."

Hawk quickly slipped out of the baggy tan sleep breeches and into his tight blue linen pair. He found the tight pants were easier for climbing the rigging. He tied a red sash around his waist, slipped his sheathed dagger into it, and pulled on a white cotton shirt. As usual, he left it unbuttoned. He didn't wear a scarf or hat on his head, and his blond hair was still untamed from sleep.

As he emerged from the cabin, he sensed something amiss. The ship was listing to port like it was taking on water. The pirates that weren't manning the cannons rushed up and down through the hatches, carrying various items. Hawk quickly climbed up to the main deck. He instantly noticed the sails in total disarray, most torn and some removed. Men took pieces of canvas and wood and placed them into empty barrels. At least four of these barrels were spaced about the upper decks.

"What—" said Hawk. Two explosions roared from beneath the main deck. They were from cannons, but no ship was attacking. The schooner rocked hard to port, then back to starboard. "What's going on?" he called out to Captain Bloodstone.

"The art of deception, me boy," Bloodstone replied with a wink. "Hoist the flag!" he called out to the pirate closest to the main mast. Hawk watched as the flag was raised. Only it wasn't theirs; it was a Spanish flag.

"I think this is the craziest scheme you have ever had," Mr. Bones said as he and Andre approached the two.

Bloodstone laughed. "Don't want me men to get bored, I reckon."

"Do you know how long it will take to repair the hull and sails—what is left of the sails, that is?" Mr. Bones was as serious as Hawk had seen him.

"That be why we're in the blasted schooner, Bones," Bloodstone said, his temper flashing. "Besides, ye might not need to."

"What's going on?" Hawk demanded, looking back and forth between the three men.

"Our captain had the crew move all the cargo to the port side, causing the ship to list," said Mr. Bones. "Then he had them destroy most of the sails and instructed Mr. Andre to have two cannon balls shot through the starboard hull to make it appear we were attacked. Now, I assume we will set those barrels of wood and canvas ablaze to make it look like we are burning."

Hawk stared incredulously at Bloodstone. "Why are you doing all this?"

"There be a Spanish galleon, belly bulgin' with loot, I wager, sailin' this way out of the Windward Passage. I imagine they'll stop to help a fellow Spanish ship in distress." A grin on Bloodstone's face replaced the scowl that Mr. Bones had earned. "Andre, ye be ready below deck?"

"But of course, my Captain." Andre was clearly excited at the prospect of another battle.

"Hawk, get up to the crow's nest and be ready with the muskets. Ye'll know what to do when the time comes. Aye, good day for some killin'." Bloodstone walked away, shouting orders to any pirate he passed.

Hawk's heart started racing again. He was finally going to be in a battle! He was excited and scared at the same time. He had shot plenty of targets and animals over the past couple of years but never a person. He scampered up the ratlines and climbed into the crow's nest. Four muskets stayed in it at all times. He confirmed they were all loaded and then waited nervously for events to unfold.

Hawk could observe all the activity on the decks below from this vantage point. Lamp oil was poured into the four barrels, then set ablaze. The flames were fairly small, but the sails released a thick black smoke. A longboat was lowered into the water, and Diablo and three other pirates climbed into it. Fifty pirates on the main deck grabbed blunderbusses and crouched below the railing on the port side, causing the boat to list even more. The remainder followed Andre below deck.

Hawk scanned the horizon and soon spotted the sails in the distance. The ship was a massive three-masted galleon. He had never seen a ship so big; it was easily three times larger than their ship. The wind filled the galleon's large square sails, and their schooner was anchored with no sails raised, so the big ship approached quickly. He crouched down inside the nest, barely peaking above the rail to watch the ship close. *How will we defeat that monster?*

Hawk watched as the galleon halted just before the longboat. Since his ship was silent and no wind blew, he could hear the exchange.

"Ahoy in the longboat!" the galleon captain called down to the boat almost directly beneath him. "I am Captain Cortez, and this is my first mate, Hernandez. What is your situation?"

"We were attacked by pirates—the devil himself, Bloodstone, no less!" Diablo shouted.

"And how did you escape?" Hernandez called down from beside the captain.

"We managed to get a few good shots in his hull. He was taking on water, and with the condition of our ship, he didn't risk boarding."

"Are you the captain, sir?" Cortez asked.

"Our captain was killed, with most everyone else. I am the quartermaster, Diablo." While they were speaking, the current was drawing the galleon closer. Soon it was only thirty feet away from the schooner, with the longboat crowded in between. "Can you have your men board the schooner and look for survivors? We only had room for us four. Also, if you'll throw down some ropes, we'll get off this boat before we're smashed to death."

"Hernandez, get everyone over here. The current will soon have us close enough for the gangplank." Cortez unfurled a rope ladder over the side.

Hernandez scowled but quickly shouted orders to the men on the main deck. They left their posts at the cannons or set down their muskets and gathered together behind the captain. "What kind of name is Diablo, for an honest Spaniard?"

Diablo stood up in the longboat and spat into the water. "Never met an honest Spaniard," he replied, his hands on his hips, very close to two of his flintlocks.

"Those are some unkind words for someone seeking rescue," Hernandez said, glancing at his captain.

"In fact, the only honest Spaniard is a dead one," Diablo said. The other three pirates moved their hands to their pistol's hilts.

"You go too far, friend!" Cortez shouted. "Another comment like that, and we shall leave you to die in that boat."

"I should think not." Suddenly Diablo's hands reached down, grabbed two pistols, and raised them high in front of him. He cocked the hammers and fired both in one fluid motion, one at the captain and one at his first mate. The captain was struck in his right shoulder. He staggered backward and grabbed for his own pistol. Hernandez wasn't as lucky. A gaping hole opened in the center of his breastbone. He stared down in horror and then toppled backward on the deck.

As the men on the galleon started to react to the attack, six cannons from the schooner fired. Since the ship was listing hard to port, the cannons were aimed at the galleon's main deck, despite being on the gun deck of the schooner. They were loaded with canister shot, which consisted of musket balls and nails. The deadly spray tore through the Spanish sailors.

As soon as the cannons erupted, Hawk grabbed a musket and stood. He saw Captain Cortez, somehow missed by the shrapnel, lean over the rail with his pistol pointed at Diablo. Hawk quickly trained the musket on the man's chest. Although the adrenalin was rushing through his body and his heart was pounding, he had no time to think about missing the shot. He inhaled deeply and then slowly exhaled. He squeezed the trigger, and a second later, the ball struck the captain on the left side of his chest.

Once again, Cortez staggered backward, away from the rail. He dropped his pistol and clutched at the wound that quickly soaked his white silk shirt with red blood. He turned and stared directly at Hawk. Hawk had grabbed another musket and was prepared to fire again. But then he froze. The look on the Spanish captain's face wasn't one of anger or fear; it was shock and sadness. Cortez's mouth opened as if he was trying to speak to Hawk.

For Hawk, time was barely moving. The sounds of battle faded to a distant murmur. Pirates and sailors were just blurs on the periphery. It was now just him and the Spanish captain, locked in a death stare. Cortez dropped to both knees, eyes still locked onto the young pirate's. His hands dropped. Slowly, ever so slowly, he leaned over to the side, finally collapsing to the deck. He no longer stared at Hawk, but his eyes and mouth remained open—for eternity.

Hawk also collapsed to his knees. He was covered in sweat, dizzy and light-headed, and nauseated. Suddenly, he lurched forward and vomited onto the floor of the crow's nest. He finished and collapsed, with his back to the battle. He pulled his feet up, folded his arms across his knees, and buried his head into his forearms. He cried like he hadn't since his first night on the *Bloody Seas*.

Hawk couldn't block out the sounds from the battle below. He had watched enough battles to know that the first round of blasts was the blunderbusses. The large guns were deadly at close range, and multiple targets would be hit with every shot. The second round of shots was the muskets. Their bullets would almost all find a target at that range. Then he heard the yells and shouts as the pirates boarded the galleon, some swinging from ratlines and dropping onto the deck and others climbing over the railings. Diablo and the three pirates in the longboat would have climbed the rope ladder by now and joined the others. They would quickly overwhelm the overmatched crew with flintlocks and cutlasses.

The cries and screams quickly died out, and the battle was soon over. Hawk heard Spider shout the orders to lash the two ships together and extend a gangplank. Then he heard Bloodstone.

"Arrr!" Bloodstone bellowed loudly. "Any of ye Spanish dogs that want to live can go over to me ship. She still be seaworthy. I be takin' this one. Me crew, grab all your valuables and get your sorry hides over to our new ship."

Hawk finally stood on weak legs and peered over the edge of the crow's nest. The pirates went streaming over the gangplank, carrying weapons, crates, and personal items. The Spanish sailors steadily filed over to the pirate ship. Hawk slowly climbed down to the deck below. He was weak and shaken and didn't share in the pirates' elation. He found Wesley, and they headed over to the galleon together. They stayed clear of the other pirates and started moving their few possessions into the cabin closest to the galley on the gun deck. They returned to the main deck to watch the remainder of the encounter.

Bloodstone sent Andre and a large group of pirates below deck on the galleon, and another group was busy in motion about the main deck. Soon the crews had completed the swap. Bloodstone had the galleon's sails hoisted. The other ship had now leveled off some, the sailors apparently having repositioned the cargo in the hold. They'd also thrown the smoking barrels overboard and worked on getting some sails back into place.

"Ho, Spaniards! Ye forgot somethin'. Don't let it be said that I be a selfish pirate. Mr. Diablo?" Suddenly, the cannons on the main deck fired at the schooner. A few seconds later, the ones on the gun deck fired. At that distance, they tore through the unsuspecting ship from top to bottom. Some sailors were probably killed, but those shots were meant to destroy the hull. And they were successful. As the galleon sailed away, the schooner began listing to starboard; this time, it wasn't a ruse. The hold was quickly filling with water.

***

"What's wrong, lad?" Wesley asked Hawk, entering their new cabin. Hawk had slipped back to it just after Bloodstone attacked the schooner.

Hawk lay in the hammock facing the wall. "I...I shot someone," he said, trying to hold back the tears.

"Ah, I see." Wesley sat down in a chair close by. The previous occupants had the cabin furnished well. "You never forget your first kill."

"It was horrible! I...I saw his face. He just stared at me. He looked so...so sad."

"Killin' ain't an easy thing to do, that's for sure. Gets easier, though," Wesley said somberly. "And he would have killed you if he'd had the opportunity. It was a battle, Hawk."

"Why do we do it?" Hawk asked, rolling over on his back and staring at the ceiling.

"Do what?"

Before Hawk could reply, the cabin door swung open, and Captain Bloodstone strolled in. He was puffing on a long, curved pipe, as he liked to do after a battle. Wesley stood up and vacated his chair for the captain. He went and sat down at a desk against the far wall.

"What be wrong with ye, Hawk? Heck of a shot out there. A captain, no less! Saved Diablo too, I'd wager." Bloodstone sat down in the empty chair. He stretched his feet out, leaned back to rest his neck and head against the high back, and puffed the sweet-smelling tobacco smoke into the air.

"Why do we attack ships and kill innocent people and take their loot?" said Hawk.

Bloodstone suddenly sat up straight and leaned forward. "Innocent people?" Bloodstone roared. "Innocent people? There ain't a cursed one of those Spanish curs innocent! They've killed, enslaved, and robbed innocent people for two hundred years; ye can bet your life. All the gold and silver they haul back to Spain is sticky with the blood of innocent men and women! They all lost their innocence the first day they left Spain."

Hawk sat up in the hammock, leaning his back against the wall. "Really?" He suddenly felt a little better.

Bloodstone breathed deeply and sighed. "They've killed thousands of natives that weren't even armed, me lad. Least those bilge rats were armed and on a ship prepared for battle. They knew the day they left Spain what they risked, they did. If they weren't stealin' loot from innocent people, they wouldn't be attacked by me or any other pirates."

"So, that captain had probably killed lots of innocent people?"

"Aye, Hawk, I'd wager hundreds, least had his men do it. Cowards those Spaniards are. Brave against unarmed men and women, not too brave against a crew of armed pirates. Ye done a right good deed today, Hawk."

Hawk managed a smile. "Thank you, Captain. Shot him right in the chest, I did."

Bloodstone chuckled softly. "Let me tell ye another story 'bout the bloody Spaniards." Bloodstone inhaled deeply from his pipe. He blew out a smoke ring that hovered in front of his face for a moment before drifting up to the ceiling. "Ye see, me and my parents were on a voyage from New Spain to North Carolina. I reckon I be 'bout your age in those days. We were tryin' to get away from the Spanish Main. Our ship was set upon by a cursed Spanish warship. My father and the menfolk were slaughtered before our very eyes. The women and children, being mostly Indian or part Indian, were set off to Cuba. We were forced to work in the sugarcane fields like dogs.

"Me and my mother were there for a year or two. We were both beaten most daily, nearly starved to death too. Then one day, one of the devils drank too much. He started bullyin' me mother worse than usual. Got right fresh with her; he did. Then he started tryin' to rip her clothes off and have his way with her right there in the daylight. Well, I had all I could take of the devil. I picked up a large smooth stone, charged him, and struck him in the side of the head. Blood spattered all over the three of us. He fell to the ground, and I set upon him. Smashed his skull in, I did.

"More of them dogs came runnin'. Me mother was shot and killed. I managed to smash another one's skull and then fled. I ran as fast as me legs could carry me for hours. I finally reached a beach, and by the gods, a pirate ship be sailin' close by. They spotted me, covered in blood, realized I wasn't a Spaniard and took me aboard. I still clutched that bloody stone in me hand. The pirates named me Bloodstone, and Cap'n Christopher White took me in, much like I did ye. And to this day, I've been tryin' to pay those devils back for what they did to me and my family."

Hawk's eyes were wide, and his mouth hung open as he listened to the captain's tale. "Wow, that's some story! No wonder you hate those Spaniards."

"Aye, me lad. As should ye. Don't forget they killed your family too." Bloodstone stood up and walked out of the cabin.

Hawk never grieved for another dead Spaniard.

CHAPTER V

"Not Bloodstone?" Captain Nathaniel Cord asked James.

Lieutenant James Wellington lowered the spyglass. He had been excited when he saw the black ship. But Bloodstone wasn't the only pirate who painted his ships black. "No. How can we not come across that cowardly dog?"

"Ah, it's a big sea, my boy. But one of our fleet will eventually find him. The sea gets smaller each day."

"I just hope we get to him first. I want to personally make him pay," James said, his quick temper flashing.

"I hope so too—for the sake of all the poor pirate scum you encounter between now and then." Cord smiled.

Captain Cord and the USS Enterprise had rescued James from the burning British merchant ship some six years prior. The USS *Enterprise* was part of the New Orleans Squadron and served the United States in the war with England from 1812 to 1815. They had patrolled the east coast, as they were when they found James, and fought numerous battles with the British navy. James was forced to learn quickly on a ship engaged in a war, and he impressed the captain from the start with his eagerness to learn, especially when it came to combat.

After the Battle of New Orleans in 1815, the war ended, and they were assigned to hunt pirates in the Caribbean, something James had desperately wanted. Cord helped James with his education, having him read any book they came across and maintain the official ship's log. James also quickly learned everything he could know on a ship and was soon one of the best gunners and fighters onboard. For most sailors, it was just a job. For James, it was his life. He was also continually driven by a burning desire for revenge. Just recently, at sixteen, Cord promoted him to lieutenant.

Cord frequently tried to temper James's rage toward pirates. The navy wanted to capture pirate ships with as little fight as possible and then try the pirates in a courtroom. If convicted, they were hanged. It was a good message to dissuade others from becoming pirates. James preferred to kill everyone aboard a pirate ship and then sink it, saving a lot of time and money.

Cord repeatedly pointed out two flaws with that strategy. One, if the pirates knew that surrender was not an option, they would fight harder and to the death, causing more navy casualties. Two, usually a few pirates aboard each ship were innocent of piracy. They were usually the skilled men— navigators, cooks, carpenters, gunners, musicians, and surgeons —forced to join the crew when their ships were captured.

Every so often, Cord would let James decide how to attack a pirate ship and determine the fate of its crew. He said it was part of his training to become a captain someday. This was one of those times. They were far from land, and no one would witness the battle and outcome. The crew all liked James as long as they continued to have success and few casualties. James had an excellent military mind and devised sound, although usually daring, plans.

"Well, Mr. Wellington, what say you?"

"Burn and slash. We should be able to catch her before she reaches shallow water. Let's load some chain shot in the swivel guns and shred her sails when we're within range. Load and man all the starboard guns for a broadside soon after. Every hand on deck needs a grenadoe or stinkpot, with a blunderbuss or muskatoon close by. When the smoke and flames clear, we'll board."

Captain Cord stared at the pirate ship for a moment and finally nodded.

James grinned and studied the pirate ship further. It was just a schooner. The *Enterprise* was one of a new class of navy frigates. It had three masts of square sails, fifty guns, and three hundred sailors. The schooner was no match, and most likely the pirates would try to surrender or escape. Their brutal defeat would send a strong message to other pirates that a new era was dawning.

The *Enterprise* sailed with the wind, as did the pirate ship, but with three masts and larger sails, it steadily gained on the smaller vessel. James stood on the forecastle, in between the five swivel guns. The ships were soon close enough to see the pirates scurrying about the deck. They had no trail guns, though, so they could do nothing in their current position.

"Fire!" James shouted loudly as soon as they were within range. The five guns fired, sending the chained balls hurling into the masts and sails. Most of the sails sustained some damage, and the schooner slowed significantly as the canvas flapped loosely in the wind. James's heart began to pound as the battle started. He loved when the captain gave him control. He lived for these moments—making the heartless, cowardly pirate scum pay the ultimate price. He hoped and prayed that one day it would be Bloodstone's ship he encountered.

"Hard to port! Ready the guns!" he shouted. His orders echoed through the men behind him until they had reached the navigator and the gunners below deck. The *Enterprise* turned to the port side of the schooner. With its superior speed, it began to overtake the floundering ship. The navigator had the bow of the navy ship pointing at a forty-five-degree angle to the port hull of the pirate ship. "Fire the guns!" shouted James.

The *Enterprise* was slightly behind the schooner and at such an angle that most of its cannons could be pointed at the pirate ship. Only a few cannons near the stern of the pirate ship had a chance of hitting the frigate's bow. Twenty cannons fired their projectiles into the schooner. Around fifteen balls struck the ship's hull, rails, and deck. Pirate bodies flew across the deck, and pieces of wood scattered in all directions. Screams rang out from above and below deck.

Two of the cannons on the schooner managed to return fire.

One ball sailed harmlessly in front of the *Enterprise*. The other one struck halfway down the hull near the bow. James knew no men were in that part of the hold. "Come along side! Throw grenadoes at will."

The pirates hadn't had time to recover and find weapons before the grenadoes began bouncing onto the deck. Gunpowder and metal scraps filled some of the grenadoes. The metal tore through the pirates as the gunpowder set fire to the deck. The others were stinkpots and emitted a thick smoke with a revolting smell that caused physical illness.

James grinned. Sometimes it was too easy. "Ready the blunderbusses!" The pirates who hadn't fallen ran about wildly in the smoke. Some coughed and vomited while others threw buckets of water on the flames. A stray shot or two were fired, but none found a mark on the *Enterprise*.

"Fire!" James yelled.

The blunderbusses fired their multiple musket balls into the smoke-shrouded pirates. More screams rang out; more bodies fell. Now the two ships were side by side.

"Grapple and prepare to board!" James commanded. He grabbed the two flintlock pistols hanging from his belt. The sailors threw ropes with iron grappling hooks tied to the ends. The hooks struck the pirate ship's deck and were pulled until they caught onto the rail. The sailors tugged hard, drawing the two ships together, and then lashed the ropes to the belaying pins on the railing of their ship.

They waited momentarily for the smoke to begin to clear. Then James led the charge, running and leaping over the railing of both ships. Before he landed, he fired both pistols at dazed pirates. By the time his feet struck the deck, the pistols bounced by his side, and his cutlass was in hand. His blade was a silver blur. His crew quickly filled the deck beside him.

Many pirates tried to surrender, but James recalled the images of his unarmed father being callously shot and the deaths of the captain and the rest of the good people on the merchant ship years before. He imagined what kind of torturous fate his brother Henry probably met. No, these pirates were not that same brutal crew of Bloodstone, but today they would have to do. The sailors steadily advanced to the far side of the deck. Soon all the pirates were dead, except for a few that had jumped overboard. Most pirates couldn't swim, and even the ones who could had nowhere to go.

James led his men down through the hatches and onto the lower decks. They encountered a few more pirates on the gun deck, but they didn't offer much resistance. Once all the pirates were dead, the sailors went down to the hold, quickly grabbed any valuables, headed back up to the main deck, and returned to the *Enterprise*. The cannons had been reloaded by then and were angled down at the waterline of the schooner. They fired again. This time all the balls struck the hull. The *Enterprise* sailed away as the pirate ship slowly disappeared into the depths.

"I'm glad you are on our side," Captain Cord said when James was back by his side watching the other ship sink. "That was brutally efficient."

"It's good to have the men get experience like this," said James, his face expressionless. "We barely took damage and didn't lose a sailor. They'll be ready when we find Bloodstone."

CHAPTER VI

"Nice shot," Diablo said after Hawk finally emerged from Wesley's cabin for supper.

"Thank you," Hawk replied, shocked that Diablo was speaking to him.

"It's a little tougher when you're not perched one hundred yards away in the crow's nest, though. Oh, and by the way, you didn't save my life. He'd had my dagger in his throat a second after your bullet struck him." Diablo continued past, not waiting for a reply.

A grand celebration was held aboard the galleon that night. It was a rare feat for a pirate to take a galleon, unheard of with only one ship—a schooner. The cargo was also a massive sum of gold and silver bars, doubloons, pieces of eight, gemstones, and jewelry. It was the richest haul Bloodstone had ever taken. Even Wesley wandered out onto the deck to listen to the music and singing and watch the dancing. He drank some, but not to excess. Most of the other pirates crossed way over the line of excess that night. Bloodstone stayed out a little longer than usual, even dancing a quick comical jig in the midst of his crew. This was the shining gem in his treasure trove of a pirating career.

The huge ship barely made it past the trees in the lagoon before it had to anchor. The crew used several longboats to ferry the loot and themselves to shore. The party continued the first night back at the Rock, with the shore-bound crew getting their chance to celebrate. It was several weeks before the pirates sailed again, other than to sell the galleon to the British in Jamaica and buy another schooner and sloop with the money.

The pirates also made several trips to New Orleans. Hawk still didn't know precisely what took place in that legendary city, but he knew the men came back very happy and very broke. Most of the pirates also upgraded their wardrobes with their newfound wealth.

**

Hawk continued to participate in battles over the next two years. He was still confined to the crow's nest but quickly earned the reputation for being one of the best shots with a musket. The first few people he killed still caused him some squeamishness, but he no longer mourned for them. He would just remember Bloodstone's tales of Spanish brutality and what Bloodstone told him the Spanish did to his father and brother, and he was ready to shoot again. Eventually, he no longer felt anything. However, he only targeted men attacking or threatening his fellow pirates. Even Spaniards deserved better than to be shot without cause or warning.

His melee skills were getting honed, too, with Bloodstone still his primary trainer. The captain was getting older by pirate standards but was still arguably the best swordsman. He made up for what he had lost in speed in cunning and brute strength. Hawk was quicker now but couldn't match the mental processes honed by thirty years of fighting. Sooner or later, he made a mistake or fell into a trap, and Bloodstone made him pay. But he was getting closer and was fueled by the desire to be the best.

By age fourteen, he was growing into a man. He was lean and muscular and already stood nearly six feet tall. His hair was still blond and hung down to his shoulders in the back. The pirate life had matured him well beyond his years, and he carried himself with an air of command. As many of the pirate crew turned over, mainly through death and injury, the new men looked to him almost like a quartermaster—and a possible heir to Bloodstone. They ignored his age and respected his knowledge and skill. He was also intimidating from an intellectual standpoint—able to read books, write, and interpret maps and charts. He knew the ship's workings inside and out from working with the officers. The only thing he hadn't done was fight hand to hand.

***

"Come in, lad."

Hawk entered Bloodstone's cabin on the *Bloody Seas*, shutting the door behind him, and sat down in a chair on the near side of Bloodstone's desk. "You wanted to see me, sir?"

"Aye. So, ye think you're gettin' good with that cutlass?" Bloodstone looked up from his map, relit his pipe, and stared at Hawk.

"Pretty good, sir."

"And I s'ppose you're itchin' to fight for real?"

Hawk leaned forward, his eyes widening. "Aye! That's the only way I can get better. There's only so much I can learn practicing."

Bloodstone chuckled. "I reckon it be 'bout time. Can't protect ye forever. I'd killed twenty with a blade by your age, I'd wager."

"When can I fight?" Hawk asked eagerly.

"We be comin' up fast on a small Spanish merchantman. I figure she be as good as any to cut your teeth on. No trickery this time. We'll come up broadside, fire a few rounds, and then swing over. Stay back till the first wave is aboard, then drop in behind. Keep your back to the rail, or our crew, and just fight one at a time."

Hawk stood up, trying to suppress his exuberance. "Yes, sir!" he said enthusiastically and went to prepare for his first battle.

***

Hawk again stood in the crow's nest and watched the *Bloody Seas*, which was much faster with its three masts fully rigged, quickly gain on the two-masted merchantman. He was as nervous and excited as he had ever been. He knew most of the crew respected him. But some, especially Diablo, resented he never had to get dirty in a fight. He merely stood in the crow's nest and picked off sailors from a distance. Now, he would finally have a chance to prove his true fighting prowess.

The *Bloody Seas* sailed up broadside to the merchantman.

Only a dozen men were on the main deck. Many times merchantmen only had twenty or thirty sailors and few cannons, so they made easy targets for the pirates. Most didn't put up a fight. Almost all ninety-nine pirates, except for the ones manning the cannons on the lower deck, were gathered on the main deck or up in the rigging.

"Ho, Spaniards!" Bloodstone called across to the other ship. Both ships had reefed their sails and slowed their speed. They were only thirty feet apart. "I wish to parley with your cap'n."

The man that stepped forward from the group of sailors was dressed like a Spanish naval officer, not a merchant captain. "I am Javier Ramirez, captain of this humble merchant vessel. And whom am I speaking with?"

"Cap'n Bloodstone it be. I s'ppose ye heard of me?"

Hawk surveyed the merchant crew a little more closely. Something didn't feel right. Some of the sailors wore military clothing. That was seen frequently on pirate ships and warships but not typically on merchantmen. He trusted that Bloodstone would have the same apprehension.

"Aye, I believe I have. I've heard that you are a cowardly man, though very brave against unarmed men, women, and children —a plague on the Caribbean and a black mark on humanity itself." Captain Ramirez stared unflinchingly at the massive pirate.

Hawk saw Bloodstone whisper to Diablo, and Diablo gave some nods and hand gestures to several pirates. One ran over to the hatch and disappeared below deck.

"Ye got a right sharp tongue there, Spaniard. And here I was in a kind mood." Bloodstone rested his right hand on a pistol handle and his left on the hilt of his cutlass. "But if ye'll give up your loot without a fight, I might be able to overlook your rudeness."

"A very generous offer indeed, Mr. Bloodstone. Let me confer with my men here and let you know our decision." Captain Ramirez turned to the three sailors close to him, wearing similar uniforms.

Bloodstone leaned over and whispered something to Diablo again. Hawk couldn't hear it, but he assumed it was to be ready for an attack. He kneeled in the crow's nest and trained his loaded musket on Captain Ramirez.

Ramirez finally turned back around to face the pirates. "We have reached a decision, sir."

"I figured ye'd be reasonable like," Bloodstone said.

"Fire!" Ramirez roared. He and the sailors closest drew their pistols and shot at the pirates. At the same time, eight cannons fired from the deck below. The balls from the pistols nearly all found a target, with the pirates grouped so close together. Several pirates were wounded, and others dropped to the deck. Ramirez's shot grazed Bloodstone's left shoulder. The cannon balls wreaked havoc on the gun deck and the cannons of the *Bloody Seas*. Screams and small explosions rang out below deck as the hull was ripped apart.

A second after the sailors fired their weapons, Hawk's musket ball struck the captain's head. He was dead before he hit the deck. Hawk didn't allow himself to think about the horror of the situation, the pirates falling, or the screams below deck. He quickly grabbed the next musket and fired again, picking off another man in uniform.

Captain Bloodstone roared with rage and began firing his pistols into the sailors. The other pirates quickly recovered from the shock and rushed to the weapon racks against the rail. Soon the blunderbusses were roaring, doing significant damage at that range. Sailors began dropping and scurrying for cover. A few cannons managed to fire from the gun deck, striking the side of the merchant vessel.

Hawk knew that most of his cannons, and the pirates manning them, were unusable now and that the merchant ship would be ready to fire again soon. They had to get to the other ship and neutralize the enemy. Bloodstone must have realized the same thing as he shouted, "No quarter!" and led the charge to the other ship. The pirates on the ratlines and rigging began swinging over the water between the two ships and dropping onto the merchant deck. Others threw grappling hooks over the other ship's railing and pulled the two ships together. Then they climbed onto the railing and leaped over the narrowing gap.

More sailors were now coming up through the hatches on the merchant ship and joining their remaining comrades. Hawk guessed they had abandoned the cannons when they realized that sinking the *Bloody Seas* would leave the pirates no option of retreat, and they might fight even harder to take the merchant ship. The Spaniard's only hope was to repulse the pirates, inflicting enough injury and death to force them back to their ship. Some had pistols drawn, other cutlasses and sabers. Hawk now knew without a doubt that many of the sailors were marines—trained soldiers frequently aboard warships.

Hawk fired the remainder of the muskets, trying to help the first pirates land safely. Although the pirates were well-armed, seasoned fighters, they were initially badly outnumbered as the Spaniards swarmed. He scampered through the rigging until he found a long rope which he quickly cut with his dagger. He then drew a pistol and launched himself through the air. As he flew, he cocked the pistol and shot down into the Spaniards, wounding one in the shoulder. He let go of the rope and fell the remaining ten feet, landing beside his pirate comrades.

He threw his pistol down and drew his cutlass. Then he froze, his heart trying to pound out of his chest. His legs and arms were weak, his sword heavy. It suddenly struck him that he was in a real fight now. He would have died at the end of every practice battle with Bloodstone if they'd been fighting for real. Now it *was* real. He could get hurt. He could die. He had no margin for error now, and almost any lesson learned would be learned too late. Swords and axes swung and clanged all around him. Men grunted, roared, and screamed. The wounded still fought, while the dying and dead littered the deck.

"Not in the crow's nest anymore, swab," a voice said from just behind his right shoulder.

He didn't turn to look—it could only be one person. His hesitation turned to rage. As he had grown into a man, he was getting closer and closer to standing up to Diablo. In a different situation, this might have been the day. But now he had to focus his anger somewhere else. A uniformed marine suddenly appeared around the left flank of the pirates. He spotted young Hawk not engaged and charged with cutlass raised.

Hawk quickly raised his cutlass to block the overhand blow. He kicked his right leg out, striking his opponent's left knee. The marine stumbled backward, nearly falling. Any hesitation and nervousness in Hawk ended with the first swing of the sword. Now he relied on his training and instincts. He slashed viciously toward the man's left side. The marine managed to block it but barely in time. Hawk pulled his blade back and quickly swung at his other side. Again the sailor barely managed to deflect the blade. Hawk steadily drove him back and kept him on the defensive.

Hawk next brought a powerful one-handed blow straight down at the sailor's head. The sailor blocked it, holding his weapon with both hands. Hawk swung one more blow straight down. This time, as soon as the blades made contact, Hawk reached his left hand down to his waist, drew his dagger, and plunged it into his adversary's side, right below the ribs. The marine saw it coming, but too late, with his sword locked overhead. He removed one hand from his cutlass to clutch at his side. Realizing his fatal mistake, he looked back at his attacker, an appeal for mercy in his eyes. He found none. Hawk swung a final blow with his cutlass to the right side of the sailor's neck. He collapsed to the deck in a quickly spreading pool of red.

"Not bad, me lad," another voice said.

Hawk turned to see Bloodstone standing beside him. The pirates gained the upper hand and began pushing the sailors and marines back toward the middle of the deck. The enemy still had the numbers—more came up from below deck—but most of the marines were dead. The merchant sailors all fought because they knew they would die regardless, but they were overmatched.

Hawk engaged his next attacker. This one was dressed in regular seaman garb. Hawk almost felt sorry for him but only for a moment. He knew many pirates lay wounded and dead back on the *Bloody Seas*. If Ramirez hadn't attacked first, most of the sailors would have been spared. Hawk swung a few wide blows from side to side, forcing the man to block. After a few overhead blows, he feinted to the right, forcing the sailor to start moving his blade to counter. Then he stopped his swing and plunged his sword through the man's stomach and partially out his back.

Hawk, Bloodstone, and Diablo fought side-by-side-by-side and, along with the now large throng of pirates, quickly finished the grisly job. Hawk slew two more sailors before the battle was done. His training had paid off well. He realized that Bloodstone was indeed an elite fighter. That he hadn't ever defeated him in practice didn't mean he couldn't dispatch most anyone else. Bloodstone emphasized the art of surprise and using tactics like kicking, punching, and using two weapons. It worked well in an actual fight.

"Looks like I can manage OK out of the crow's nest after all," Hawk said to Diablo as he wiped his blade clean on a fallen sailor's shirt and sheathed it. For a moment, Hawk thought Diablo might attack him.

"I'd say you're still better with a mop, swab," Diablo said and walked away.

The pirates quickly stripped the merchantman of any loot, which wasn't much other than some silver, a little gold, and some sugar cane. Then they returned to their ship to inspect the damage and help the wounded.

Six dead pirates lay on the deck of the *Bloody Seas*. A small crowd gathered around one. Hawk nervously pushed his way through the circle of silent pirates. He gasped when he saw Spider lying on the deck, a hole in his left breast. Other than Wesley, Hawk had been closer to Spider than any other pirate —helping him with the rigging and sails almost daily. Tears instantly filled his eyes. He had seen a lot of dead pirates during his six years with Bloodstone's crew but had never lost anyone close.

"Hawk, below deck," a pirate's voice rang out as he climbed

up through the hatch.

Hawk quickly turned and headed to the lower deck. Eight more dead bodies were strewn about the gun deck. He climbed down to the orlop, which was crowded with the wounded. He headed straight to the infirmary, brushing past the line of wounded waiting their turn, and entered the room. Mr. Bones was inside, his face pale and shining with sweat. On one of the tables lay Andre. Hawk quickly noticed that his right leg was mangled beyond repair. Andre was surprisingly calm but obviously shaken.

"Great, now we'll have two peg-legs clacking about the ship," Hawk said, approaching the table. "What a racket!"

"Aye, I will still be better than most, with only one leg," Andre said, smiling weakly. "Let's get it over with." He placed the leather-wrapped hilt of his dagger in his mouth and bit down.

Hawk held down his leg, and Mr. Bones quickly sawed if off with a hand saw and sewed up the stump. "Go get some rest, and I will fashion you a new leg as soon as I get everyone else mended," Mr. Bones said. Hawk helped Andre up and, placing his arm around the Frenchman, assisted him out of the room and to an open hammock. He returned to help Mr. Bones care for the rest of the wounded, including Bloodstone, though the captain's grazed shoulder was a minor wound.

The ship was severely damaged, but the holes were above the waterline. Diablo temporarily assumed Spider's duties and soon had the ship moving again toward open water. They didn't celebrate their victory. The bodies from below deck were brought up to the main deck and placed beside the others. Chain shot was attached to their legs, and they were prepared for burial at sea.

Two hours later, once the wounded were patched up as well as possible, Bloodstone gathered all hands to the main deck. He addressed the somber crew. "Tis a sad day indeed, mates, and a black spot on our victory. By blasted treachery and deceit, we've lost fourteen brothers. One of them be our bosun, Spider. I take the blame for these deaths. T'was I that tried to parley right civilized like with a Spanish fork-tongued devil. The cowards set a trap, with marines loaded aboard a merchant vessel. Won't happen again, I swear by the blazes! But when we be back at the Rock, ye can decide whether I deserve to be your cap'n or not. Now, Mr. Wesley, say a kind word for these poor souls."

Wesley stepped forward, standing in front of the bodies. "Ashes to ashes, dust to dust. God, please forgive these men for their wrongs and such. I'm sure they had good hearts and intentions. If it pleases thee, open the gate and let the sorry lot into heaven. Amen."

The bodies were then picked up one by one and tossed overboard. They quickly sank into the murky water. Then each pirate fired one pistol into the air in honor of the fallen. The group promptly disbanded, and the ship set sail for the Rock. Hawk and Wesley walked back together to their cabin.

Hawk sat down in the high-back leather chair and Wesley at the table. "Sad day," Wesley said, shaking his head.

Hawk fought back his tears. "Yeah, it is." The two sat in silence for a moment. "Wesley?"

"Yes, Hawk?" Wesley had only recently begun calling him Hawk instead of lad or Henry.

"Do you think those men will go to heaven, especially Spider?"

Wesley rubbed thoughtfully at his scruffy beard. "It's hard to say. They all did a might share of killin' and stealin' in their time. Not to mention cursin', lyin', gamblin', and adulterizin'. I'd say they all broke 'bout every law and commandment there is a time or two. But such things aren't for us to decide. Only God knows what was in their hearts and souls."

"So if they don't go to heaven, they go to hell?" Hawk was hoping for a better answer.

"Yeah. I reckon they do. I don't think there's much in between. But some of them might like one as well as the other." Wesley chuckled softly.

"Why do they all do it?

"What's that?"

"Pirating. What makes all these men want to do this when they can be maimed, killed, or go to hell?" Hawk and Wesley engaged in many such conversations over the years. They both enjoyed each other's company, and none of the other pirates had similar deep thoughts about life and death.

Wesley paused and shifted in his chair. "Times are tough all around the world. There aren't many jobs, 'specially for folks in the countryside. Money and food are hard to come by, and the workin' conditions are brutal if you can find a job. Most of these men were sailors workin' on merchant or navy ships. Many were forced into it through impressment. Life is hard on those ships, much harder than ours. They get very little pay and are frequently abused and even killed by their captains. Bloodstone is a hard man, 'specially on the Spanish, but if he takes you onboard, it's not a bad deal. You get plenty of loot, lots of freedom, and all the adventure you can stomach. You're free to take your money and leave whenever you want. So piratin' is a big step up for many."

"How did you end up here?"

Wesley smiled and shook his head, "Now, that's a right long tale and not for tonight."

***

The *Bloody Seas* returned uneventfully to the Rock two days later. That night Bloodstone called a meeting of all the pirates in the middle of the fort. A huge bonfire was built, and everyone gathered around it. The mood had changed somewhat. Everyone had time to grieve, and it had been several days without a good night of music, rum, and celebrating. Even Andre appeared to be getting along well with his wooden leg. Several other pirates had lost limbs after the battle, mostly hands and arms. Supper had been served, and several rum barrels were rolled down to the congregation. Excitement was building when Captain Bloodstone stepped inside the circle near the fire.

"Arrr!" Bloodstone growled, getting everyone's attention. "It's been a tough week, to be sure. Lost some good men and our bosun to boot. Before we be gettin' to the business at hand,

I'd like to recognize some good fortune from our battle. For those of ye that didn't see it first hand, our lad Hawk tasted his first swordplay. Fought like the devil, he did. Smartly killed four Spanish vermin with his blade, not countin' those he shot from the crow's nest. 'Cause of his deeds, I hereby declare him no longer a swab or cabin boy but a pirate!"

The throng of pirates cheered loudly. Hawk scanned the faces in the crowd. If there had been reservations about his fighting prowess or courage, they were gone.

"And if this be me last act as cap'n, I want to put to the vote Hawk replacin' Spider as me bosun."

The pirate crew cheered even louder, and several fired pistols into the air. Hawk was surprised but apparently not as much as Diablo. Hawk saw the shock on the pirate's face as he stared daggers through the captain.

Bloodstone continued, "Those in favor say aye."

The crowd roared 'aye' as one.

"Anyone opposed say nay."

The roar died down as everyone glanced around.

Bloodstone stared directly at Diablo. Diablo's face was stone. "Then so be it. Hawk is bosun!"

He gestured to Diablo. "Mr. Diablo, the next vote." Bloodstone stepped back and let Diablo step forward.

"Because of the results of the last battle, Captain Bloodstone has asked that we vote to see if he remains our captain. All those in favor of him remaining captain?"

The crowd roared 'aye' as loud as they had for Hawk.

"Opposed?"

No one spoke.

"Captain Bloodstone remains our captain!"

CHAPTER VII

It was some celebration at the Rock that night. The barrels of rum were opened and quickly emptied. The fiddles, penny whistles, and lyres played loudly, and the pirates sang and danced with gusto.

Bloodstone brought a large wooden tankard over to Hawk. "You're a man today, Hawk, and a pirate. It be time ye took your first taste of grog."

Hawk grasped the mug and peered inside, swirling the liquid around and taking an experimental sniff. He slowly brought the mug to his lips and let the liquid touch his tongue. The rum was watered down to make grog, but it still burned as he swallowed. Several pirates close by witnessed him drinking and cheered and encouraged him to drink more. He held his breath and turned the tankard up, managing not to gag as the liquid burned its way down his throat and into his stomach. Bloodstone laughed and cheered loudly.

Hawk's head was very soon spinning, but he found himself uncontrollably happy. He danced and sang, laughed, yelled and shouted, listened to the tales of debauchery that he had never been privy too, and drank. Everyone stayed outside that night, even Bloodstone and Wesley, and celebrated beneath the stars. Diablo was even seen dancing and laughing a time or two. The recent battle and fallen men were quickly forgotten. For that night, Bloodstone and his crew ruled the world, and all was right.

Hawk woke up the next morning face down on the ground beside the burned-out fire. He slowly pushed up to his elbows and forearms and looked around, trying to remember the events of the night before. Many other pirate bodies lay strewn about the ground inside the fort, looking like a massacre had taken place during the night. The sun was already up and blazing hot. Hawk's head pounded, and he was nauseated. He slowly stood, nearly falling back down in the process. He stumbled to his new cabin, Spider's old one, and collapsed into the hammock. Chores could wait. *Cursed grog!*

The next day, just after lunch, half the crew started getting ready for a trip to New Orleans—the first in many months. Most bathed in the fresh water ponds on the island and changed into their city clothes. These were usually the clothing from plundered ships that weren't sold or worn aboard the *Bloody Seas*. The pirates reveled in dressing and acting like the upper class when in towns. The other half of the crew would go the next day. All the men were excited over returning to their favorite haunt.

Bloodstone strolled into Hawk's cabin without knocking. "So, ye goin' or sittin' here playin' in the dirt?"

"I get to go?" Hawk asked, his voice loud with excitement.

"Aye, s'ppose it's time. After all, I reckon if you're old enough to kill a man and drink grog, you're old enough for a woman."

"A woman?" Hawk had never been around women. He barely remembered his mother.

Bloodstone laughed. "Get cleaned up and meet us at the beach."

Hawk joined his companions half an hour later. He was dressed in black leather pants and boots, a loose-sleeved white shirt, a red sash around the waist, and a black waistcoat. He wore no head covering, as usual. He and most of the other pirates had not only bathed but also used the perfume they'd taken from some of their prey. Most of the pirates appeared like respectable sailors or navy officers. Bloodstone had undergone the most shocking change. He wore tall black boots, white breeches, a white ruffled shirt, a blue waistcoat, a gold scarf around his waist, a blue doublet with gold trim and buttons, and a blue tricorne with gold trim. His hair and beard were neatly trimmed and combed.

They sailed west on the *Gator*, the schooner named in honor of Razortooth, with the mainland in the distance on their starboard side. Hawk was almost as nervous as he had been going into his recent first swordfight. He wasn't sure exactly what happened in New Orleans, but he'd heard enough to know it was an adventure in its own right. With the good wind, it was just a few hours before they turned, and Hobbs headed straight for the landmass. Soon the mouth of a vast river opened up before them.

"The mighty Mississippi," Mr. Bones said, coming up to stand on the bow beside Hawk.

The *Gator* continued sailing up the river, around several large bends, for over an hour. Finally, they came to a long row of docks on the starboard side. Over a hundred ships of all sizes and shapes were docked on the riverside. Hobbs steered them to an open berth, and a few pirates quickly leaped onto the dock and moored the ship to large wooden posts with thick hawsers.

"All right, ye bunch of heathens!" Bloodstone roared from the gangplank. "Be back here by noon tomorrow, or ye'll be left behind. No getting' into somethin' ye can't get out of. Ye know where to find me 'tween now and then."

The forty pirates quickly crossed the gangplank to the dock and dispersed into the city. Hawk stayed with Bones, and they made the short walk from the docks to a large open square surrounded by buildings. "Jackson Square," Bones said, holding his arms open wide.

Colored brick, cobblestones, and wood boardwalks covered the ground of the square. Smells assaulted Hawk's nose, but unlike those on the pirate ship, these smells were wonderful —sugarcane, peanuts, fruits, and vegetables. Open tables were spaced about selling the sources of the odors, along with clothing, jewelry, trinkets, and dozens of other items. Buildings, many two and three stories tall, lined the edges of the square. Some had sunken arcades and recessed courtyards in front. Iron poles were scattered about with unlit oil lanterns on top.

Bones guided him past the many restaurants, coffee houses, taverns, gaming houses, stores, and warehouses. Some restaurants had tables outside in their courtyards where people were busy eating supper. The square was crowded with people— some were clearly sailors, and many others were finely dressed men and women. The women wore long colorful dresses and smelled of sweet perfume, and the men wore fancy suits.

He also saw some horse-drawn coaches, with a man seated on a bench in front of the cart guiding the horses and people sitting inside the enclosed cart behind. Hawk had never seen horses before but recognized them from some of the books he'd read. He was mostly silent as he absorbed the sights and smells. His world had been so small and limited all his life. New Orleans was totally foreign to him—and exciting.

They made their way toward three huge buildings on the plaza's north side. The one in the middle had ten large columns in front supporting the high roof. "St. Louis Cathedral," Bones said before Hawk could ask. "The building on the left is the Cabildo—the old city hall. On the right, the Presbytere—the new city hall."

Bones led him onto a street beside the cathedral. "Pirate's Alley," he called out. Tall buildings lined both sides of the street, primarily alehouses and restaurants. A few booths and tables were set up selling wares. Halfway down, Bones stopped at a three-story building with a sign hanging over the door reading, "The Treasure Cove." "Bloodstone and most of the pirates will be in here. This can be a rough place, so it would be best to lay low and just listen. There are women and rooms here, and most of us will stay the night. You'll be expected to do the same. Enjoy."

The inside of the building wasn't too crowded since it wasn't even dark outside yet. It was easy to locate their crewmembers. The rum was already flowing, and they were talking and laughing loudly. Round tables filled the large open room. A long counter stood in front of the left wall, with a doorway in the wall behind it. Bloodstone and about two dozen of the crew sat at a group of tables that had been slid close together. Women servers walked around the room in colorful dresses that billowed from the waist to the floor and were cut low in the front. Hawk and Bones sat in two empty chairs at one of the tables.

"Well, lookey here! Me new bosun! Hey, Madame Cynthia, get the Hawk some rum! And some hot grub."

"Make it ale," Hawk said. After seeing the alehouses, he wanted to try it. Plus, he didn't want a repeat of the night before.

Madame Cynthia walked over to Hawk a few minutes later and set a tankard of ale in front of him. She was an older but attractive lady. Her red hair was wound up into a bun on the top, and she wore a blue, white-trimmed dress. "What have we here, Captain? Where have you been hiding, Mr. Hawk?"

Hawk's cheeks instantly grew warm. "Uh...just on the ship... and island," he stammered. The nearby pirates burst into loud laughter and issued some catcalls.

"Hmmm. I might take this one for myself tonight," Cynthia said, looking from Hawk to Bloodstone."

"Ye'd kill the poor boy," Bloodstone said to even louder laughter. "Better stick with a man that can handle ye."

"Yeah. I suppose you're right, Captain. But I do have a good companion for Mr. Hawk. She's not too much older than him and very gentle." She looked back at Hawk and brushed his cheek with the back of her hand. His cheeks burned even hotter. "Maybe one day...when you can handle me." She turned and walked off, swinging her hips side to side.

Hawk quickly drank a swig of ale, which he liked much better than the rum, and waited for the pirates to grow tired of teasing him. Soon they did, and all listened to Bloodstone tell stories. He told them about a privateer most had heard of, Jean Lafitte. Lafitte used to have a base on nearby Grande Terre and up to fifty ships and a thousand men at one time. He stole from the Spanish ships and brought the goods to New Orleans. His brother, Pierre, ran a nearby warehouse that sold the goods.

Some years earlier, Lafitte had fallen out of favor with the local merchants trying to make an honest living. The US Navy overran his base and forced him and his crew to leave. When the war with England started, Andrew Jackson, the US general in charge of fighting the British, sought Lafitte's aid. With the help and skill of his men, the United States repelled the British attack and ended the war. Lafitte then moved his fleet to Galveston Island, off the coast of New Spain.

Even though Lafitte had been gone for years, Bloodstone and his crew still had to pretend to be merchant sailors and fishermen to avoid being mistaken for some of Lafitte's crew or other pirates. Hawk realized that was why Bloodstone had dressed up like a naval officer and referred to himself as Captain Blackburn.

As the night wore on, the pirates consumed more and more rum and ale. They were also served hot, fresh food—slabs of beef, pork ribs, and pieces of chicken, as well as cooked vegetables and hunks of bread that were actually soft. Wesley could cook well but didn't usually have the option of serving food this good. Many women served drinks; some came by and just talked with the men. Occasionally, one of the pirates would get up and follow a woman up the spiral staircase in the corner of the room. Eventually, only a handful of pirates remained. Hawk felt good from the ale but not out of control like he had been with the grog.

Madame Cynthia finally returned to the table with a young woman in tow. Her companion had long reddish-brown hair, pale skin, and green eyes. She wore a low-cut green dress, similar in style to Cynthia's, with gold lace trim. She was the most beautiful woman Hawk had ever seen, although, before tonight, that was none. She glanced at Hawk briefly and then stared down shyly at the floor.

"Mr. Hawk, this is Anna. She'll be your...companion for the night. Now, Cap'n, are you ready for your companion?"

"Thought ye'd never ask," Bloodstone laughed. He slammed his mug down on the table. "Well, Hawk, this week ye became a bosun. Tonight, ye become a man!" Bloodstone stood up and followed Madame Cynthia, slapping her on the rear more than once as she led him up the spiral staircase.

"Are you ready to go upstairs?" Anna asked, smiling shyly. Her voice was sweet and pure.

Hawk's heart started pounding as hard as it did at the start of a battle. He nodded, smiled nervously, and followed her across the room and up the stairs. He really didn't know what was to happen next. He just knew everyone else was going up the stairs with women. She turned left at the top of the stairs and led him down the hall to the last door on the right. She opened the door and entered, with Hawk following after. The room was small and sparsely furnished, with only a table with an oil lamp burning on it, a couple of chairs, a bed, and a washbasin with a mirror above it in the corner. Old, torn curtains covered the window in the wall opposite the door. The room was dusty and smelled of must.

Anna shut and locked the door and walked over to sit on the edge of the bed. Then she patted the bed beside her, and Hawk slowly walked over and sat down. He stared down at his boots and the dusty floor. Her sweet, flowery perfume quickly found his nose. She smelled wonderful.

"So, how old are you, Mr. Hawk?" She asked sweetly, staring at the side of his face.

He thought briefly about lying, but he was sure his behavior would betray him. "Fourteen."

"Wow, so young!"

"How old are you?" he said, a little defensively.

"A woman does not reveal her age, silly boy! But older than you." Her laugh was musical. "I assume this is your first time?"

Hawk finally looked up and turned to gaze upon the beautiful creature beside him. Her skin was soft and smooth, contrasting with the tough, leathered faces of pirates and sailors. Her large green eyes flickered in the lantern light. Her lips were full and pink, glistening slightly with moisture. He glanced briefly at her ample cleavage and the exposed tops of her shapely breasts. He quickly looked back up at her face. She smiled, showing perfect white teeth, also rarely seen on a ship.

Anna laughed, a little louder than before. "Am I that hideous, Mr. Hawk? You look at me like I am a sea monster!"

Hawk's cheeks burned even hotter than they had downstairs. "Uh...no! You're...you're the most beautiful thing I've ever seen!"

"Hmmm...thing?" She quickly spoke again before Hawk suffered even longer. "Thank you very much. You are a very handsome young man and certainly not like your sailor companions."

"Uh, thank you." Hawk looked away, not wanting to keep rudely staring at her beautiful face.

"Well, Mr. Hawk, should we get started?" Anna reached out and laid her left hand on top of his right, her fingers wrapping around the edge of the palm and rubbing softly.

Her hand was warm and smooth on Hawk's rough, calloused skin. Tingles raced up from his hand to his arm and quickly spread throughout the rest of his body. The hair stood up on his arms and the back of his neck as if it were cold in the room. He wondered for a moment if she was a siren or some other magical creature—like he'd read about with Wesley—casting a spell over him. He slowly turned his hand over, allowing their palms to touch and his fingers to squeeze her hand too. He slowly looked up and gazed into her mesmerizing eyes. "Can we just talk for a while first?" he whispered.

The sweet, young, attractive sailor intrigued Anna. She had been forced into prostitution when she was not much older than Hawk. She had sold her body to more sailors and pirates than she cared to count. None of her encounters had ever gone like this, though. None of her patrons wanted to hold hands or talk. They were mostly animals. She was also a little concerned. She felt something with the touch of Hawk's young yet strong hand. Chills ran up her arm, and her heart fluttered quickly. "The night is yours. What would you like to talk about, Mr. Hawk?"

"Well, first, I'm just Hawk, not Mr. Hawk." He grinned. He was slowly gaining his composure and feeling a little more at ease. He continued holding her hand and lightly stroked it with his fingertips. "How does someone as beautiful and kind as you end up doing this…working here?"

It was Anna's turn to look away from him and down at the floor. "That is a long story you do not wish to hear."

"Yes, I really do want to hear. Please tell me."

She had never told her story to anyone other than Madame Cynthia, but for some reason, she felt at ease with Hawk. She found herself talking before she could reconsider. "My father was a wealthy fur trader. He traveled around a large area, trapping and hunting animals, and sold their pelts back in town. My mother went on a long trip with him, and my uncle watched over me.

"After a couple of weeks, we received word that Indians had killed them. My uncle sold everything my father had, took the money, and disappeared. I had no money or food and had to live on the streets begging for a couple of months until Madame Cynthia found me. She gave me clothes, food, and a place to stay. She taught me how to talk and act like a lady—she told me that even though our patrons were rude and crude, they did not want the same in a woman. In exchange, I had to work for her and take care of men."

Hawk thought he saw tears in Anna's eyes as she turned away to look toward the lantern. He would have never guessed she hadn't come from royalty by her speech and mannerisms. "That's a terrible story. I'm sorry about your family." Without thinking, he removed his hand from hers and placed it on her back. He rubbed it through her dress.

The tingling sensation on her back snapped Anna back into the present. She quickly wiped the corners of her eyes and turned around to face Hawk. The tingling was turning to heat, spreading all over. "Now your story, Hawk."

He told her his story, except he carefully skirted around the pirating part since he'd heard about the price on Lafitte's head. He explained that he worked aboard a merchant ship. Everything else he told was the truth, but he was vague regarding the Rock and how they obtained their merchandise.

"So, it sounds like we have a lot in common," he said.

"Yes, I suppose we do. But I believe you have more freedom and get to experience adventures. And you are not just a plaything for nasty sailors."

"Nasty sailors like me?" Hawk asked, flashing his smile.

"You know what I mean," Anna responded, playfully slapping his leg.

"I'm not sure if I would consider my life freedom. I'm pretty much confined to the ship most of the time. And life on a ship is not as fun as it sounds. The work is hard, the food terrible, and the smells unbearable. You're at the mercy of the weather and winds, and sometimes the wind won't blow for days or even weeks. Disease is a constant worry. The Rock is nice, but we cannot stay there often. We always have to find more goods to sell for money."

"I guess we both were dealt a bad hand," she replied softly.

"It also struck me for the first time today, as we entered the city, that there is so much I haven't seen or done. I saw my first horse today and a horse-drawn carriage. I saw my first town, with stone streets and markets and restaurants. And I just met my first woman!"

Anna laughed. "And you are getting ready to experience something else new." Anna slowly leaned toward Hawk.

Hawk didn't move as Anna closed the distance between them. He wasn't sure exactly what was going to happen next. He was scared, but he knew he wanted to experience more with that young woman beside him. Instinctively, at the last moment, he leaned in to meet her. Her soft, warm, moist lips touched his. The sensation was incredible. The tingles he had experienced at the touch of her hand were nothing compared to now. It felt like even the hair on his head stood. He closed his eyes and enjoyed her lips gliding across his. She was soft and gentle at first and then began to press them more firmly against his. He didn't know what he was doing, but he tried to move his lips together with hers. Soon he felt an incredible desire stirring. The rush of sensations and emotions was almost overwhelming.

Anna didn't know what possessed her to kiss the young sailor. Madame Cynthia had taught her early on not to kiss any of the men she entertained. She said kissing led to feelings, and she didn't want or need any feelings for sailors. Maybe it was just his naivety and innocence, but she was drawn to Hawk. He was definitely inexperienced at kissing, but the touch of his lips still excited her. A warm flush soon spread over her body. As she kissed him more passionately, Hawk seemed to catch on, and he began to kiss her back. For the first time ever, she actually wanted to make love to someone, not just do her duty.

Anna finally broke off the kiss and stood. Hawk opened his eyes and stared at her, silhouetted in the lantern light. She placed her hands at the top of her dress and started to pull it down.

"Whoa! What are you doing?" he said.

She laughed. "Why, disrobing, of course."

"Why?"

"You really are a naïve one! That is what comes next."

"Sit back down. Please," he said, patting the bed beside him.

Anna slowly lowered back down on the bed. "What would you have me do, Hawk?"

"Let's lie down together and talk and hold hands and press our lips together some more," Hawk said with a big grin. He crawled behind her and lay down on the bed, his head on the old, lumpy pillow and his right arm underneath it.

Anna laughed and joined him. "So, what should we talk about now?"

Hawk experimentally reached his left arm around her and pulled her close. He ran his hand through her long, thick hair and stroked the soft skin of her neck and shoulders. She reached her arm around him and rubbed his muscled back through his shirt and waistcoat.

"What are your plans in life?" he said.

"Plans? Plans for what?"

"You're not going to do...work here forever, are you?" Hawk's left hand continued to roam over her body from her shoulder down her arm to her side and hip.

"I have not really thought about it. I save what money I can, but Madame Cynthia takes a large portion for my room, food, and clothing. I am nowhere near being able to leave. There are very few jobs for women too. Unless, of course, I find a rich man to steal me away." She laughed. She raised her hand to run it through Hawk's wavy blond hair and touch his cheek.

"And where would this rich man whisk you away to?" Hawk found it occasionally hard to concentrate with Anna's caresses. His skin prickled at almost every touch.

"Hmmm. I would not be tough to please—maybe to a big farm in the country. He would build me a brand-new log cabin in the middle." Anna's voice quickened with excitement as she momentarily allowed her mind to escape her life. "We would own horses that we would ride almost daily across our land. There would be a forest and a river, and we would occasionally sleep out under the stars and spend hours on the riverbank. We would have lots of farm animals and crops for food and to sell, and we would help each other with the chores. It would be our own private paradise. Then, we would have to raise children to enjoy it with us and help with the farm."

"I believe you have thought about it," Hawk laughed. "That's a good plan, though."

Anna's smile slowly disappeared. "No. Not a plan. Just a foolish girl's dream. Now, what is your plan for your future?" Anna enjoyed talking to Hawk, but his hand touching her body had her mind on other things. He was so close, yet so far away.

"I'd never thought about anything except pir...being a sailor." He silently cursed himself for his slip of the tongue. "Until this trip. Now I wonder how much more is out there that I've never seen. I've saved up some money too, but like you, I doubt I have enough to leave the ship. And if I did leave, I wouldn't even know how to survive in this city or anywhere else. But I do like the sound of your dream. The only thing I would add is occasionally leaving the farm to go on trips, exploring the world."

"I guess we are both just foolish dreamers," Anna whispered.

"No. Dreams can come true. Maybe one day I'll be the rich man to steal you away to that farm!"

Anna laughed loudly. "Should I pack a bag and be ready for you?"

Hawk playfully slapped her hip. "No. It will take a while. Just don't let go of that dream." He leaned forward and gently kissed her. He wasn't sure if he had figured it out yet, but it definitely felt right. Anna moaned softly as she kissed him back. Their wet lips slid back in forth, moving in perfect unison now. They continued to caress each other through their clothing. They kissed, touched, talked, and finally slept—clothed—for a few hours. Anna faced away from Hawk, holding the hand on the arm he kept wrapped tightly around her. She felt safe and secure for one of the first nights ever—although it was a restless night, as both of their minds were occupied with much more than sleep.

The last couple of hours of sleep were finally deep. It was rare for Hawk to get to sleep in a warm bed and one that was not moving with the waves. When he finally awoke the next morning, he was alone. He quickly pulled on his boots and headed downstairs. Madame Cynthia met him at the bar. "So, did you have a good time, Mr. Hawk?"

"Uh, yes, the best, ma'am!" He scanned the room, but it was nearly empty. "Where is Anna?"

"I'm glad. You'll have to come back soon. I'm sure Anna would like to see you again. I had to send her out to run some errands. Captain Blackburn has already paid, and he and the rest of your crew have returned to your ship."

Hawk couldn't conceal his disappointment. He nodded to Madame Cynthia and quickly returned to the ship. As he walked back through the square, he wished he could stay for the entire day. The square was much less busy in the early morning, and the shops were just opening. The smells of the evening before were already starting to waft through the warm, thick air again.

His thoughts then shifted to Anna. He wondered where she

might be and how she felt about him and the night they spent together. He could still feel her soft skin, taste her warm luscious lips, and smell her sweet perfume. He would be counting down the days until he could see her again. He was also going to work hard at saving his money. He now received a share and a half of plunder since he was a boatswain, or bosun, as the crew called him. Somehow, someway, he would become rich and rescue Anna from her current existence.

CHAPTER VIII

It seemed a long voyage back to the Rock, with all the teasing and questions Hawk received from the rest of the crew. He was sure his cheeks glowed red the entire trip. Even Bloodstone threw in his fair share of comments. "Did she let ye swab 'er decks, lad?" The pirates roared with laughter.

"Hawk, is it true your flintlock went off before it cleared your breeches?" asked Lucky, a pirate sporting a hook for his left hand. Another roar of laughter erupted from his mates.

"Now, mates, we are being a little hard on Mr. Hawk. I am sure he mastered the fair young maiden the same way he mastered firing a musket," Mr. Bones said.

Hawk stood up straight and puffed his chest out. "Thank you, Mr. Bones."

"Aye," said Bones. "Grabbed hold tightly with both hands, closed his eyes, and prayed she would not kill him."

The crew erupted in laughter again, with some actually falling to the deck. Even Bloodstone doubled over and slapped his knee. Hawk quickly scurried up a ratline to check the sails and rigging. He stayed at the mast tops until they reached the Rock.

***

"Wesley!" Hawk shouted, running into Wesley's cabin.

The old man looked up from his desk and the book he read, peering over his glasses. "Ah, yes, fresh back from your first night in town."

"I had the best night of my life!" Hawk ran and leaped onto the bed like he had so many years before. Only this time, his emotions were much different.

Wesley chuckled. "The first fresh-faced lass usually does that to you."

"No. I met the best girl in the world! We talked and held hands and pressed our lips together!"

"Kissed?"

"I guess that's it! But I felt all tingly and had chills, and the hairs on my arm stood when she just touched me! I can't even describe all the feelings I have for her. My stomach's churning like a whirlpool, and my head spins like I've drunk too much rum again." The words left Hawk's mouth as fast as he thought them.

"Whoa. Heave to there, lad!" Wesley's smile disappeared, and he shook his head.

"What's wrong? Is something wrong with me? Am I sick?"

"Aye, I reckon you have a touch of somethin', all right. I'm afraid you've fallen head over tail in love."

"Love?" Hawk asked, his smile also disappearing.

"Aye. I reckon what you're feelin' is love," Wesley said somberly.

"Is love bad?"

"Oh, it's fine while it lasts. Never does, though. And love messes with people's heads. It's caused more murders, wars, and heartaches than anything 'cept religion, I'd wager."

Hawk was silent as he mulled over Wesley's words. For a moment, his emotions were dampened. "Have you ever been in love?"

Wesley stared at him as if deciding whether to share his story. "Aye, that I have. A sad tale too."

"Please tell it to me!" Hawk pleaded.

"All right then, sit back and listen. When I was a lad, 'bout your age, I was a sailor on an English privateer ship. We had a charter from the king to attack Spanish ships and take the loot they brought back from the New World. I lost my leg a couple of years into it, and they made me the cook. The gold and silver was plentiful back then and the fat galleons ripe for the pickin'. I saved up a good sum of money to leave that life one day while I was still a young man.

"In London between voyages, I met the prettiest young lass you've ever seen. Her name was Emily. Ah, her voice was like a siren's, and she smelled as sweet as a field of honeysuckle. Her skin was like silk. I felt just like what you described. We were married and bought a little house. I was more determined than ever to save enough money to leave the sailor life behind and be with her every day and night.

"We sailed all the way to Havana on one trip, gone for several months. I thought about my sweet Emily every night, even dreamed 'bout her on most. When we finally returned to England, I rushed home to my little cottage. I found it empty —all my loot and possessions were gone, as well as sweet little Emily. I never saw her again. After that, I gave up my dreams of leavin' this life and of love and women. Sure, I've had my share of women over the years, but just for a night here and there. Nothing but trouble they are." Wesley spat on the floor beside his chair.

"That certainly is a sad tale. But surely all women aren't like that. You might have found another one that would have loved you as much as you loved her," Hawk said.

"My heart was in pieces for nearly a year after that. Don't know that it ever totally healed, or at least it healed a little blacker and colder. I'll never risk it again. If it gets broke again, it'll be from a musket ball or cutlass."

They were both silent for a few minutes.

"Well, my Anna wouldn't do that to me," Hawk finally said. "I can't help how I feel, no matter how bad your being in love turned out. I'm going to save up my money too, and when I have enough, we'll run away and live happily ever after on a little farm." Hawk's excitement was suddenly rekindled.

Wesley chucked again. "All this from one night together, huh?"

"I have given my word and made up my mind." Hawk climbed off the bed and headed to the door. He didn't want Wesley to dampen his mood any further.

"Just keep your wits about you, boy. If it happens, it happens, but until then, you're a pirate with duties to perform."

Hawk walked out, closing the door firmly behind him.

"Lover boy," a voice called out.

Hawk looked up to see Diablo emerging from his cabin. He wore a blue and red military outfit. He was leading the men that didn't go to New Orleans the night before into town that night. Hawk ignored him and headed toward his cabin.

"Hawk, what was your lass's name? I might have to show her what a real man can do tonight."

Hawk suddenly whirled around, his hand on the hilt of his cutlass. "Stay away from her!"

Diablo laughed. "You're a little on edge, my boy. And I'll tip her well. Oh, and don't pull that blade out unless you intend to use it."

"If I pull it out, it will be used. And if you lay a hand on Anna, it will come out."

The two men stared at each other for what seemed like minutes. Finally, Diablo grinned, tipped his hat, and headed toward the gate. Hawk stormed into his cabin, overwhelmed by his many conflicting emotions.

***

In the following months, Hawk's fighting skills and prowess only improved with experience. Diablo usually led the pirates into battle, but Hawk was close behind. Hawk and Diablo had occasional run-ins, but they knew Bloodstone wouldn't tolerate fighting among pirates in his crew. They would either be marooned or forced to duel to the death. Neither was quite confident enough for a duel. So they poked and prodded but avoided coming to blows.

Hawk continued to think about Anna every night in his hammock. They did visit the Rock a time or two over the next couple of years, but they didn't return to New Orleans. The New Orleans Squadron continued adding ships and gaining strength and intensifying its pirate hunting. Visiting a US city like New Orleans, which was frequented by many navy ships and officers, became increasingly riskier.

Bloodstone expanded his area of operations to make them more challenging for the navy to find. He also started visiting different cities to sell merchandise and spend their coin—Tortuga, Havana, Port-au-Prince, Santo Domingo, and Kingston. They used extra caution and took more time with their disguises in the Spanish towns. Kingston was British-owned, so they spent most of their time there.

Officially, Kingston was against piracy. Any pirates caught were hung at Gallows Point on the island of Port Royal, which had been a pirate haven many years before. Unofficially, pirates brought in cheap goods for the merchants. Even better, most goods came from Spanish galleons and merchant ships. So the Kingston officials and soldiers didn't look for pirates but had to deal with them if they found any. Kingston had enough taverns, gambling houses, and brothels to keep the pirates happy. Hawk partook in the drink and occasionally gambling, but never the women. He couldn't do that to Anna, even though he knew she was with many other men.

Hawk continued to amass a small fortune in gold and silver. Most of his comrades spent all their loot on alcohol, gambling, and women. That's why most pirates could never leave the trade. The more they made, the more they spent, and the more they had to make. Hawk had to spend a little on food, drink, and clothing, but he stashed away the rest. Although the visions of Anna faded somewhat, he still thought of her almost nightly. He still enjoyed the battles and the crew's admiration, but his mind was with Anna, and dry land, during the quiet moments.

***

Hawk knew Captain Bloodstone didn't make many mistakes, or else he wouldn't have lived so long in the pirating business. His greatest occurred during this time away from New Orleans and the Rock. During their long voyage, they used several different uninhabited Caribbean islands for their bases of operation. Most infamous pirate hideouts, like New Providence, Tortuga, and Port Royal, had been cleared out. The US Navy had also started searching unpopulated islands. Setting up a long-term base was not a good option for survival, and the voyage to the Rock was too long to make regularly. So, they just searched for a safe-looking harbor to use long enough to careen the *Bloody Seas* and make repairs.

Many of these islands had shallow harbors, and the *Bloody Seas* had a deep draft. That made it challenging to careen her and to transfer items from ship to shore. Bloodstone wanted a smaller, faster ship to better navigate the small islands and escape the British naval vessels if necessary. He spotted the perfect twenty-gun, two-masted Bermuda sloop on one trip while searching for Spanish prey. Bloodstone fell in love with the ship and had to have it.

The only problem was that the sloop belonged to the Royal Navy. Bloodstone put taking the ship to a crew vote. Always up for a new challenge, the crew voted in favor of taking it. Hawk secretly disagreed. The Spanish were their prey and the ones he could justify attacking. Hawk had no issues with the British, especially since his family was from England. But he didn't want to vote against the crew. He did privately ask Bloodstone to show mercy on the sailors.

Bloodstone used his tactic of flying the same flag as the prey, in this case, a Union Jack they found aboard a Spanish merchantman some time back. They hailed the sloop, easily sailed close, and put the *Bloody Seas* broadside. By the time Bloodstone revealed their true intentions, the sloop captain knew he couldn't match the firepower of the pirates or escape. In return for not resisting, not risking damaging his new ship, and to appease Hawk, Bloodstone offered to maroon them on a nearby island. The area was a busy sailing lane, so marooning would not be the death sentence it typically was.

Bloodstone sailed the *Bloody Seas* and his new prize, the *Cobra*, named for its speed, to a nearby haunt. Bones and a select crew stayed behind on the island to customize the *Cobra*. They ripped out cabins and upper decks and removed as much weight as possible. Bloodstone also instructed Bones to mount oars inside the cannon ports so the cannons could be rolled back and the ship rowed if the winds were not in their favor. Hawk decided to stay with Bones and assist, as Bloodstone and his crew returned to the sea to hunt Spanish. Another trip to Kingston was also in their near future.

***

"There they be!" a young pirate, Benjamin, called out from the top of a palm tree.

The *Bloody Seas* had been gone for the two weeks that the work on the *Cobra* had proceeded. That was a little long for a typical treasure and carousing run. Hawk had been close to taking the *Cobra* out to search for them. Pirates gathered on the beach from makeshift huts and shelters and from performing various tasks about the new ship to greet their captain and crewmates.

The *Bloody Seas* dropped anchor, and a longboat was lowered into the water. A group of pirates quickly climbed in and rowed to shore.

Hawk stood in front of the crowd to greet them. "Where's Captain? And Diablo?"

Wesley and Andre limped to shore, followed by Billy, Bones, and a half dozen other pirates. "Let's go to your hut and talk," Wesley said. Hawk had never seen that look on his face before. Andre, Billy, and Bones followed Hawk and Wesley to the makeshift, thatch-roofed hut Hawk was using as a cabin. The rest of the pirates gathered around the other six to learn what information they could.

"It's bad, Hawk, really bad," Wesley said, breathing slightly hard from the short but brisk walk.

"What happened?"

"We took a nice Spanish prize nigh a week ago. Course, the boys all wanted to head to Kingston to celebrate. One night of celebratin' led to two. The second night, Diablo, Bloodstone, Billy, and a few mates left us to seek a new tavern. Little did they know it was a favorite haunt of the Royal Navy and city garrison. Devil take me, who do you s'ppose was in there that very night?

The crew of that sloop out there! Apparently, they had already been rescued from their maroonin' and returned to Kingston. That cursed captain made Bloodstone and Diablo right away. All 'cept Billy was immediately taken off in chains to the prison.

"Billy managed to slip off without bein' caught and found us before the garrison did. We made haste to the *Bloody Seas* and set sail straight away. From what we heard, they were to be tried the next day and hung at Gallows Point a week later if convicted." Wesley's face was pale and sweat-covered by the time he finished the story.

Hawk collapsed into a chair beside the small table in the middle of the room. He was stunned by the news that Bloodstone, Diablo, and two other pirates would be hung and distraught that he'd helped talk Bloodstone into showing mercy on the British sloop crew.

He nodded to the other chairs around the table, and the others quickly sat down.

"So, when do you think the hanging will be?" said Hawk.

Wesley scratched his beard. "It took us four days to sail back here. I s'ppose that'd make it three days."

"Blast! Can we sail back there in three days?" Hawk stared at the table and rubbed his hand through his thick hair.

"Not in the *Bloody Seas*. The winds won't be any better going back. Wouldn't do no good anyway unless you just want to watch Bloodstone and the others swing."

"Mr. Bones, can we sail from here to Port Royal in three days on the *Cobra*?"

Bones glanced briefly at the stern faces of Wesley, Billy, and Andre and then back to Hawk. "It would be tight and might require some rowing, but I would say with a good crew, it could be done."

"What are you thinking, Hawk?" Andre said.

"We're going to rescue them. It's my fault that we let that British crew live. I can't let Bloodstone and the rest, even Diablo, swing for that."

"You're mad, Hawk!" Wesley exclaimed in a tone that

surprised Hawk. "And just what is your plan?"

"That's what we're going to figure out. Who knows Port Royal and Jamaica the best?"

"Uh, that would be me, sir. I lived most of my life in Jamaica before goin' on account," Billy replied.

"Good. Gentlemen, we'll stay in this cabin until we have a plan. Then we'll have the crew vote. But regardless, with a crew or not, I'm leaving before sunset for Port Royal."

***

The *Cobra* set sail shortly before sunset, just as Hawk had promised. The crew had unanimously voted in favor of the plan. None questioned Hawk's assumption of leadership, with the captain and quartermaster not present for duty. He didn't put being temporary captain to a vote; he just took charge. Bones, Andre, Billy, Wesley, and forty pirates joined Hawk. Fourteen pirates manned the oars when the wind wasn't behind them. The remainder worked the sails. Hawk spent much of the next three days and nights with his officers finalizing the plan.

CHAPTER IX

The air already hung hot and thick above Port Royal as the sun climbed above the haze over the eastern horizon. The crowd was filing into Gallows Point to see the hanging of the most famous pirate since Calico Jack Rackham almost a hundred years prior. The common people walked, while the wealthiest arrived in horse-drawn carriages. A large contingent of garrison soldiers was mixed among the crowd. Most were more interested in watching the hanging than ensuring the other spectators were orderly.

Port Royal was a shell of its former self since the earthquake had destroyed it many years before. But today, the large crowd and buzz in the air made it feel as vital as ever. Many boats crowded the docks and filled the channel between Port Royal and Kingston. The berth closest to the shore remained open, waiting for the ship from Kingston that would soon arrive with the governor, executioner, and prisoners.

The gallows consisted of a large, elevated wooden platform, with a long beam running nearly the entire length ten feet above. Five nooses hung down from the beam. A lever at the end of one of the side support beams would cause the portion of the platform beneath the nooses to drop away, allowing the victims to fall through the platform and break their necks.

Garrison soldiers formed a hundred-foot perimeter around the platform, keeping the area clear of spectators. They also maintained a wide pathway open from the circle to the docks. Two horse-drawn carts, with a man sitting on each horse, sat at the eastern edge of the circle just behind the soldiers, waiting to haul the bodies off after the ceremony was complete.

A cheer erupted through the now large crowd. All eyes turned toward a beautiful schooner that approached the docks. The ship was in pristine condition, its rails and gunport trim painted gold and the boards of the brown hull polished until the sun reflected off them. The sails were new and glowed a brilliant white in the sunlight. Ten shiny bronze cannons shone in the open ports. It sailed effortlessly across the glassy water and soon glided to the open berth. A gangplank was quickly extended, and a small party crossed from the deck to the dock.

At the edge of the docks, two drummers began to tap their drums. The garrison captain led the small column, dressed in his finest bright red military uniform. Behind him walked the governor, dressed in white silk stockings, maroon velvet breeches, a white silk and lace-trimmed ruffled shirt, a maroon waistcoat, and a long maroon velvet coat with polished brass buttons and gold trim. A golden sash circled his waist. His face was red and puffy, already gleaming with sweat, and a powdered wig adorned his head. The executioner was next—a burly, bearded man that bore a slight resemblance to Bloodstone. Two garrison soldiers followed, with the four convicted pirates next, their hands chained behind their backs. Two more soldiers brought up the rear.

Captain Bloodstone was the first prisoner. He'd been stripped of his fine town clothes and wore a plain gray linen shirt and pants. His head was bare, and his hair was tossed wildly about his head and shoulders. Despite not wearing his black pirate garb or being armed, he was still an intimidating man. He grinned at the cheering crowd lining the narrow path that led to the gallows. Diablo followed, dressed in similar clothing. His grin was more of a sneer, and he spat several times as they walked. Stephen Martin and Jeremiah Parker stared at their feet, their fear evident.

The crowd turned from cheering the governor and soldiers to jeering the pirates as the procession made its way to the gallows. The garrison captain led them up the stairs and across the back of the platform. The crowd fell silent as the executioner, governor, and captain stepped forward to the front.

"Mr. Executioner, what are the crimes that these men have been convicted of?" the governor asked in a loud but high-pitched voice.

The executioner's baritone voice boomed across the entire square. "Governor Worthington, these men—Captain Bloodstone, his quartermaster, Diablo, Stephen Martin, and Jeremiah Parker—have been convicted of murder, theft, and acts of piracy against the Royal Navy. Their sentence is hanging until deceased."

An excited murmur spread through the crowd. Soon, random shouts and chants erupted. Gallows Point had a long history of pirate hangings, but the frequency had decreased since the golden age of piracy had ended many years before. Captain Bloodstone was a well-known name. The one-eyed Diablo had also earned a reputation for his cruelty and brutality.

***

As the crowd roared and cheered, no one noticed four sailors climbing into the body-carts, two into each. Not even two of the men having pegs for legs drew attention. One man stayed in each cart while the other two slid onto the backs of the horses. Before the riders could even turn in surprise, their throats were slit. The thuds of their bodies hitting the ground and the shuffling of the horses went unnoticed by the enthralled crowd.

***

The soldiers on the platform pushed the four pirates forward to stand before the nooses. "Do the convicted have any last words?" the executioner said in his booming voice. The noise of the crowd quieted to a dull murmur. The other three pirates turned to their captain.

Captain Bloodstone somberly surveyed the exuberant throng. His eyes fell briefly upon the two carts. A slight grin appeared, and he turned back to the crowd in front of the gallows. "Arrr!" Bloodstone roared loudly as if he was addressing his crew. "I reckon I do."

The crowd suddenly fell completely silent as the legendary pirate spoke. "I used to only hunt those thievin', cursed Spanish devils and took back their stolen loot. Made a good run of it, I did. Never had anything 'gainst the British." He spat onto the platform in front of him. "I reckon that be changed now. When I get back to me ship, and back to the sea, I'll be killin' ye, British cowards, too."

The crowd erupted with shouts and boos.

The governor's face went pale, or at least paler. "Get this over with," he said to the captain and executioner. The soldiers placed the nooses around the necks of the four pirates and slid the knots down until they were tight. The governor, captain, and soldiers returned to the back edge of the gallows, and the executioner walked over to the lever.

The two body-carts began to roll forward, nudging the soldiers in front to the side. They were somewhat surprised since the drivers typically waited until after the pirates were dead. But they quickly turned their attention back to the gallows. If the drivers were not following the ceremonial protocol, they would have to answer to the governor after. Once the carts cleared the soldiers, the riders spurred their horses into a near gallop.

The crowd's noise was so loud that scant attention was paid to the carts and their occupants. The drummers from the dock now stood just inside the cleared perimeter and began playing a drum roll. The executioner placed his hand on the lever. The sailors in the back of each cart rose up to their knees, each bringing up a musket. Two shots rang out just as the lever was pulled, and the platform broke away.

The four pirates fell. Bloodstone and Diablo totally disappeared through the gallows, landing on the ground below, the musket balls severing their ropes. The other two pirate's bodies dropped halfway down, and their momentum halted as the nooses snapped their necks.

Chaos erupted on the gallows and within the crowd. It took a moment for everyone, including the executioner, governor, and garrison soldiers, to realize what had happened. The two carts were now in front of the gallows, and Diablo and Bloodstone charged out from beneath the platform and were snatched into the carts by Hawk and Andre. Wesley and Billy, the two drivers, spurred their horses harder and galloped toward the open path to the docks.

As the garrison soldiers began to recover from shock, most drew their weapons. Then commotion erupted from their ranks. Bodies started falling as daggers were plunged into their backs. Twenty-six of the pirate crew of the *Cobra* had positioned themselves just behind the soldiers along the path. The soldiers were torn between stopping the carts and defending themselves from the attackers behind. A couple did get off shots, but none hit the carts or their occupants. As the carts sped past, many pirates in the crowd broke free of the soldiers and leaped onto them. Once onboard, they turned, drew their flintlocks, and began firing at the pursuing soldiers. The remainder of the pirates followed behind the carts, shooting and stabbing at any soldiers nearby. The spectators remained frozen in shock.

The two carts sped toward the *Cobra*, which had sailed up during the ceremony and wedged in beside the governor's schooner. The drivers halted the carts on the dock in front of the sloop, and their passengers quickly disembarked. Several muskets fired behind them, the balls sailing harmlessly past. Hawk helped Wesley off his horse, Billy helped Andre out of the wagon, and the pirates crossed the gangplank to the *Cobra*.

Once aboard, the pirates grabbed the loaded guns leaning against the rails and fired into the garrison soldiers chasing the remaining pirates. The last pirates ran and leaped from the dock to the ship as their mates continued to fire the muskets, blunderbusses, and flintlocks. Bloodstone and Diablo were still shackled, so they, Wesley, and Andre hurried below deck, with Andre shouting orders to the gunners.

The ten cannons on the port side fired into the side of the governor's schooner. At point blank range, the middle of the beautifully polished hull was shattered. Then the cannons were quickly rolled back and secured, and fourteen pirates assumed their positions and started rowing. The last group of garrison soldiers reached the dock just as the two swivel guns on the Cobra's bow fired canister shot, sending the soldiers either collapsing onto the dock or fleeing back into the crowd. No more shots were fired as the *Cobra* rowed into open water and unfurled the sails to catch the strong wind. None of the cannons fired from the many forts spaced around the Jamaican coast. Word could not travel as fast as the sloop. If any other ships followed, they were quickly left behind.

CHAPTER X

Once the *Cobra* was in open waters and running before the wind, the celebration began. Bloodstone and Diablo had their chains cut, and all the pirates gathered on deck to celebrate. Although they had lost Stephen and Jeremiah and five other pirates at Gallows Point, Hawk had pulled off something that had never been done—rescuing someone from the gallows, and two people at that.

"Well, blow me down!" Bloodstone roared, a tankard of rum in his hand. "What a bloody fool of a plan, Hawk!"

"Would you rather us go back?" Hawk asked, grinning. The pirates howled and laughed around them.

Bloodstone clapped him hard on the back. "Don't reckon me neck is ready for that yet. Foolish, but the bravest plan I've ever seen, no doubt. Drink one to the Hawk, boys!" The pirates all raised their mugs and tankards of rum and shouted in salute. Even Diablo nodded his head toward Hawk and extended his cup before drinking deeply.

With Billy's knowledge of Port Royal, and a quick scouting of Gallows Point by Hawk and his officers, Hawk came up with the exact plan the night before the hanging. Just hours before the execution, Billy had contacted some old friends in Kingston. One had a connection in the prison and passed word of the plan to Bloodstone and Diablo. Although some good men were lost, it went as well as it possibly could have. There were a hundred ways the scheme could have ended with most, or all, of their deaths.

"Where did ye learn to shoot a musket like that?" Bloodstone asked a few minutes later.

"From the other shooter, of course," Hawk replied, nodding at Andre.

"And could ye make that shot again?"

"One out of four." Hawk laughed.

Bloodstone shook his head and chuckled. "And Wesley, how in the blazes do ye ride a horse with one leg?"

"Very carefully, Cap'n. Very carefully." Wesley laughed. "I guess I haven't totally forgotten my old ridin' days in England. I'm glad the ride wasn't much longer, though."

They didn't have time for a proper celebration when they reached their current hideout. Bloodstone said the Royal Navy would be scouring the islands in full force. The exploits of Hawk and his crew would quickly spread across the Caribbean. It was a massive embarrassment for Jamaica and, by association, England and their King. It was now time to see how the atmosphere in New Orleans was.

"Hawk, me boy, I need someone to cap'n the *Cobra* back to the Rock," Bloodstone said when the men began boarding the ships. "I reckon ye've earned it. Take a hand to be your quartermaster, and ye can keep most of the men ye took to the gallows with you. I'll be takin' Diablo, Wesley, and Andre with me, of course."

"I'll race you back," Hawk said.

Hawk quickly sought out Billy among the throng of pirates on the beach. "Ho, Billy," he called out when he spotted him.

Billy scampered across the beach to Hawk. He wasn't much older than Hawk but was a skilled and experienced pirate. Had it not been for Hawk, he might have replaced Spider as bosun. Hawk had been impressed with Billy during the rescue. He had a quick mind and was absolutely fearless. He had been an apprentice blacksmith before pirating and, as a result, was very knowledgeable about weapons and skilled with a dagger and cutlass. He was also skilled with a horse, as he had shown.

"Yes, sir," Billy said. He was a few inches shorter than Hawk and clean-shaven with short black hair and big blue eyes. He was slight of frame but wiry and strong.

"I need a quartermaster for the trip back to the Rock," Hawk said.

Billy's eyes widened in shock. "Me, sir?"

"If you would. You proved yourself back at the gallows, and I need someone I can trust."

"Uh…OK…I guess," Billy stammered.

"Good! You'll be a fine mate." Hawk grinned and clapped Billy firmly on the shoulder. "Now, let's get these bilge rats rounded up and on the sloop."

***

After many months of absence, the *Bloody Seas and the Cobra* sailed uneventfully back to the Rock. There was a buzz about the *Cobra*, and Hawk assumed on the *Bloody Seas*, over Hawk's daring plan and rescue of their captain and quartermaster. It was a legendary exploit and would be remembered long after the time of piracy had ended.

Hawk tried to ignore the talk, but he knew his status was elevated among the crew, even with most of the older pirates who favored Diablo. The younger crew members clearly idolized him. He was only the bosun, though, and tried to stay focused on his duties. Although for this short trip, he did enjoy acting as the captain.

Hawk and the *Cobra* arrived at the inlet first. He sounded the horn to have the trees raised. He saw no response. After a few more tries, he fired his flintlock into the air. Still nothing. He cursed and had his men row the *Cobra* to the starboard shore. Three quickly hopped off to man the wench. The ship was then rowed to the main part of the island on the port side, where three more men rushed into the thick vegetation to operate that wench.

Slowly the trees rose out of the water, and the *Cobra* sailed into the harbor. Hawk knew immediately that something was amiss. The *Gator* and sloop were missing, and no pirates were there to greet them. Lookouts were always stationed near the wenches on the outer part of the inlet or in the beach area. He sailed the *Cobra* almost to the shore, its shallow draft allowing it to go much closer than the larger ships.

He and his men quickly leaped or climbed down to the water and waded to the beach. Although he knew the *Bloody Seas* was close behind, Hawk didn't wait. He drew a flintlock and led the way to the jungle path. "Be ready, men!" he shouted. His crew followed single file behind.

The trail was more overgrown than usual, and Hawk had to use his cutlass to clear the way in spots. He felt sick to his stomach. They had been gone a long time, longer than any other voyage before. Pirates didn't do well with idle time, especially with no captain. Lewis Walker had been left in charge. He had been a captain on a merchant ship they captured a couple of years prior. He seemed a capable sailor and leader, and Bloodstone was grooming him for bigger things.

The party hurried up the trail and soon arrived at the fort. The gate was closed, and no one was visible upon the walls. Hawk strode up to the thick wooden door and rapped hard with the butt of his pistol. Nothing stirred on the other side. He repeated even harder. "Open the blasted gate! It's Hawk."

Finally, he heard noises on the other side—muffled voices, followed by the heavy wooden post that held the door shut being removed. The gate slowly swung open.

Hawk quickly strode in and surveyed the scene. "What's going on here?" he demanded of the first two pirates he saw. The men before him were pale and skinny and didn't look well.

"Thank the gods. It's you, Hawk!" the first one, Jimmy, said excitedly, his eyes wild and darting.

"Aye, ye came back to save us!" the other said, looking similarly crazed.

Hawk knew getting answers from these two would be tough. "Where's Walker?"

"He's dead, sir," Jimmy stammered.

"Dead? How?" Hawk demanded. By now, several more pirates had stumbled out of various huts. They all appeared ragged and emaciated, shuffling weakly down to meet Hawk and his crew.

Bloodstone and Diablo had also arrived, followed by the crew of the *Bloody Seas.* The two crews fanned out into a large circle around Jimmy and the dozen or so pirates.

"By the blazes, Jimmy, what be goin' on?" Bloodstone roared. Like Hawk, he had a flintlock in his hand. "Where be the *Gator* and the rest of me men?"

"Sir, it's a terrible tale. The *Gator,* she was sunk by a US Navy frigate and—"

"Why was she away from the Rock?" Diablo said.

"Well, Mr. Diablo, we were dangerously short of supplies, and we feared somethin' bad had befallen you. So Walker took me and a crew and sailed to New Orleans. We traded for supplies and were headin' back home when we spied a small merchantman sailin' to the city. Without even puttin' it to a vote, Walker ordered us to attack. We were barely out of sight of New Orleans! A large US Navy frigate, one of them new ones with all the guns, spotted us on their way out. They swooped in with guns a blazin' before we even boarded the merchant. They killed us all, including Walker, 'cept four. They told us to get into the rowboat and proceeded to sink the *Gator.* The captain, a man named Cord, and his lieutenant, James, told us to tell all the pirates their time be over. Mentioned you and Kragg; they did."

"What in the blazes was he thinkin'?" Bloodstone roared.

"I don't know, cap'n," Jimmy replied, kicking nervously at the ground.

"And did any of ye tell them ye were part of me crew?"

"No, sir," Jimmy replied. "We didn't speak a word. We just started rowin' and rowed hard for a week back here, nearly dying of thirst in the process."

"What happened to the men that stayed behind?" Hawk asked.

"We came back and told 'em the story. They were upset and feared you were dead, and now the *Gator* was lost. One morning we woke up and found that all the crew, except ten of us, was gone. They'd loaded all the loot, weapons, and food they could carry into the sloop and sailed away. We think that Elijah Wright was the leader. We ran out of ammo soon after and have been tryin' to survive on fruits and plants. But the fruit ran out a couple of weeks ago, and as you can see, we're not far from death, and most of us have the scurvy."

"Curse that English devil to hades!" Bloodstone roared. He dropped his flintlock and turned to Diablo. "Diablo, secure the fort and take some men out to get some meat. Bones, tend to the sick and see what ye can do for 'em," Bloodstone ordered, and he stormed off to his hut. The pirates began restoring order to the fort, and most went out to hunt and fish.

Hawk gave Bloodstone a couple of hours to cool off before finally going to his cabin. He knocked softly on the door.

"Come in," a voice grumbled from within.

Hawk entered and found Bloodstone sitting at his table, a tankard of rum in his hand. He could tell it wasn't the captain's first cup. Hawk sat down in a chair on the other side. Bloodstone slid the tankard over to him, stood up, and grabbed another off the top of the rum cask. He quickly filled it and sat back down.

They drank in silence for several minutes. Hawk waited for Bloodstone to speak first.

"I pity ye, Hawk," the captain finally said.

"Pity me? Why?"

"Ye come along too late. The time of pirates be comin' to an end, I'm afraid." Bloodstone drank another swig of rum.

"This is just a setback. We'll get more men, ships, and loot."

Bloodstone shook his head. "That cursed New Orleans Squadron will hunt us all down, Hawk—already searchin' the islands. And now the Royal Navy will be trackin' us like dogs. There's nary a safe port or harbor left for an honest pirate. Our world is shrinkin' by the day."

Hawk looked at Bloodstone, who was staring into his tankard. For the first time, his captain appeared old and tired. "You're the craftiest pirate ever. We'll figure out something."

"Ah, to have lived a hundred years ago, when pirates ruled the Caribbean! Almost every port welcomed 'em with open arms.

As long as they preyed on the Spaniards and French, no nation would touch 'em. The golden age, they call it. We could have ruled the world, me boy!" Bloodstone downed the remainder of his drink and quickly refilled it.

"We can make this the new golden age, Captain."

"By the powers, we can't even be seen in New Orleans now, thanks to that scurvy dog Walker!" Bloodstone slammed his tankard on the table; the contents sloshed out over the sides. "And even if it's not totally over, it's close for me. I'm old. Look around ye, Hawk. Piratin' be a young man's game. I've lived much longer than most and much longer than I deserve. And with me 'bout gettin' hanged, and now that cursed Walker, me crew's probably 'bout ready to depose me anyway. It'll be your crew soon, me boy, mark me words."

"It's your crew, sir. I would never betray you and try to take your place." Hawk leaned forward in his seat to stare into the captain's bloodshot eyes.

Bloodstone chuckled softly, his rum breath strong. "Ye won't have to do a thing, me lad. They'll pick ye. But I'm afraid it'll be a short run, no matter how good you are. The navy will get stronger. And they'll keep comin'—huntin' pirates and escortin' merchants. And soon they'll search all the islands, mark me words. There'll be nowhere left to hide. A hundred years too late, blast it!"

Hawk was thoughtful for a moment. "We just need a plan. We need a way to get back on our feet and turn the tide against the US."

"What ye got in mind?"

"Maybe it's time to hunt the hunter," Hawk said, taking a swig of rum.

Bloodstone looked up from wiping rum from the table and stared at Hawk. "Ye are a crazy one, that be for sure. Those new frigates carry fifty or more guns and a crew of three hundred, and they be buildin' more by the day. We'd need many more ships and men."

"Or perhaps not," Hawk said, flashing a grin.

"What be ye thinkin', Hawk?"

Hawk had a plan but knew it would be better for Bloodstone to come up with it himself. It was really their only option. "I'll leave that plan to you. You taught me everything I know. But while you're thinking, I have a request."

"S'ppose you're right. Maybe we ain't dead yet. What be your request?" Bloodstone was beginning to rock in his chair, obviously impaired from the rum.

"Let me take the *Cobra* and a small crew to New Orleans. We're in desperate need of supplies and news of what's happened since we've been gone and the impact of Walker's blunder." Hawk knew he had to ask quickly before Bloodstone passed out.

"I don't know, me boy. Might be too dangerous."

"No one will recognize me. I'll take Billy and some of the younger crew too. Besides, our ship is obviously not a ship of war or a pirate vessel. I'll leave in the morning and be back in three days. You can tell me the plan then," Hawk pleaded, sitting on the edge of his chair.

"I s'ppose that sweet young lass at the Cove has nothin' to do with your visit?" Bloodstone asked.

"Well, they do have excellent food and drink there. And I'll need a place to lay my head after all, and—"

"Ye old dog! But ye saved me neck. I reckon I can trust ye on a mission such as this. Three days, Hawk."

Hawk floated back to his hut. He couldn't have stopped grinning if he wanted to. Despite the events he had learned of today and Bloodstone's words, he would get to see his sweet Anna again. Right then, nothing else mattered.

CHAPTER XI

"Bloodstone?" Captain Cord asked.

The *Enterprise* had been a terror to pirates since getting assigned as the flagship of the New Orleans Squadron. Most recently, they attacked Galveston Island and drove Lafitte and his pirates out. "Unfortunately not. Looks like it might be one of Kragg's, though." James responded, squinting into the spyglass. With Lafitte on the run, Bloodstone and Bartholomew Kragg were the two most powerful pirate captains remaining in the Caribbean. James knew if they could take them out, most of the remaining pirates would disappear.

"Your plan?" Cord said.

James was glad to be allowed to lead the attack again, "Let's show our colors—the Jolly Roger. Load the canister shot and ready the grenadoes. Have all the men get down out of sight with a grenadoe in hand and a blunderbuss close by. I'll take care of the rest." James walked off to prepare his weapons, while Cord began performing his duties like he was the junior officer.

The *Enterprise* had the wind behind it and headed on a perpendicular course toward the black schooner. The pirate ship flew a black flag with a red devil holding a pitchfork. It was definitely one of Bartholomew Kragg's ships. It was too small to be his flagship, so it was likely just one of his captains. Kragg had more ships and men than Bloodstone and was nearly as feared but not as clever. With Kragg, it was just a matter of sheer numbers and brutality. With Bloodstone, it was intelligence, cunning, and pure evil.

The danger with James's plan was that the pirate ship

was already broadside to the *Enterprise*. The enemy vessel could fire first, with all its cannons. However, that wasn't the norm for pirate encounters. Typically, the two pirate captains would parley with each other. Although there were rivalries, they usually realized they had a bigger, much more powerful common enemy. In a dispute, the two captains would usually face off and have a duel. This pirate captain would have no such opportunity.

As the *Enterprise* quickly closed the distance, the schooner didn't fire its guns. James saw a lot of activity on the decks, though, and most of the pirates lined the port railing. He knew they were leery but probably not expecting what he had planned. He grabbed a flintlock in each hand and crossed them behind his back.

The navigator brought the *Enterprise* about hard to port, and they were soon broadside to the pirate ship. James stood at the gangway, with fifty of his men crouched to either side of him behind the gunwale. A pirate stepped forward from the throng on the schooner and stood directly across from him. The ships continued to drift together, now only twenty feet of water separating them.

"Ho, pirate, what means ye overtakin' me in such a hurry?" the other captain called out. "And where be your crew?" The pirate captain wore a red doublet, customary of Kragg and his captains, with black breeches and boots. He wore an old, worn black tricorne on his head.

Although James wore a navy uniform, it wasn't unusual for pirates to wear the uniforms of their victims. "Arrr! This be the first wind to blow in weeks. Been dead in the water, we have. Lost most of me men to the fever and thirst. The livin' ones be dyin' below deck. Been survivin' on bilge rats, maggots, and fouled water, I have. I hailed ye to see if ye can help a pirate mate and his dyin' crew."

The pirate captain scanned from bow to stern and then turned back to James. "Your ship 'pears to be shipshape, as do ye. What be your name, Cap'n?"

A slightly different plan came to James's mind. He almost grinned. "Ye should know me. I be the fiercest pirate of all, Cap'n Bloodstone. I see ye fly Kragg's colors. What be your name, Cap'n?"

The pirate captain placed his hand above his eyes and squinted. "Ye don't look much like Bloodstone. I'm Captain Grant."

"And have ye ever seen him before?" James roared.

"Don't reckon I have. Heard about him, though. Big beast of a man with black hair and beard dressed in black. Ye look more like a swab without a hair on your chin." The pirate crew behind him laughed loudly at the insult.

"And what do ye reckon Bloodstone would do if he were insulted by a cowardly servin' wench of a captain of Kragg's?"

Captain Grant's hands dropped to the hilts of two pistols hanging from his belt. His crew likewise tensed and placed their hands near weapons. "I be in a generous mood today. Seein' you're by yourself on that ship, I suggest ye sail away. Else I decide to brave the disease and take your ship for Kragg."

"That be a right kind offer, it is. If I weren't Cap'n Bloodstone, I'd take ye up on it. But I'm afraid I have only one word in response."

"And what word be that?"

"Fire!" James brought both cocked pistols forward and fired, one at Captain Grant and one at the closest pirate that appeared to be an officer. Both pirates fell to the deck, either dead or dying. Before the other pirates could draw their weapons, the *Enterprise* crew stood and launched the grenadoes. They had lit the fuses behind the rail as soon as they realized the conversation was over. The grenadoes hit the pirate ship deck and exploded, sending fire and scraps of metal in all directions. The pirates were so close together that the damage was devastating. Then the cannons roared from the deck below. The canister shot spewed its deadly contents into the pirates screaming and running about to avoid the grenadoes.

The sailors then grabbed the blunderbusses and tried to find targets.

"Hold!" James shouted.

Only a handful of pirates remained on the schooner's deck, and they were desperately seeking cover. Captain Cord appeared beside James, looking at him questioningly.

"Yo, pirate crew, who be in charge now?" said James. The flapping of sails and slapping of water against hulls was the only reply. "Don't make me board ye to figure it out!"

A timid pirate poked his head over the railing next to the forecastle. "I think that would be me. I'm the bosun. You killed the captain and quartermaster."

"I be in a generous mood today too, just like your cap'n was. If ye throw all your weapons in the sea, including your shot, I'll let ye live."

The remaining pirates appeared from various hiding places about the deck. They huddled together for a moment and then began tossing cutlasses, daggers, pistols, muskets, and blunderbusses into the water. The cannons below were rolled back out of the gunports, and cannon balls soon started splashing into the ocean. After ten minutes, the splashing stopped.

"That's all, Cap'n," the bosun called out.

"Thank ye. Never let it be said that Captain Bloodstone doesn't have a heart. Ye sail back to Cap'n Kragg and tell him the Spanish Main ain't big enough for the both of us. Now get ye gone before I change my mind."

The few remaining pirates scurried about the deck, and the two ships disengaged.

James turned to Captain Cord. "Well? What do ye think?"

"Nice pirate talk. Do you think they believe you are Captain Bloodstone?"

"No. Those fellows over there don't. But by the time they get back to Kragg and have to explain how they lost their captain, quartermaster, two-thirds of their crew, and all their weapons without firing a single cannon, I'll have been Bloodstone and on the *Bloody Seas* no less. Kragg wouldn't accept them losing to an anonymous pirate."

Cord clapped James on the shoulder. "Bloody genius! Now you will have Kragg and Bloodstone in an all-out pirate war."

"And we'll be there to congratulate the victors. Now, let's do some more hunting."

CHAPTER XII

Hawk immediately noticed a difference in the ships anchored at the New Orleans docks. In the past, pirates did little to disguise their heavily armed pirate ships, other than not flying their colors. Now, most ships were clearly either merchant or navy. Luckily, their sloop wouldn't attract any attention, nor would the young sailors that disembarked.

"Billy, take half the men and trade our goods for food and supplies. Buy the rest," Hawk said, handing Billy a leather pouch of coins. "Spread out and gather information tonight. Make time for a little fun after."

Billy took the pouch and quickly rounded up ten men. They began bringing boxes and crates out of the hold and headed off to visit some of their regular merchants. The sun hung low in the sky, and the merchants would close soon.

"All right, ye lot o' scallywags." Hawk did his best imitation of Bloodstone. "I want you to spread out to your usual haunts. If you haven't been here before, pick a direction; you'll find a new one soon. But before you get too far into drink and women, listen for any talk of Bloodstone, pirates, or the navy. Our lives could depend on what you hear tonight. I need you all back here by sunrise. I have a short mission for you then." Hawk strode onto the dock and toward the Treasure Cove without waiting to see the pirates' reactions.

The Treasure Cove hadn't changed much since the last time Hawk was there. It might have been a little more crowded, and the occupants a little better dressed and respectable, but it was the same. He excitedly scanned the room for Anna but didn't see her. His heart skipped a few beats. *What if she's gone?*

He found a small, unoccupied table in the corner, sat down with his back against the wall, and did his best to eavesdrop on the nearby patrons. It wasn't hard since most were in at least some state of drunkenness and tried to talk above the din. Finally, Madame Cynthia noticed the new patron and approached his table.

"May I help you, handsome?" she asked sweetly.

Hawk looked up and grinned. "Hello, Miss Cynthia."

"Well, I'll be!" she exclaimed. She quickly leaned down and hugged him. She smelled sweet, despite the odor of food, alcohol, and smoke in the room. "Let's see...Hawk!"

"You're good."

"My, you've grown into quite the strapping man!" She laughed when she saw Hawk's cheeks redden. "Now, where is that old Captain Blood...Blackburn?"

Hawk was surprised at the slip and that she must know who Bloodstone really was. "He didn't make this trip. It's been a while since we've been here, and he wanted me to check how the market was for...honest sailors."

Cynthia flashed a quick grin, followed by a wink. "That was probably wise. It's definitely not as good trading here as it used to be. Despite saving New Orleans's arse in the war, Lafitte and his crew still aren't welcome here."

"I figured as much," Hawk replied, shaking his head. "I heard one of Captain Bloodstone's ships was sunk close by recently." He spoke louder now, so their whispering wouldn't draw attention.

"Confounded fools! They say the ship attacked a merchantman just out of sight of the city—an American merchantman no less. The *Enterprise* took them out in quick fashion."

"What is the *Enterprise*?"

"It's the pride of the American Navy and the flagship of the New Orleans Squadron. It's sailed by Captain Cord and his Lieutenant, James Wellington. They say they are as ruthless as Bloodstone himself, especially the younger man, James. They'd rather convict and punish the pirates on their ship than wait for a judge and gallows. I heard they just chased Lafitte and his men out of their stronghold on Galveston Island." Cynthia's eyes looked a little glassy just for a moment. "I'll be back with some ale and a plate of food."

Hawk mulled over her words. That was the first time he'd heard James's last name. He always thought of his brother when he heard the name *James*. It was a common name, though. However, something sounded familiar about *Wellington*. He searched his memories until Cynthia returned with his tankard of ale and a plate with a large slab of roast beef, boiled potatoes, and some kind of greens.

"Now that the business is out of the way, I suppose you would like to inquire about a certain sweet, young lady?" She reached out and rubbed his thick blond hair as she had two years prior.

Hawk quickly forgot about James Wellington and grinned. "I think I might like to say hello."

Cynthia laughed loudly. "I bet you would. Finish your meal and get some ale in your belly. I'll have her come by and visit."

"Oh, Madame Cynthia," Hawk called out as she turned to leave. She quickly turned back around. Hawk reached into his waistcoat and produced a gold coin. "This is for the food and drink and for Anna tonight and tomorrow. Also, pack some food and drink and throw in an old blanket. I'll pick it up in the morning."

Cynthia quickly scooped up the coin and grinned. "For this, you can have her tomorrow night too. The food will be in a basket behind the counter."

Hawk didn't gather much more news as he ate his supper and drank his ale. His eyes scanned the room until he finally spotted Anna emerging from the kitchen behind the bar. She appeared almost the same as she had two years ago, only dressed in a blue and white lace dress this time. Her eyes searched the room and then met his, and she walked quickly over to his table.

"Hello, Mr. Hawk," she said in her sweet, musical voice. She stared shyly at the ground.

"Hello? I thought you might be more excited."

"It has been a long time," she said unemotionally.

Hawk tried to hide his disappointment. His fantasy had involved her running over, wrapping her arms around him, and kissing him passionately on the lips. He didn't expect this. Apparently, he hadn't been on her mind as much as she had been on his. "Can we go upstairs and talk?"

"Madame Cynthia said you had paid, so we can do as you wish." She turned and led him up the stairs and into a different room this time, although the interior was almost identical. She sat on the bed, staring straight ahead, and Hawk quickly joined her.

Hawk reached over and caressed her smooth, soft cheek with his left hand. He gently turned her head until she looked at him. "Anna, it's me. What's wrong?"

"It's you? Who are you? Oh, you're the young boy that filled my head with crazy dreams two years ago—the one that promised to come back and rescue me from...this. Not only didn't you rescue me, you never even came back to see me!" She pulled her head back away from his hand and stared at the floor, her eyes glassy.

Hawk was stunned by her honest and cold response. She didn't sound like the sweet, proper young lady from his last visit. He suppressed the frustration that was quickly building. "Anna, I've thought about you every night. You don't know how bad I wanted to see you again."

"Then why didn't you come to see me?"

"We...our ship...we sailed to a different area to find new places to...trade. We just returned yesterday, and I came to town to find out news of the trading conditions here. Anna, you have to understand that I'm not the ship's captain. I'm just the bosun. I have to go where the others vote to go." Hawk reached his right hand over and placed it on top of her small, warm left hand.

"That story doesn't make sense. Just what kind of trade do you and your ship engage in?" She now turned to face him.

Hawk was silent for a moment. Despite her anger and sorrow, she was still a beautiful creature. His heart fluttered as he inhaled her perfume again. "Almost anything really—cloth, weapons, spirits, food...."

Anna quickly wiped a tear from the corner of her left eye. "Are you a pirate? Don't lie to me, Hawk."

"Let me tell you the entire story."

Anna turned, pulled her hand away from his, and placed both hands over her face. She sobbed softly.

"Anna, please just listen; then you can judge." Hawk waited a moment for her sobbing to subside. When he knew she was listening, he told her his life story.

They were both silent for a few minutes after he'd finished. "I don't know, Hawk. You're a criminal. You have killed and stolen your entire life," Anna said softly.

"What was I to do, Anna? I was eight years old when Bloodstone rescued me. I had no family left or place to go. Other than the Rock, I never even set foot on land until I met you last time. Was I to subdue or kill one hundred pirates, take the ship, and sail it blindly, hoping to find land I could escape to? It's the only life I've known.

"But two years ago, when I finally did realize that there is life outside the ship and the Rock, I did start dreaming of leaving it behind. I've been saving every coin I earn so that one day I can keep my promise to you."

Anna finally turned to face him again. Although he was still innocent, he was a grown man now. He was even more handsome and strong than two years ago. She had cursed his name and memory for most of the past year. But now, face-to-face, she struggled to keep the same feelings from two years ago from returning. For some inexplicable reason, she was drawn to him like she had been to no other man. "I don't know, Hawk. I don't know if I can accept how you make a living."

Hawk experienced a quick flash of anger. He inhaled deeply before he calmly spoke. "Anna, you questioning me being a pirate would be the same as me questioning what you do for a living. I could easily ask you why you haven't run away, why you haven't done something different. I could say I can't accept that you've been with hundreds, if not thousands, of pirates and sailors."

Now anger flashed in Anna's eyes, but Hawk continued before she spoke. "But I don't. You told me your story last time, and I accepted it. As long as you're with me, there are no other men. We can't influence each other's pasts. We can't change each other's or our own. All we can do is live in the present and try to change our futures. We both want out of our current lives. We want to start over fresh and lead new lives. I *will* leave this life behind and start a new one. But I want you to be a part of the new one. Yes, two years have passed. And two or more might pass again before I can leave it behind. But we are young. We will still be young in two years. We have our entire lives ahead of us. Please, just judge the man sitting here beside you. Judge what you're feeling right now. Don't judge the pirate you've never met."

Anna's face and eyes softened. This time it was she who reached out and placed a hand on one of his. "I want to trust you, Hawk. I want to believe in you." She squeezed his hand gently.

"Then just do it." Hawk placed his right hand behind her head and gently pulled her close. He leaned forward until their lips met. They were even softer and warmer than he remembered. Tingling instantly spread from his lips to his entire body, leaving chill bumps in its wake. They were both hesitant and tentative for a moment, then slowly, their fears and concerns melted away. Hawk reached his other hand around to softly stroke her right cheek as their kisses became firmer and more intense. Hawk's face and skin transitioned from warm to hot despite the chills. If anything, kissing Anna was even better this time than it had been the first time.

Hawk's kiss and touch had the same effect on Anna as it had two years ago—her heard raced; a thin layer of perspiration coated her skin; her body trembled as her skin prickled. She still had never experienced any desire with any of the men she had to sleep with. Sex was a job. Now she was being swept away by a man who was still a virgin. All her pain and anger at him not coming back sooner was gone. He was right. He was here now; that was the only moment she could control.

They continued to kiss as Hawk lay down on the bed, pulling her down beside him. Their hands began to explore each other's body through their clothing. Soon, both were panting—their hearts beating wildly together. Anna moved Hawk's hand from her side to her breast. He started to resist, but she kept her hand on his, guiding him.

Finally, it was Anna's turn to break off the kissing. She stood up and gazed down at Hawk. "Do not say a word," she said, stopping Hawk's protests in his throat. She reached behind her neck and untied her dress. She then pulled the silk material off her shoulders, allowing it to drop to the floor around her ankles.

Hawk couldn't have spoken even if he'd tried. The light from the lamp flickered across her perfect body, making it appear as if her skin pulsed and moved. He'd never seen a naked woman before, but he knew she had to be a perfect one. Her pale, smooth skin was flawless. Her breasts were firm and round, her stomach flat, and her curvy hips eventually gave way to long, lean legs. His body's reaction was overpowering. Lust and desire replaced any fear or doubt. He wasn't sure exactly what came next, but he would enjoy figuring it out.

Anna smiled at Hawk's stunned expression and open mouth. The hunger in his eyes only further fueled her own. She almost felt like she was the virgin. She leaned over, placed her hands on his shoulders, and kissed him passionately. Now he wouldn't need to try to speak. She pulled his waistcoat off and then unbuttoned his silk shirt. She then pushed him back onto the pillows and untied the sash around his waist. Hawk didn't protest as she next removed his breeches and boots and threw them on the floor.

Anna straightened up and admired Hawk's body in the dim lamplight. His body could have been chiseled out of stone. He was tan, lean, and muscular. The numerous scars only made him that much more manly. He was so strong, yet his touch so soft and gentle. His thick blond hair was ruffled from their touching and kissing. His blue eyes stared at her with desire, and his lips were full and glistening from her kisses. She'd been with hundreds of men but never a perfect one.

Anna slowly climbed onto the bed and lay down beside him. "Do not worry, Mr. Hawk. I will teach you." Anna whispered softly into his ear. They just kissed at first, enjoying the sensation of their hot naked bodies pressing and moving together and letting their hands discover areas previously untouched. But soon, the desire was too much, and kissing and touching weren't enough.

Anna quickly discovered the difference between having sex and making love. With her gentle guidance, Hawk quickly learned how to touch her in ways she had never been touched. The rush of emotions was almost too much as they made love that night. It was as if their minds and bodies merged into one. She was pleased in ways she had never dreamed of. Hawk was young and very virile, and they made love several times until late into the night. Finally exhausted, they collapsed into each other's arms. The last thing Hawk told her was that she was spending tomorrow with him, and they were doing something wonderful. As tired as she was, she hardly slept in Hawk's strong arms, waiting on the sun to rise.

CHAPTER XIII

When Hawk awoke, it took a moment to realize where he was. Then he quickly rolled over and was relieved to see Anna still lying beside him, sleeping soundly. He replayed the events of the night before in his mind as he stared at the beautiful woman beside him. He was still overwhelmed with emotion. First, there was the physical pleasure, which was better than he'd ever imagined. Second, there were the other feelings that came from touching her, and now, just gazing upon her—the butterflies in his stomach, his swimming head, and his racing heart. He had been a little worried over the past two years that maybe he'd built up Anna—and his feelings for her—too much based on just one short night together. But after a second night, he realized she was even better than he'd dreamed.

He reached over and lightly touched her long, soft hair. Then he stroked her cheek and lightly brushed her slightly parted lips. She stirred then and, in a moment, opened her eyes. She slowly turned her head to stare at him. As soon as her eyes focused, she smiled.

"Good morning, beautiful," Hawk said, leaning over and kissing her. He would have liked to enjoy another lovemaking session but knew they didn't have time. "It's time for our big day."

"What do you have in mind, Mr. Hawk?" she asked, rising up on her elbows.

"It's a surprise. Now, we need to make haste."

They kissed again, and Anna quickly hurried off to her room to freshen up. Hawk poured water from the nearby bucket into the basin and washed as well as he could while standing. Then he dressed and headed downstairs. He found the basket behind the counter and waited on Anna until she joined him, wearing a tight beige dress, a low-cut pair of boots, and a white, wide-brimmed hat.

They walked quickly through the square, with Hawk carrying the basket in his right hand and holding Anna's hand in his left. Few people were stirring yet, as the sun was still a few minutes from rising. Hawk was pleased that Anna seemed so excited. They arrived at the ship just as the last few pirates stumbled sleepily onboard.

"We are going sailing!" Anna said.

"Just for the morning. Then we have other plans after that."

The ten members of his crew milled about the main deck, staring at Hawk and Anna in surprise. They shared several grins, elbows, and whispers among them. Their hangovers appeared to ease at this bit of excitement.

"All right, ye bunch of bilge rats! Act like you've sailed before! Haul in those mooring lines and make ready to sail. Then you six get below deck and man the oars; you other four stay up top and man the sails. I'll take the helm." The pirates quickly set about their tasks. Hawk winked at Anna and led her to the quarterdeck.

By the time Hawk grasped the large wheel, the ship was moving. A little wind caught the sails, and the oarsmen rowed hard. Hawk steered around the bends of the river and toward the open sea. The sun had risen, and the river and nearby marshes glowed orange.

"Oh my, this is wonderful!" Anna exclaimed. She walked around the entire deck, taking in the view from each side and the stern. She finally returned to stand beside Hawk.

"First time on a ship, I take it?"

"Oh yes! I love it, though! My stomach feels a little strange, but it is great. The men obey you like you are their captain," Anna said. She placed her right arm through the bend in his left.

Hawk smiled. "I am, for this voyage at least. Here, would you like to steer a pirate ship?" Hawk grasped her hands and placed them on the helm.

Anna was concerned for a moment, then once she started turning the big wheel, she laughed. "Arrr! I am Anna, the Pirate Queen!"

Hawk laughed loudly. Now that she was away from the tavern and her job, her personality truly started to show. He stood beside her and wrapped his right arm around her waist. "And I'm Hawk, your Pirate King! Now, my dear, as pirate queen, you may act as such. You can talk and act however you'd like today...and every day with me."

Anna grinned and then turned her attention back to guiding the sloop down the river and into the open water. She was amazed at her first sight of the sea. She could have never imagined anything so vast.

Hawk shouted for Jimmy, who was close by on the main deck, to come man the helm. He had been impressed with Jimmy's honesty and bravery at the Rock and wanted to see how he handled himself on the ship. Hawk then led Anna to the bow. They stood against the front rail, at the base of the bowsprit, talking, laughing, and enjoying the thick, salty air.

"It's funny," Hawk said. "You've never been on the sea, and I've hardly ever been on the land. And we're both fascinated with what has become boring for the other."

"This is wonderful, but I think I'd be happy on land or sea as long as you were by my side." She leaned back against him and turned her head to look up. He leaned down and kissed her.

After a couple of hours, a small island came into view, and Jimmy steered the *Cobra* toward it. Hawk had taken a break from Anna along the way and told Jimmy and several of the crew what the plan was. The speck of land was one of several small islands not far from New Orleans and not too far from the Rock. Hawk had explored all the islands between the Rock and New Orleans over the years. This one was similar to their stronghold, with its hardwood forest and lagoons, but it was much smaller and surrounded by water that was too shallow for a ship like the

Bloody Seas to get close. The *Cobra* could sail almost to the beach.

Hawk disappeared into his cabin and changed into his everyday pirate garb. Now he wore a baldric, stretching from his shoulder to his waist, over top his white linen shirt. It held two flintlocks, his dagger, and a cutlass.

When he reappeared on the main deck, Anna looked him over from head to toe and grinned. "So, this is pirate Hawk?"

He laughed. "Do I look brave and dashing?"

"Yes...and a little scary. Do you need all those weapons?" Her mirth gave way to concern.

"Hopefully not today. But you never know. These are dangerous times. Especially for honest pirates."

He turned to the helm. "Ho, Jimmy!"

"Yes, sir," Jimmy called back.

"I need for you to be back here by sundown today."

"Aye, Captain," Jimmy said heartily.

"I'm not your captain. And Jimmy, I'm counting on you. Sundown."

"You can count on me, sir."

The ship sailed as close to the white, sandy beach as it could safely go. Hawk shouted commands to the pirates nearby, and soon a longboat was lowered over the side and into the water.

Hawk dropped a rope ladder over the rail. "I'll go down first," he said to Anna. "Jimmy will drop the basket down to me, and then you can follow. I'll help you into the boat." He swung his legs over the rail.

Anna watched Hawk scramble down the ladder. He stood in the boat as Jimmy dropped the basket over the side. Hawk caught it effortlessly and placed it in the front of the boat. He then nodded to Anna. She frowned, not wanting to climb down the unsteady ladder. Hawk smiled up at her. "Come down, my lovely pirate queen!"

Anna finally shook her head and displayed the smallest of grins. Jimmy held onto her arm as she tentatively climbed onto the unstable ladder. She paused a moment and then inched her way down, glad that Hawk and the boat were below her.

"Hmmm. I like this view," Hawk said as her feet reached the rung just above his head.

"You'll see the view of the bottom of my boot in just a moment," she said, not entirely joking.

Hawk laughed. When her feet were almost to the boat, Hawk reached up and placed both hands on her waist. He gently lowered her to stand in front of him on the rocking vessel. "Ho there, Miss Anna," he said, smiling at her until she finally smiled back. "It will get better, don't worry."

"It had better!" Anna was actually very happy and excited now that she'd made it down the rope.

Hawk motioned for her to sit on the board closest to the back of the boat, and he sat down in the middle and grabbed the two oars. He began rowing with long, powerful strokes. Anna liked watching his muscles strain beneath his thin white shirt. It was unbuttoned halfway, exposing his bare, muscular chest.

Her gaze darted away when he caught her staring. The sea was a beautiful, nearly clear blue. The sky above was close to the same color, with a few large billowy clouds floating past on the gentle warm breeze. Her heart raced as she accepted the reality that she would spend the day away from the tavern, Madame Cynthia, and dirty sailors. And she got to spend it on a beautiful island with her handsome pirate. Small waves soon caught the boat and sped it toward the white beach.

When the boat hit ground, Hawk leaped out, grabbed the bow, and pulled it farther up the beach. He helped Anna out onto the warm sand and then gave her a big hug and a long, slow kiss.

"What is this place?" she finally said.

"I'm not sure if it has a name, but it's not far from the Rock. I've only been here a couple of times, usually hunting and gathering fruit. I love it, though. The waters are too shallow for the big ships."

"And what are we going to do?"

"Whatever you like. I had the madame pack us a meal in this basket. I thought we would walk to a small pond in the woods near the island's center and eat there. Maybe we can enjoy some swimming too."

"Oh, that sounds perfect!" She kissed Hawk again.

He grabbed the basket from the boat and led her up the beach to an old animal trail leading into a stand of palm trees. Anna's head constantly swiveled. She had never seen anything except New Orleans. She soaked in all the new sensations like a sponge —the smell of the ocean and lush vegetation, the texture of the leaves and trunks of the trees, the warm breeze, the sounds of birds singing and animals scurrying out of their way.

She reached a hand inside the bend in one of Hawk's arms. "I've never felt like this!"

Hawk turned to look at her beaming face. "Like what?"

"I don't know—just so…so excited…so happy! I never knew a person could feel this way."

"And to think you were so rude to me last night," Hawk laughed.

Anna pinched his bicep. "You didn't tell me we were going to a beautiful island." She laughed too.

The palms gave way to a thicker patch of oak trees. It was shady and cooler here, with only occasional shafts of sunlight penetrating the dense foliage. Anna loved the earthy smell. Finally, they arrived at a large oval pond. The water was a dark, murky, blue-green color. A thick patch of reeds covered the far side of the water. Several clumps of white flowers dotted the banks, and a bed of ferns surrounded the water and flowers.

"Wow, this is lovely!" Anna exclaimed. She gave him a quick peck on the lips.

Hawk walked to a thick, semi-shaded patch of ferns on the near side of the water and set the basket down. He opened it, removed an old, stained cotton blanket, and spread it over the ferns. He then distributed the basket's contents on the blanket —a loaf of soft bread, a block of cheese, hunks of roast beef, a couple of apples, two onion bottles of red wine, and two silver goblets. The madame had done well, although, for a doubloon, she still came out much ahead.

"Are you hungry, my dear?" Hawk asked, motioning for her

to join him on the blanket.

Anna ran over and kneeled beside Hawk. She couldn't stop grinning. Every moment they were together, things only got better. She watched as he removed his dagger and placed it beside him. He then took off his baldric, laid it on one corner of the blanket, and removed his boots. Only sixteen, he was full of confidence. She quickly removed her boots too and sat down beside him.

Hawk wrapped his right arm around her, and she laid her head on his shoulder. It was a warm day but comfortable in the shady forest. They stared at the pond in silence. Bullfrogs croaked from the direction of the patch of reeds, and birds called out from the tree limbs somewhere overhead. An occasional rustling in the leaves indicated some kind of forest creature scurrying about.

"You're quiet. Is everything OK?" Hawk asked, turning to look at Anna. Her cheek and hair glowed in a ray of sunlight.

"Oh, Hawk, I cannot even speak! I have too many emotions flowing through me. I want to cry; I want to scream; I want to laugh; I want to run and jump around like a little girl. I don't know what's wrong with me." She gazed at him, tears welling up in her eyes.

"But it's a good feeling, right?"

"Very, very good! Just a little overwhelming."

Hawk leaned over and kissed her gently. It very quickly turned passionate, and Hawk felt the blood rush to his face and other parts of his body. He had planned on them eating first, but desire quickly swept him away. He gently laid her down on the blanket while continuing to kiss her. Soon they were panting as they stopped only long enough to remove each other's clothing. In moments, they were making love. Now that the nervousness was gone, it was even better than the night before. There was also something special about being in nature and their bodies getting caressed by the sun's rays and kissed by the soft breeze.

When they finished, they lay on their backs, Hawk's arm beneath Anna's head, and stared at the patterns of leaves on the limbs above. The gentle breeze cooled them off and quickly dried their sweat. After several minutes, Hawk rolled over, kissed her, and then sat up. "I bet you're hungry."

Anna sat up, too, grabbing her dress and placing it over her lap. "Famished."

Hawk also placed his shirt over his lap and began making their lunch, consisting of beef and cheese sandwiches, apples, and sweet red wine. They hadn't eaten since the evening before and had definitely worked up a good appetite. After the feast, they lay down on the blanket to let it settle.

"This is so amazing," Anna said softly.

"This place is nice," Hawk replied, his eyes closed.

"No. Not just this place. I guess it is the…the freedom. I don't remember what it is like not to have chores to do. I have nothing that I have to do today. For this moment, we're totally free. We can do whatever we want. I don't have to pretend to be someone I'm not. Of course, I guess you're used to having freedom."

Hawk was silent for a moment. "Not really. Pirates have chores and jobs, whether on the ship or on land. While you do have some free time at night on the ship and when you're at a hideout, you're still not free to come and go as you please. You also never have privacy. There are always mates nearby, even in my cabin and hut. This kind of freedom is much better." He paused for another moment. "Really, Anna, our lives aren't that different."

"I think that's one reason I'm so attracted to you. It does sound like we're both slaves to our lives in many ways—forced into them and unable to escape. Now we're both old enough to realize there are other options and other lives we could lead." She turned her head to gaze at him.

Hawk rolled his head over and grinned. "You're very right, my dear." He gave her a quick kiss. "So, is your dream still the same one you told me about last time?"

"Yes! And this day has just made me realize that reality could be even better than my dreams. Now I'll add a pond to my dream, though." She laughed. "Can you imagine having our own piece of land? Enjoying privacy like this? Doing what we wanted when we wanted? Sure, we would have chores to do, but chores we wanted to do."

Hawk laughed at her excitement. "Yeah, I've been thinking about your dream a lot. With each voyage, I grow more tired of the pirate life. It's no longer exciting, even after a great battle or big haul. Well, it's only exciting because the more loot I receive, the sooner I can leave the life behind. I'm just so ready to do something different: sleep in a bed that doesn't move during the night, breathe air that's not heavy with salt or tainted with foul odors, and not have to wonder each day if that day will be my last."

"You wouldn't get bored, leaving all the adventure and fighting behind to be stuck on land with me?" Anna asked, her lower lip pushed out a little.

"Tired of this? Spending every moment in paradise with the sweetest, most beautiful woman ever? Not on your life! It would be heaven on earth."

"Oh, Hawk!" She rolled over on top of him and kissed him forcefully.

"And would you not miss all the excitement of the tavern and meeting and entertaining all those handsome sailors?" Hawk asked when they finally ended the kiss.

Anna lightly smacked his cheek. "You would be all the excitement I needed. And you're handsome enough. You'd do." She laughed. Suddenly she leaped to her feet, dropped her dress, and ran down to the pond, diving in headfirst.

In a moment, she reappeared, shaking the water from her long hair. She smiled and motioned for Hawk to join her. He laughed and quickly obeyed. He dove in and swam beneath the surface until he could see her white legs in the murky water. He bit her thigh playfully, almost receiving a surprised knee in the face. He then slowly kissed his way up her body until he eventually stood in front of her in the chest-deep water. Her naked body was warm against his, despite the cold water surrounding them. They kissed each other passionately for several minutes, their wet lips sliding together effortlessly.

"Want me to teach you how to swim?" Hawk asked when they finally paused to catch their breaths.

"I had heard pirates cannot swim," she said playfully.

"I'm not your ordinary pirate." Hawk pinched her hip beneath the water.

"So, are you now the Seahawk?"

Hawk turned and swam to the edge of the pond. He reached it quickly with long, powerful strokes. It was true that most pirates and sailors couldn't swim, and falling off a ship in a storm or battle was usually a death sentence. But Hawk had mastered the skill, as well as most other skills. He might die in a battle, but not from the water. He turned and swam back to her. "Now, your turn."

Hawk held his strong arms beneath her stomach and instructed her how to move her arms and legs. He walked with her, supporting most of her weight as she kicked and paddled. There was a lot of playful splashing, laughing, touching, and kissing, but she soon learned the basics.

As she practiced swimming on her own, Hawk waded out to the blanket and sat down to drink some wine. He smiled as he watched her splash about. He loved the carefree Anna—so much different from the one at the Treasure Cove. Suddenly, another movement caught Hawk's eye. It came from within the patch of reeds. When he scanned the patch, he only saw some ripples and bubbles. He dismissed it and turned back to Anna.

Then he thought about Razortooth. "Anna! Swim this way as fast as you can!"

Anna stopped swimming and let her feet hit the sand below. "What's the matter?"

Hawk knew she would never make it. He grabbed his dagger and ran full speed to the pond's edge. "Swim!" he yelled as he leaped as high and far as his powerful legs could propel him. He disappeared headfirst into the water, almost at Anna.

As Hawk dove into the water, Anna felt something big strike her left thigh. Several sharp pains quickly followed the blunt force. She screamed and tried to run. A great commotion churned the water just behind her.

Suddenly, Hawk reappeared. In his arms was a massive grayish-green scaled head. Its mouth was open, filled with razor-sharp white teeth. Hawk's left arm was bleeding in several spots. Anna knew from hearing sailor's tales that it was an alligator. "Hawk!"

"Get to shore!" Hawk shouted. The alligator started rolling its body, and they soon disappeared beneath the surface. A small red stain appeared in the water, a mixture of his and Anna's blood.

Anna ran out of the water and onto the shore. She realized the beast's teeth had punctured her leg in several places. Blood streamed down her leg and dripped onto the ferns. Hawk must have reached the alligator just before it completed the bite on her leg. His arm had paid the price. The pair continued to roll and thrash beneath the water and moved back and forth across the pond. Occasionally, Hawk broke the surface, gasped for air, and disappeared again. Other times, the alligator's tail or back would momentarily appear and quickly disappear.

The red stain in the middle of the pond began to spread much faster. Neither combatant had broken the surface in over a minute. The churning and splashing in the water slowed until nothing moved at all.

"Hawk!" Anna screamed, tears flowing down her face. Still nothing. Then she saw the alligator's body appear at the surface —without Hawk attached to it. "No!" she screamed.

She sobbed and stared at the water's still surface for what seemed like minutes. Then, something moved in the water just in front of her. Hawk's head appeared first, followed by the rest of his body, as he crawled up onto the bank, rolled over, and collapsed onto his back beside her. He still held his bloodied dagger in his outstretched right arm. Anna realized that the alligator wasn't swimming but floating, and the blood was spreading from its neck. Hawk's arm still bled profusely too. He also had gashes in his side and on one of his legs. He lay there panting hard, his eyes closed.

Anna knelt over him. "Hawk! Are you OK?"

Hawk slowly opened his eyes, blinked hard a few times, and focused on her. "I've been better," he whispered, grinning weakly.

"Oh, Hawk! You saved my life! You're so brave and strong!" She leaned down farther and kissed him.

"If I'd known I'd ended up like this, I might have changed my mind," Hawk chuckled softly.

Anna slapped him playfully on his unharmed arm.

"How is your leg?" he asked, suddenly remembering her getting struck first.

"It has a few holes and hurts, but I think I will be OK."

Hawk slowly sat up and surveyed his wounds and then Anna's. "Let's patch ourselves up, dress, and head back to the beach. The ship will be here soon. I can clean our wounds and stitch them up on the way back to New Orleans. I've had lots of training with Mr. Bones."

They moved up to the blanket, and Hawk quickly cut his shirt into different size strips. He tied one around Anna's leg. The wounds were deep but had almost quit bleeding. Anna helped him secure another one around his arm. His leg and side weren't too bad. They put their clothes back on, packed the basket, and limped back down the trail to the beach. It was later than they realized, and Jimmy and Billy had just swum to the shore in preparations to go find them.

"Hawk! What happened to you?" Jimmy looked at Hawk and Anna and quickly scanned the trees behind them.

"I think I found Razortooth's brother," Hawk chuckled. He told his story to Jimmy and Billy.

"Wow! You killed an alligator with your bare hands?"

"Well, I had help from a dagger. I'm glad you two came to shore, though...now you can row us back to the *Cobra*."

The four climbed into the boat, and Jimmy and Billy rowed them back to the ship and helped them board. Onboard, the story quickly spread until every man had heard it. Hawk's legend continued to grow. The crew almost fell over themselves, trying either to be of assistance or to get out of his and Anna's way. Hawk led Anna to his cabin and grabbed the alcohol, needle, catgut, and bandages. A painful half hour later, their wounds were cleaned, stitched, and bandaged, and Hawk changed back into his city clothes.

Hawk let Billy and Jimmy handle most of the duties for their short voyage back. He and Anna sat on the ship's bow, arms around each other, and watched the sun set, its orange rays dancing off the calm water. Despite their pain and discomfort, it was a perfect end to a nearly perfect day.

"Well, other than getting bit by an alligator, did you have a good night and day?" Hawk asked.

Anna's head lay against his shoulder. "Oh, yes, Hawk. It was the most wonderful night and day of my life!" She squeezed his arm, the uninjured one, tightly.

"Good. Once we get back to New Orleans, I'm going to walk you to the Cove, and then my crew and I will have to sail back to the Rock."

Anna was silent for a moment. "When will I see you again?" she asked softly and lifted her head to look at him.

"I'm not sure. I have a feeling Bloodstone has something big planned for us. I told you about our current situation. I don't have enough money stashed away yet for me to leave. Just know this, Anna. I swear that I will come back for you. One way or the other, I will come back rich enough for us to disappear into our dream. It might be a year…it might be five years, but I will be back." He leaned forward and kissed her. He felt her warm tears run down her cheeks onto his. He was pretty sure some of his tears joined them.

"Please hurry," she whispered.

"I will. But now you've at least had a taste of what it will be like together. It's no longer a dream. You've touched it—held it in your hands. Now you have memories to live on, not just dreams. And one day, all this time we've waited will be long forgotten."

"And you have just had a small taste of what waits for you."

CHAPTER XIV

That night, Hawk, Diablo, Bones, Andre, Hobbs, and Bloodstone gathered around the large table in Bloodstone's cabin. They had spent the first-hour drinking rum, talking of Hawk's trip and recent fight, and swapping stories of the sea. Finally, Bloodstone called the meeting to order.

"Arrr! It be time for business, me mates. As ye know, we be short of men and money. The times, they also be a changin'. The New Orleans Squadron, led by that devil Cord and the *Enterprise*, be a scourge to pirates. They have at least a dozen ships now and be addin' more all the time. They also be searchin' all the islands. Ain't no hideouts safe now." He paused and swallowed a large swig of rum. "The way I reckon it, we have two choices to ponder. One be to leave the trade and become honest men."

"That ain't an option," Diablo said.

"Aye, I reckon it ain't, for sure. The second be to do somethin' big—to even the odds or least buy some time." Bloodstone sat back in his chair and puffed sweet-smelling tobacco smoke from his long pipe.

"And what do you propose?" Andre asked.

"There be three parts to me plan. First, we need men and loot. As ye know, slave ships be more common than treasure ships. In the past, we set free those that we didn't kill. As bad as it pains me, I propose we offer quarter to all ships we attack, slave or merchant, if they'll join us. If they think they won't die, I reckon most won't fight. The blacks will join without pause. We take 'em all, sailors and slaves, and their loot. We train 'em how to shoot, and we buy more weapons. That be the first part."

The officers exchanged glances and nods. Hawk knew that he and everyone except Diablo secretly disagreed with Bloodstone killing the innocent sailors.

"And the second part?" Bones asked.

"The second part ye won't like as much. We need to make an alliance…with Kragg."

That statement brought an eruption of exclamations and chatter from the officers. Diablo's voice rose above the rest. "We can't trust that devil! He's as much our enemy as Cord!"

"Why would you suggest that?" said Andre. "The crew will vote you out in a heartbeat."

"Let's hear him out," Hawk said, staring coldly at the others. He had been right, and Bloodstone had arrived at the same plan he had.

"It do leave a bad taste to even utter such, that be for sure. But I suggest it, because of the third part of me plan. I want to kill Cord and sink the *Enterprise*. We can't do that with just the *Bloody Seas*, and we don't have time to capture and man an extra frigate. We join up with Kragg for one battle. If we take out the squadron's flagship, that'll set the entire fleet back. Plus, it'll give pause to the navy officers and hope to all pirates. It'll at least buy us some years. If we do nothin', we'll all be hangin' in a years' time."

The officers sat in silence, mulling over Bloodstone's plan. Hawk surmised that as bad as they wanted to object, they realized they were in desperate straits. Bloodstone's last statement rang all too true. The noose would quickly tighten around their necks if something didn't slow down the navy.

"Let's hear the rest of the plan," Diablo said.

Hawk and Diablo were the last two to leave Bloodstone's cabin. As Hawk turned to walk to his, Diablo firmly grabbed his arm.

Hawk spun around, jerking his arm free of the firm grip. "What?" Hawk barked.

"You're becoming quite the hero, aren't you?" Diablo hissed.

"I just do my job and look out for my crew."

"Your crew? *Your* crew? This will never be your crew, swab! The old man is going to get himself killed—probably very soon. When he's gone, I'll be captain." Diablo flashed his evil grin.

"That will be for the men to decide." Hawk was tired and not in the mood to deal with Diablo.

Diablo ignored Hawk's words and continued, "I'll be a fair captain to you, though. You'll have the choice of me killing you or marooning you on a deserted island. Well, actually, I think I'll stick with killing. You'd find some way to escape the deserted island and become even more of a legend."

Hawk leaned close, his face inches from Diablo's. "Look, if you want to fight like a man, then let's go right here. If not, then turn and walk away. I don't have time for your drivel."

Diablo's smug grin shifted into a fierce scowl. His hand dropped to the hilt of his cutlass. "Watch your back, swab. It's going to be a dangerous battle." Diablo turned and walked toward his cabin. Hawk shook his head and limped to his.

The following day, Bloodstone and his officers presented the plan to the entire crew in the middle of the fort. The men were likewise skeptical of making a deal with Kragg. But once they heard the whole plan and understood the alternative, they voted in favor of it.

***

Bloodstone and his crew thrived over the next few months. They did have to be vigilant to avoid contact with the *Enterprise* and the other frigates. The West Indies Squadron replaced the New Orleans Squadron, with the *Enterprise* still as the flagship. The larger squadron included new ships, such as: USS *John Adams*, USS *Congress*, USS *Lynx*, and USS *Nonsuch*. They heard the tales of many other pirate ships being taken and their crews hanged.

The slave ships were easy targets, though. They were lightly defended and rarely escorted. Once word spread that Bloodstone offered quarter, many sailors and slaves eagerly went on account. Soon Bloodstone's crew swelled to nearly 180 men. Thirty stayed at the Rock, and 150 manned the *Bloody Seas*. The captain resisted the urge to add more ships to his fleet. The more vessels he had sailing, the more risk of one getting caught. Another reason teaming up with Kragg was a good plan was that he could share the risk.

Hawk thought of Anna every day and especially every night. And his personal stash was growing very quickly. If he managed to survive the coming battle, he could see being able to leave pirating behind in the next year or so. They would still have most of their lives to spend together. He just had to stay alive long enough to get that opportunity.

CHAPTER XV

"I don't have a good feeling about this," James said.

"You should be ecstatic, my boy. This is your chance to finally face Bloodstone and exact your revenge," Cord said, scanning the horizon for sails.

"I don't trust that Vasquez."

Two days prior, a small Spanish sloop had hailed them just off the coast of Cuba. One of the sailors, Vasquez, came aboard to speak to Cord and James. With a patch over his left eye, he appeared more like a pirate than a sailor. He told them that he was the first mate aboard a Spanish merchantman. They had a cargo full of gold and silver and were headed back to Spain. His captain had learned that Captain Bloodstone's *Bloody Seas* was praying on ships around the Bahamas. No Spanish warships were in the area to escort them, and he didn't trust the British navy after they'd failed at hanging Bloodstone and his quartermaster at Port Royal. They had heard of the mighty US Navy ships hunting pirates in the area, so he was requesting an escort. They would be passing through in two days. He offered gold for the escort, whether or not they encountered pirates.

Cord asked where his ship was, and Vasquez explained that it was in Havana preparing for the voyage. That's when they learned no escort ships were available. James and Cord knew the relationship between Spain and the United States wasn't strong enough to travel to Havana to investigate. After discussing it with James, Cord offered not to escort the ship, which would scare Bloodstone away, but to sail around the westernmost tip of Grand Bahama Island. If Bloodstone attacked, the *Enterprise* would swoop in from behind. A day and time were agreed upon when the merchantman would pass the island.

"No matter," Cord said. "Even if it is a trap, the *Bloody Seas* is no match for the *Enterprise*. We will be ready. Very soon, Captain Bloodstone, Diablo, and his Hawk will die. After Bloodstone is gone, we will hunt down Kragg. The end of the pirates is near, James, very near." Cord clapped James on the shoulder.

James stared out over the water thoughtfully. The legend of Bloodstone's bosun, the Hawk, had spread all over the country through word of mouth and newspapers. The Hawk had rescued Bloodstone and Diablo from hanging at Port Royal. His shooting and fighting prowess were also legendary, based on reports from the few sailors that survived Bloodstone's attacks. Diablo had been the most feared of Bloodstone's crew, but he was all but forgotten since the appearance of Hawk. James remembered Diablo's role in the attack on his ship so many years ago. He hated him almost as much as Bloodstone. He didn't know this Hawk, but the bosun would face his wrath too, as would all Bloodstone's crew.

The *Enterprise* had passed the town of Freeport and continued toward the island's western end. If the attack were going to happen, it would happen just around the western tip. If not, the merchantman would hit open water and escape the pirate's normal hunting range. Suddenly, James heard the unmistakable distant booms of cannon fire.

"Unfurl the sails!" Cord cried out.

They had only been running at half-mast so as not to arrive in the channel too soon. Now the sails were fully raised, and they caught more wind, speeding them northwestward.

"All hands prepare for battle!" yelled James. Sailors began rushing about the deck, loading and preparing the muskets, blunderbusses, flintlocks, and cannons. Others climbed quickly down through the hatches to the gun deck to prepare the remainder of the cannons.

"This is it, James! The moment you have waited for all your life," Cord said, grinning.

James couldn't help but grin back, despite his still-lingering concerns. Both men checked their flintlocks and other weapons and prepared for the battle of their lives.

As the tip of the long island neared, they spotted the stern of a large frigate, painted black. Soon the sails and flag came into view. The flag was the legendary white skull with red eyes on a black background. The ship was broadside to them. Behind that ship, the front half of another frigate was visible, turned broadside to the *Bloody Seas*. The two were locked into a cannon battle, and smoke hung heavy in the air, obscuring the damage either ship was giving or receiving.

"The *Bloody Seas*!" Cord exclaimed. "What is wrong, my boy? You should be jubilant."

"Something isn't right. That other frigate doesn't look like a Spanish merchantman."

"No matter if it is a merchant or a pirate. Bloodstone and his men are fully engaged in a battle. We will sail up beside the *Bloody Seas* unnoticed and give them a full broadside. Once she sinks, we will deal with the other ship if necessary. Today will go down in history, James."

James was still uneasy, but the *Enterprise* was a formidable ship. And they had finally found Bloodstone and the *Bloody Seas*. Soon he felt his usual excitement building over an impending battle—his heart raced as the adrenaline coursed through his body. He clutched the railing and waited impatiently for the wind to carry them into the battle.

As they closed the distance, he could make out the pirate crew. They all were facing the starboard side of their ship and the foe they engaged, and none appeared to notice the approaching *Enterprise*. Their ship seemed in surprisingly good shape to be locked into a long cannon battle, though. The other ship was of similar size but was too far away and too smoke-obscured to make out its crew or condition.

Cord shouted orders across the deck. "Ready the guns! Helmsman, bring us alongside. Reef and trim the sails." The ship slowed considerably as the sails were lowered and turned.

They silently drifted behind the *Bloody Seas* and came about into a broadside position. Still, no pirates turned to discover them, despite their proximity.

Just before Cord could shout the order to fire, the fourteen cannons on the port side of the pirate ship erupted. The six from the main deck fired canister shot, spraying the main deck of the *Enterprise* with flying pieces of metal. Explosions from below deck indicated explosive shot was fired from the eight cannons on the gun deck. Screams rang out from around James and Cord and more from below deck. Before their shock wore off, eight cannons from the front half of the other ship fired. It was farther away, but at least five balls hit the bow of their ship.

James now realized that it was indeed a trap. Pirates had been crouching below the gunwale on the main deck and manning the cannons on the gun deck. They had probably just been manning a few cannons on the starboard side to shoot harmlessly over the other ship. Now the other ship hoisted its topsails, catching enough wind to pull out from behind the *Bloody Seas*. James could now see its colors—a red devil with a pitchfork. It was *Hell's Fury*, Kragg's flagship. They were now facing the two greatest pirate captains of the era.

"Kragg!" Cord yelled. "Fire!"

James hoped they had enough men and undamaged cannons left. Twenty of the twenty-six cannons on the ship's port side fired into the *Bloody Seas*. The damage was massive, destroying most of the Bloody Seas' gun deck and cannons. Explosive shot set fire to large parts of the main deck and sails. Having a crew of three hundred was a huge advantage to the navy frigate—plenty of sailors could step up and replace the fallen. The cannons on both decks were quickly reloaded, and damaged ones were rolled away and replaced with ones from the ship's starboard side.

***

Captain Bloodstone, Hawk, and Diablo stood together on the flaming deck. The trap had worked perfectly so far, but the *Enterprise* was a formidable ship with twice as many men as theirs. Bloodstone shouted orders that were relayed below decks to pump the water from the hold to the main deck to help fight the fires. Other men rushed about with sand and buckets of water. The main deck cannons were pretty much ruined, and the death toll was high. He ordered the gun deck cannons to be reloaded with explosive shot, and the remainder of the men opened fire with muskets and blunderbusses. The two ships slowly drifted together and would soon be within grappling range.

Hawk felt helpless as he watched the cannon battle unfold. The remainder of *Hell's Fury's* cannons fired at the *Enterprise*. Only about half the shot hit the upper deck, doing minimal damage to the structure and sailors but damaging the foremast and its sails. Fourteen of the *Enterprise's* cannons returned fire at *Hell's Fury*. Despite the distance, most made contact. They fired a combination of canister and explosive shot, and the loss of life and damage was great. The main mast was hit, the deck set ablaze, and holes ripped open in the hull. Six more cannons fired into the hull of the *Bloody Seas*, opening more huge gashes in the side, some low enough to take on more water.

Hawk led the crew in firing muskets at gun crews on the *Enterprise*, trying to prevent more cannon fire. They were accurate and dropped men, but more stepped up to take their places. Less than fifty pirates stood on the deck of the *Bloody Seas* and still hundreds on the *Enterprise*. The pirates then tossed all the grenadoes and stinkpots onto the *Enterprise's* main deck. That finally disrupted the sailors enough to halt them from reloading the cannons.

"What do we do?" Hawk shouted to Bloodstone. Typically, they would board the other ship at this point. But no matter how skilled they were as fighters, they couldn't overcome those odds.

"Hang me!" Bloodstone shouted, spitting onto the deck. "Where in the blazes is Kragg?" He rushed to the ship's starboard side, Hawk and Diablo following.

"Kragg!" Bloodstone shouted to the *Hell's Fury*.

The giant redheaded pirate, dressed in white breeches, a red shirt, a long blue coat, and a black tricorne hat, made his way through the throng of pirates dousing flames and loading cannons. "Aye?" he shouted back.

"Get your bloody ship into place and attack those navy dogs!"

Kragg laughed loudly. "I think me men tire of fightin' today. Ye can take the glory, Bloodstone."

"Ye can fight, or by the gods, I'll pull your cowardly heart from your chest and feed it to you!" Bloodstone yelled, his face glowing red.

Suddenly, the remaining sails on *Hell's Fury* were hoisted. The breeze quickly filled them, and the ship began to move away. "Save me a spot in hell," said Kragg. "This is for attacking me schooner and killing Captain Grant. Did ye think I'd forget?"

Before Bloodstone could reply, half a dozen cannons fired from *Hell's Fury*. Ball and chain shot tore through the sails and rigging, doing tremendous damage. Kragg laughed loudly again and turned and strode toward the helm of his ship. It moved faster now, turning to the northwest and away from the battle.

"Curse his hide! If I die today, lads, someone has to kill that mangy cur for me!" The three rushed back to the battle with the *Enterprise.*

When they rejoined the fight, the navy sailors had thrown grappling hooks over their rail and pulled the two ships together. A surge of sailors leaped over the railing onto the *Bloody Seas'* deck. The pirates with flintlocks fired them into the charging sailors and then drew their cutlasses. Diablo, Bloodstone, and Hawk wordlessly split up to lead their badly outnumbered crew. Hawk tried to keep the sailors from surrounding the pirates to the stern, and Diablo did the same toward the bow. Bloodstone attempted to keep the middle of the ranks from collapsing.

The badly outnumbered pirates fought bravely; they were more experienced and better trained with the cutlasses than the sailors. The deck quickly became slick with blood, water, and sand. The pirates even started pushing the onslaught back toward the *Enterprise.* Then more sailors swung and leaped aboard. The gun crews from below deck were now all on the main deck. The ones that couldn't find room to board the *Bloody*

Seas stayed on the main deck and shot at any pirate they had a clean shot at.

***

After the navy crew withstood the pirate counter surge, James began to push his way through the ranks until he reached the main group of pirates. Bloodstone was easy to spot, towering above his crew. The pirates were skilled; James gave them that. But he was fresh, and fueled by nine years of pent-up hatred and hostility. His blade was a blur, dealing death on all sides.

The pirates charged again as the remaining men from below deck abandoned the pumps and cannons and made their way through the hatches. The mass of bodies moved back and forth, almost like water sloshing in the hold. But inevitably, the pirates were driven toward the starboard rail. Once they were cornered and pinned, the battle would soon be over.

***

Hawk fought like a mad man, leaving a pile of bodies surrounding him. He would have lost count of the sailors he killed had he been counting. In a brief break in the fighting, as more sailors surged aboard to replace the ones he had killed, he surveyed the scene on both ships. Only four-dozen pirates were alive on the main deck. There were almost twice as many sailors, plus the *Enterprise's* deck was still full of more waiting their turn. These sailors were highly trained and much better fighters than they encountered on merchant ships.

For the first time in his life, Hawk contemplated his own death. He had never been truly pushed before or in a no-win situation. The alligator had been a little frightening, but he worried more about losing a limb than dying. He had fought plenty of battles with sword and gun, but his confidence never allowed him to think about losing, not since his first battle.

Then a vision of Anna appeared in his mind. They were together again on the blanket by the pond, holding each other after just making love. She smiled her sweet smile and stared into his eyes. He wondered what she would do when she found out he broke his promise and died before returning to her. He imagined her crying. She might not have another way out of her life of prostitution. He might be her only hope for a better and happy future.

He had to do something to turn the tide, or it would soon be too late. He recalled every battle he had fought and all the cunning and trickery Bloodstone had ever used. Then an idea hit him. It was foolish and had a slim chance of succeeding, but it was at least something. He turned and bolted toward the quarterdeck before the next wave of sailors could reach him. He scampered up the ladder, ran across the deck, and with several long strides, dove over the rail and disappeared headfirst into the sea below.

***

James finally found himself standing before the mighty Captain Bloodstone. He was even more imposing and intimidating up close, standing several inches taller than James and much broader. But he panted hard and was covered in blood —some of it his own. For a moment, neither man attacked.

"You devil!" James shouted, years of repressed rage boiling out. "You killed my father, brother, and many good men on our ship. I've hunted you for nine long years so I could finally avenge my family!" The fighting around them slowed, and the din quieted somewhat.

"Arrr! I don't doubt I killed 'em, but they like as not deserved it," Bloodstone replied, flashing an evil grin.

"They were unarmed! We were just sailing to the New World on a merchant ship. My brother was eight years old!"

The shouting had now halted all the fighting. The two crews moved back, forming a circle with pirates on one side and sailors on the other. The men on the *Enterprise*, with Cord in front, pressed against the railing, watching the impending duel.

"I've never killed any eight-year-old boys. But if ye be set on killin' me, then I s'ppose we best get to it."

James wondered momentarily why Bloodstone would lie about killing Henry. But Bloodstone swung an overhand blow at him, and he had to quickly raise his cutlass to block it.

Instantly, all the years of anger and hostility surged through his body and into his sword arm. He knew Bloodstone was tired and wounded. James had fought some but was much fresher than his opponent. He went on the offensive, raining blows down on Bloodstone from every angle. The crowd surrounding them erupted in yells and cheers.

Bloodstone was able to keep up with James and block all his attacks. They were probably equally skilled with a blade, although the pirate was slowly forced to give some ground, despite his size advantage. His exhaustion was evident, and James was much stronger and younger. But James knew the pirate captain wouldn't go down easily.

James swung a hard overhand blow at Bloodstone's head. Bloodstone blocked it just in time, and their swords locked together. James pressed down hard with his cutlass, using both hands and all his strength. Bloodstone's blade slowly lowered toward his head, now bare since his hat had long since fallen off. Suddenly, Bloodstone leaned backward, removed one hand from his blade, and reached for a dagger on his baldric. He had the sword drawn and swinging toward James before the lieutenant could react.

Just before the blade struck James's exposed side, Bloodstone's right foot slipped in a puddle of blood on the already slick deck. The pirate captain collapsed onto his right knee and nearly fell from the force of the dagger swing and James's sword pressing down in front of his chest. The slip gave James just enough time to leap back, and the dagger blade only slashed his shirt. James landed and quickly jabbed his sword into Bloodstone's left knee. Bloodstone howled in pain. James quickly pulled his blade free and landed a short, quick stab into Bloodstone's left shoulder, which was still extended from the dagger swing.

The big pirate teetered backward, nearly falling onto his back. He managed to regain his feet and held both blades in front of him. His left knee was damaged badly, and he had to shift most of his weight to his right leg. James strode confidently forward. Bloodstone flung his dagger underhanded at the sailor's midsection, but James was ready and quick. He effortlessly swung his blade down and sent the dagger flying to the deck.

The sailors on both ships now cheered and yelled loudly. The pirates were mostly silent, watching in horror and shock. James swung a series of blows at Bloodstone's right side. The pirate shifted more weight to his right leg and managed to block the blows. Then James suddenly kicked his right leg out and struck Bloodstone hard on the left knee. The leg instantly buckled.

Bloodstone collapsed heavily onto both knees. He struggled to rise but was too weak and wounded. He struck at James's legs a few times, but the sailor was too quick. James grinned, and his blade became a silver blur. He heard the roar from the sailors behind him. Bloodstone was late on a block, and James's cutlass dug deep into his right shoulder. When Bloodstone reached for a flintlock in his baldric, James nearly severed his left arm just above the wrist. Another blow struck his right arm and sent his cutlass flying.

It seemed time had nearly stopped for James as he rained the last few blows onto the man who'd destroyed his life and killed his family. For a second, he almost felt pity for him. Bloodstone was on both knees, defenseless and bleeding from numerous cuts and slashes. His eyes almost looked sad, not angry. Then James replayed the image of Bloodstone coldly shooting his father. He imagined what torture Henry probably endured before his death. He raised his sword over his head, holding the hilt with both hands.

"I'm James. James Wellington. This is for my father, Peter Wellington!" His blade dropped and cut deeply into the side of Bloodstone's neck. Still, Bloodstone remained on his knees, blood pouring down his shirt and onto his breeches. "And for my brother, Henry." James was puzzled at the look of surprise on Bloodstone's pale and bloody face.

The pirate opened his mouth. "Haw—"

James swung his cutlass one more time, hitting the same

deep gash. Bloodstone's huge head balanced on his shoulders for a few seconds. Then as the pirate captain's body tumbled backward, his head rolled forward. It landed at James's feet, its mouth still open, trying to finish his last word.

James wanted to collapse onto the deck too. He was exhausted—physically and mentally. For most of his life, he had dreamed of this day. He now had avenged his father, brother, and innocent people on that ship so long ago. He was elated and relieved but also felt strange, somehow empty. He turned, sheathed his sword, and walked back through the sailors, who parted to give him a wide path. "Finish them," he said, breaking the silence.

The men resumed the fight. The action started slow and then steadily built into the loud roar of battle. James didn't look back as the sailors rushed past him to get at the remaining pirates. As James reached the rail, a massive explosion erupted from deep within the stern of the *Enterprise*. A gaping hole ripped open from the inside, and flames rolled out. Many of the men on the *Enterprise* were knocked off their feet. James realized in horror that the explosion was in the magazine. He instantly wondered if another ship had attacked them and if this was another part of the pirate's trap. More explosions followed, tearing out more of the hull and the deck above. The battle aboard the *Bloody Seas* halted once more, and all eyes turned to the *Enterprise*.

James quickly leaped over the railing back onto the deck of his ship and followed Cord and the other sailors down through the hatches to the hold. He knew they had to act quickly if they were to save the ship. More sailors followed them, returning from the *Bloody Seas*, all forgetting about the remaining pirates.

***

At first, no one noticed Hawk emerging from the hatch closest to the bow of the *Enterprise*. He shoved two flintlocks into the red sash around his waist, placed a dagger in his teeth, and scampered up the closest ratline to the main mast. He paused to cut the rigging up to the crow's nest.

He glanced over to the *Bloody Seas* when he heard a shout he recognized. Billy had spotted him. The remaining, startled sailors on the *Bloody Seas* started running back toward their ship, not knowing how many pirates might be aboard. The pirates began yelling and cheering behind them.

Hawk spotted Diablo too. Diablo started shouting commands to the small crew of remaining pirates, and they ran to the starboard rail. The gun racks on that side of the ship were still full of loaded blunderbusses and muskets that the pirates never had a chance to use before the assault began. Soon they were firing shots into the sailors retreating back to the *Enterprise*. The volley was devastating from that close range.

Hawk turned back to his task, relieved to know that Billy, Diablo, and some of his crew were still alive. He had slashed all the lines he could reach, devastating the rigging. He then dove into the air with his dagger held tightly in both hands. The blade stabbed into the mainsail, and he slid down it, splitting it in half as he fell. He let go of the dagger as it reached the spar and dropped lightly to his feet on the deck below. He snatched a cutlass from among the dead sailor's bodies, then ran and jumped onto the Enterprise's rail. Pausing momentarily, he leaped onto the deck of the *Bloody Seas*, crashing into the few remaining sailors.

He went to work dispatching them with his blade. The pirates rushed forward to help, and soon the deck was clear of sailors. Hawk and the other pirates quickly began cutting the grappling lines.

"Some of you grab the pikes and push us free," said Hawk. "You four get down below and man the pumps. Tell Bones to get to work patching holes. Billy, hoist the sails and have Hobbs steer us leeward!"

Diablo helped Hawk get the men rushing about to set sail. Soon their ship started drifting away from the *Enterprise*. Its crew was still below deck, trying to extinguish the flames and patch the holes. Hawk stood at the port rail and stared at the damaged frigate. He wasn't sure the sailors and ship would survive. The fire was still raging, and an occasional explosion still boomed. It would be a challenging voyage to safety if they didn't sink. Then he saw two sailors climb up through one of the hatches. He recognized them as Captain Cord and his lieutenant, James. They rushed to the rail, their shock evident.

***

James saw the shirtless pirate standing against the rail of the *Bloody Seas*. He surmised he was the one that had blown up the magazine and destroyed the mainsail and rigging. As he studied his blond hair and face, he noticed the birthmark on his left breast. They were still close enough for him to see that it resembled a bird. His mind instantly raced back to his childhood and his little brother, Henry. *Henry had a birthmark...just like... that.*

His conversation with Bloodstone came rushing back to him. Bloodstone had said he never killed any eight-year-old boys. Then he remembered the last word that Bloodstone had tried to speak when he had mentioned Henry's name: "Haw—" *Hawk? Henry?* "Noooo!" he shouted.

CHAPTER XVI

Diablo approached Hawk at the center of the main deck once they were under sail. Hawk tensed and placed his hand on his cutlass. This was not the time for a confrontation. Diablo actually flashed a grin that wasn't a sneer. "As bad as it pains me, I will give you credit for saving all of us."

"You're welcome. Look, let's just get this wreck back to the Rock, regroup, and then we can get a plan together."

Diablo nodded and walked off to see to the many tasks taking place. Hawk climbed down to the lower decks to inspect the damage. Luckily, Bones had been working on patching the holes on the lower decks while the battle raged. Water was still several feet deep in the hold, though, and more was coming in from holes yet to be repaired. Most of the powder and stores were ruined. Several men rotated working the pumps, trying to keep the water level from rising until the holes were patched.

Hawk's heart leaped into his throat when he saw Andre's body. He was apparently killed in the first broadside. Most cannons were heavily damaged, and many ports, the surrounding hull, and the deck were destroyed. They would be basically defenseless if they encountered another navy ship or Kragg. Hawk then made his way to Wesley's cabin. He slowly opened the door, praying the old sailor had survived.

Wesley sat at his table, pointing a flintlock at the door, a dagger in front of him. When he saw Hawk, he set the flintlock down beside the blade. "Thank the gods! I haven't fought in many years, but I wasn't lettin' 'em bilge rats hang me. You're a sight for sore eyes, to be sure. How bad is it?"

Hawk dropped wearily into another chair. "Bad. Bloodstone is dead."

Wesley dropped his eyes to the table and shook his head. "Poor ol' devil. I s'ppose it was well past his turn. Can't live forever, that's for sure."

"And Andre. Looks like there are less than fifty of us left, counting the wounded."

"Devil, take me! And the *Enterprise*?"

Hawk recounted the battle and Kragg's betrayal. Wesley cursed and spit on the floor at that news. Then Hawk shared his diving into the water and swimming underneath the *Enterprise* to the other side. The ship was listing enough that he was able to grab the edge of a gunport and climb inside onto the gun deck. The only sailors he encountered were dead or dying, so he grabbed a linstock and made his way down to the hold to the magazine. He cut a hole in a powder keg and ran out a long line of black powder halfway across the deck. He lit the powder, scurried back up to the bow of the gun deck, and hid behind a cannon until the explosions started. Soon after, the sailors, along with Cord and James, climbed down the ladders at the far hatches and made their way below, no one looking toward his hiding place. When they were all below, he made his way to the main deck and began destroying the sails.

Wesley grinned and shook his head. "I knew you were special, but you keep outdoin' yourself, my boy. I've never heard a smarter and braver act for the likes of me."

"I just wasn't ready to die yet, and that's the only plan I could conjure up. Luckily, it somehow worked. So much death, though."

"Aye. Our luck has definitely been bad lately," Wesley said, shaking his head.

"You know, the night we returned from Port Royal, I spent some time with Bloodstone in his cabin," said Hawk. "He kept talking about pirating coming to an end and reflecting on the golden age a hundred years ago. I think he knew his time was short."

Wesley scratched his scruffy beard. "The old devil had his faults, to be sure, but he was a wise man. Had an uncanny ability to predict the future."

"Our working with Kragg to attempt to sink the *Enterprise* was our best plan for trying to extend the pirate age," said Hawk.

"'Bout the only chance we had, I reckon."

"We might have sunk it or pretty much destroyed it anyway. But you know, I don't think it will make a difference. There are at least four more frigates just like it, and more are being built. Like Bloodstone said, there's not a safe harbor left for pirates. Sure, we could regroup and sail around a couple more years, but it's basically over." Hawk leaned back, his hands behind his head, staring at the ceiling.

"Aye. I'd like to say somethin' reassurin' to you. But I'd say you and Bloodstone are right. Not much of a livin' to be had for honest pirates, huh?" Wesley chucked softly. He stood and poured them both a tankard of rum from a small cask. He sat back down and placed one in front of Hawk. They drank in silence for a few minutes.

"So, what's your plan? Just callin' it quits now?" Wesley finally asked.

Hawk stared at Wesley for a moment and swallowed a large swig of rum. "Not quite yet. Bloodstone told us that if he was killed, we should go after Kragg and make him pay for his treachery."

"We don't have the ship or men for that!" Wesley exclaimed.

"No. Kragg would win in an all-out battle. Yet he has to die. I'm working on a plan."

Wesley laughed and finished his rum. "You and your bloody plans!"

Hawk left Wesley and helped tend to the wounded pirates in the infirmary as Bones was occupied mending the ship. That night, as the *Bloody Seas* limped back to the Rock, the crew gathered on the main deck. All the dead pirates were laid in rows, nearly one hundred bodies. They placed Bloodstone's body in the center of the first row. Chain shot was wrapped around their legs, as was the crew's custom. It used nearly all their remaining shot. The officers stood in front of the bodies, against the starboard rail. Wesley read a few verses from the Bible.

Hawk stepped forward when Wesley was done. "These men fought hard and died like men. Let's remember and honor their bravery and deeds. Captain Bloodstone was the fiercest pirate captain ever to sail the seas. For twenty years, he reigned supreme, causing men to fear the very mention of his name. If not for an unfortunate slip, he'd be standing here tonight. When we get back to the Rock, we will elect a new captain to lead us. But none can replace Captain Bloodstone. May God watch over these men in their next journey."

Hawk stepped back and nodded to Diablo. Diablo frowned and then stepped forward. "They lived hard, fought hard, and died bravely. I hope hell knows what's coming."

Some chuckling and laughing interrupted the somber ceremony. Then the pirates grabbed their dead mates and tossed them into the ocean. Bloodstone was saved until last, and Diablo and Hawk did the honors. His head had been placed inside a canvas bag and tied to the chain at his feet.

The wind was generous, and they made decent speed back toward the Rock. Once the ship was out of danger, Hawk knew that word had spread among the pirates of how he had saved them. He didn't like the extra attention, but the excitement over his deeds took the crew's mind off losing so much life and their current situation. Soon he even heard whispers that he couldn't die, and as Bloodstone had stated so long ago, he was marked by the gods. If only that were true…

***

When the *Bloody Seas* limped into the harbor at the Rock, the men on the beach quickly fell silent, stopping the celebration at seeing their crew return on the heavily damaged ship. They watched in shock as only fifty men made their way to the beach, Captain Bloodstone and Andre not among them. The pirates all walked and limped up the trail to the fort, the healthy helping the injured. Hawk instructed everyone to eat and then meet around the bonfire after. He asked the officers, along with Billy and Jimmy, to join him in Bloodstone's cabin.

Once seated around the table, Hawk poured them all tankards of rum, sat down, and then spoke. "I don't need to state the obvious. I have several proposals to make, and then we can have the entire crew vote."

Diablo stared at him, unblinking. His scowl was fierce.

"First, I propose that Jimmy take Andre's place as gunner." Jimmy had proven himself as a solid and dependable pirate and gained the favor of Bloodstone and Hawk. Everyone nodded in approval. "Next, I propose that Billy be the new bosun."

"Bosun?" Diablo roared. "So, I s'ppose I know what's coming next."

"I propose I be elected the new captain," Hawk said flatly, staring at Diablo.

"Over my dead body! I should be the captain. I've been a pirate since before you were even swab material. Not to mention I've always been Bloodstone's right-hand man," Diablo stood up and placed both fists on the table.

"Let us hear him out," Bones said, glancing from Diablo to Hawk. Diablo glared at Bones for a moment and slowly sat again.

"There's a reason I want to be captain, Diablo. If I'm elected, I will then have the men vote on going after Kragg. He must pay for his cowardice."

"I can do that as well as you," Diablo shot back.

Wesley shook his head. "I don't know how either of you fools propose to do that with a handful of wounded men and a broken ship."

Bones and Hobbs murmured in agreement while Jimmy and Billy were silent, taking in the exchange with wide eyes.

"*We* are not going to fight him," Hawk said.

"Then what are you proposin', lad?"

"I am going to challenge Kragg to a duel to the death. His crew can't be happy with his treachery. They know that their only hope, as well as ours, is to join together against the United States. Kragg will have no choice but to accept my challenge.

I will further propose that the survivor become the captain of both crews. Now, Diablo, would you rather do that in my place?"

Diablo muttered something under his breath and finally shook his head.

Hawk knew that Diablo couldn't accept that offer. He was a good fighter but wouldn't voluntarily challenge Kragg. Hawk was younger, stronger, and quicker. And if Kragg killed Hawk, Diablo could probably organize a mutiny against Kragg for his treachery against Bloodstone. The only thing that worried Hawk was what Diablo would do if he won. He was just as liable to try a mutiny against him. But he couldn't worry about that now. One plan at a time...

"I don't know, Hawk. Heaven forbid, but what if Kragg kills you?" Wesley asked.

"I'll do my best to see that doesn't happen. But if it does, join his crew. Then organize a mutiny as soon as you can. His crew will be ready to turn on him. Diablo, you could have your long-awaited captaincy then."

Hawk read a lot into Diablo's smirk.

The men around the table voted unanimously for all Hawk's suggestions. They then proceeded to the bonfire and the congregation of pirates. Hawk presented the proposals to the assembly, to which they all enthusiastically voted in favor. If some favored Diablo's becoming captain, they didn't openly express it. The chant "Hawk, Hawk, Hawk," filled the air. Soon some pirates fetched casks of rum, and the celebration started. The musicians played, and the pirates danced and drank late into the night.

The next day, Hawk put every available hand to helping him and Bones repair the *Bloody Seas*. He wanted to set sail the following day by sunrise. Hawk figured that Kragg would be at his hideout for several days. Kragg wouldn't have known the battle's outcome, and if the *Enterprise* had sunk the *Bloody Seas*, he would be their next target. *Hell's Fury* also needed repairs. It was doubtful Kragg would be in any hurry to get back on the water—keeping his men drunk and happy on land was better than the options at sea.

The *Bloody Seas* left the cove and unfurled its sails at daylight the next morning. All eighty remaining pirates were onboard —healthy, injured, old, and sick. Hawk knew that the coming events would forever change the fates of his crew, Kragg's, and probably all pirates. All needed to be present, for better or worse.

Hawk had learned the location of Kragg's home base during the parleying before the attack on the *Enterprise*. Kragg used one of the many islands in the Turks and Caicos, north of Hispaniola. On the several-day voyage to the islands, they didn't show their colors and generally skirted ships of any type. The *Bloody Seas* was sailable but definitely not battle ready. Only half the cannons were operational, and they hadn't had time to replace their powder and shot. The crew was unusually subdued—all knew what was at stake.

CHAPTER XVII

Late evening on the fourth day, Hawk spotted the island Kragg had named "Devil's Island." The two rock peaks rising from the center did resemble horns. The water on the approach to the island was shallow and filled with small rocky islands and submerged coral. It required all Hobbs's years of experience to navigate the frigate through the maze, with Billy helping spot from the crow's nest. Had their ship been fully armed and the hold full of booty, they would have had trouble approaching the protected harbor.

As they squeezed between two fairly large rock islands, they spotted the deep, clear harbor just ahead. *Hell's Fury* lay on its side on the left side of the cove, repairs and careening in full swing. Two schooners and a sloop were anchored at other points in the large bay. There were no walls or fort, but the broad, deep beach did hold a number of huts and wooden buildings similar to those inside the fort at the Rock. Most of Kragg's men appeared to be working on the *Fury*.

Horns suddenly sounded on rocky outcrops on each side of the harbor. The pirates on the beach began scurrying about, and more joined them from the huts and buildings, most holding muskets, pistols, or cutlasses. Some climbed into the two longboats and began rowing out to the schooners. They would be too late and of little consequence if the *Bloody Seas* were bent on attacking.

The *Bloody Seas* sailed in as close as was safe and then came about hard to port until it was broadside to the beach. The sails were furled and the anchor dropped. By this time, it appeared that Kragg's entire crew was on the shore. Kragg himself, in the same clothes he had worn in the battle, pushed his way to the front of the throng. Hawk stood against the starboard rail, flanked by his officers. Most of his crew formed a semicircle behind them.

For a moment, Hawk was tempted to change his plan and fire a broadside at Kragg and his crew. The damage would be devastating. Follow it up with a musket volley, and there would be few left standing. He was surprised at the laxness of Kragg's defenses. Obviously, he didn't expect anyone to navigate their way to his harbor. But destroying Kragg's crew wouldn't help him at all. That would just make the US Navy's job easier. He had to try his plan.

"Cap'n Bloodstone and crew, so glad ye survived that battle," Kragg called out. "I hope ye sent those navy vermin to the bottom of the sea!"

Hawk waited for the hisses and mumbling from his crew to die down before he spoke. "Thanks to your treachery, Captain Bloodstone and many of his crew are dead. I am Hawk, the new captain of the *Bloody Seas*."

"Treachery? Me cannons must have misfired. They were pointed o'er your bow at the *Enterprise*. We had to sail with haste 'cause we were takin' on water."

"Spare our crews and me your lies. You did two things no decent pirate would ever do—double-cross a fellow pirate and help out the navy. I have no idea why your crew has let you remain their captain or even continue living. You are the biggest coward I have ever encountered." The crew behind Hawk erupted in cheers and laughter. Kragg's crew was strangely silent.

"Double-cross? Need I 'mind ye 'bout your captain's cowardly attack on me ship a few years back? Ye killed a lot o' good men for no reason." Kragg gave up any pretense of being nice.

"You're mad. We have never attacked any of your ships or any other pirate. The only treachery was from you, you bilge-sucking devil. And today, you will pay for it!"

"So, you're just goin' to slaughter me and all these good men? Looks like ye would be the coward."

"No. I have no quarrel with your men," Hawk replied calmly. "Just you. Both of our crews have suffered enough. The only hope for all pirates is for our two crews to join together. Then we might have enough men and ships to hurt the navy, or at least stay alive a little longer." He scanned the faces of Kragg's pirates.

"And who would captain this crew?" Kragg retorted.

"The winner of our duel. The fight is between us, not our crews. I challenge you to a duel to the death. The winner becomes captain of both crews. My crew has already voted and accepted my proposal. I suggest you put it to a vote with yours."

Kragg growled and spat into the sand at his feet. Before he even turned to his crew, one of his men shouted, "Aye." The verbal assent quickly spread through the throng.

"You and your men row ashore, and me and you will have this duel."

"No. I will come alone. Then if you attempt treachery again, my crew will kill everyone on this beach." Hawk didn't wait for a reply. He had the longboat lowered and scrambled down into it and rowed ashore. When he reached the beach and exited the boat, Kragg's crew had moved back to leave a large clear area for the two combatants. Kragg already had his cutlass, a much heavier and bigger blade than Hawk's, in hand.

"I want this to be a fair fight," Hawk said. "We both discard all our weapons except our cutlasses." He drew his cutlass and tossed his baldric into the boat.

Kragg cursed under his breath, but he, too, removed his baldric. He tossed it up the beach to the feet of his crew.

The two men circled each other in the sand, wet and hard-packed from the recent high tide. Hawk was barefoot, having known not to wear his boots in the sand. Kragg still wore his knee-high black leather boots. Hawk hoped that would give him an advantage before the battle was over.

Suddenly, Kragg leaped forward and jabbed his cutlass at Hawk. The speed of the attack, and the surprising quickness of the big pirate, caught Hawk off guard. He stepped back, but slightly too late. The cutlass penetrated his shirt and bit into his side. He didn't think it was serious, but he felt warm blood soaking into the white cloth.

Kragg continued the attack, steadily driving Hawk back toward the water with a flurry of blows. Another quick jab, amid a flurry of slashes, penetrated Hawk's biceps on his left arm. A trail of blood soon appeared on his sleeve. Kragg laughed a booming, terrifying laugh. Hawk's crew had fallen silent. Surprisingly, only a handful of Kragg's men were cheering.

Hawk was becoming concerned. He felt like he had during so many sparing sessions with Bloodstone. He had thought he was a much better fighter now, if not one of the best. But Kragg kept him on the defensive. Hawk was accustomed to using his quickness and aggression to keep his opponents off balance. Unless Kragg tired and slowed on his own, Hawk had to think of something quick to turn the tide. One slip or mistake on his part and the fight, and his life, would be over.

Slipping. The thought suddenly gave Hawk an idea. The water was washing over his bare feet as Kragg continued his onslaught. He parried his blows and waited for the next overhand one. When Kragg swung a hard blow down at his head, Hawk reached up and blocked it with his sword. Instead of trying to knock the blade away, he let Kragg's blade stay on top of his. Kragg leaned forward and pressed down with both hands on the hilt of his cutlass. His grin was fierce, and his hot breath reeked. Hawk's blade continued to lower toward his bare head.

Suddenly, Hawk spun to the left, causing Kragg's blade to slide off his. Kragg was leaning forward and pressing down so hard that his momentum caused him to lurch forward. His boots sank into the wet sand, and he lost his balance, flapping his arms as he fought against falling face down in the waves. Hawk completed his spin and struck Kragg on his broad back with his blade. It bit deeply all the way across.

The crew of the *Bloody Seas* erupted in yells and cheers. Had Hawk been able to stab, the fight would be over. As it was, his blow was deep but not debilitating. Kragg regained his balance and turned around to face Hawk before he could strike again. But now Hawk was able to go on the offensive, and Kragg's boots continued to sink in the watery sand. Hawk danced nimbly in front of him, jabbing and flicking his sword in all directions. Soon Kragg's shirt and pants were cut in several places, along with the skin beneath.

A moment later, Hawk landed an overhand blow onto Kragg's extended blade. They were in the same situation they had been in a few minutes before, only their roles were reversed. Hawk began leaning forward and bearing down on Kragg's blade, just as Kragg had done. Hawk was hoping Kragg would try to copy his defensive move.

Kragg let his sword drop slightly, encouraging Hawk to commit further. Hawk knew he was baiting him into the spin move. Hawk suddenly leaned forward even further. Then, in a blinding quick move, Hawk raised his knee and drove it hard into Kragg's stomach. Kragg was driven backward and almost doubled over. Their blades separated, and once again, Kragg fought for his balance.

Kragg looked up just in time to see Hawk's blade rushing toward him. His block attempt was much too slow, and Hawk's blade drove through Kragg's chest to the hilt. Hawk's face was mere inches from Kragg's when the blade finally stopped. Kragg stared down in shock at his chest and then back up at Hawk.

"I'd stay away from Bloodstone in hell," Hawk whispered.

The blood gurgling up into his throat and mouth drowned Kragg's last words. Hawk let go of his sword, and the giant pirate toppled into the surf. The young captain turned, walked a few steps out of the water onto the hard sand, and collapsed wearily onto his knees. He was exhausted from the battle and nearly overwhelmed by the events of the past couple of weeks. Cheers erupted from both crews, and soon shouts of "Hawk" rang out from the beach and ship.

Hawk closed his eyes and tried to come to grips with the moment. Then gunfire erupted from behind him on the *Bloody*

Seas. The shouts and cheering stopped on the ship and the beach. Slowly, Hawk stood and turned to face his ship. He saw a scuffle on the main deck. He couldn't determine precisely what was happening, but after several more shots, the scuffle and movement stopped.

Most of the crew had been pushed back to the middle of the main deck. A dozen or more pirates formed a semicircle between them and the railing, flintlocks leveled. Diablo strode over to the rail and stared at Hawk, his evil grin visible even from that distance. He held a musket.

"Splendid battle, Hawk! Once again, you've added to your legend. I'm afraid, though, that I get to write the final chapter of your story."

"What are you doing, Diablo?" Hawk wearily called out.

"Doing what should have been done long ago. I am now the captain of the *Bloody Seas*, Hell's Fury, and the men behind you. Any that don't agree will meet your fate." Diablo rested the musket on the rail and took aim at the defenseless Hawk.

"You're a madman and a fool! These men will never follow you." Hawk prepared himself for the death that he had so long eluded. Once again, his mind traveled to Anna. The vision of her he could always conjure was as strong as reality. He held her head and kissed her lips. His life was of no consequence. It was just the thought of what would happen with her life and of never being able to see her again that made him sad.

"They have no choice, and that is no concern of yours. Oh, Hawk, I need to tell you something before you die. Bloodstone didn't rescue you from your ship." Diablo smiled.

"What are you talking about?"

"So naïve. He attacked your family's ship. You and your cowardly family were hiding in the captain's cabin. You rushed out, brandishing that confounded wooden sword of yours, and confronted Bloodstone. Of course, I wanted to kill you, but that cursed Bloodstone wouldn't let me. Your father came scurrying out of the cabin, trying to save his sweet, brave son." Diablo paused for a moment, seeming to enjoy the emotion on Hawk's face. "Bloodstone had you whisked away to the *Bloody Seas* and then proceeded to kill your unarmed, restrained father in cold blood. He would also have killed your cowardly brother if a navy frigate hadn't interfered."

Hawk fell to his knees again. "You're lying!" he shouted, even though he knew Diablo wasn't. That story made more sense than the one he had been told all his life. He had spent his life serving and trying to please the man who killed his father and brother.

"I couldn't make it up, Hawk. Oh, and you know the funny part? That lieutenant on the *Enterprise*, the one that killed Bloodstone, said his name is James Wellington. He said Bloodstone killed his brother and father nine years ago. You have to love the sense of humor of the gods, Hawk. James is your brother. Apparently, Cord rescued him before the ship sank."

"No!" Hawk placed his head in his hands, overwhelmed by Diablo's words. It was too much. He almost looked forward to the musket ball that would end his life. He closed his eyes and waited.

Diablo laughed loudly. "Yes, it would have been even more humorous had you two fought and one killed the other, only to find out it was his own brother he had slain. Alas, that won't happen. But don't worry, Hawk; James is my next victim. I want to finish the job of killing your family." Diablo cocked the hammer on the musket and took aim at the easy target on the beach.

Hawk opened his eyes briefly, wondering about the delay, and saw a commotion behind Diablo. A man pushed his way out of the throng in the middle of the ship and charged him. Diablo turned just as two flintlocks fired. The man collapsed to his knees just behind him. Diablo laughed and turned back around. "Oh, Hawk, Wesley's dead."

Diablo aimed the musket again. Hawk couldn't see which two of Diablo's supporters had shot Wesley. He hadn't even thought about Wesley, Hobbs, Bones, Jimmy, Billy, and other pirates loyal to him. He guessed many would die that day or already had in the initial struggle. A tear ran down his cheek. He prayed the bullet would end his life quickly, before more tears fell.

The musket fired, flame and smoke issuing from the barrel, but the shot flew somewhere high overhead. Diablo suddenly straightened. His mouth opened, but no words came forth. He stared down at the dagger blade that had just appeared out of his bare chest. Blood trickled out both sides of his mouth, and his eyes were wide with shock and rage. The dagger disappeared, and he collapsed, vanishing behind the rail.

Another man stood in Diablo's place. It was Wesley, holding a bloody dagger in his crimson hand. Blood soaked his white shirt on both sides of his chest. He pointed the blade toward Hawk, smiled weakly, and collapsed behind the rail.

Another commotion ensued on the deck. Diablo's conspirators stood in shock, having just watched their leader die. They offered little resistance as the pirate crew charged and subdued them. Very soon, the mutiny was over. Billy appeared at the rail, raised his dagger, and shouted, "Hawk." The chant was quickly echoed by the pirates behind him and then spread to Kragg's crew on the beach. Hawk stayed on his knees, staring numbly at the sand in front of him.

CHAPTER XVIII

"Good morning, handsome," a sweet voice whispered in Hawk's ear.

He opened his eyes and slowly turned his head toward the source. Anna lay beside him, raised up on her elbow. They were lying in a bed in a room he didn't recognize. She was as beautiful as he had ever seen her. A sun ray danced on her face and hair through an open window, making her glow.

"Where am I?"

"You're in bed with me, silly." She laughed her sweet laugh.

"I can't remember how I got here. The last thing I remember is being on Devil's Island. What's happened to my crew?" Hawk looked around the room and searched his memory for some clue as to how he had arrived.

"They are close. Much closer than you realize."

Suddenly, Anna's right arm swung into view. Hawk saw the flash of silver but was too slow to stop it from descending and plunging into him. He stared down in horror at the dagger hilt protruding from his chest, Anna's small hand still clutching it. He looked back up at her. "Why?" he managed to whisper.

"I want you to join me in hell!" Suddenly Anna's face began to transform. It was now Diablo lying beside him, his cruel smile present again.

Hawk awoke screaming and sat straight up in bed. The hut door swung open, and a man he didn't recognize rushed in.

"Are you OK, Mr. Hawk?"

Hawk blinked several times and then looked down at his chest. He saw no blade and breathed a few times deeply as his racing heart began to slow. He realized his head was pounding with a headache, and he was a little dizzy. He recognized that feeling—*rum!* He looked around and surveyed the interior of a small, thatched hut. The sun shone behind the pirate greeting him, outlining his body in gold. The pirate had a rough, weathered, but friendly face. He had a short-cropped white beard and white hair poked out from beneath the black scarf on his head. He was barefoot and wore baggy blue breeches, a white shirt, and a faded blue waistcoat. He wasn't a large man, but Hawk had no doubt he had been in a scrap or two. "Who are you?"

"Beggin' your pardon, sir. I'm Jack—Jack Roberts. I was Mr. Kragg's quartermaster. Don't guess ye 'member too much 'bout last night?"

Hawk searched his memory, just as he had in his dream. He only remembered a mob of pirates helping him to his feet. Barrels of rum quickly made their way to the beach, and he drank and drank as his crew joined Kragg's, and the celebration began. He vaguely remembered staggering to Kragg's old hut, and there the memories ended.

"Not much," Hawk croaked. His mouth and throat were dry. "What officers are left from my crew?"

"Let's see. There's Billy, a right quick lad, Bones, not a bad man for a Brit. I think that be all. Oh, and I believe a Jimmy."

"Wesley? Hobbs?"

"I'm afraid Wesley just had enough strength left to kill that Diablo. Fittin' name if there ever be one. Was Hobbs your navigator? If so, he was killed in the mutiny. Luckily, Bones was below deck and survived."

Hawk's stomach turned. He had hoped more of his memories had been nightmares. Wesley had saved his life and probably the lives of most of the other pirates. Poor Hobbs—hadn't fought a day in his life and was killed. Jimmy and Billy were young and still inexperienced as officers. That just left Bones as the only real tie to the past. Then he remembered Diablo's words about Bloodstone slaying his father and his brother, James, still alive.

He recalled seeing James on the deck of the *Enterprise* as they sailed away. Did James know he was his brother?

"How about the mutineers?"

"They joined Diablo, Bloodstone, and Kragg. Your crew didn't exactly follow their articles, but I'd say it was a just enough endin'," Jack said and added a wink.

"How many men do you have? And supplies, treasure, and all that?"

"Round one hundred and fifty, give er take a few. The navy's been hittin' us hard, even before the last battle. Now treasure be another story. Kragg had it in his articles that a quarter of each haul was held out; the rest was divided among the men. He said that would give us somethin' to tide us over should we need to lay low for a while. Personally, I think the ol' dog was gonna steal it for himself someday and disappear. Would you like to see?"

"Sure. I need to clear my head anyway."

"Oh, here, take this first." Jack handed Hawk his baldric.

Hawk instantly noticed a new pistol hanging from it, a golden, double-barreled flintlock. A double-barreled flintlock was rare and a golden one legendary. He drew the weapon and studied it in awe.

"Kragg took it from a rich cap'n aboard an East India Company ship off the coast of Africa. Richest haul we ever had, I'd wager. It was Kragg's prized possession. And now it's yours."

Hawk finally sheathed it and slung the baldric over his shoulder, noting his prized dagger was still in it too. He followed Jack out of the hut and onto the beach. It appeared like the two crews were working together reasonably well. The *Bloody Seas* had been pulled to the beach's other side and laid over for careening and further repair. *Hell's Fury* was still being repaired but appeared close to seaworthy. The pirates they passed grinned and offered some kind of acknowledgment. Both crews shared an excitement that had been absent for some time

Jack led them up the beach and onto a small trail that wound through the dense vegetation. Soon they came to the base of a small, rocky mountain reminiscent of the Rock. A small round cave led into the stone. Jack lit an oil lantern just inside the entrance.

"This was a volcano at one time. There are caves all through it," Jack reported, leading him back into the smooth tunnel. After a short distance, the tunnel turned to the right and ended at a wooden door. Jack produced two keys and unlocked the lock in the door and another lock joining two pieces of chain over the front. "Borrowed the keys from Kragg last night," he grinned.

After a moment, he pulled the heavy door open, handed Hawk the lantern, and nodded for him to enter. Hawk walked into the small round room and nearly gasped. Stacks of gold and silver bars lined the back wall, and several large chests sat on the floor, some with the lids open. They were filled with doubloons, pieces of eight, jewelry, and gems. This was probably more treasure than Bloodstone had taken in his entire career, successful though it had been by most standards. Other crates and barrels were stacked around the sides, which Hawk figured were also full of expensive goods.

"The ol' devil had a good run," Jack chuckled.

Hawk realized it was more than enough treasure for him and Anna to live out the rest of their lives comfortably. He could just take his share and disappear, leaving all the pirates and the pirate life far behind. While that idea was perfect for him, what would the nearly two hundred men looking for him to lead them do? He knew of no one else that could lead them, other than to their deaths. Even though he didn't know Kragg's crew, he still felt an obligation. He didn't want to see both crews hanged.

"Jack, can I trust you?"

"Yes, sir, that ye can."

"Of course, I don't suppose you'd tell me if I couldn't?"

"It'd be a dangerous game askin' a lyin' backstabber if he lies or backstabs, Cap'n," Jack replied with a wink.

Hawk had just met this Jack, but he liked him. He would have to rely on his ability to judge people—he had no time to do otherwise. "I need a quartermaster. Billy's a good man and shows a lot of promise, but this isn't the time for training. I need someone who's done it all. Plus, I need the loyalty of both crews. Would you be interested? And I assume you are well-liked by your crew?"

"I was hopin' you'd ask. At your service, Cap'n," Jack said with a mock salute. "And, of course, they love me. How could they not? Now, do we have a plan yet?"

"Not yet. Walk with me to the top of one of the peaks at the harbor's entrance." Jack locked the treasure room door and led Hawk out of the cave.

A trail close to the beach wound through the vegetation around the harbor. It gradually climbed the rocky ridge to the right and ended at a flat stone outcropping overlooking the harbor, beach, and sea. Three pirates quickly stood when they saw the two. They had polished horns hanging around their necks.

"Good morning, men," Hawk said. "Would you mind taking a walk for an hour or so? Me and Jack will keep lookout for you."

The men smiled, nodded, and disappeared down the trail.

Hawk sat down on the cliff's edge, letting his legs dangle over the side. He stared out onto the calm, shimmering, sapphire sea. The sun was up but still low in the sky, its orange rays dancing on the water. The air was still cool, but a warm breeze hinted that it would soon be hot. The sky was deep blue, with only a few white clouds hanging low on the horizon.

"What be on your mind, Hawk," Jack asked, sitting beside him.

Hawk glanced at Jack for a moment and then back to the sea. From here, he could see all the small rocky islands and many shallow patches on the approach. It was indeed a tricky harbor to reach. "What I tell you stays with us, or I'll make Kragg seem like a priest."

"It'll die with me, Cap'n."

"Jack, I've been trying to find a way out for several years now."

"A way out?" Jack asked.

"This is all I've done since Bloodstone kidnapped me at just eight years of age. I never knew of any other life until I went to New Orleans for the first time. I didn't see much, but enough to know that there's a lot of world out there on the land. And I met a girl."

"Ah, a beautiful young lass," Jack said. "They'll definitely change your way of thinkin', to be sure."

"I promised her once I had made enough money, I would leave this life and take her away somewhere far from the sea. We would buy a nice plot of land, build a farm, start a family, and live happily ever after." Hawk looked up at Jack. The man reminded him a little of Wesley.

"A good dream it is," said Jack.

"But it doesn't have to just be a dream! I could take my share of the treasure, give the rest to you and your men, and make it happen."

"You could, indeed. But, Hawk, you must realize that ye might be the greatest pirate cap'n ever. I've sailed ten years with Kragg, and I know of all Bloodstone's deeds. I even sailed with Lafitte for a time. All of 'em right fine pirates. But, Hawk, you're special. I've heard of all your feats, and you're only seventeen years old. You're smarter than the rest—and more cunning. And, apparently, you just won't die." Jack chuckled.

"Bloody lucky, more like it. But it's like Bloodstone said, I'd have been good a hundred years ago. The time of pirates is over. You know it. We might have sunk the *Enterprise*, but there are more out there just like it and even more being built. We can't go back, Jack. The US isn't going back. We're two hundred against a nation. Sure, we could buy some time, but how long until we're shot or hanged?"

Jack was silent. He grabbed a piece of long grass and chewed absently on the end. "I don't know, Hawk. I guess the times are changin'."

"Have you ever thought about doing anything else?"

Jack nodded. "Actually did. I started off workin' on a merchantman. I was young and wide-eyed and thought the sea was full of adventure. I slaved on a merchantman for nigh ten years, I reckon. I had some adventures, but it was a hard life. If you think a pirate ship is tough, try a merchantman. On one voyage, Lafitte attacked us off the coast of New Spain. He was a fair pirate and gave us crewmen a choice of joining him or going free. I thought I'd had my fill of the sea, so I turned down Lafitte, and he let me go in Galveston.

"I got a job as a carpenter since I had so much experience on the ship and met a sweet, pretty young lass in town. We bought a little piece of land, and I built our house. I had everything I wanted."

Hawk thought instantly of Wesley and his story of his young bride. "But apparently, it didn't work out."

"Turns out it wasn't what I really wanted. As hard as life on a ship was, I missed the freedom, the open sea, drinkin', gamblin', and swappin' stories with my mates. I missed it all. I hooked up with one of Lafitte's ships and went on account. There I found my true freedom and adventure. A couple of years later, I heard of Kragg and joined his crew in New Orleans. I didn't like being tied to the land as much as Lafitte was in Baratavia." Jack had a slight smile as he reminisced his past.

"And the girl?" Hawk asked.

"Oh, she was glad to see me go. No woman wants a man that has his mind somewhere else. You see, Hawk, the key is figurin' out what your heart really wants. If you're stuck on the sea, the land sounds good. If you're stuck on land, the sea sounds good. But once you find your place, you'll know it. Mine is piratin'."

Now Jack really reminded him of Wesley. He was a wise old pirate. "And how will I know where my heart wants to be?"

"Oh, you'll probably have to run off with your lass and give the landlubber dream a go. You'll be miserable on the sea and only half a man if not. Just don't be surprised if you hear the sea callin' your name one day—she's a powerful mistress who never truly releases you. You'll know where your heart lies if one day you grow so tired of your borin', perfect life that it makes your belly turn. If adventure and glory beckon to you and you can't sleep at night for relivin' your past. Or if you do sleep, then the dreams come. And then you'll find yourself resentin' that sweet, pretty lass for takin' you away from the life you really wanted."

Both men were silent for some time. Hawk looked over his shoulder to watch his crew work on the ships and move about the beach. They reminded him of ants from this distance. Gulls and osprey dove into the surf below, catching their breakfast. The air was warmer now, but it was still a pleasant day.

"So you're saying I should go?" Hawk finally asked.

"No...least not now. Hawk, I know ye don't owe any of us pirates anything. But you've given these men hope for the first time in a long time. They want to follow a legend for a while. They want one last go at it before their time is up. And you've just been a cap'n for a week now. I know you're bound to have dreamed about bein' a cap'n. It's all yours now. You're more powerful than Bloodstone or Kragg. If you walk away now, that will only lead even more to you missin' the sea and wonderin' what might have been. Regret is even worse than longin'. I say you stay with us for a year. Let's go raise some cane, make some noise, and finish writin' the legend of the Hawk. At the end of a year, if you're still bent on seein' your girl, leave us and go off to do as you want."

Hawk mulled over Jack's words. Like Wesley, he made a lot of sense. He had worked his entire life to reach this moment. He was a pirate captain and probably the last great one. If he left now, he would always wonder what it would have been like, what he missed. His captaincy thus far consisted of one short voyage and one duel. With Bloodstone, Kragg, and Diablo gone, it was truly his crew now. He did hate to postpone his dream with Anna, but one more year would pass quickly. They still had the rest of their lives to spend together.

Also, what would happen to all his men if he left now? Most would continue piracy but without a strong leader. They would be easy prey for Cord, James, and the rest of the fleet. If he told them ahead of time that he was leaving, they could plan their futures. They could save money if needed, and he could split up the treasure from the cave, so all could at least have a fresh start.

Maybe he could even work out getting them pardons before he left.

His mind also turned to James. All his life, Bloodstone and the pirates had been his family. Now he had a real family— a brother he could barely remember—if James had somehow survived. Somehow, he had to get to James. But getting to a lieutenant on a US Navy ship, bent on eradicating pirates, would not be easy. Not without the visit ending at the end of a noose, anyway. He had to figure out how to talk to James before he ran away with Anna. *Why is life so complicated?*

"What do you think the point of all this is?" said Hawk.

"Point of what, Cap'n?"

"I don't know—life?"

Jack scratched at his beard and appeared to think deeply. "Don't know that I've ever given much thought to it, Cap'n." He stared out over the glimmering sea for a few minutes. "I guess if I had to say, it'd be makin' a name for yourself and leavin' your mark on the world—to have people speak your name long after your body's at the bottom of the sea."

Hawk mulled over his words for a few moments but chose not to discuss it further. "Do we have enough men to sail both ships? I'll need you to captain *Hell's Fury*. I can make Billy my temporary quartermaster. I have Jimmy as gunner and Bones as carpenter and surgeon. I need a navigator and cook, and it wouldn't hurt to have another surgeon. You'll need a full crew."

Jack smiled. "Edward Hill is as fine a navigator as you've ever met. Charles Miller could stitch up a fly. Ol' Smokey can stir up a pot of lobscouse as good as any, I reckon. I can put me a crew together, and we can fully man both. Wouldn't hurt to pick up a few more hands along the way, though."

Hawk nodded and stood. He turned to look down upon the beach and ships. "Oh, we need new ship names too. Those names died with their captains."

Jack stood too. "Any ideas, sir?"

"The *Bloody Seas* will now be the *Seahawk*. You can name the other."

Jack picked at his beard thoughtfully. "How 'bout the *Phoenix*, Cap'n? Us pirates have been reborn and are risin' from the ashes."

Hawk smiled. Apparently, Jack also liked to read. "Excellent. Now, no word to the crew of our one-year deal yet. I don't want it to leak out to the navy that they only have a year to deal with me. When the time comes, I'll tell everyone, and we'll divide up the treasure.

"We need to make some major changes to these ships. Let's go talk to Bones and your carpenter. Then we need to pack everything up. We won't be coming back here."

"Yes, sir!" Jack said enthusiastically, saluting. "Where are we headin', Cap'n?"

"I need to make a quick stop at New Orleans. After, I'm not sure. But I do know this: the men better be ready. It'll be a year like no other."

***

At sunrise a week later, the *Seahawk*—with the black paint removed—and the *Phoenix* made their way out of the Devil's Island harbor. The *Seahawk's* and *Phoenix's* upper decks—quarter and forecastle—had been removed. The main decks were now flat, similar to a navy frigate, and cannons lined the main deck and gun deck. Each ship carried fifty cannons now between those two decks. They didn't have enough men aboard either vessel to man all the cannons, but just the sight of them would strike fear into most. The ships would be much faster now with the extra weight removed. They were fully repaired, armed, and stocked with food. Both their crews went about their chores with excitement. Their wounds were mostly healed, and they had eaten and drank their fill for days. They were ready to get back to pirating.

Hawk used Wesley's old cabin on the gun deck. The other officers' cabins were on the orlop deck below. The *Phoenix* was set up similarly, with Jack also having a cabin on the gun deck. Although he was the acting captain on the *Phoenix*, he and both crew's knew Hawk was the leader.

As Hawk stood on the bow, hands on his hips, he couldn't help but feel a little excited. First, he was going to get to see Anna again. Second, he was a pirate captain. Although he had liked and respected Captain Bloodstone, at least until Diablo's confession, he disagreed with his brutality and some of his tactics. Not having Diablo's aggressive, confrontational, and negative presence also lifted the mood of all. At least at the moment, and before any battles had been fought, Hawk was beloved by his pirate crew. The time of pirates might almost be over, and his reign as captain would be short, but for today and the coming year, it was going to be a new golden age.

CHAPTER XIX

"I've missed you so much!" Anna exclaimed. She reached her hands around Hawk's head and pulled him down to kiss him.

Hawk wrapped his arms around her waist and pulled her closer. He loved the sensation of her body pressed against his, warm even through their clothing. He also remembered just how much he enjoyed her kisses. It was amazing how they instantly had such a powerful effect on him. Chills crawled up his spine as his heart raced again. "Hmmm. And I missed you too!"

"Are you here to finally take me away?" she asked once they broke the kiss off to breathe.

"Anna, let's sit down."

Anna frowned but followed him to the bed and sat beside him, as he had done the first time they were together. She went from exuberance to fighting back tears. Hawk told her what had happened since their day on the island, mainly of the past few weeks' events. He held her hand and gazed into her eyes as he spoke.

"So, you should be free now for us to start our new life?" Anna asked, a glimmer of hope returning.

Hawk told her the remainder of his story and his plan. Now she could no longer hold back the tears. "Anna, I swear, one more year, and I'm done."

"It's always one more year or two more years! You have all the money we need now. You owe those cutthroat savages nothing!" Anna pulled away and placed her head in her hands.

"I owe it to them and to me. I don't want to be like Jack.

If I leave the sea behind, I want it to be forever. I don't want us to end up being torn apart because I'm wondering too hard about what might have been. Yes, we could run away together—tonight, for that matter. But that wouldn't be fair to either of us. I have to leave the right way, with no what-ifs. Does that make any sense?"

Anna wiped her eyes on the top of her red dress. "I don't know, Hawk. Part of me understands. But part of me doesn't know if I can take another year. You've no idea how bad I hate my life now. The hope you give me lasts a while, but then I have to wonder if you're still alive or coming back. Look how many pirates have been killed over the past couple of years.

"It's so hard to get out of bed each morning and face this life of misery. There is never a good day in this job—never anything to look forward to. Most women in this business don't do it all their lives. They get married or find some way out. You're my way out, Hawk. Or so I hope. But if you're not my way out, then I have to try to find another."

"Well, I don't want you lying with another man until I return," Hawk replied, nauseous from witnessing Anna's pain.

"Then what would you have me do? Beg for crumbs on the street again?" Anna looked at him with eyes red and glassy.

Hawk reached inside his shirt and withdrew a large leather pouch attached to a leather cord around his neck. He lifted the cord over his head and handed the heavy bag to Anna. "Tonight is your last night working here."

Anna's mouth dropped open as she held the bag. Her hands shook as she opened it to reveal it was stuffed with gold doubloons and pieces of eight—more money than most people would earn in their entire lives. She closed it back and stared at Hawk, unable to speak.

"After I leave in the morning, take this money and find a place to live. You can get another job or even start your own business. This will be enough to last you for many years. If I'm not back by this time next year, then something has happened, and I won't be coming back. Then you can do whatever you want with the money and your life. Can you do that for me, Anna? I haven't let you down so far."

Anna leaned over and hugged him tightly. After a moment, Hawk gently pushed her head back so he could kiss her. They kissed for several minutes. "While I would take you over the money, you have no idea how happy you've made me! I'll wait a year for you, Hawk, and longer if you ask. But please, please just try to come back to me."

"Well, you know the legend of the Hawk wouldn't be complete if I died now, would it? I'll come back for you, Anna, and it will all have been worth it. Just leave word with Madame Cynthia once you get settled, so I know where to find you. And please be careful not to let people know about the money. I don't want something to happen to you."

Hawk spent the night with Anna. They made love and held each other most of the night, only drifting off to sleep in the early hours of the next morning. After Hawk left, Anna went to pack and to tell Madame Cynthia she was leaving. She could wait one more year now.

***

It didn't take long for Hawk to make his name as a pirate captain. His two ships became the terror of the Caribbean. Although once word spread that quarter would be given to any that didn't resist, most ships surrendered at first sight of the pirate ships. They allowed the fittest men, or the most skilled, to join the crews. After a few months, both ships had crews of nearly two hundred. The few ships that did resist quickly paid the price. The Hawk was soon known from Boston to New Spain. Stories from survivors of his attacks were printed in the newspapers of every city.

Although Hawk and his crew were thriving, piracy was still declining. Earlier that year, piracy was dealt a significant blow. Spanish privateers near Honduras attacked Jean Lafitte. Although it was never confirmed and his body was never found, it was rumored that Lafitte was killed in the battle. Others said he escaped and just disappeared. But either way, another one of the greatest pirates of the day was gone.

Hawk spotted US Navy ships more frequently, and more vessels were steadily added to the West Indies Squadron. But his ships were as fast or faster than the frigates and larger schooners. The corvettes, sloops, and gunboats wouldn't challenge them, at least not alone. Since they didn't have a regular hideout and usually just anchored somewhere long enough to careen, restock supplies, and sell merchandise, they were challenging for the navy to track down. Hawk also expanded their range from North Carolina to Brazil. They took ships from the United States, England, Spain, France, and Portugal.

Six months after the death of Bloodstone, Hawk learned from a group of US sailors that had recently joined his crew that Captain Cord had been promoted to Commodore of the West Indies Squadron. James was promoted to captain of his own ship, the USS *Avenger*. The *Enterprise* had sunk after her magazine exploded. James, Cord, and a handful of sailors had barely escaped in a longboat.

Hawk quickly amassed a fortune in gold and silver. His men could all have been rich, but as with most pirates, the more they made, the more they spent on women, gambling, and drink. Hawk thought increasingly of a way to leave the pirate life and join Anna. He often wondered what Anna was doing now that she had her freedom. Hopefully, she was running her own tavern. At least she no longer had to lie with men for her money. He had rescued her even if he died before ever seeing her again.

***

Early the following year, most of the West Indies Squadron withdrew from their base at St. Thomas. Disease had run rampant on their ships, forcing them to return to the United States mainland. Although disease was always a concern on ships, fresh food and water helped Hawk's crew avoid it. With the fleet gone, little could slow down Hawk and his crew. Even the Spanish man-o'-wars that escorted some of the treasure ships were no match for Hawk's two ships.

In less than a year, Hawk and his crew captured over a hundred ships. It was hard to imagine growing bored with one of the greatest pirate campaigns of all time, but Hawk was. Even his crew grumbled some over the lack of fighting. The treasure and lifestyle were great, but so many ships surrendered, and the ones that didn't were subdued so quickly that they experienced minimal fighting and killing. Hawk refused to be the bloodthirsty killer that Bloodstone and Kragg had been. Since he had learned that it was Bloodstone, and not the Spanish, who had killed his father, he no longer hated the Spanish or any other country. He merely wanted what they carried in their holds. It was never personal.

It was hard for Hawk not to become overconfident. All he heard from his men, those of the ships he captured, and from the cities and ports they visited was how great the Hawk was. He had never been defeated in a fight or battle. Even in the fight with the *Enterprise*, he had saved the day. He had done things no one had ever done, living or dead. His legend was already growing greater than the infamous pirates from the golden age —Blackbeard, Avery, Kidd, and Roberts. Only Lafitte's legend was possibly greater than his in the modern era. With Lafitte dead, Hawk was the only one still adding to his story.

One night after taking a big prize, Hawk addressed his crew. He had drunk a little more grog than usual and felt particularly good. "Hail to the greatest pirate crew in history!" He raised his tankard to the men around him. The men cheered and raised their goblets, mugs, and tankards. "The only thing that can stop us now is a mistake or God himself." The crew cheered again. "Hawk doesn't make mistakes, and I'm not sure even God wants to tangle with these two ships!"

CHAPTER XX

A couple of months later, and close to a year since he left Anna, the *Seahawk* was careening on a small island near Devil's Island. They had found a deep water, protected cove on the island's north side. Jack had sailed the *Phoenix* to Havana to sell some merchandise and buy supplies. By flying a Spanish flag, they could come and go in Cuba as they pleased.

Hawk stared up at the southern sky as it turned black well before sunset. The clouds rolled and churned, and the wind kicked up through the palm trees behind the beach. It took Hawk only a moment to recognize the impending danger. Hurricanes were not an uncommon sight while sailing the Caribbean. But, as with most other things, Hawk had been lucky and managed to avoid or survive all the ones he'd encountered. This time, he couldn't run.

By the time Hawk found Billy, the rain was pouring and the wind gusting. "Round up the crew and head into the trees!" said Hawk. "Make sure all are off the *Seahawk*."

The *Seahawk* had been leaned to one side and secured by the anchor and numerous ropes stretching from the railing to nearby trees. The beach was totally open and unprotected, so the only hope of shelter was in the trees. Hawk waited on the beach, squinting into the sheets of rain until all his men had dispersed into the forest. Streaks of lightning lit the skies, and thunder boomed close by.

Hawk started to flee into the palms too, but then thought about his ship. If the ropes broke or the trees they were tied to fell, the boat would probably be washed out to sea. If it didn't sink, it could be dashed on the rocks or lost for good. Being marooned on this island was not how he was going out.

Billy came rushing out of the trees to see what was keeping Hawk. "Come on, sir! You'll be blown out to sea. We've found some good dunes to shelter behind."

"I'm going onboard the ship," Hawk shouted above the gusting wind. "Those ropes will never hold, and I'm not losing her."

"You can't man that ship by yourself! And it will be a miracle if it's not smashed to pieces on the rocks," Billy screamed.

"Won't be the first miracle! Go find shelter, and I'll see you in the morning." Hawk turned and sprinted toward the ship, the wind almost knocking him off his feet a few times. It was too dark and raining too hard to determine if Billy had made it back into the trees. Hawk scrambled up a rope ladder that hung over the side. He was slammed into the hull once or twice but finally reached the sloped deck.

The ship was already rocking in the surf and straining against the ropes. Hawk instantly realized the ship was too vulnerable laid on its side. The hull would likely be split open and the masts destroyed if it were washed farther onto the beach. He also knew he couldn't turn the capstan by himself to reel the anchor back into the ship. He grabbed an axe and quickly started chopping at the anchor's hawser line, the frequent flashes of lightning providing enough light to see. The wind battered against him, and the rain stung his face and hands.

He finally severed the rope, and the entire ship lurched. The deck's angle flattened out as the ship leaned more upright. He then rushed about the deck cutting the remainder of the ropes attached to the distant trees. He was startled to see movement at the side of the ship. Then a bright flash of lightning illuminated Billy leading a small group of pirates over the rail.

"What are you doing?" Hawk shouted.

"Apparently, sailing in a hurricane!" Billy shouted back.

Hawk saw Jimmy, Edward, Charles, Smokey, and three other pirates behind Billy.

"Bones said he'd be here to patch the heap up when we return," said Billy.

Hawk shook his head and laughed. He was upset but admired the loyalty of his crew. Most pirates were only out for themselves. His crew was more like a large family.

He pointed to three of the pirates. "You men finish cutting these ropes! Edward, man the helm. Sail her just out of the harbor and keep her turned directly leeward. Billy, raise just enough sail to escape the surf."

The pirates quickly set about their chores, and the ship was soon upright and being tossed roughly in the waves. Once the sails were at half-mast, the wind instantly filled them and began driving the ship out of the surf and toward open water. "Find a spot and tie yourself to a mast or rail!" Hawk shouted. Most used the loose pieces of rope still tied to the railing to secure themselves, leaving enough slack to move around but not enough that they could be washed overboard.

The ship seemed small, tossing about in the vast, rough sea. Waves crashed over the sides, battering the frail men and threatening to snap the ropes that bound them to the ship. Anything loose was swept into the water. It required all Edward's skill as a navigator to steer into the large waves and keep the ship from getting turned broadside to the wind. That would have resulted in a quick death for them all. Hawk stood beside Edward, shouting commands and helping him turn the wheel. His worst fear was the masts snapping in half.

After what seemed like hours, the wind and rain suddenly stopped, as did the lightning. Thunder still rumbled around them, but the stillness of the air and sea was eerie.

"Eye of the storm!" Hawk shouted to the crew. "Check the sails and rigging, then secure yourselves and brace for the second half."

The calm didn't last long. The winds soon picked up again, and the rain and gale returned with a vengeance. The hurricane raged most of the night, but the ship and the small crew somehow survived. By the time the sky began to lighten, the storm had passed.

The ship had taken a lot of damage to the rigging and sails, but the masts held, and the hull was intact. Hawk knew the lower decks would be a disaster, but he and his crew had survived. The island was still in sight far astern, although they had sailed much farther than he thought. He had Edward swing the ship about and head back to the island, hoping to find most of his crew alive.

It took several hours to search the entire island. Many trees had fallen, and some were just gone, carried away by the angry sea. Nearly two-dozen pirates were dead or missing. Falling trees had crushed some, and flying limbs had struck others. Waves had apparently claimed the rest. They quickly buried their fallen comrades without ceremony, repaired the sails and rigging, reattached the anchor, and loaded up the *Seahawk*. The lower decks would be repaired and straightened up during the voyage.

The sky was blue and the sun hot when the *Seahawk* departed from the island and sailed toward Havana. Once on the open water, little evidence remained that such a massive storm had passed through just twelve hours earlier. Hawk was worried about Jack. He was supposed to have left Havana the night before and been back by noon. It was two hours past now, and they had seen no sign of him. Both ships shared the same charts, so Hawk knew the route Jack would have taken.

Halfway there, Hawk began noticing debris in the water—here a barrel, there a crate. His heart sank. The debris field left the charted course and led north; likely, the storm had carried the ship that way. Edward guided the ship to follow the trail. More wooden objects floated in the water on both sides, along with some pieces of sails. Then they saw the bodies. They floated face down in the water, rising and falling with the gentle swells. Hawk stood at the base of the bowsprit, desperately hoping against fading hope that somehow his ship, and most of his crew, survived.

"Longboat ho, two points starboard," Billy called down from the crow's nest.

Edward steered the boat toward Billy's setting. Soon, Hawk spotted the longboat ahead, with a number of people onboard. He also saw large pieces of debris floating close to it with other objects, hopefully, live pirates, clinging to them.

The *Seahawk* reached the small boat a half hour later. Hawk was relieved to see Jack with ten other pirates. There were, indeed, more pirates sitting on, and clinging to, pieces of the ship—barrels, crates, and even a long section of one of the masts. Three dozen pirates were plucked from the sea onto the safety of the *Seahawk.*

Jack and his quartermaster, Samuel Mortensen—Mort as he was called—were the only officers to have survived. Once he was sure all his remaining crew was onboard, Jack rushed over to Hawk. "You're a sight for sore eyes, Cap'n. Never seen anything move so fast. We tried to turn this way and that but couldn't escape it. Once our mainmast broke in two, we were doomed. The rudder snapped next, then we drifted broadside to it. Wasn't long until we were upside down and sinking fast. Ol' Matthew went down with the ship, still trying to steer that broken rudder. Those of us who could swim, or float long enough, ended up together in the debris. The longboat somehow broke free during the sinking, and some of us climbed aboard." Jack was shaking from cold and clearly rattled from the ordeal.

"That's a shame to lose that ship and all those men," Hawk said.

"Aye, Cap'n, a bloody shame. What about you? How'd you escape it?" Jack surveyed the *Seahawk.*

Hawk told the story of the past night and morning. "Yesterday, we had two ships and almost four hundred men. Today, we have one ship and barely over two hundred."

"We'll get it all back, sir. The squadron is still mostly back in the States. We can take another frigate or nice schooner or two, and men are lining up to join the great Hawk. Like you said, not even God can stop the Hawk."

Mort nodded behind him.

"I think God has spoken loud and clear. Gather what supplies you can from the water and meet me in my cabin. Bring Billy, Jimmy, and Mort." Hawk turned and walked toward the helm, leaving Jack to his task.

***

Billy, Jack, Jimmy, and Mort entered Hawk's cabin several hours later. Hawk looked up from a chart he studied at the end of the large, polished table and nodded for them to sit. "I'll get straight to the point. Jack and I had a conversation a year ago, back when I defeated Kragg."

"Hawk! Shouldn't we talk first?" said Jack.

Hawk glared at Jack and then turned back to the officers. "I wanted to leave the trade then. I wanted to leave the sea and retire to the land with my sweet Anna. Jack persuaded me to stay and give my captaincy a good shot. We decided I owed it to both crews, and I agreed I'd give it a year. After a year, if I still wanted to leave, I would divide all the loot, and we could all head our separate ways."

Billy, Jimmy, and Mort exchanged glances and then turned to Jack, who was staring down at his hands, fidgeting in front of him on the table. "What are you saying, Cap'n?" Billy asked.

"It's time to get out with our lives and health. The West Indies Squadron is starting to return, and they will have more ships and men this time. Bloodstone, Kragg, and now Lafitte are all dead. Captain Cofresi and I are the only other captains of mention, and we're being hunted like never before." Hawk leaned back in his chair, placed his hands behind his neck, and stared at the oil lamp overhead.

"But they're still no match for us!" said Jack. "We just need to replace the *Phoenix* and add some hands."

"We gave it a good run, boys. We've taken a hundred ships in the past year and have never been defeated in a battle. But now, even God is telling us it's time to quit. We could take another ship and find some men to sail it. But for how long? Six months? A year? The sea's getting smaller by the day. Sooner or later, they'd catch us, and probably sooner. I can't do that to any of you. We need to get out while we can. There's enough treasure to make every one of us wealthy." Hawk closed his eyes, saw Anna's smile, and heard her sweet laugh for a moment.

"Even if that be so, how do you s'ppose we all go free?" Jack asked. "They won't just let the famous Hawk and his crew walk away and take on honest lives."

"You're right. But I will get pardons for all of you," Hawk opened his eyes and looked at Jack.

"And just why would the US be so kind?"

"I have something they want." Hawk grinned weakly.

"And what do you have that they'd let us all go free for?"

"Me."

CHAPTER XXI

The *Seahawk* sailed into the harbor as soon as Hawk spotted the schooner, the USS *Beagle*, which he had been tailing for several days, waiting for an opportunity to take it. The schooner was small and had a shallow draft, so it was perfect for sailing close to all the small islands searching for pirates.

Hawk had hoped to simply sail up and send over a boarding party while its crew was busy searching the island. Unfortunately, by the time they reached firing range, the sailors had returned, and the longboat had just been pulled onboard. But it was no matter. The schooner only had thirty sailors or so and three guns. They would be foolish to resist.

Hawk watched as sailors on the schooner grabbed their weapons and waited on the much larger frigate to drift in beside them. A man stood in front of the crew dressed as a naval officer. He had no weapon in his hands, although he had two flintlocks and a cutlass in his belt. The *Seahawk* lowered its sails and dropped anchor ten yards from the navy ship. Billy quickly hoisted Hawk's flag.

Hawk strode through the throng of pirates to the railing. "Who is the captain of the *Beagle*?" he called out.

The well-dressed man on the other ship cleared his throat. "Lieutenant Platt. And you must be the famous Hawk."

"I am. I don't want to destroy your ship or kill any of your sailors."

"So then, you are willing to surrender without a fight?"

Hawk's crew erupted in laughter. Hawk glanced at his crew briefly, smiled, and turned back to Lieutenant Platt. "I have twenty cannons loaded and prepared to fire into your ship. Forty men behind me have loaded blunderbusses aimed at your men, and they have grenadoes and flintlocks close at hand. I don't think we will be surrendering."

Lieutenant Platt's gaze traveled from one end of the pirate ship to the other and back to Hawk. "What is your offer then?"

"I want your ship. You can take what supplies you need, all your crew, and stay on that island behind you. I'm sure another squadron ship will find you soon," Hawk said, growing a little impatient with the overconfident captain.

"I'm afraid I cannot accept that offer. Perhaps we can give you some food and water, if you need it, and maybe some powder, but not my ship."

Hawk felt the blood rush to his face. One broadside would reduce the *Beagle* to splinters. But he needed a United States ship for his plan. He really didn't want to slaughter the sailors, either. They were just doing their jobs, which meant following a foolish captain for now. "Would you and your crew rather be shot or stabbed? It makes no difference to me, but I will have your ship." The men behind Hawk took aim at the sailors on the schooner, eager for a fight.

Platt turned to look at the men behind him. Some words were exchanged and several nods. Finally, he turned back to Hawk. "I think we'd rather kill your crew face-to-face if you please."

"Grapple it!" Hawk roared. Within moments, the grappling lines were tossed onto the Beagle and pulled tight until the hooks bit into its rail. "If a sailor touches a rope, shoot him in the head!"

Hawk hoped once he sent a few dozen skilled pirates aboard, and killed the lieutenant if necessary, the rest of the crew would surrender. They had to know his reputation for being fair and honest. As the ships were pulled together, Platt and his crew retreated to the middle of the deck and waited with their cutlasses and sabers drawn.

Without a word, Hawk ran and vaulted over the rail of the

Seahawk, flew over the rail of the *Beagle*, and landed lightly on the schooner's deck, cutlass in hand. His crew roared loudly and followed him. Hawk slowed now, motioning for his men to hold back. He wanted to give Platt one last chance. "Do you wish to reconsider before I kill you?"

"I think you have a problem, Mr. Hawk," Platt said smugly.

"And just what is that?" Hawk asked with no patience remaining.

"You have a battle on two fronts."

"What?"

Suddenly, cannon fire erupted from behind the pirates. Hawk turned to see the *Seahawk* rock violently. On the other side was a large navy schooner, much larger than the *Beagle*. While all the pirates had been watching the unfolding confrontation, the other schooner had sailed silently into range and fired a broadside. Instinct caused Hawk to turn just in time to knock aside a thrust from Platt's cutlass. He hoped that Jack, Jimmy, and Billy knew what to do because he had to deal with the crew of the Beagle.

Hawk saw the surprise on Platt's face at how quickly he had turned and blocked his thrust. Hawk attacked the lieutenant savagely and soon overwhelmed him. When his sword snapped Platt's smaller blade in two, a quick thrust into his chest ended the fight.

The pirates around Hawk charged the sailors with a berserker-type rage. The sailors held their own for a moment, but after seeing their leader slain, they quickly retreated. Half leaped off the railing behind them and into the water below. The rest were quickly slain. Hawk instructed a half dozen pirates to stay on the Beagle and led the remainder back onto his ship just as the *Seahawk's* cannons roared, firing into the other thirty-gun schooner.

By the time Hawk regained the deck of his ship, the pirates onboard were already firing blunderbusses into the sailors on the navy ship. They had only fired a handful of cannons but had significantly damaged the ship. Hawk couldn't determine the extent of the damage the *Seahawk* had taken, but it didn't appear to be taking on water.

The sailors returned fire, striking many of the pirates around Hawk. More cannons erupted from the *Seahawk* as the men below deck finished loading the portside cannons. The shots ranged from the waterline to the gunwale of the navy ship, now discernable as the USS *Grampus*. Splinters of wood flew into the men, scattering them about the deck.

Hawk led his men in throwing grenadoes and stinkpots. The sailors took heavy casualties from the fire and debris, and the clouds of toxic smoke interrupted their reloading the guns. Before Hawk and his crew could take advantage of the confusion on the *Grampus*, its cannons fired again. The *Seahawk* was rocked hard once more. Hawk knew from the sound below that the damage was great. He drew his flintlock and fired at the closest sailor. His men quickly followed suit. The pistols were much less accurate, but enough found their mark.

The *Grampus* began unfurling its sails and disengaged from the fight. The *Seahawk* managed a couple of more cannon shots into it, right at the waterline. The schooner limped away, clearly taking on water. A man dressed as its captain shouted from the railing just before it was out of hearing range, "The end is near, Hawk!"

Hawk realized the *Grampus* only wanted to cripple the *Seahawk*. The search would begin in earnest now for the Squadron. Hawk cursed and hurried below deck to inspect the damage. The ship was taking on water in the hold, but just right at the waterline. Bones was already on the repairs. The damage to the hull was extensive, but nothing that couldn't be fixed. A half-dozen pirate bodies were strewn about the gun deck. He returned to the main deck where a dozen more pirates had been killed and many more wounded. The wounded were helped to the infirmary for Charles to patch them up.

"Billy, set sail to Devil's Island and make haste repairing the ship," said Hawk. "The navy has searched that island a time or two, but that's no guarantee they won't be back. We'll try to return before you're ready to sail again. Jack, gather a small crew and meet me on the *Beagle*. We need to complete my plan. By the way, yet another sign."

***

The USS *Beagle* glided smoothly into the harbor of St. Thomas. A number of the West Indies Squadron vessels were currently at the docks. The navy had recovered from the illness that had ravaged their fleet the prior year and was now returning to their pirate-hunting missions.

Hawk, dressed in the clothing of Lieutenant Platt, spotted the ship he was looking for, the USS *Avenger*. He had Jack sail the *Beagle* several berths away from the large frigate. The docks had minimal activity at the moment, with only a few sailors coming and going from the ships. The *Avenger* had more activity than most, and it appeared like it was preparing to sail.

Jack and Hawk disembarked and fell in unnoticed behind a large group of sailors heading to the *Avenger*. They followed the sailors onboard the large ship, joining many more already performing their tasks about the ship. A ship as large as the *Avenger* typically carried three hundred sailors, and men came and went on the navy vessels, so the crews were not as close as those of a pirate ship. It wasn't hard to blend in. Hawk appeared important in Platt's clothing, and no one looked twice as he and Jack climbed down to the gun deck. The ship was laid out very similarly to the *Seahawk*, so Hawk knew precisely where the captain's cabin was.

Hawk opened the door without knocking and walked inside, with Jack following close behind and shutting the door. The cabin was large, taking up most of the last quarter of the stern end of the deck. A lone man sat at the end of the large, polished table in the middle of the room. He wore an open white shirt and a navy waistcoat with brass buttons. He looked up absently from a map he was marking with a feather quill and ink.

"Lieutenant Platt? Who are you?" The man demanded, quickly standing up from the table. He wore navy linen pants to match his vest.

"Are you James Wellington?" Hawk asked, approaching the near end of the table. Jack stayed back near the door.

"Yes. Now, who are you, and what do you want?" James demanded, his hand resting on the handle of his flintlock.

"Hawk. Or Henry Wellington if you'd rather." Hawk unbuttoned the top few buttons of his shirt and stretched it open to reveal the birthmark on the left side of his chest.

James stared in stunned silence. "My brother..." he said softly.

"I believe so. And we need to talk." Hawk pulled out a chair and calmly sat down.

"You are the most wanted pirate in the Caribbean, and I'm a captain in the West Indies Squadron, whose mission is to track down and kill or capture pirates. And you killed hundreds of navy sailors, attempted to kill a commodore and me, and destroyed the *Enterprise*. Tell me why I shouldn't kill you right now?"

"We're brothers. And you'd be dead before you cocked your flintlock. We have a lot to talk about, brother. After we talk, you can then decide what course of action to pursue."

James finally dropped down into his chair, still shaken. He knew after the battle with Bloodstone that his brother was likely alive. But he never expected to be face-to-face with him. Hawk was his brother and only living relative. Yet, he was also the most infamous pirate of the era and responsible for the deaths of countless men, the destruction of hundreds of ships, and the stealing of unimaginable loot. James's head swam with the conflicting emotions.

Hawk didn't wait for James to speak. "Tell me what you remember...before we were separated."

James's memory of that fateful day was still vivid, and he recounted every word and act to Hawk. Hawk remembered most of it, until he was whisked away to the *Bloody Seas*. James described Bloodstone shooting their father in the chest and even killing his own man on purpose in the process. Then the pirates spotted the USS *Enterprise* approaching, set fire to the ship with explosive shot, and sailed off before the *Enterprise* could attack. James finally snapped out of his paralyzing fear and managed to run and dive out of one of the cabin windows before the flames totally engulfed the ship. The *Enterprise*, and Captain Cord, found him floating near the burning wreckage. He was the only survivor.

Hawk shook his head and stared down. It was a moment before he could reply. "I never knew what happened after I was taken aboard the *Bloody Seas* until after I slew Kragg. That's when Diablo told me the story during his mutiny. He didn't share the details, though. Bloodstone had said that a Spanish warship had attacked my family's ship and killed Father and you, and the pirates rescued me.

"Soon, being a pirate was the only way of life I knew. I learned to hate the Spanish, like Bloodstone and his crew did." Hawk shared Bloodstone's tales about the Spanish. He fell silent as he relived his past in his mind.

James finally spoke. "I grew up with the hatred of Bloodstone and all pirates. Cord took me as his son, and I've been in the navy ever since. We defended the east coast against the Royal Navy, which Cord was doing when he found me, and then defeated them at New Orleans. After the Battle of New Orleans, we were commissioned to hunt pirates. I guess you know the rest. I was made captain of this ship shortly after the battle with Bloodstone."

"What a cruel irony," said Hawk. "Two brothers separated as children, growing up on opposite sides. The gods have a terrible sense of humor."

"You said you grew up hating the Spanish. But you and Bloodstone attacked and killed more than just the Spaniards."

"In the later years. But you can justify anything. Most of the merchant ships are hauling ill-gotten spoils too. Look at the United States. The English stole that land from the Indians by force. I didn't agree with everything Bloodstone did. But what was I to do? Mutiny? Leave the only life I knew? For what? I never knew what a town looked like until I was fourteen and went to

New Orleans. It was then I met Anna and decided I wanted to leave this life and run away inland with her." Hawk studied his brother. His hair was brown, and he was two years older, but they definitely shared a resemblance.

"Why didn't you leave then?" James asked, carefully evaluating everything his younger brother, the pirate captain, said.

"Money. I promised Anna I would come back for her when I had enough money for us to live comfortably for the rest of our lives. I was close before our battle with you and the *Enterprise*. Then, of course, I had to avenge Bloodstone and confront Kragg. I then felt obligated to lead the combined crew for a while—one last run."

"And now?"

"I'm done. I have enough money, and I've had my fill of being a pirate captain. I want out."

"And that's why you're here?"

"Aye. I want to make a deal."

"There's no way I can let you and your entire crew go, even though you are my brother. With your time serving with Bloodstone and now on your own, you've taken more ships and killed more people than any pirate in recent history, maybe ever. Even the president mentions you by name. I would be court-martialed, if not hanged, if I were to let you go—Cord would see to it himself. Besides, you and your crew would be hunted even if I did. You and Anna would never know peace and security."

"Oh, by the way, I took the *Beagle* too. Unfortunately, Lieutenant Platt and his men didn't want to let me borrow the ship, and we had to kill a few. The *Grampus* sailed up, though, and tore my ship up pretty good, if it makes you feel any better."

"What?" James roared, leaning forward.

"I had to have a way of coming to talk to you. I tried every way possible to ask nicely for it." Hawk turned to the older pirate. "Jack, do you mind going out and mingling with the nice sailors? I need to talk to my brother in private."

"But Cap'n! He could shoot you dead as you sit," Jack said.

"As I should," James said.

Hawk laughed. "He's not that quick. It will be fine. I'll join you in a bit."

Jack shook his head and turned and left the cabin, shutting the door hard behind him.

Hawk turned back to face his brother. "Would they take my life in exchange for my crew getting pardoned?"

"What? How can you offer up your life? What of your dream with Anna?"

"You said I could never go free. But there is no one of any fame in my crew. I'm the only one the Unites States wants. And if I'm gone, my crew will walk away. There's no one left to lead them, and I have enough loot to keep them all happy and out of trouble." Hawk leaned forward and folded his arms on the table.

"So, you'll just turn yourself in, right here, just like that, to be hanged?" James asked, shocked at Hawk's suggestion.

"Well, not right here. And maybe not just like that. I have a plan...of course." Hawk spent a few minutes describing his plan to his brother.

James shook his head when Hawk had finished. "I don't know, brother. A lot could go wrong."

"Do you have another plan other than killing me now?"

"No."

"James, you know you're no different than me. If our roles had been reversed, we'd have ended up on opposite sides of this table. I played the hand I was dealt, as did you."

"I didn't kill innocent people," James said flatly.

"Really? I've heard stories of your time on the *Enterprise*. They say entire pirate crews without so much as one man taken alive. So you knew without a doubt that none of those men had been forced to be aboard those ships? Were no innocent navigators, cooks, musicians, surgeons, or carpenters taken for their skills? What about the British soldiers you killed in the war? None of them were pressed into service?"

James was silent, staring at the table.

"And for the record," said Hawk. "Since I've been captain, I've offered to let any crew that didn't resist go free. I have never liked killing, James. Sure, I've done my share, and I'm right good at it. But I've never liked it, other than Kragg, that is. The truth is, both of our hands are stained with blood. And some of it was from innocent people. Killing is killing, brother. The difference is only what side you're on."

James stood up abruptly. Hawk tensed for a moment until James turned and walked back to a cabinet behind him. He produced a large bottle of reddish-brown liquid and filled two silver goblets. He set one in front of Hawk, then returned to his seat with his. "I will mull your plan. For now, let's drink and be brothers. That's fine brandy, given to me by the governor of North Carolina. Smoothest you've ever tasted."

Hawk was surprised at the change in James but pleasantly so. He swirled the liquid in his cup, sniffed, and then sipped it. "The *only* brandy I've ever tasted. Don't you know we pirates are all about the rum? It is good, though. How long do we have before you sail?"

"We sail when I say we sail. I am the captain, after all." James laughed. "You think Jack will be OK?"

"I'd worry more about your crew."

For two hours, the two long-lost brothers talked and laughed like...brothers. They swapped stories about their lives and filled in the missing details. They mostly avoided their battles' tales and spoke about the men they knew, humorous stories, likes and dislikes, hopes, and dreams. As the brandy flowed, they laughed more. Soon they sat side by side and even shared a rowdy song or two.

A knock on the door interrupted their revelry. "Come in," James called out with a slight slur.

A young officer opened the door and entered. His face was pale, and red hair showed from beneath his tricorne hat. "Is everything OK, Captain?"

"It's great, First Mate Smith," James said, eliciting a smile from Hawk. "Just sharing a little brandy with an old friend."

"When will you be ready to sail, sir? The ship is prepared."

Thomas Smith stared hard at Hawk as he spoke.

"Oh, no real hurry, Thomas. Give us an hour or two."

Thomas frowned, glanced at Hawk again, and turned and left the cabin.

"A worrisome lad, huh?" Hawk asked, laughing and taking a large swig of brandy.

"You have no idea."

Despite having been apart for much longer than they had been together, living opposite lives all along, they both experienced the bond that only brothers can share. Their minds worked the same and thought the same. For a time, they forgot the real world. They didn't even notice the red-faced Jack glaring through the window many times during those two hours.

CHAPTER XXII

Jackson Square buzzed with excitement, the most excitement since the British had been defeated in the Battle of New Orleans. The crowd began at the docks and spread to the center of the square. Armed soldiers and sailors lined a long clear lane and kept the throng pushed back. In the middle of the square, in front of the St. Louis Cathedral, a large platform had been erected, similar to a gallows. Governor Hawthorne himself sat behind a table at the back of the platform. A magistrate sat beside him, and Commodore Cord stood close behind with several of his captains. They were surrounded by some of the governor's personal attendants and two-dozen soldiers and sailors.

The anxious crowd all stared toward the docks, where they could see at least some part of the *Seahawk*. James Wellington and a large contingent of sailors stood at the gangplank, waiting for the pirate crew to depart their ship for the last time. Finally, the pirates walked single file off the ship. When a pirate reached the dock, he handed his weapons to two sailors flanking James, and another sailor searched him for hidden weapons. Then the pirate walked down the lane through the excited crowd to the platform, up the wooden steps on the near side, and stood before the governor. He signed a piece of paper affirming that he would never again engage in piracy. Then he received a signed pardon from the magistrate and exited the stage on the far side. The pirate could wait and watch his mates go through the same process or disappear into the city streets. Most chose the latter.

Two weeks prior, word had spread of a deal between the

famous pirate captain, Hawk, and Captain Wellington of the USS *Avenger*. Hawk would turn himself in for trial and sure hanging, and his crew would receive a full pardon in exchange. James had gone to the commodore, the commodore to the governor, the governor to the president, and they had all approved the plan. They all knew that defeating Hawk and his crew, even with the past month's events, would be no easy task, and they would lose many men and ships. None of Hawk's crew was of particular note—no more Hawk's or Diablo's. Hawk was the last of the great pirate captains. Once he was gone, there would just be some mopping up of a few small, weak pirate crews in the Caribbean.

Hawk's trial wouldn't be today. After all his men were pardoned, he would be charged with his crimes by the governor and magistrate, taken away in irons, and jailed until a trial date was set. He would probably be tried and hanged within a week or two. That would be an even greater spectacle than today. But today, just seeing the famous Hawk was enough.

Most of the crowd halfway expected the Hawk and his crew to have some kind of attack planned. All had heard of Hawk's daring rescue of Captain Bloodstone at Port Royal. But as the pirates continued to file past, the crowd's apprehension eased. Hawk couldn't do much alone and had little to gain by attacking anyone in New Orleans. After an hour or so, all 180 pirates had received their pardons, including Hawk's first mate, Jack, and his quartermaster, Billy. The crowd now breathlessly waited for Captain Hawk to make his walk down the gangplank and surrender his weapons.

After several agonizing minutes, Hawk finally appeared on the deck of the *Seahawk*. He wore one of his more common outfits—tight black leather pants, knee-high boots, a red sash belt, and a white silk shirt unbuttoned halfway. His blond hair glowed gold in the sunlight. The baldric across his chest held two pistols and a dagger, and a cutlass was at his side.

He walked over to the rail and surveyed the huge crowd stretched from the dock to the square. The throng suddenly fell silent as they waited for the famous captain to make a move.

Some still thought he could somehow fight and defeat all the soldiers and sailors there. But after a moment, he gracefully strode across the deck to the gangway. He paused and surveyed James and the surrounding sailors, and then his gaze moved past them to the ships on the other side of the dock. Finally, he walked down the gangplank, moving with the grace and ease of a lion.

Hawk reached the bottom of the ramp, where the two sailors extended their hands for his weapons. James stood in front of him, his gaze solemn and unreadable. Hawk handed the first sailor a flintlock and the second one his cutlass. He drew out his golden, double-barreled pistol next. The eyes of the sailors widened as the rays of the sun reflected off the polished barrel. Then, in a blur of motion, he leaped forward, grabbed James, and spun him around. Hawk wrapped his left arm around James' neck, and his right hand pressed the flintlock to his temple. The sailors around him drew their weapons in a near panic. A gasp spread throughout the crowd. Most couldn't see what had happened, but they knew all wasn't going according to plan.

"Make a move, and you'll be covered with his brains!" Hawk shouted. James tried to wrestle free, but Hawk's grip was tight. Hawk pressed the tips of the barrels harder into James's temple, and he stopped resisting. Hawk quickly turned and walked backward through the sailors, half dragging James with him.

Hawk stopped at the far edge of the dock. "Tell Cord not to follow us, or James will die. If no one follows, I'll free him somewhere along the way." He then quickly dragged him down another gangplank onto a small catboat.

The sailors watched frozen from the dock as more soldiers and sailors rushed down the lane and joined them. The commodore and governor followed close behind. Hawk kept his pistol to his brother's head as James unfurled the sails on the single mast. The two men then walked to the tiller, and Hawk made the navy captain steer the ship into the river. The wind was blowing steady from the west, aiding the strong current. The catboat quickly passed out of flintlock and musket range.

"You can probably pull those barrels out of my temple just a bit," James said once he was sure they were out of sight of the town. "Nice pistol, by the way."

"Maybe just a bit, but I'm still going to keep it in hand. We'll surely pass some ships on the way out. Oh, and it was a gift from Kragg." Hawk moved behind James and opened a hatch in the deck.

"Do you think they bought it?" James asked, sailing the catboat smoothly and swiftly down the river.

Hawk now squatted above the deck and peered down the ladder. "Probably—for now anyway."

James turned to see what Hawk was doing and saw a female's head poke just above the deck. Hawk leaned down and kissed the woman. After some quite conversation, she disappeared back down the ladder. Hawk closed the hatch again and went to check the sails. "It will be your return that will be the test."

"Yes, you are right. You may get me court-martialed or hanged before this is over with. How is Anna?"

"She's good," said Hawk. "Anxious to get into the fresh air, of course. You should just come with us, brother. You have no business in the navy now." He turned the boom slightly to keep the wind square in the sails.

"Sounds tempting. I would kind of like to finish up the pirate eradicating, though. Cofresi is still out there and a few more scoundrels. I guess I'm in a similar situation as you were last year—I need to leave the right way."

They did pass a couple of ships on their way down the river and out to sea, but none were navy. Their little catboat wouldn't draw much attention either way, and none would be able to confirm if James was a hostage. When they reached the sea, they headed east. Hawk opened the hatch again, and Anna climbed out onto the deck this time. They embraced and exchanged a lengthy kiss.

"I cannot believe it!" Anna exclaimed. Hawk had snuck into the town the night before and found Anna running a small tavern several streets away from the Treasure Cove. She had packed a few belongings, and Hawk whisked her away to the small hold of the catboat. He stayed with her until close to sunrise.

"I told you I'd come back for you someday. That someday ended up being a few years late, but I am a man of my word." Hawk laughed and hugged her again.

James cleared his throat from the helm.

"Oh, Anna, meet my brother, James."

Anna bypassed James's outstretched hand and hugged him. "I'm pleased to meet you, James. And I want to thank you for helping us."

"Against my better judgment, ma'am. He forced me to drink brandy and agree to this scheme."

"Well, either way, thank you very much."

"You are very welcome and very sweet, Anna. Why in the world are you running away with this scallywag?"

"Hey, watch it now!" said Hawk. "I'm a retired scallywag." He put his arm around Anna.

They sailed all day and into the night, taking turns steering and working the sails, including Anna. Soon after dark, the stars appeared. It was an unusually clear night, and Anna couldn't help but stare at the sky, fascinated by the millions of twinkling flecks of light. At one point, she and Hawk lay down on the deck on some old wool blankets that Hawk found in the hold. His right arm was beneath her head, providing a pillow. James manned the helm and used the stars to guide his way around the many islands in their path.

"What was that? That star moved across the sky and disappeared," Anna said excitedly.

"A shooting star," Hawk said. "Some people say they are an omen."

"Good or bad?"

Hawk reached over and found her left hand. "Good. It means we're heading off to a great and happy future."

Anna laughed and leaned over to kiss him. Hawk pointed out some of the constellations he knew—Orion, his favorite, Cygnus, the Big Dipper, Pisces, and Andromeda, among others. She snuggled close and barely listened after the first couple. She just enjoyed the warmth of his body in the cool night and listened to his strong heartbeat.

Hawk eventually stood and disappeared below deck. When he returned, he wore different clothes—nondescript beige canvas trousers, a dirty white cotton shirt, work boots, and a floppy hat. He still wore his baldric, with his dagger and pistol sheathed in it, and a leather satchel over one shoulder hanging under his arm. "Do I look like a famous pirate captain now?"

Anna and James both laughed. "If not for the weapons, I would almost think you were an honest man," James said.

"Almost," Anna added, still laughing.

"Oh, James, my clothes are below, as well as the chicken," Hawk said. James nodded in reply.

Hawk relieved James at the helm, and James went to sit and talk with Anna. They shared their life stories and what they knew about the Hawk, which really wasn't much. But they quickly discovered they had a bond, almost like brother and sister. For the short voyage, all the uncertainty and danger disappeared. The three all were light-hearted and free. It almost seemed too soon when, around midnight, Hawk steered the boat toward land and the twinkling lights of a small town.

The few lamps on the docks helped Hawk guide the boat silently to an open berth. Several larger merchant ships were docked there, the kind that transported goods up and down the east and gulf coasts of the United States. Some of the smaller ones even traveled up and down the larger rivers to trade with the small towns along the way. James quickly jumped out and moored the boat to a post on the dock. The docks were quiet, as was the town. Hawk extended the gangplank, and he and Anna joined James.

"Come with us, brother," Hawk said.

"I'll have to pass for now. I'm sure we will see each other again, though."

"I hope so. We still have a lot of catching up to do. Finish your pirate hunting and come visit, or build a house beside ours."

"Sounds good. Now, I'll need your pistol and dagger," James said, extending his hands.

"Why?" Hawk asked with some apprehension.

"First, you are no longer a pirate. If you walk down these streets with weapons like those, everyone here will know who you are. Second, if I'm going to tell everyone I killed you, I'll need proof. The Hawk would never voluntarily give up his prized weapons."

The last part of the plan was for James to say he fought with Hawk and killed him. His body fell off the small boat and apparently sank in the darkness. He would use the blood from the chicken to stain Henry's shirt and his own clothing. It wasn't a perfect plan, but James had an exemplary record and was known throughout the fleet for his hatred of pirates. Also, very few knew that Hawk was his brother, and none in the navy. There would likely be some questioning, and some doubt, but he thought he could weather the storm.

Hawk shook his head and removed the baldric. He took out the dagger and stared at it reverently. It was his first real weapon. It had saved his life numerous times and was always by his side. He had never thought about parting with it as part of the plan. But James was right, and he really didn't need anything tying him to his past. He had enough memories.

He sheathed it and drew the golden pistol. He also loved that weapon. He had made it famous over the past year. But it didn't have the same meaning as his dagger. It was just a rare and valuable possession. He definitely couldn't wear that on his person in his new life. He finally sheathed it too and handed the baldric to James. Hawk kept the satchel containing a few supplies and all his gold, silver, and gems. "Treat them well," he said to James with a wry smile.

"Please come visit soon, James," said Anna. "I'd like to get to know you better. And you brothers should stay close now that you've finally found each other again." She hugged James.

"I will, Anna. Now, a quick hug for my brother." James

stepped forward and hugged Hawk.

"I'm glad you're telling everyone that you killed me and not hugged me to death," Hawk said after the hug had ended. "Good luck, James."

"You too, Hawk. Enjoy your new life."

"I will. Oh, and it's Henry now. The Hawk is dead."

CHAPTER XXIII

Henry and Anna walked hand in hand across the dock and onto the street. Pascagoula was a small town, and they were on the main dirt lane that led from the docks through the middle of it. Lamps burned at regular intervals, providing dim light and creating large, dancing shadows. A few smaller dirt lanes bisected it, leading off into near darkness. A two-story inn was on the right side of the road about halfway through town.

Henry and Anna entered through the double doors, causing a bell in front of one to ring. A large counter stretched the room's length on the left, and the wall behind was lined with bottle-filled shelves with a doorway cut in the middle. Empty tables and chairs filled the room to the right. A wide flight of stairs in front of them led up to the second story and a balcony that skirted the room. A few lanterns burned around the room, providing dim lighting.

After a moment, an older man in a long white gown and white cloth hat shuffled through the doorway behind the bar. He had obviously been sleeping and rubbed at his eyes as he reached the counter. "A little late for travelers," he said gruffly.

"A story too long for a night so late," Henry replied. He quickly produced a doubloon and laid it on the counter. "How about a room for the night and no questions asked?"

The man's eyes widened, and the drowsiness instantly disappeared. The coin quickly vanished, and he produced a key from under the counter. "Room thirteen—up the stairs and to the right."

"Thank you, sir." Henry took the key, and they climbed the

stairs and found their room. It wasn't much bigger or nicer than the rooms at the Treasure Cove but would do for a few hours of sleep.

Very quickly, they were both undressed and in the firm bed. There were times when they were apart for the long periods when Henry almost forgot the feel of Anna's body, the smell of her perfume, and the taste of her lips and skin. But after only a moment together, it all came rushing back as if they had never been separated. He wondered how he could ever forget the warm, smooth, soft touch of her skin against his and her sweet, flowery scent. Hopefully, he would never have to forget again.

"I've missed you so much," Henry said, squeezing her tightly against him.

"Not as much as I have you, Hawk. Or, I mean, Henry." She kissed him softly. All thoughts of just talking and cuddling for a while instantly vanished. Their bodies were soon on fire as the heat of lust swept them away. The soft kisses quickly grew rough and forceful as they groped each other's body. It was Anna who soon rolled on top of Henry. They made love until early in the morning. Their talking would have to wait until the day because they both collapsed into slumber soon after.

The next morning they went downstairs and sat at a table in the corner of the common room. An older lady in a worn, faded yellow dress rushed about serving breakfast to the other patrons. Henry and Anna ordered a meal of chicken eggs—not the turtle eggs Henry was accustomed to—sausage, hard biscuits, and strong black coffee.

They ate mostly in silence and tried to eavesdrop on as many conversations as possible. Most stories just dealt with small-town affairs, cotton farming, and other mundane subjects. Word of the pirate's surrender, and Hawk's escape, hadn't made its way to the town yet.

"Ma'am," Henry said when the server returned to check on them. "Is there a good town a little farther inland where a man and woman could buy a little piece of land and settle down?"

The server stared at him for a moment as if gauging his

intent. "There are little towns all up the rivers north of here. Traders sail their boats up and down them, pedaling their wares. I've heard a little bit about a town named River Junction a couple of days' ride north—not far from where the Leaf River joins the Chickasawhay to form the Pascagoula. It's supposed to be growing pretty fast."

"And land?"

"Plentiful. A lot of land was taken from the Indians all over the state. Just ask around when you get to whatever town you settle on." She turned and hurried away.

Henry paid for their food, and they left the inn. The day was warm and humid and the sky deep blue. A thick, salty breeze blew in from the sea. The town was quaint and friendly, but Henry knew it wouldn't be safe for them to stay that close to the sea long. Sooner or later, someone from a visiting ship would recognize him. He hoped the locals would quickly forget the strangers.

A couple of hours later, after purchasing supplies, a flintlock, and a dagger at the general store and horses at the stable, as well as receiving some basic riding lessons, they rode out of the small town. Henry rode a black stallion he named Tempest and Anna a gray mare she called Destiny. The dirt road led out of town and followed the Pascagoula River. The land was wet and marshy, and the road soon deteriorated into just a worn trail. The mosquitoes were buzzing loudly, and it was sweltering and sticky. After several hours, they finally left the marsh behind and found more solid footing. They began to see cotton farms worked by black slaves. Henry had never liked the idea of slavery. Although a lot of pirates kept them, Bloodstone never had. The old captain and his mother had basically been slaves, so Bloodstone hated the practice. In fact, he freed all the ones that didn't want to go on account.

They only passed a few travelers, some on foot, some on horses pulling carts of cotton back toward the town, and several flat-bottomed barges drifting down the river to Pascagoula or the sea. They passed through one small town on this side of the river and spotted another on the other side a few miles farther up the path. They didn't stop in the one they passed through, though. Henry didn't want more people to notice them than necessary until they were further inland.

As the hours passed, the flat land gave way to some rolling hills, and Cypress trees and spruce pines began to appear. They stopped in a little stand of loblolly pines for lunch, both needing a break from riding in the saddles—already their legs and posteriors were getting sore. Henry spread a blanket and meal on the ground, and they sat down to eat.

"Bring back any memories?" Henry asked, making them both a sandwich of meat and cheese.

Anna grinned. "Yes, but let's hope there are no alligators. And I don't believe this is private enough for other activities. Even if either one of us were fit for such right now."

"I'm sure there are no alligators. And I can always handle some activity. But you might be right on the privacy." Henry laughed and slapped Anna's hip playfully.

"You rogue!" Anna exclaimed, smacking his hand.

"Retired rogue," Henry said, still grinning.

They packed up and continued their journey up the river. They talked and laughed light-heartedly as they began to accept the reality that, after so many years of dreaming, they were finally free and running away together. Although there would always be a slight chance of Henry getting recognized, that chance decreased the further inland they went.

Close to sunset, Henry led them a mile away from the river and into a small forest of oak and spruce trees. They had plenty of wood and shelter here, and soon Henry had a large fire burning. They roasted some beef strips over the fire and enjoyed a couple of apples. Had they had time, Henry could easily have killed some fresh game to eat—the deer and turkey were plentiful.

He had planned on using the tarp for shelter, but the night was warm and the sky clear, so they slept in the open, wrapped up in their blanket. They didn't make love that night, but they still enjoyed lying together and experiencing each other's body heat. The noises of the forest animals in the darkness startled Anna, but she felt entirely safe with her head lying on Henry's chest. An animal or bandit in the dark wouldn't stop the greatest pirate captain alive.

They both awoke very stiff and sore the following morning; the insides of their thighs and posteriors were the worst. The thought of another day's ride wasn't appealing, but they had little choice. They ate a cold breakfast, packed their belongings, refilled their canteens in a nearby stream, and mounted.

"I think I'll go back to a ship!" Henry said. He received an immediate scowl from Anna.

The promising sunrise was quickly erased by dark, threatening clouds rolling in from the west. The wind began picking up, and thunder boomed in the distance, reminding Henry of cannon fire. Large drops of rain began falling, and the intensity increased until it was soon a downpour.

Henry had his floppy hat, and Anna wore a round white hat with flowers on one side. The hats helped keep the rain from their eyes, but that was about it. They were riding in an area of open, rolling land, with only a few trees and little shelter within sight. Henry wasn't worried about himself. Pirates spent much of their lives in rain and storms, trying not to be washed overboard to their death. But Anna...she was such a dainty young lady who had barely been out in any weather.

Henry glanced over at her. She had her head down, and the rain had soaked her completely, causing her brown dress to cling to her shapely body. He was glad she hadn't worn a white one. He reached over and grabbed her arm. "Are you OK?"

Anna looked up, the rain now striking her face. Then she suddenly burst out laughing. She held her arms over her head, looked up at the sky, and laughed.

"Are you mad?" Henry asked, shaking his head but also smiling.

"I've never been on a horse in a downpour!" she shouted above the roar of the wind and rain. "This is most wonderful."

"You're definitely mad."

Henry spurred his horse in front of hers and led them into the shelter of a large oak tree. He quickly jumped down, tied both horses to the trunk, and grabbed Anna's waist, easily lifting her off. With her feet still off the ground, he wrapped his arms around her and kissed her. Their lips glided effortlessly together, slick from the rain. They were cool, but only for a moment.

"What was that for?" Anna asked when Henry finally lowered her feet to the ground.

"For you being so wonderful and happy and beautiful...and to help warm you up."

"Well, aren't you the sweet one today!" She kissed him again and then pushed him away. "Ever danced in the rain?"

"I've seen a few pirates dance jigs on the deck in the rain," Henry said, still marveling at Anna's exuberance.

"Well, then dance me a jig, Mr. Wellington."

"Uh, no thanks."

"Ah, come now. Surely a big, mean, fearless former pirate captain isn't afraid of dancing in the rain," Anna taunted. She then held her dress up, almost to her knees, and began to imitate some of the dancing she had seen on weekend nights when musicians played at the Treasure Cove.

Henry shook his head yet again. "Do I even know you, Ms. Stevens?"

"Not even vaguely." Anna smiled, twirling around quickly to cause her dress to flare into a wide circle at the base.

"I was afraid of that." He finally laughed and joined her. He figured he could do at least as well as drunken pirates. Both forgot their soreness and danced, laughed, and carried on in the rain for some time. Eventually, their energy wore down. They ate a quick meal and continued their northward journey in the rain and thunder.

As the day wore on, Anna's fascination with the rain ended. They were both cold and miserable, with few breaks in the downpour. Several times lightning flashed close to them, frightening their horses. They passed through another small town, again not stopping even for shelter. Finally, near dark, Henry spotted a thick grove of pine trees at the top of the ridge to their right. They left the trail and rode into the sanctuary. The pines were so thick that some spots on the ground actually weren't totally soaked.

Henry found a cluster of four trees close together and used his rope to secure the corners of the tarp to the trees. He then spread the blanket out on the ground beneath. It was damp but much drier than out in the open. Anna was skeptical, but Henry convinced her to remove all her clothes, and he did the same. He hung their clothes from another length of rope he tied beneath the tarp, and then they lay together on the blanket, folding it on top of them.

Soon their body heat chased away the cold. It was almost dark now, especially beneath the tarp underneath the thick pine canopy. They lay face-to-face, rubbing the other's back to warm them. Once they were warm, their rubbing gradually transitioned to gentle caressing. Wet, passionate kisses joined the touching.

"This looks very private," Henry whispered, gently kissing and sucking her earlobe.

"Indeed it does," Anna whispered back, biting and raking his earlobe with her teeth.

Henry rolled on top of Anna, their now hot bodies pressed firmly together beneath the damp blanket. They could still hear the rain falling around them, but if any drops struck them or the blanket, they went unnoticed. Anna kept thinking that someday their lovemaking would lose its fire and intensity—that it would become ordinary and mundane. While someday that might happen, that day was definitely not today. She was quickly swept away in a flood of desire and lust. She was pleased as only Henry could please her. They eventually finished and fell asleep in each other's arms, not even realizing they hadn't eaten supper.

CHAPTER XXIV

They woke early the following morning and were relieved to see shafts of golden sunlight penetrating the pine trees in several places. The morning was cool, but the storm appeared to have finally moved on. After dressing in their cold, damp clothes, they ate most of the remaining food, and Henry fed the horses the last two apples to give them a break from only eating grass the past two days.

"How far do you think it is?" Anna asked after they'd mounted their horses.

"I would think we should be there before dark. We lost some time yesterday, but it looks like a good travel day today."

They rode back to the river and proceeded north. The trail was now barely more than an animal path. The day was very warm and humid, but the sun did dry out their clothes and boots. They were still sore, but their bodies seemed to be adjusting to the riding. They talked and laughed as the rode, enjoying their third day together.

They stopped under a large oak beside the river for lunch. "I hope we reach the town soon. If not, I might have to do some hunting," Henry said as they finished the last two biscuits and scraps of meat. As they relaxed and enjoyed watching the waters of the Pascagoula, they heard a rumble coming from the north.

Henry hopped up and strode over to his horse. Anna followed, staying close behind him. Within a couple of minutes, two horses rounded the bend in the river and galloped toward them. Two large, scruffy men spurred the beasts hard as they rode. They wore long leather coats, hats, and knee-high boots, and both sported scraggily dirty beards. They slowed as they noticed Henry and Anna and stopped their horses when they were beside them on the trail.

"You fellows look to be in a hurry," Henry said politely.

The larger, tanned, dark-haired man glanced at his smaller, paler, brown-haired companion. The other grinned and stared down at Anna, who was almost hidden behind Henry. "Aye," said the black-haired man, with a grin missing several teeth. "Seems we're always in a hurry for one reason or such. But we try to make time for strangers."

Henry nodded. "That's mighty nice of you, I suppose. And just why is it that you stopped for us strangers?" He casually leaned against his horse, his left arm resting on the side of the saddle. His right arm was by his side, hiding the dagger's hilt sticking out of his belt.

"Ye see, we like to help people," the man said and spit brown saliva on the ground beside his horse.

"And just what kind of help are you offering?" Henry asked. He shifted his body slightly to make sure Anna was totally behind him.

"We'll help lighten your load a little." The big man pulled out a flintlock from inside his coat and leveled it at Henry, cocking the hammer. The other man did the same.

"Thanks, but we're fine," Henry replied, not moving.

"Not your choice. Throw that satchel and pack over here. Slow and easy like."

"I think you two should keep riding down the trail," Henry said, still not moving.

"Henry, just let them have it," Anna whispered from behind him.

"Look. You can give us your bags now, and you two can live. If we have to take them, you die, and we take your woman with us," the big man replied, leaning forward on his saddle.

"How long do I have to decide?" Henry asked, ignoring whispered protests behind him. He glanced from the speaker to his partner.

"I'll count to three."

"I'm impressed." Henry felt his old bravery and swagger return. These men were no hardened pirates or pirate hunters, though.

The first man growled, and his face reddened. "One...two..."

He never reached three. Henry's right hand suddenly moved at his side. A flash of silver struck the big man in the chest. The pale man glanced quickly at his partner as he gasped and clutched at the dagger hilt. Before he could turn back to Henry, Henry's left arm swung around from the saddle and fired his own pistol. The man stared down at his chest for a moment, then tumbled from his horse. The big man now lay slumped over the neck of his.

Henry turned to Anna. She had her face covered with her hands. "Are you OK?" he asked.

She was sobbing now.

He gently pulled her hands away from her face. "It's OK. They're dead."

"Why...why didn't you just give them your bags?" she asked between sobs.

"That satchel contains all our money. What kind of life would we have with no money?"

"We would still...still have each other. We could work." She slowly regained her composure.

"That's not our dream, and we've waited too long already. Those men weren't going to take it away from us," Henry said, a little surprised at Anna's reaction.

"Is that money worth dying for?"

Henry shrugged. "I knew I could kill them both without us being harmed."

"How did you know?" Anna asked, wiping away the last of her tears.

"Anna. You know my past."

"And I thought we were leaving that behind."

"We are," he said, placing his hands on hers. "Anna, I'm done killing unless it is to defend my family. And now you're my family. But those men probably would have killed me and taken you anyway."

"My protector, huh?"

"Always."

Henry searched the saddlebags on the strangers' horses and found a large canvas bag in each full of gold and silver coins, as well as some jewelry. Anna frowned as she watched Henry. He brought the sacks back over to his horse and tucked them into his saddlebags. He looked at her face and knew what she was thinking. "They are obviously thieves. We'll find someone to turn these into in River Junction, as well as their horses. Maybe they even stole the loot from there."

Henry retrieved his dagger from the first man's chest, then pulled his body off the horse and dragged it down to the river, shoving it into the water. He also threw the second man into the water and then tied the reins of a horse to each of their saddles. He opened his satchel and reloaded his flintlock. "We'll take them to River Junction with us." They remounted and continued their journey, leading the thieves' horses behind them.

After about an hour, they saw another group of men riding hard toward them on horseback. Henry led Anna off the trail side and positioned himself in front of her again, and they waited for the six riders to arrive. The men slowed and stopped their horses on the trail when they reached the couple, just as the other two men had done. Henry was a little nervous this time. Six armed men would be tough to take single-handedly, with only a dagger and a flintlock.

The leader of the group walked his horse up to Henry's. His curly black hair, sprinkled with a little gray, stuck out from a floppy hat similar to Henry's. Black sideburns ran down past his ears. He had piercing hazel eyes, a thin black mustache, and a patch of neatly trimmed hair on his chin. His pale skin was in strong contrast to his black hair. He nodded to Anna and then to Henry. "Begging your pardon, but have you seen two large men riding hard down this trail? Probably came through an hour or two ago." His accent was French. He stared at the horses behind them.

"Indeed we did," Henry said, glancing from the Frenchman to the men behind him. He hoped they weren't the partners of the first two and didn't want to reveal too much information if they were. "What is your business with them?"

The Frenchman stared at Henry for a moment before responding. "They robbed the general store and some patrons in River Junction—killed two innocent people, stole their horses, and headed this way. We're going to track them down, retrieve the loot, and hang them from the nearest tree—along with anyone that aids them."

"So, you are a soldier or lawman?"

The Frenchman scowled. "Neither. I run the saloon and inn and help look after the town. I'm John Lafleur. Now, we are obviously in a hurry. Tell me about these men."

Henry judged that John was telling the truth. He reached into his saddlebags and produced the two sacks. "Here, this will save you some time," he said, holding the bags out to John.

John's eyes widened as he looked from Henry to Anna and back to Henry. The men behind him also didn't hide their surprise. "And how did you two come by the stolen loot?" John grabbed the two sacks and quickly stuffed them into his saddlebags.

Henry didn't see an advantage in lying at this point. "They tried to rob us too. I warned them to ride on, but they persisted and threatened to kill me and take Anna. I couldn't allow that. Their bodies are floating down the river ten miles back. We brought their horses with us."

John tried to stare through Henry with his gaze. "You mean to tell me you single-handedly killed two vicious killers?" The men behind him whispered and stared at Henry with amazement.

"Well, I don't know about vicious killers. But I did have to kill them."

"What is your name, stranger?"

"Henry. Henry We-Williams. This is Anna Stevens. We're

actually heading to River Junction."

"What business do you have in River Junction?"

"We're looking for a place to live. We heard it's a nice part of the country."

John relaxed a little and leaned back on his horse. "Pleased to meet you, Henry and Anna. Oh, it is a beautiful town. We could use some young people like yourselves, especially one who can handle himself like you. You're welcome to follow me back into town if you'd like. It's only an hour's ride."

"That would be great. That is a lot of coin for a general store," Henry commented.

"Our town does well in trade," John said with a scowl. "I suppose we owe you a reward for retrieving this money. I'm sure Albert would give you ten percent. Some of the others might chip in too."

"No thank you, John."

"No money? What can we do to repay you?"

"Maybe you could help me find a piece of land. I'll also need a little help building a house," Henry said.

Anna smiled behind him.

"Well, that's easy enough. I just so happen to own quite a bit of land around there. And I'm sure we can find some volunteers to help you build. Follow me, then."

John instructed two men to take the extra horses, and they all rode to River Junction.

CHAPTER XXV

The path continued to transition into more of a defined dirt road, and they passed more houses and farms as they went, along with a few travelers. Henry took a liking to John as they rode and talked. John told them about River Junction and the people there. The town had only been around for a few years, and he had helped it to grow and prosper. People traveling up and down the river occasionally stopped for supplies or to spend the night, and some ended up staying.

Many residents worked for the local saw mill, which John owned. They cut pine logs and sold them to the river traders who regularly sailed barges up and down the river. The traders resold the lumber at Pascagoula, Biloxi, or to larger traders that sailed ships to New Orleans and other cities in the Spanish Main. Others farmed cotton or soybeans and sold their products to the river traders. John also owned some of his own barges that hauled lumber, cotton, and soybeans down the river to sell. They brought back supplies and goods in return.

"Do you own everything in River Junction?" Henry finally asked.

"Let's just say I am heavily invested," John replied with a wink and grin as they approached a large wooden bridge spanning the Pascagoula. "So, where are you and Anna from?"

Henry used the time John was describing his town to contrive a story. He knew John or someone would be able to discern that he had spent a lot of time on a ship by his rolling gait, or sea legs as they were known. He also knew that he would have difficulty not slipping up if he invented a story that didn't involve the sea and sailing. "I used to work on a merchantman, sailing from New Orleans to Boston and everywhere in between. I met sweet, young Anna in New Orleans a year or so ago, working at a saloon. We saved up our money and decided to run off together. I was tired of sea life, and Anna wanted out of the city. So, we caught a boat to Pascagoula and learned of your town." It was a little close to the real story, but at least now he could explain away most questions that might arise.

"Ah, you left the trade too soon," John replied, staring at Henry thoughtfully.

"What do you mean?"

"I hear the end of the pirates is nigh. Word has it that the great Hawk and his crew all surrendered in New Orleans a few days past. The men were to receive pardons, and Hawk was to hang."

It was all Henry could do to keep his face expressionless upon hearing that John had already heard about Hawk. "I hadn't heard that. So, did Hawk hang?"

"I'm surprised you weren't there to see the men surrender. It sounds like the timing was close," John continued to stare at him with his unnerving gaze.

"I guess we left a day or two before. I left out a few details of our voyage. We did make several stops along the coast on the way to Pascagoula and spent a night in Biloxi while the captain traded goods there. Then we stayed two nights in Pascagoula before our journey up here. So I suppose it's been a week or more since we left."

"Ah, I see. Well, anyway, they say this Hawk captured a navy captain, I believe a James Wellington, and sailed off with him in a small boat." John finally turned away from Henry as they crossed over the bridge, their horses' hooves clacking loudly.

"They say that Hawk is a crafty one. Did they find him or James?" Henry's heart slowed a little, but he would definitely have to be careful around John.

"Last I heard, neither had turned up. We get our news from the river traders. I suppose we'll hear more in a day or two."

"Oh. Now, what's your story? How does a Frenchman end up running a saloon in River Junction, Mississippi?" Henry asked.

John chuckled. "That is a long story indeed. The short version is that I'm a businessman and a trader and have done my share of traveling. I, too, spent some time on a merchant ship back in the day. In my travels, I saw a good opportunity in lumber and farming in this part of the country where I knew could make a little money and live in a beautiful, quiet, peaceful town."

"I want the long version someday."

"And I yours." John laughed.

River Junction was similar to Pascagoula, only a little smaller. A wide dirt lane passed through the town, with large wooden buildings lining both sides and two narrower roads bisecting it. The buildings appeared to be a mixture of stores and warehouses. Smaller buildings and single-story homes lined the side streets. It seemed that a lot of the residents lived in the town.

Henry noticed at least one difference from Pascagoula, though. He spotted armed men standing at the entrance of the town and milling around some of the buildings. He even caught movement on the tops of others. They tried to blend in with the regular citizens but couldn't fool Henry's keen eyes. He wondered if they were stationed in response to the robbery or were a fixture in River Junction. He decided not to ask John about them, at least not yet.

John led them to the largest building, a three-story structure in the middle of town. A short flight of stairs led up to a porch that ran across the front, and a sign above the door read, "Fleuve Maison." They hitched their horses to posts outside, walked up the stairs, and entered through the swinging double doors.

"The River House," John said as they entered. The inside appeared similar to most saloons. A few people occupied the round tables and chairs that filled the room, and a counter ran the length of the far wall with stools in front of it. An older man tended the bar, and a young, attractive, dark-haired woman wiped the tables and served the patrons.

"George, prepare our guests a feast of a supper," John called to the man behind the counter. Then he turned to the young lady. "And Madame Rosa, take good care of them."

"Thank you very much for your hospitality," Hawk said.

"You are more than welcome. I have some business to attend to, but I'll be down in a bit to speak more with you. Enjoy your meal." John turned and quickly disappeared up a flight of stairs in the corner of the room, with three of his companions following.

Henry grinned at Anna. She had been silent on their ride with John, content to listen to the men talk. "What do you think of John?" Henry knew Anna was a good judge of character from dealing with men all her life.

"I'm not sure yet. He's definitely not telling us everything. I don't know whether I trust him or not. And you?"

"I agree. There's more than meets the eye. He's likable, though. I suppose we'll find out quickly enough if he isn't trustworthy. But we might have picked the perfect town if he is honest."

"It's definitely a beautiful town and countryside. I cannot wait for a bath and a bed, though!"

"We had our bath yesterday. Remember?"

"You might have had your pir—" She caught herself. "Sailor bath. But it was no bath for a lady!"

Rosa brought them large tankards of ale as they waited for their food. Before long, she began serving the feast—roast venison, beef, and pork, along with potatoes, boiled greens, and soft bread with butter. All the food was seasoned and flavored like nothing they had ever tasted. They scarcely spoke as they gorged, not realizing how famished they were. Rosa made sure the bowls, and their tankards, stayed full. It was the best meal either of them had ever eaten.

As Henry and Anna ate, more people began filing in. It was close to dark, so Henry assumed they were coming by for a drink or supper after work. Soon, a steady buzz of conversation spread throughout the room. They received some odd glances, but most people spoke to them or smiled. It appeared to be a friendly town.

Soon they were both full and feeling good from the drink but also very tired from their trip. They were relieved when John finally reappeared, his companions no longer with him.

"Well, did you enjoy our food?" John asked, sitting at the table with them.

"The best meal either of us has ever eaten," Anna said.

John raised his eyebrows and then smiled. "That's good. And the ale?"

"Just as good," Henry chimed in.

"Good. Now, would you two like to stay for some entertainment? The musicians will be here soon, and we'll have some singing and dancing."

"That does sound lovely, but begging your pardon, we're both exhausted," said Anna with a sweet but tired smile. "It's been a long, rough journey for us."

John smiled warmly. "Ah, but of course. Where are my manners? Go ask George for a room key. I think you'll find the room comfortable. There is a tub in your room. Just tell George when you are ready for a bath, and he'll send a couple of our ladies to fill it for you. Then in the morning, we can go look at some land." He seemed friendlier and more inviting than he had on the trail.

"Let me give you some money for the meal and room," Henry said, reaching for his satchel.

"Nonsense. This is part of your reward. Just a coin in the purse for the money you returned to us. Now, I must speak to my guests. You two have a good night, and I will see you in the morning." John stood and headed off to a table behind them.

Their room was up the stairs on the second floor. Henry pushed the door open, and they both froze in the doorway. The room within was nicer than any either had ever seen. Plush red carpet covered the floor, and the wooden walls and ceiling were smooth and painted white. A large desk sat against one wall, with a high-backed red velvet chair in front and a chest of drawers against another. A bathtub sat in the near corner, with a table beside it and a mirror behind. The bed was large and covered with clean, thick white blankets. Oil lamps burned on the bedside table and desk, and several candles flickered in sconces around the room.

Anna glanced at Henry, laughed, then ran and dove onto the bed. It was as soft as it appeared. She rolled over and gazed up at him. "Can we just live here?"

Henry laughed, shut the door, and ran and dove onto the bed beside her. "Maybe we can ask him who his decorator is and where he bought this furniture."

"I'm tired, but I hate to dirty this clean bed. Should we take a bath?"

Henry frowned.

"Don't tell me you've never had a bath!"

"Does rain, ocean, or pond count?"

"You silly rogue! Go tell George we'd like our bath drawn."

Henry wasn't sure about taking a bath, but he went downstairs and informed George. A few minutes later, a couple of young ladies entered and filled the tub with large metal buckets full of hot water. After several trips, the tub was three-quarters full. The women sprinkled some perfumed powder into the water and left the couple alone.

Within seconds, Henry and Anna were undressed and sitting in the tub. Being naked in a tub of hot water with his beautiful Anna made Henry forget his doubts. They laughed and splashed and washed each other. After the water had grown cold, they dried each other off with soft towels that the ladies had left on the table beside the tub and then climbed naked into the comfortable bed. Despite being tired and sore, they couldn't resist each other. They made love and then slept the best sleep of their lives, not waking until well after the sun had risen.

A knock on the door finally roused them. Henry rolled out of bed, slipped on his breeches, and cracked the door open. A young woman stood outside with her arms full of clothing. He wasn't sure if she was one of the ones from last night.

"Pardon me, sir, but Mr. Lafleur asked me to bring some clean clothes for you and your companion. We will clean your soiled ones while you are out today."

Henry opened the door wider and took the clothes, and the woman smiled and quickly disappeared. He brought the clothes in, and he and Anna dressed. His attire consisted of brown linen pants, a white cotton shirt, leather shoes, and a belt. Anna had a yellow dress with dressy leather shoes and a yellow hat. The dress came to just slightly below her knees, which would help for riding and walking outdoors.

They went downstairs, relaxed and refreshed, and enjoyed a delicious breakfast. John met them soon after.

"Good morning. I hope the room was to your liking?"

"Unbelievable," Anna said.

"You have been much too generous," Henry added.

"Nonsense. You are very important guests. The entire town has now heard of your bravery. The room and food are nothing compared to the reward you could have had. So, Mr. Williams, tell me about this land you seek. Do you want to farm cotton? Or soybeans? I can set you up with the land and find enough blacks to work it for you."

"No. No slaves, and nothing that big. We'd like to grow enough crops to eat and maybe raise some cattle or hogs. I assume you raise those around here?"

"Cattle and hogs, huh? We raise a few. Not a lot of money in it, though. So you will need some pastureland and water?"

"Water would definitely be good—maybe a creek or river and pond if possible. And some stands of hardwoods and rolling hills. We'd like enough land to ride our horses."

"Hmmm. You might be in luck. Most farmers here want a lot of flat, open land for their cotton. Hills and trees are of no interest. And water is plentiful—many little streams feed the Leaf River. Let's ride a little way and see what we can find."

John led them down the main road and out the other end of town. The dirt road narrowed a little but was still a good road and obviously well used. The day was going to be hot and sunny, but it felt less humid than it had closer to the coast. As they rode, they saw many cotton and soybean fields. They passed an occasional horse-drawn, flat wagon loaded with either bales of cotton or cut pieces of lumber heading to town. John explained that the docks were right in the town where the barges were loaded and unloaded.

Several smaller roads forked off to the left of the main road leading to the various farms. When the land around them became hillier and more trees began to appear, John led them off the main road onto a poorly defined trail. After a mile or so, the path entered a large patch of pine trees. It was a mature forest, and the riding was shaded and easy.

The ground gradually rose until they exited the forest. Once out of the pines, the land opened up and sloped down for a hundred yards to a flat bottom that was a hundred yards wide and several hundred yards long. The land was grown up with bushes and weeds, and several large trees grew here and there on the upper end. On the west and north sides of the bottom, the land sloped up until it reached a hardwood forest. To the south, the land gradually rose into hills, with one big hill obstructing the view of what lay beyond.

"This land was logged long ago, before I arrived here. It's hardly big enough for cotton or soybeans and a little far from town. There is a creek that flows through the trees in front of us. It exits on the other side of that hill, fills a large pond, and keeps going to the southeast. It would take a little work to clear the brush and build a house, but would this work for you?"

"Oh, it's perfect!" Anna exclaimed, riding up between the men. She began gesturing at the various features. "We could build a house between those two big trees for shade. Over there, we could plant a garden. Then we could have animals on the hills and around the pond and creek."

Henry laughed at Anna's excitement. "I guess you have our answer. How much do you want for it?"

"I have some ideas on that. Why don't we head back to town

and me and you talk some business?" John said.

Henry felt sick to his stomach, not liking the sound of that. "OK," he finally said.

Anna was too excited to care about the delay. She talked to Henry and John about all her ideas for the land. Henry was still excited too, but a little daunted, both by John's business talk and all the work he would need to do to make Anna's dream come true. When they returned to the hotel, Anna went to the room while Henry walked up to the third floor with John and the same three men that had been with him the day before. The entire third floor was John's living quarters and business office.

"Let's talk, Henry," John said as they sat at a large table in the middle of his office. The office had a large desk and chair in front of the far wall, with a couple of padded chairs in front of it. Book-laden bookcases lined the white walls, with several paintings covering the bare spaces. All the furniture was expensive, and thick blue, plush carpet hid the floor. Lamps and candles provided plenty of light.

"These are some of my loyal men," said John. "Levi, Ferdinand, and Philip. Henry, I can use another good man to help run things. Managing a town isn't easy business—yesterday's incident with the bandits illustrates that. I am a good judge of character. You can definitely handle yourself and are a sharp, dependable, and trustworthy man. I could use you."

"Those men weren't bandits, were they?" Henry asked, staring hard at John to gauge his reaction.

John glanced quickly at Philip and then returned his gaze to Henry. "Why would you ask that?"

"I saw the armed men you have stationed about the town. If two bandits just rode in, stole the money, and rode out, you wouldn't have had time to position that many men throughout town before pursuing them. And if all those men were already stationed in town, two ordinary bandits wouldn't have attempted robbery, or if they did, they wouldn't have escaped."

"I did mention sharp—very observant, Henry. They were my men. Philip handles matters of…security for me. Those men had apparently plotted for a while to steal the money that came back from a big lumber sale in Biloxi, several barge loads worth. They ambushed and killed the two barge pilots on their way from the docks to here and rode out of town before anyone could get a clean shot at them. That's what also makes your killing them more impressive. They were trained killers, not just hapless thieves. Not bad for a retired sailor and future farmer."

"I've been in a scrap or two over the years," Henry replied flatly. "And why do you say I'm honest and trustworthy? Because I returned the money?"

"You returned *all* the money. It would have been very tempting to say that it was not all there when you found it. And I would have thought nothing of it. But it was all there, every piece of eight."

"So, what are you asking of me now?"

"Come work for me."

"Doing what?"

"Oh, I don't know. A little bit of everything. You could help with security, trade, and business matters. If you did, I could let you have that piece of land for free, plus pay you very handsomely."

Henry looked from John to the other three men. They all smiled and awaited his response. "I am very honored you asked. But Anna and I have been planning to settle down, build a little farm, and start a family for years. Maybe I'll change my mind at some point, but for now, I just need some rest and relaxation. If you need my help on something specific, though, let me know. I'm indebted to you already."

John smiled. "Fair enough then. It will still be good having you and Anna around and about town. If you should ever change your mind...."

"So, about the land?" said Henry.

"Tell you what. I'll still give you the land. I'll even provide the materials and labor for your house and farm. But if you sell any of your crops or animals, you have to do it through me. I'll take ten percent and give you the rest upon sale. Levi there is my builder, and he's in charge of the logging operation. Ferdinand is my head agriculture manager and can help clear your land and supply you with livestock. Do we have a deal?"

Henry rubbed his chin and looked at the men again. "Sounds fair enough. Deal." He stood up and shook John's hand.

"Welcome to River Junction," John replied, grinning.

CHAPTER XXVI

The next day, Ferdinand, Levi, and several workers helped Henry start clearing the land for a house and garden, using sickles and horse-drawn plows to clear a small patch and leaving the rest grown up. Ferdinand explained that the horses and cattle would eat that vegetation. The following day they started on the house. Henry had never built a house but had a lot of experience repairing and modifying ships. Once he understood the basics of framing, he got along fine.

He and Anna stayed at the River House at night. Within a week, the house was finished. Henry hadn't let Anna see it yet but did take her to visit some of the warehouses in town to pick out furniture. It wasn't quite as nice as John's, but Henry soon had the small house furnished and decorated very handsomely.

Henry insisted on blindfolding Anna in the pine forest and then leading her into the clearing. "OK. You may remove it."

Anna removed the scarf, and her mouth fell open as she stared at the transformed piece of land and new house. She couldn't speak as tears streamed down her cheeks. The house sat nestled between three large trees and faced south, toward the hills. It was one story with stairs leading to a porch that stretched across the front, supported by columns leading to a sloped roof. It wasn't painted, but the red cedar logs glowed orange in the sunlight. Two windows were on the front side and one on each of the other walls. A well had been dug on the near side and a privy built beside a tree in the back. A wide, clear path led down the hill to the house.

"Are those good tears or bad?" Henry asked.

"Oh, Henry! It's wonderful! Even better than I dreamed!" Anna nudged her horse next to his and leaned over to kiss him. "I cannot believe this day is finally here—the first day of the rest of our lives!"

They galloped down the hill to the house, dismounted from their horses, and ran up porch steps. Henry opened the door and led Anna inside. In one half of the first room stood a large dining table surrounded by wooden chairs. In the other half was a large plush couch, two padded chairs, and a small table. The couch and chairs faced a fireplace in the far wall to the right. A door on the other side of the big table led into a kitchen with a new wood stove, numerous cabinets, and a basin. A small hallway straight ahead led to the two bedrooms. One was furnished as a bedroom and the other as an office. Colorful rugs covered most of the floors in every room except the kitchen. A painting of the ocean hung in the main room. The walls were unpainted, but the cedar was pretty in its own right.

"Will it do?" Henry asked after the tour.

Anna grabbed him and hugged him tightly, the tears flowing again. "I love you, Henry! It's so wonderful!"

Henry placed his head on top of hers. He even blinked away a tear or two. "I love you too, Anna."

They walked back onto the porch and sat in two rocking chairs. The roof blocked the sun, and the hot summer air was tempered by the shade and a steady breeze. They held hands and rocked as they surveyed their land.

"I just realized something," Henry said after a few moments.

"What's that, dear?" said Anna, smiling at him.

"This is the first time in my life that I've had nothing to do, nowhere to be, and no one wanting to kill me—other than our picnic. Even there, we had a time limit, and an alligator tried to eat me."

Anna laughed. "Hmmm...and the same for me, except for the killing part. I think I'm rather fond of it."

"Yeah, me too. I mean, there is still a lot to be done but nothing we can't do ourselves. We have more than enough money to buy anything we need, and the farming will just give us something to do."

"You don't think we'll become bored and unhappy, do you?" Anna asked, her smile fading.

Henry let go of her hand, lightly brushed the side of her face, and then leaned over and gave her a quick, gentle kiss. "Bored being in paradise with you? I don't think so."

"Good answer," Anna said, her smile returning. "Now we need to start figuring out what all we need for our house."

"What's all that stuff in there?" Henry asked, raising his voice in feigned displeasure.

"Just furniture, silly. We need food, curtains for the windows, more hangings and paintings for the walls, pots and pans and cooking utensils, soap, perfume, clothes—"

"OK! OK!" said Henry. "You get a list together, and we'll go into town in the morning."

"Oh, and parchment and quills and ink and..." Anna laughed at Henry's scowl.

A little later, they explored the land on their horses. The northern boundary was the forest. The west border was the creek that flowed about a hundred yards into the mature woods. Squirrels scurried about on the ground and in the trees, chattering loudly at their intrusion, and deer trails crisscrossed the woods. The water could either be called a big creek or a small river, ranging from six to twelve feet wide. Henry saw plenty of deep pools that he knew had to be full of fish. One end eventually flowed into the Leaf River: the other wound through the forest and into the hilly fields to the south.

The river fed into a large pond just beyond the big hill that kept them from seeing their house. On the other side of the pond, it continued across the field and into the pine forest, creating their southern border. The eastern edge was about halfway into the pines. It was a perfect piece of land for what they needed, and private. People wouldn't be coming that way unless they were lost or looking for them.

They returned to the porch in time to watch the sun set

behind the hill and the forest to the west. "I still cannot believe we're finally here!" Anna said, the last rays of the sun kissing her face as she gazed at Henry. "I've dreamed about it for so long. Yet as time passed, I had less and less hope that the dream would ever come true."

"I know what you mean. There were many battles when I thought I would die and never be able to share this with you. I think that's probably the main reason I didn't die. I had to see this through."

"It seems like I was working at the Treasure Cove just yesterday. By this time, the sailors and fishermen would be straggling in. I would have to serve and wait on them through their meals and then…."

"There is no more 'and then,'" Henry said. "I'm your only 'and then' from now on."

"You're a very wonderful 'and then,' Henry…Williams." Anna laughed and reached over to rub his thick hair.

Henry grabbed her hand and pulled it down to his face. He gazed at her as he gently kissed her fingers. At first, it was playful and teasing. Then he started kissing with more intensity. He flicked his tongue against her fingertips and worked in some playful sucking along with the kissing. Anna's cheeks reddened as she watched Henry's lips and mouth work on her hand. He was so romantic and sensual. The innocent boy of years ago was long gone. Playful and funny quickly transitioned into seductive and erotic. A few seconds of Henry's kisses set her body on fire like no man had ever been able to do with hours.

Henry stood and gently pulled her out of the chair, scooped her into his arms, and carried her into the house, not bothering to lock the door. "I think it's time to explore the bedroom again."

"You beast!"

"Retired beast."

***

The next few weeks were busy as they bought supplies for the house, and Henry built fences and pens for their future livestock. While Henry was working in the fields, Anna worked in the house. After everything was arranged and decorated like she wanted, she turned her attention to cooking. Henry showed her what he had picked up from Wesley over the years. She also spent some time with George at the River House when Henry was in town talking business with Levi, Ferdinand, and John. She soon became a very good cook.

Although the work was hard and the days long, they loved it. They took frequent breaks to sit together and talk and to give a hug or kiss. Many hours were spent on the bank of the pond, eating lunch on a blanket as they had so long ago on the island. Naked swims followed on some days. In the evenings, they went for walks, rode their horses, or sat on the porch and rocked. Of course, they always found time for lovemaking, pretty much anywhere and everywhere on their land, and especially on the pond banks.

Over the past few years, Henry had some doubts about what would happen when he and Anna were together all the time. After all, they really didn't know each other well. He also thought about the cautionary tales of Wesley and Jack. But so far, it had gone even better than he had imagined. Anna was intelligent, quick-witted, and had a good sense of humor. She was also a strong, independent, and spirited woman. She begged to ride to town by herself almost daily, but Henry hadn't let her yet.

It was that spirit that led her to come to Henry one day after lunch and make an unusual request for a woman. "I want to learn how to shoot your guns."

Henry laughed. "That would be scary."

Anna smacked him on the shoulder. "I'm serious! A girl needs to know how to protect herself. What if Indians or bandits attack while you're off in town talking with your men friends?"

Henry still smiled, but it actually wasn't a bad idea. "Are you sure? Those muskets kick hard, and you're just a dainty little thing." Henry had bought several guns in town over the past few weeks.

"I'm a strong woman! I can handle your little guns," Anna

said, grinning.

"OK. We will go shooting then."

Henry placed some empty onion bottles on the fence posts nearest the house. He started with the musket and first showed her how to load it. He then handed the heavy gun to Anna and let her get used to the weight and then stood behind her and showed her how to aim and half-cock the hammer, pulling it back into the first notch. He then instructed her to pull the hammer back one more notch. "OK. Take a deep breath. Now, place your finger gently on the trigger. As you slowly exhale, squeeze it."

A moment later, the gun roared, and a flash of fire erupted from the barrel. The gun barrel rose up in the air several feet from the recoil, and Anna stepped backward. When the smoke cleared, the bottle was no longer on the fence post. "I hit it! I hit it!" Anna exclaimed.

Henry smiled and gave her a hug. "Let's see if it was luck. Now, load the gun like I showed you and try again." With a little guidance, she quickly had the gun reloaded and fired again at another bottle. It was the same result.

"Maybe I can outshoot you, Captain," Anna exclaimed.

"Let's not get carried away." Henry was impressed with her shooting. They shot the musket several more times until Henry finally had to show off his aim by shooting just the tip off one bottle. They then switched to loading and firing the flintlocks, which was pretty much the same procedure. She had a little more trouble aiming them but quickly caught on.

"Maybe you *should* have been a pirate queen," Henry said as they carried the guns back to the house.

Anna's hand and shoulder were already sore from the shooting. "Don't forget that, either," she replied, making a shooting motion toward him with her hand.

***

The next phase of their new life was creating the farm. Ferdinand helped Henry pick out cattle, hogs, and chickens and taught him how to care for them and milk the cows. Henry installed a hand pump, similar to the ones on ships, to pump water from the pond to nearby troughs. The hogs had their own pen, as did the chickens. He built a hen house for the laying hens so Anna could gather eggs each morning.

Ferdinand also helped Henry plant a garden. It was only early summer, and Ferdinand assured him that all the plants would produce by fall. A month after finding River Junction, Anna and Henry were finally settled into their perfect new life.

CHAPTER XXVII

Henry and Anna were married in a small Christian church at the end of the town. Nearly the entire town showed up for their wedding, even though they hadn't met most of the townspeople yet. Everyone was excited to have new people move to the area, and they all had heard of Henry killing the "bandits." Anna was radiant in a long, billowing white dress, and Henry was dashing in a fine black suit.

After the service, with everyone gathered at the River House, Anna was introduced to the wives. Ferdinand was married to Caroline, Levi to Lilly, Philip to Elizabeth, and John had a lady friend named Sarah. Anna soon found herself at the table with them as Henry drank with the men. They were all friendly enough and readily shared news and gossip about the town and the people gathered in the room. Anna soon knew much more than she needed to about almost everyone. The ladies invited her to have tea with them on Tuesday and Thursday mornings at the small clothing store Sarah owned.

***

The remainder of the summer was great for Anna. She and Henry were as happy as two people could be. When she wasn't working in the house on chores and cooking, she would help him tend to the garden and animals. She just wanted to be close to him as much as possible. He was sweet and caring to her, and she always felt safe and secure with him around. The work was hard, but it kept them busy, and they still made time to relax and enjoy each other's company. Henry even hung a couple of hammocks behind the house between four trees, and they lay out there sometimes during the day and on warm nights.

Even before they ran off together, Anna had worried about Henry becoming bored with life away from pirating. He had lived a life that few could imagine, rising to the status of a legendary pirate captain. His name had been known from England to the Spanish Main. He had probably taken more ships and more treasure than any pirate who'd ever lived. His life had been pure adventure and excitement since he was eight. But he seemed content with their new life.

Henry bought some books from the general store and taught Anna how to read. At night, they usually sat together on the couch, by the light of the oil lamps, and read. Anna loved Shakespeare, especially *Romeo and Juliet*. Henry liked *Don Quixote* and *Robinson Crusoe*. They also read frequently out of the Bible, taking turns reading verses to each other. Henry didn't talk much about his religious beliefs, but Anna believed in God and the Bible. She knew they had both committed many sins in their pasts but hoped God would forgive them, especially since they were living well now.

Things slowed down as summer transitioned to fall. They harvested all the vegetables from the garden, and Henry learned how to slaughter cattle and hogs and process the meat. They always ate well, with their homegrown vegetables and meat and Anna's blossoming cooking skills. Henry actually spilled out of his lean pirate body and gained a few pounds around his midsection.

Henry began hunting and fishing with the extra time. It gave him something to do, provided more meat, and kept his shooting skills sharp. Anna wanted to learn how to hunt, too, so Henry began taking her with him. She was an uncanny shot. It took her a few tries to adjust to hitting a moving target, but she soon picked it up. The river had trout, and the pond had catfish and bass. Henry made them both fishing poles, and they also became proficient at catching fish.

They rode into town at least weekly for supplies and to visit. Henry would go to the River House and Anna usually to Sarah's

Clothiers. Sometimes all the couples met at the River House for supper. Although Henry and Anna loved being in each other's company every day and night, it was nice to see and talk to other people too. Occasionally, some of the men, with or without their wives, would stop by the farm to visit. River Junction was a close-knit town, and all the residents watched out for one another.

***

Fall gave way to winter, with much shorter and wetter days. Henry found himself feeling a little strange. Restlessness was building inside, and he felt a tight knot in the pit of his stomach most of the time. He didn't sleep well at night. He became bored with feeding and tending to the animals and even grew tired of hunting and fishing. They had all the meat they could eat for a long time—salted and cured so it wouldn't spoil. Their piece of land was a good size, but he knew it as well as the back of his hand.

He still loved Anna and being with her, but lately, kissing, touching, and making love wasn't the same as it had been in the beginning. Their lovemaking transitioned from every day or two to once or twice a week. It was enjoyable, but her touch and kiss slowly lost some of their effect on him. He longed for the days of tingles, chills, and racing hearts. He tried to experience it again, but those special feelings were gone no matter how hard he tried.

"Are we going to read?" Anna asked shortly after Henry came in from feeding the cattle. Darkness came early now, even earlier that day since it was cloudy and rainy.

Henry had removed his wet boots and sat on the couch in front of the fire, warming his feet. He stared into the flames, his mind lost in their flickering depths.

"Henry?"

He slowly turned to see Anna standing beside him. "Oh, I'm sorry, Anna. Just daydreaming, I guess."

Anna frowned but was afraid to ask what his thoughts were about. "So, are we going to read tonight?" She sat down on the couch beside him.

Henry glanced at her thoughtfully for a moment and then turned back to the flames. "I don't think so."

"Oh. Would you like to play cards?"

Henry grunted a response that Anna took to mean no.

"Would you like to go to bed early and...um...cuddle?" Anna placed her hand playfully on his knee.

"No," Henry said gruffly.

Anna tried her best to remain cheerful. "My, you're grumpy today."

"Can I not just sit in front of the fire and relax?" he replied curtly.

Anna stood. "Well, I believe I'll go to bed. Come join me soon." She bent over and kissed him. She received only a quick, emotionless peck in return. She quickly walked down the hall to the bedroom, tears in her eyes.

Henry went into the kitchen to retrieve a bottle of rum. He didn't drink much at home but kept a supply just in case. As the cold, dreary winter set in, he experienced more and more just-in-case days. He sat in front of the fire and drank deeply from the bottle. He drifted in and out of memories and dreams. The flickering flames morphed from lanterns on ship decks to bonfires at the Rock to burning ships in battle. He finally woke a couple of hours before dawn. The fire was burned out, and he headed to bed. Luckily, Anna was still asleep. He felt terrible after the times that he snapped at her, and he knew she was just being kind and supportive. He would try to do better.

***

Henry's sleep was restless for the next few weeks. Many nights, he woke up in the middle of the night and couldn't fall back to sleep. Occasionally, he slipped out of bed and went out onto the porch. One particular night, he went outside and sat in one of the rocking chairs. The air was cool and the sky clear. He rocked and stared at the stars in the southern sky, and his mind drifted back to so many nights on the sea, sleeping underneath those same stars. He knew which stars could guide him to

Nassau, Havana, or Hispaniola. He wondered if any pirates still sailed the sea, chasing the fat galleons, or if the squadron had slain them all.

Then he thought of James. Was he still in the fleet, or had he gotten out? Or was he even still alive? He hoped to see him someday riding through the gate and down to their house. Henry had only been around him a few times but loved him as only brothers can love. How great it would be for James to live close by, along with a wife that Anna could befriend.

"What are you doing?" Anna asked as she walked through the door. "It's cold out here."

"I couldn't sleep. I just came out to look at the stars."

Anna sat down in the chair beside him, a blanket wrapped around her. She reached over, grabbed Henry's hand, and stared at the stars. A shooting star streaked across the sky, disappearing over the pines. "Remember the first one we saw?"

"Indeed I do."

"And its omen came true. We did head off to a happy and great future," Anna said, trying to discern her husband's face in the dim light. Henry stared straight ahead and didn't respond. "You are happy, aren't you?"

"Oh, of course. Sorry, my mind just drifted off for a minute. I am very happy." Henry squeezed her hand and smiled in the starlight.

"Your mind seems to drift a lot lately. Do you want to go back to bed?"

"Sure, let's go."

***

Two days later, he went into town for a few supplies. Anna decided to stay home; she hadn't been feeling well lately. Henry said he would try to be back not long after dark. Neither he nor Anna worried too much about her being alone since she was skilled with a gun. While she had never shot at a person, neither of them was concerned that she could if necessary.

"Ale tonight?" John asked as Rosa came over to the table.

"Rum," Henry said shortly.

"Rum? Wow, rough day?" John asked, nodding to Rosa to get the drinks.

"Just a rough time in general."

"Animals, OK?" Ferdinand asked.

"They're still alive," said Henry, finally flashing a wry grin.

"Hmmm. I bet I know what troubles you," John said. Rosa had returned with their drinks.

Henry swirled the rum in his mug, sniffed, and then turned it up. He drank half of it in one gulp. "And just what is that?"

"You're bored; restless. You've lived an exciting life as a... sailor, traveling the world, visiting many ports, and meeting many people. Your days were never exactly the same. Now, you're cooped up on a small piece of land, doing the same thing every day."

Ferdinand, Levi, and Phillip nodded or grunted in agreement.

"I think you're wrong. I'm with the most beautiful woman in the world, whom I love with all my heart. I don't have to sleep on a foul ship with a hundred unwashed men. I don't have to worry about dying daily or wondering where my next coin is coming from. I can work as hard or easy as I want, as long as my animals don't starve. I'm living the perfect life." Henry finished his rum and waved at Rosa for another.

"Oh. Just thirsty for rum then, huh?' John said, staring through him as he was prone to do.

"Aye. Just thirsty, I guess. And tired of the rain."

"Well, let me know if you'd like to talk someday."

The men sat and talked and drank for several hours. Henry slowly began to feel a little better and more relaxed as the rum flowed. His companions started drinking to match him. It was Saturday night, and most didn't have to work the next day. They soon began asking Henry to share some stories of the sea and his adventures as a sailor.

Henry finally obliged. He knew it was dangerous, but he found himself wanting to talk about the sea, to relive the memories. He started with some of the pirate tales he had heard about other pirates over the years. And John chipped in his share of stories. It seemed that he had encountered a few pirates during his life too. He was particularly knowledgeable of Jean and Pierre Lafitte. He said he knew of the Lafitte brothers from his time as a merchant in New Orleans.

A few other townspeople—mainly Levi, Ferdinand, and Philip—shared stories too. Henry had noticed before that he wasn't the only one in town who walked on sea legs. He didn't inquire into anyone's past, though, because he didn't want to share his own. It seemed to be the way in this town. Everyone just had a current role, and that was all anyone needed to know.

Soon, Henry ran out of tales about other pirates and moved on to Bloodstone and Hawk stories—much to the delight of the listeners. Even John seemed to take a keen interest. Henry, of course, said that he had just heard the tales from other sailors over the years. But the details were incredible, and he was a great storyteller. Gradually, a crowd of men had pulled up chairs around their table to listen. The entire room fell silent when he told of Hawk rescuing Bloodstone and Diablo from the gallows of Port Royal, a story all had heard or read about. Then he recounted the famous battle with Cord, Bloodstone, and Kragg.

"Some say the Hawk is immortal, that he can't be killed," Jacob, the burly town blacksmith, said after hearing about Hawk defeating Kragg. Some murmured in agreement.

"Unfortunately, not. Word is, Captain Wellington killed him after Hawk's escape from New Orleans," Levi replied, also receiving some support from the crowd.

"Don't think they ever found the body, though, did they?" John asked, looking at Henry as he spoke.

"I bet the ol' devil is still alive, plottin' and plannin' his next move," Abe added, one of John's hired guns posted about town.

"What do you think, Mr. Henry," asked Bartolomeus, or Bart, as everyone knew him. The Dutchman was John's main riverboat captain. Henry had noticed that many nationalities were represented here, which was a little unusual for a small town in Mississippi. They all seemed to know John well.

"Hard to say. He definitely had a way of surviving dire situations. But even if he survived, what's he going to do? The time of pirates is done. It's a new day, men." Most grumbled in reply and were mostly silent as the story telling wound down. Henry suddenly realized that it must be close to midnight. He quickly stood, excused himself, and walked out with a slight stagger to find his wagon.

It was a long ride home on the dark paths to their house. Luckily, the moon was mostly full and gave enough light to navigate by. He tried to creep into the house and to the bedroom. A lamp was burning on the table beside the bed. As he removed his shoes and clothes and gently sat down, a voice behind him spoke.

"Do you know how worried I've been?" Anna asked.

Henry cringed, cursed himself, and slowly slid into the bed. "I'm sorry, dear. A lot of men were there, and we started swapping stories and drinking a little too much." He finally rolled on his side to face her. Her eyes glistened in the flickering light and were red from crying.

"Pirate stories?"

Henry swallowed hard. "Ended up with some."

"Henry!"

"I just told them they were stories I had heard. John had his share of stories about Lafitte and other pirates too. It was fine, Anna."

She was quiet and rolled onto her back to stare at the ceiling.

"What's wrong, Anna? I told you I was sorry. I've never stayed out like that before. I guess I just needed to let off a little pent-up energy."

"You miss it."

"Miss what?"

"Pirating. I know you've been restless. You haven't been yourself lately. I've seen how your mind is somewhere else most of the time. I've heard you toss and turn and get up in the night. I saw you staring at the stars the other night." Anna turned her head to stare at him again. A tear rolled out of her eye and raced for the pillow.

"Anna, that part of my life is over…forever. I have been a little restless lately, but I guess it's just the winter coming on and all the rain. This is new to both of us. It gets dark early now, and there are no crops to tend. I guess it's just boredom."

"So, you're bored with our new life? And with me?"

Henry sighed. He was still experiencing the effects of the rum and really needed sleep. He was also trying to be patient with Anna. But he was not used to getting questioned about his comings and goings. He inhaled deeply and tried to remember how much he loved her. He reached out and touched her check with his hand, wiped away a tear, and stroked her hair. "I love our life…and you, Anna."

She smiled weakly and placed her hand on his and squeezed it. He slid one arm under her head, the other around her, and pressed his body against hers. They fell asleep with the lamp still burning.

**

Henry tried to get his mind back to the farm and his marriage over the next couple of weeks. He found chores to keep him preoccupied, even if the chores weren't really necessary. At night, he went back to reading with Anna or cuddling on the couch. He did start staying up later than Anna, though, and enjoyed a few drinks in front of the fire. He found he could sleep better with some spirits in him. Some nights he fell asleep on the couch. Anna wasn't happy the next morning, but he tried to make up for it during the day and evening.

**

He went back into town two weeks after his last late night out. After trying to be a good husband and staying busy with chores, he built up a lot of frustration he needed to let out with the guys. He told Anna he would probably be a little late, but he needed some man time. She seemed OK with it.

He arrived at the River House just before dark. He bought a bottle of rum from George and headed upstairs to seek John. He had decided to take him up on his offer to talk. Maybe John did know what he was going through. The door to John's office was open, and Henry found him at the table, working through a pile of papers. Henry shut the door behind him and sat down at the far end.

John looked up and smiled as he watched Henry take a swig from the bottle. "Another rum night, huh?"

"Aye." Henry tilted the bottle toward John.

John stood and walked around the table to sit beside him. "You might be a bad influence on me." John drank deeply and handed the bottle back. "Well, are you ready to talk?"

"I guess it won't hurt."

"I was right, wasn't I? You miss the sea and your former life."

"I guess that's some of it. It's been hard with the winter here and being cooped up inside most of the time. Life on a merchantman was tough but usually not boring. And the chores and tasks kept me busy all year." Henry took another drink and passed the bottle again.

"Well, it's only your first winter," John said, his friendly smile already making Henry feel a little better. "Those feelings will pass. Give it time. And spring will be here before you know it."

"Yeah, I'm sure you're right."

"But that's not all, is it?" John asked, staring intently at Henry.

Henry looked up at him, debating whether to say more.

"Is it Anna?"

Henry marveled at John's perceptiveness. "I don't know, John. I've loved Anna ever since we met. All I have thought about for years is being with her. And it's been great most of the time we've been together."

"Most of the time?"

"Until recently. I don't know. It just doesn't feel the same with her. I used to get chills every time she touched me. The hairs on my arms and the back of my neck would stand with her kisses. My stomach fluttered just seeing her naked. I was content being with her every minute of every day." Henry was surprised he was revealing so much.

"And now...you're bored," said John. "You don't experience the same excitement with every touch and kiss. Lying together isn't quite as...interesting. Sometimes you just want to go out alone and not be with her every minute. Sometimes you don't even want to...lie with her."

"How do you know all this?"

John laughed. "Because it happens to every man and woman."

"It's happened to you?"

"Yes. I met my Madeline some years ago. She was the most beautiful lass I'd ever seen—fair skin, dark black hair, and fierce blue eyes. I thought I had taken ill the first time we kissed, my body shook so. It seemed like we had known each other forever. We could talk all day and make love all night—every night. I thought it would stay like that forever once we married or even get better." A slight smile of reminiscence played across John's face.

"And it didn't?"

"It did for a while. But with time, some of those feelings faded. I found myself putting more time into work. We had a child together, and the romance declined even more. We didn't talk as much or do things together as we did when we were courting. We got along well enough and liked each other, but I was afraid we had fallen out of love." John swallowed a large swig of rum.

"What happened?"

"I ran a warehouse on Galveston Island at the time and had a decent business going, trading with the Lafitte brothers. But because of Jean Lafitte, the US Navy sacked Galveston, and my warehouse was destroyed. I could have moved farther inland with Madeline and my son, or I could have gone back to New Orleans. But I missed the sea and my days on a merchantman. I found myself wanting to captain my own ship. I told Madeline that going back to the sea was my only option to make a living. I helped them move inland, gave them a little money to get by on, and told them I'd be back to visit as often as I could.

"I bought a large sloop, gathered a crew, and started trading about the United States and the Spanish Main. I built a successful business. But after being at sea for a good while, I started realizing what a fool I was. I could have gone with Madeline and Jean Pierre and lived a nice, full family life. I discovered back on my ship that I thought about her every free moment, just like in the early days. Despite the adventure and excitement of being a captain, my heart was with her."

"So, you fell back in love with her?" Henry asked.

"No. That's my point, Henry. I never fell out of love. Love changes during a relationship. It can't always be like it is in the beginning—it will never stay that way. In fact, those feelings aren't even love. I've had prostitutes in Port Royal make my head swim, heart race, and palms sweat. That's just your physical reaction to an attractive woman and someone new. Once the newness wears off, those feelings fade. Love is much more than that. Love is finding someone you want to spend the rest of your life with and share everything with. It's finding someone who will always be there for you—a familiar, smiling face first thing every morning and last thing every night. To put it in seaman terms, it's like having your first mate, bosun, navigator, and cook all rolled into one. But a lot softer, better looking, and better smelling!"

Both men chuckled.

"It's not always going to be passionate and exciting. But you have to stick it out through the boring and tough times to appreciate the good times." John said, passing the bottle back to Henry.

"Wow!" Henry said, swallowing another swig of rum. "Did you ever go back and try to find them?"

"No. By the time I realized my error, I figured I'd waited too long. I felt certain she had moved on and found another man. They probably both hated me by then, if my son even remembered me." He paused again. "Well, enough women talk. Think about what I said, though. If you want to return to the sea and leave Anna behind, then do it. But just make sure it's truly what you want to do. Don't end up like me."

"I've had two other men offer me the opposite advice—to choose the sea over a woman."

"And how did that turn out for them?"

"Well, one is dead, and I'm not sure about the other. But I'm guessing not too well." Henry finished the rest of the rum. He stared at the bottle for a few minutes, his mind wandering far away. Finally, he looked back up at John. "Let me ask you a question since you seem so wise."

"Sure. Anything."

"What is the purpose of our lives?

John stared at him for a few seconds as if gauging if he was serious. Finally, he laughed. "You are a deep one, my friend, especially to be so young."

"So I've been told a time or two," Henry said, but he didn't smile.

"Well, I don't know if I have ever thought about it too hard," John said, leaning back in his chair and placing his hands behind his head. "I do think that the meaning might be different for each person, though. If I had to give a broad answer, I would say that it is to give your all and try to be the best at anything you undertake. Strive to make a difference with whatever you do." He paused for a few seconds. "And enjoy the moment—the past is the past, and the future may never come. Live your life so you're ready to face death when it comes looking for you."

Henry sat in thoughtful silence for a moment. Finally, he stood. "Enough deep talk for tonight. Let's go show the landlubbers how to drink rum."

They ventured downstairs and spent some time with the other men, sharing stories and drinking more rum and ale.

**

"Let's go to the sea," Anna said late one night a few weeks later as they sat cuddling, wrapped in blankets by the fire.

The statement startled Henry. He turned to look at Anna, the light flickering on her face making it appear as if it shifted and moved. "Really? Are you sure?"

"Henry, I know this move is hard on you, although I'll never truly understand it. There is no part of my old life I miss. This is enough for me. But I don't want you to be unhappy. Maybe just seeing the sea, smelling the salty air, and watching the ships will make you feel better. Maybe we could even catch a quick ride on a merchant vessel to Biloxi or somewhere close."

Henry lay back and stared at the ceiling. His heart was racing. That idea appealed to him so strongly that it scared him a little. He rolled over, facing her, and wrapped his arm around her. "That sounds good, but only if you truly want to do it."

"If it will make you happier, then I do."

Henry kissed her. Instead of the quick pecks of recent weeks, it soon became passionate. Anna moaned slightly as she kissed him back. Neither had realized how much the desire of old had faded over the past few months. The pent-up hunger and lust quickly reappeared, and their hands roamed as clothes were removed. The heat from the fire warmed their skin, only increasing the heat their bodies generated. Soon, they were making love on the floor beside the dancing flames.

CHAPTER XXVIII

Henry and Anna arrived by barge in Pascagoula two days later on a cool, cloudy, damp morning. They bid Bart good-bye and walked off the dock and around the side until they found the white sand beach. The sun began to peak above the clouds in the eastern sky, and the air started to warm. Henry inhaled the thick, salty air deeply as he stood and stared out over the water until it merged with the gray horizon. He could barely make out the topsails of what appeared to be a three-masted ship in the distance, heading east with the wind.

Anna watched Henry but didn't speak. She didn't want to know what he was thinking as he watched the distant ship. She just hoped this trip would work. She knew that his seeing the sea again could be a mistake and might only fuel his discontent, but it was a chance worth taking. If she did nothing and pretended nothing was wrong, the desire within him would continue to build until, one day, he would just leave her. All she could do was support him and hope she was enough.

They removed their shoes and walked along the beach holding hands. "Bet you cannot catch me," Anna said, pushing Henry and taking off running into the water's edge. Henry laughed and ran after her. Anna zigzagged across the beach and through the surf, sending water spraying high around her.

She was quick, but Henry still moved like a big cat. He soon caught her and scooped her up in his arms. "Bet I can," he said and kissed her salty lips. They spent most of the day walking, looking for seashells and sharks' teeth, and frolicking on the beach and in the water. Their clothes were soaked, and it was a little cold despite the sun, but it was a good day for both.

"I take it you've never spent much time on a beach," Henry said as Anna showed him yet another oyster shell.

"Never!" she replied, laughing and running off to find another.

He smiled as he watched her run about. Sometimes he forgot how young they were. They both had lived rough lives and were forced to be adults many years too soon. He loved to watch the youthful, playful, energetic Anna. He tried to be as carefree, but he caught himself frequently glancing toward the horizon. When he'd see a ship, he'd size it up. He could discern how many knots per hour it was traveling, if it were loaded, its likely armaments, and the size of its crew. He never knew one could be in two places at once, but that's where he found himself now.

They finally made their way back to town after watching the beautiful sunset from the dock. The sunset really brought back a flood of memories for Henry. Back in the pirate life, a sunset meant the start of the evening, when the work and fighting were done, and the men could gamble, sing, and talk on the deck beneath the stars. Henry remembered all the nights he spent on the deck with Wesley, talking about life, pirating, and death. And he could almost smell Bloodstone's pipe smoke wafting across the deck behind him like a long tail.

They arrived back at the inn by dark and found a table. Already, a decent crowd was present. Soon they were drinking ale and enjoying a meal of fish, clams, scallops, and crab. The room continued to fill up as they ate. A group of obvious sailors made their way in, talking loudly and laughing, and sat at the table behind them. Henry tried his best to speak and listen to Anna, but he found himself also eavesdropping on the sailors.

He quickly learned that they had loaded a load of cotton and soybeans today on a schooner and were heading to New Orleans in the morning. Henry's heart skipped a few beats at the news. Seeing the ocean was great, but returning to New Orleans would be even better. There he could hear news of pirates, the squadron, and maybe even James.

"Henry! You're not even listening to me," Anna scolded.

"I'm sorry, Anna. I guess I'm just a little tired from chasing you around all day," Henry smiled.

Anna leaned over to look past Henry's head and saw the sailors behind him. "I know what you were doing," she said softly.

Henry leaned forward, so no one else could hear. "Anna, they're going to New Orleans in the morning. Let's go with them!"

Anna stared at Henry coldly and then stared down at her plate. It was a moment before she spoke. "I'm not going back to New Orleans. I have no fond memories of that...that place."

"I understand. But Anna, it would really help me to go there, just for the day. I can catch a ride back the following morning. I only want to hear news of the affairs of the world and maybe find out about James. I would dearly love to see my brother again."

Anna wanted to protest with everything she had. But again, she found herself in a no-win situation. If she forbade him, he might resent it and start thinking even more about going after they returned home. If he went, then he could end up not returning. But hopefully, he could hear what he needed to hear, and it would be good if he could find out what James was doing by chance. "Go."

"Are you sure? I don't have to go."

"You need to go. I'll wait here. I can shop some tomorrow and maybe go down to the beach again."

"I love you so much, Anna! It will be a good trip...for both of us. I promise."

Anna wrinkled her brow. "And you'll be sure to disguise yourself? You haven't been gone that long."

"But of course. I'm just a humble farmer from Mississippi." Henry grinned.

***

Henry stood on the schooner's bow with the wind spitting sea spray in his face. The boat was still making decent speed, and the trip wasn't long. It was hard for him to be aboard a ship and not either give orders or help with the sails or the helm. It did feel good to be back on the open sea again, though. He had hoped it wouldn't; he had hoped he wouldn't feel anything at all. But his heart was racing, palms sweating, and his mind was clear and sharp as he gripped the rail and scanned the horizon.

It rained a couple of times, but Henry's thick wool coat was warm enough, and he had been through much worse while wearing much less. He finally left the bow and paced around the entire deck a few times, visually checking the sails and rigging and inspecting the helm. It was a two-masted vessel and designed as a merchant ship. Only two-dozen sailors were aboard and very few weapons. He noted six cannons, but Henry would wager they had no powder or shot nearby. His first thought was how easy it would be to take a ship like that. His second was how quickly he could convert it for pirating.

He went and spoke to the captain, a salty old sailor that had spent most of his life on the boat. "Any pirates around these days?"

The captain manned the wheel now that they approached the mouth of the Mississippi. He apparently didn't trust anyone on his crew to navigate the river up to the city. He paused from shouting orders to his men to answer Henry. "Nah, not to speak of. Ol' Cofresi was killed earlier this year. He be 'bout the last. I s'ppose there's always a few here and there, but not enough to worry over. The squadron is all over the water now. Good time for halfway honest merchants." He chuckled and then began shouting orders again.

A couple of hours later, they were moored at a dock in New Orleans. The sun had just set behind the city, and the lamplighters were out doing their jobs as Henry entered the square. He instantly thought back to his crew's pardon and his "escape." It seemed like that was years ago. He strolled around the square, enjoying the sounds and smells. He remembered his first visit there when Bones had guided him through. And then, of course, his meeting Anna shortly after.

He left after an hour and then made his way to the Treasure

Cove. He was a little nervous going back there, but he wouldn't be easy to recognize in his heavy coat, large floppy hat, and drab farm clothes. He had also let his beard grow out since the end of summer. It was dirty blond and made him look much older than Hawk when he was "killed."

The Treasure Cove seemed about the same. However, it was a little brighter and appeared to have a new coat of paint on the walls and maybe a few newer tables and chairs. A bigger crowd was gathered now, with three-quarters of the tables full. Henry chose a small table between some larger round tables full of seamen. It looked like naval officers behind him and merchant seamen in front. He scanned the room for Madame Cynthia but didn't see her. A young serving girl came by shortly after he sat down.

"Where is Madame Cynthia?" he asked.

"She left a few months ago—said she was heading west. Madame Rebecca is in charge now. Would you like to speak to her?"

"No thanks, ma'am. How about some hot food and a tankard of ale?"

Henry drank a couple of tankards of ale and ate a hot meal as he eavesdropped on the table closest to him. The merchant sailors soon began swapping stories of their sea adventures. Henry heard Lafitte's name mentioned a time or two. He was still a legend in New Orleans. Against his better judgment, he switched from ale to rum. He continued listening until he heard a story or two about Bloodstone and then, inevitably, Hawk.

"Mind if I join you," Henry said, sliding his chair over. With the ale, and now rum, he was feeling pretty good. "I might know a story or two."

"About what? Cotton?" one of the men asked, staring at his clothing. The other seven men laughed loudly.

Henry suppressed his instant anger. He could break the speaker's neck before he even knew he had been attacked. "I heard you mention Bloodstone and the Hawk. I used to sail with a man that had been on account with them for years."

The men suddenly stopped laughing and studied the stranger a little closer.

Henry began weaving his tales but started with some of the early battles and deeds of Bloodstone and his crew that most had never heard. Bloodstone typically didn't leave survivors, so only pirates that had served with him knew the stories. Soon, other patrons were listening to him speak, and a circle of men two and three deep surrounded the table.

The rum kept flowing, and his judgment continued diminishing. He didn't pay any attention to one side of the circle parting and allowing some of the naval officers to wedge in. He came to the infamous stories of Port Royal, Kragg, and then Hawk's final escape, much to the delight of the patrons.

"You think he's still alive?" one of the sailors asked.

"No," a voice behind Henry said before he could respond.

Henry, as well as the crowd gathered around, turned to look at the speaker. He was in full naval uniform and dressed like a captain or other high-ranking officer.

"Captain James Wellington slew him like the cowardly dog he was. I heard it told that he dropped to his knees and begged and pleaded for his life before James put a ball in his chest." The officer smirked. His companions, also apparent naval officers, laughed.

Henry studied the man with his somewhat impaired vision. He looked familiar, but he couldn't quite place him. He was young, pale, and had a neatly trimmed red mustache and a patch of beard. Red hair showed around the edges of his tricorne.

"Is that true, sir?" another man at the table asked Henry.

Henry turned back to face the man who'd asked the question. "From what I've heard of the Hawk, he would never beg or grovel to anyone for anything." He turned back to the redheaded officer. "And unless James himself told the story, I would have to doubt its accuracy."

The captain pursed his lips in thinly veiled anger. "Either way, the Hawk is at the bottom of the sea, as are all the pirate scum. Now, why don't you men tell stories of current things and real heroes like James Wellington and the members of the West Indies Squadron? Don't waste your breath trying to glorify dead cowards. Although, I do wish some remained to hang. I do miss them soiling themselves as they flop about on the end of a noose." The officers laughed again.

Henry clenched his fists under the table. He could gut the arrogant captain from belly to neck and be out the door before his body hit the ground. But he bit his tongue. He had already brought too much attention to himself tonight. He turned back to the table and started asking about local affairs. The officer and his companions seemed satisfied and returned to their table.

Henry eventually asked the men what had happened to Captain Wellington. One told him that he was still the captain of the *Avenger* and was hunting down the few remaining pirates. He was based out of Pensacola, where Commodore Cord was now headquartered. He was as famous for the squadron as Hawk had been for the pirates.

Finally, around midnight, Henry finished his tankard of rum and stood. He bid his companions good night and turned to walk toward the stairs. The navy officer called out to him before he'd cleared their table. "Ho, farmer, come here for a moment."

Henry gritted his teeth. This man was pushing the limits of his restraint. He slowly turned and faced the table of officers. "Yes," he replied, glaring at the cocky redhead.

"You seem to know a lot about Bloodstone and Hawk. Did you sail with them?"

"No."

"Then how did you come by those stories and in such vivid detail? They didn't leave many survivors to tell tales."

Henry sighed. He was much too drunk and tired for this. "I worked on a merchant ship years ago. One of the crew had served with both of them. I don't recall his name."

The man stared at Henry, studying his face and actions. "And what do you do now?"

"A cattle and hog farmer. Came to town to make some merchant contacts." This night was close to turning out very bad for someone.

"A farmer, eh? And where is your farm?"

Henry knew he should have lied, but he was tired and having trouble standing steady in one spot. "Mississippi. And if that is all, I must go to bed. I'm returning there early in the morning." The officer waved his hand, dismissing him. Henry turned and quickly crossed the room and disappeared up the stairs.

***

"What was that about, Captain Smith?" an officer beside the speaker asked. He was even younger and more innocent looking than the captain.

"That man is lying. Those stories weren't secondhand," Captain Smith replied, finishing his ale.

"You think he's one of Hawk's pardoned crew?"

Captain Smith stroked his chin thoughtfully. "I don't know. I'm going to find out, though. Pack for a trip tonight, Owen— wear civilian clothes. I have a mission for you. You can prove if you are worthy of being a first mate."

"Yes, sir!" Owen replied eagerly.

***

Henry paid for a couple of biscuits and some salted ham on the way out of the Treasure Cove the following morning and headed to the docks. He was relieved that the schooner he'd sailed in on was still there, and the crew was readying the vessel for sailing. They had loaded clothing, food, and supplies to deliver along the coast until they emptied in Florida. Henry found the captain and paid for the return voyage.

As he ate his ham biscuits and watched the crew prepare the ship, he noticed another man speaking with the captain. The man carried a large sack over his shoulder and wasn't dressed as a sailor. Henry shrugged and turned away to walk to the stern of the ship to study the river. The day was dawning mild, with a clear sky. A decent breeze blew from the west, which would make it a quick and easy voyage back to Pascagoula. After the ship was unmoored and the sails unfurled, it glided into the river's current, picked up speed, and headed toward the sea.

Henry made his way to the bow and watched the water, lost in his thoughts.

"Hello, sir," a voice said from behind him.

Henry cringed and slowly turned his head to the side. The young man that had boarded last walked up to stand beside him. The lad was much too happy for this time of morning. Henry's head wasn't too clear from the night before, either. He nodded his head and turned back forward.

"Say, were you in the Treasure Cove last night telling stories?"

He had his attention now. Henry turned back to study the boy's face a little closer. He wore a long gray coat and a hat similar to some worn by businessmen in New Orleans. His face was vaguely familiar, but Henry's memories of last night were a little fuzzy. "I was there."

"I was in the back of the crowd listening. Those were some good tales, sir!"

"Just stories," Henry replied.

"Were you ever a pirate?" the boy asked, his enthusiasm grating hard on Henry's nerves.

"No. Just a seaman and now a farmer."

"Oh, sure, sounds like you were right there with the Hawk. Ever meet him?"

"No."

"You think he's dead?" the boy persisted.

"Yes. What's your name?" Henry asked, tired of getting questioned.

"Owen, sir. Owen Davis."

"And why are you on this ship, asking me questions?"

"I heard this ship was going to Pascagoula. I have relatives near there. I've been thinking about the farming business. So, you say you're a farmer?"

"Yes."

"What do you farm, if you don't mind me asking?"

"Does it matter if I mind? Cattle, hogs, chickens." Henry replied bluntly.

"Oh, I was thinking about maybe cotton or soybeans. I hear there is money in that. What do you think?" Owen asked, his smile ever present.

"I say do whatever you want to do."

"Hmmm. Whereabouts is your farm located?"

Henry leaned over the rail and rubbed his temples. The boy seemed innocent enough, but he still had to be careful. He remembered his exchange with the navy officer last night. "North of Pascagoula."

"Oh, where?"

"That, my friend, is none of your concern. Good luck to you." Henry walked away and found the nearest hatch to climb below deck. He hoped Owen would take a hint and not follow him.

The rest of the voyage was fairly uneventful. Other than a few quick exchanges, he managed to avoid Owen. The return trip felt much different to Henry. The water and salty air didn't seem the same. The searching for sails and daydreaming of the past were gone. He had known since before Bloodstone died that the times were changing. But he had never truly let go. He always held onto a glimmer of hope. Now, the glimmer had gone dark. Now, he knew that he had let go. His night in New Orleans made him realize that it was indeed a different world now—a world of authority, businessmen, and pasty-faced, wide-eyed naval officers. The world was civilized now.

But it was more than just that. Something within him had changed. He was truly at peace with leaving his old life behind. Sure, he would still have his memories, but they would be just that. He had lived more in nineteen years than most would in lifetimes. He had risen to the pinnacle of pirate life and achieved all he ever wanted to achieve. He had nothing left to do or prove as a pirate. He had fulfilled Jack's notion of the purpose of a man's life. The legend of the Hawk would live long after he was dead and buried.

His mind turned to his beautiful wife. He imagined touching her, smelling her perfumed skin, and kissing her soft, full lips. He actually found himself missing the nights by the fireplace, talking and reading. He missed hunting and riding and doing chores together. He couldn't wait for spring. The past year he had gone through the motions of farming. Now, he was ready to embrace it. He thought more about what John had said about his meaning of life. He had been the best pirate. Now, he was ready to be the best farmer, husband, and father—and he would enjoy all three roles.

The ship made a quick stop in Biloxi to unload some goods to a waiting merchant and then sailed the rest of the way to Pascagoula, arriving just after sunset. Henry made his way quickly to the inn and to the room. Anna welcomed him with open arms. "You came back!" she exclaimed, hugging him tightly and working in some kisses.

"You doubted me?"

"I'm sorry. A woman's mind can create all kinds of bad thoughts. I just kept seeing you finding your old crew, stealing a ship, and setting sail again."

"Hmmm. I hadn't thought of that." Henry smiled.

Anna struck him hard on the arm. But she was glad to see a glimpse of his sense of humor return. "Well, did you find what you needed to find?"

"Let's sit down," Henry said, walking to the bed and sitting. Anna nervously joined him. He told her about his trip, leaving out a few details of the conversation with the officer.

So, how do you feel now?"

Henry rubbed Anna's back through her dress, causing her to sigh in approval. "Anna, I won't lie to you. I had thought for a while that if piracy was still going strong, back like when Bloodstone took me, I might be tempted to return to my old life. But on this trip, I realized that my love for you would outweigh that desire and any others. This trip just reinforced that the past is in the past. I'm at peace with living in the present and looking forward to the future. I just want to spend the rest of my life with you—farming, doing chores, and raising a bunch of children."

"Oh, Henry, I love you so much!" As Anna kissed Henry, her

warm tears spreading to his cheeks. "That is all I've wanted!"

"Anna, I love you more than anything in the world. I'm sorry that I even wavered for a moment. It won't happen again. I have enough memories and stories to last a lifetime. And now I get to spend that lifetime with the beautiful young woman I love."

After they made love, Anna drifted off to sleep, but Henry lay awake—his arms wrapped around her warm, soft, naked body. He was at peace. He had finished the last chapter of his old life and was content with the new one. Sure, there would be boring days, and their love couldn't always be the wild love affair it had been in the beginning, but their bond would only strengthen. And soon, they would hopefully start a family and have children to raise and love. He'd still entertain John and his men with his stories and tales every so often, but at the night's end, he'd go home to his loving family. And that would be good enough.

They ate a quick breakfast in the morning and left the inn to find Bart at the dock, finishing securing crates and barrels of goods on the barges. Bart welcomed them aboard with a hearty handshake for Henry and a hug for Anna. Within a few minutes, the lines were unmoored, and the slaves began rowing them away from the dock. "To River Junction!" Bart's voice boomed loudly.

***

No one had noticed the cloaked Owen Davis milling about close to the docks in the predawn darkness, watching the scene intently. "River Junction," he whispered softly.

CHAPTER XXIX

A few days after they returned, Henry entered the River House at dark after finishing buying supplies. Most of the regulars were there, and they all greeted him warmly. He truly felt missed, although it might have helped that he bought the entire house a round of drinks. After a while, the musicians straggled in, and the music started. Henry, John, Ferdinand, Levi, Bart, and Jacob sat around a table, drinking some of John's fine brandy. They talked and laughed over light subjects and watched the dancers on the floor.

Henry didn't say too much about his trip to New Orleans. He gave John a look that indicated they would speak later. He shared a few stories of the old days, but they were just stories this time. They did seem almost like tales he had heard, not adventures he had lived. Soon, the crowd gathered around the table once more.

A few travelers and strangers occasionally passed through town, and most stopped by the River House for food and drink or a room for the night. A new face or two didn't draw any attention unless the person wanted attention—especially when the music was playing, drinks flowing, and people dancing and carrying on. So it was not unusual that no one noticed the young man dressed in a long gray coat with a hat pulled down low on his brow. He drank alone at a corner table behind the table drawing all the attention. Several people stood between him and the storyteller.

By midnight, most of the crowd had thinned out. John finally stood and rounded up the rest to either go to their rooms or to their homes. The young man drinking alone was the last to climb stairs. Henry and John were soon the only two left in the common room.

"All right, Henry, talk."

John walked about the room, gathering up the bottles, mugs, tankards, and dishes and carried them to the kitchen. Henry followed and helped as he told John about the trip to Pascagoula and New Orleans.

"Hmmm. So you're done with the sea, huh?" John asked when Henry had finished, and the two men stood on each side of the bar, close to the stairs.

"Aye, that I am."

"And you're sure?"

"Yes. I've left the life of pir...merchanting behind me. I'm finally at peace. I'm ready to be a married landlubber. And I'll enjoy every minute of it." He hoped somehow John hadn't caught his slip.

"You didn't start to say pirating, did you?" John asked and laughed.

"Blast it!" Henry cursed. The rum had gotten the best of him.

"I know who you are," John replied matter-of-factly.

"For how long?" Henry asked, shaking his head.

"Pretty much the entire time. Then your storytelling a few weeks ago erased any doubt." He reached over and clapped Henry on the shoulder. "Don't worry, friend. The Hawk is dead. However, I would like to hear the end of your story, including your death."

Henry glanced around the room to make sure no one was lurking. He was hesitant, but John already knew now. It would be the only time he'd share this story. He told John of James Wellington being his brother, their plot, and the final voyage.

John shook his head and laughed. "You do indeed have a sharp mind. Fine plan."

"Now, tell me how you died," Henry said.

"What are you talking about? Is that the rum?"

"Now, Jean, I've told you."

John Lafleur, or Jean Lafitte as he used to be known, shook

his head and grinned. "You dog. How long have you known?"

"About as long as you've known about me. Now, I thought you died off the coast of Honduras?"

"Very close. I attacked what I thought were two merchant ships on a dark, rainy night. Turns out they were Spanish warships. They tore us up pretty good. They ended up sinking my ship and killing most of my men. I was shot twice. A dozen of my mates and I managed to slip overboard into a longboat and rowed till we hit land. We traveled north overland for a while, away from the Spanish forts.

"We finally caught passage on a US merchant ship in another town. We told them we had been aboard a merchant ship attacked by the Spanish. They were more than willing to help us. We ended up going to New Orleans, but I knew I couldn't show my face there for long. We quickly found another ship to give us passage, a merchantman that ended up going to Pascagoula. I figured that was as good of a time as any to retire. My boys and I traveled up the river, trying to put some distance between us and the sea, and found a little town called River Junction. I had managed to escape with a sizeable stash of coin and decided to grow the town. And here I am."

"Let me guess. Ferdinand, Levi, Philip, Abe, and Bart were all pirates with you?"

John laughed. "Privateers. They and a few others. We spread the word to some of my former crews on our trading trips to New Orleans and slowly brought more men back. I don't want it to get too big, though—no use drawing too much attention to us. There are about two dozen of us here now."

"Have you ever missed the trade?" Henry asked after a pause to digest the information.

"Pretty bad my first year, like you. But this isn't a bad deal. It's not as glamorous as Baratavia or Galveston but tolerable. I can still trade, bargain, and make a little money, and I'm still in charge of men. Like you, though, I know there is no going back. A privateer, or pirate, wouldn't last more than a month or two out there now. Plus, the fact that the ships loaded with booty are gone. The Spanish have pretty much milked the New World dry. I can make more money on trade from this little town than a pirate crew could in a year, and I won't be shot or hanged."

"Aye. I agree with that. Well, I better be getting home."

"And, Henry, what say we never speak of this again?"

"Speak of what, John?" Both men laughed, and Henry left.

***

Crouching at the top of the stairs, Owen Davis quickly and quietly slipped off to his room before John, or Jean, came up the stairs heading to his third-floor quarters. His smile was huge as he closed the door to his room.

***

Spring came early to Mississippi. The weather soon warmed, and the days grew longer. Henry made his garden twice as big as the year before and added some new crops. He also seeded another field for hay. He bought more pastureland from John on the far side of the pond and added more cattle. He and Anna were happy and content and completely settled into their new life.

Anna also suggested that since Henry had so many great stories and everyone loved hearing them, he should write a book about his life as a pirate. Henry loved the idea and began writing down the details of his exciting life at night. He would talk out loud, telling Anna the stories as he wrote. Within a few months, he had a stack of paper an inch thick, filled with all his tales. He named it *The Last Pirate*. Anna told him he should try to get it published someday when they were sure that pirates, and Hawk, had faded into legend and myth and no one would come looking for the author.

***

"Henry, we need to talk," Anna said one day in April after returning from a trip into town. Henry had finally relented that spring and let her occasionally ride into town alone to spend time with the other women—as long as she had a flintlock. She had gone to see Dr. Joseph Barton since she hadn't been feeling well for a while and was frequently sick to her stomach in the mornings.

"Is everything OK?" Henry said, quickly leaping up from the rocking chair.

"I don't know," she said, looking a little pale.

"What do you mean? Did the doctor find out what is wrong with you?" Henry walked over and placed his hands on her arms.

"Yes." Anna's face was unreadable.

"Anna, please tell me what is going on! Are you OK?"

"It depends."

"On what?" Henry was growing irritated.

"If you want to be a father or not."

"A father? What?" Henry stared at Anna, not comprehending until she finally smiled.

"I'm with child, Henry. You're going to be a father!"

Henry's mouth fell open, and he scooped her up high in the air and spun her in a circle on the porch. "I can't believe it!"

"Henry, you might want to be a little more gentle," Anna said, still smiling.

"Oh, I'm sorry! Did I hurt you? Did I hurt the baby?" Henry quickly set her back down and cautiously touched her stomach.

"No, silly. We're fine. I just didn't want you to get too carried away."

Henry hugged her, careful not to squeeze her stomach too tight, and kissed her. "This is the most wonderful news ever!"

"I am so glad that you're happy. We're having a child!" Anna gazed at Henry and, for the first time ever, saw tears in his eyes.

Henry quickly wiped the tears away. "When? When will it be here?"

"In the winter. Around eight months, he thought."

"Do you need to go lie down and rest?" Henry asked, still shaking with excitement.

"For eight months?" Anna laughed. "I'm fine. I can do anything I want, at least for most of that time."

"I love you...and our baby!" Henry kissed her again.

***

A month later, Henry looked up from working in the garden

to see a man on horseback enter the gate and ride slowly down the hill toward him. He dropped the hoe and placed one hand on the handle of his flintlock and the other on his dagger. He glanced quickly at the house to make sure Anna was inside. He occasionally had visitors from town, but this didn't look like anyone he knew.

"Hello, Henry. I'm Owen, in case you don't remember," the man said as he dismounted from the horse.

Henry recognized the young man that had sailed from New Orleans with him. "What are you doing here? How did you find me?" Henry's face instantly reddened with anger. He involuntarily clenched his fists.

"I mean you no offense, sir. I have news for you."

"What news could you possibly have for me?"

"It's about your brother."

Henry grabbed Owen by his waistcoat with both hands and pulled him close. "I have no brother! And you'd better be riding back from wherever you came."

The blood drained from Owen's face. He swallowed hard but continued, "Your brother James is going to be hanged in Jackson Square at dawn two weeks from today. He has been charged with aiding in piracy and treason against the United States."

Henry could barely control his rage. He shoved Owen's chest, sending him sprawling to the ground. He rushed forward and stood over Owen before he had even come to rest. He bent down, grabbed his waistcoat, and jerked him back to his feet. His dagger was instantly in his hand and the point an inch from Owen's throat. "Tell me everything, starting from when we landed in Pascagoula!"

Owen's legs shook as he looked from the dagger's point to Henry's enraged face. "I bought a horse and followed the river north out of town. I visited my family, who live in a town a few hours north of there. They mentioned a town called River Junction and said it was a good area for farming. So, I came up here a couple of days later."

"Explain the rest!" Henry said impatiently. He touched the

point of the blade to Owen's skin.

Owen tried to lean his head back to take some pressure off the sharp dagger point. "I was in the River House having supper one night. You were there, telling your stories again. I went upstairs to my room when John closed the place up. A little bit later, I started to come back downstairs so I could go out and take a walk, as I was not sleepy. Halfway down the stairs, I happened to overhear you and John talking. I returned to my room, but not before I heard who you both were."

"Hang me!" Henry shouted, using the phrase that Bloodstone had used often over the years. "And you went and told the navy!" Henry pulled the dagger back and leveled it at Owen's heart.

"No! No, sir!" Owen shouted back. When Henry relaxed his arm a little, Owen continued. "After spending a few days here, I returned to New Orleans. I still wasn't sure about moving or farming. A couple of weeks ago, I was in the Treasure Cove and overheard Captain Smith and his officers talking about James, the Hawk, and Lafitte. I don't know how they found out. I'm guessing if I overheard you, maybe someone else did too. I came back here as soon as possible to warn you."

Henry stared intently at the trembling man before him. A layer of sweat covered Owen's face. "You seem to overhear a lot."

"A bad habit, I guess, sir."

"So, you swear to me you had nothing to do with this, and you're not setting me up for a trap?"

"No, sir! You and John seem like nice men that have left your wicked ways behind. I just wanted to let you know. Maybe you can figure out a way to save your brother like you did Bloodstone at Port Royal."

Henry ignored Owen's attempt at flattery. "Where is James now?"

"I assume they're keeping him in the brig at Pensacola until time to sail to New Orleans. I heard that Commodore Cord would personally be sailing with him and overseeing his hanging." Owen was visibly more relaxed now.

"If you're being honest, I thank you for the warning. If you are lying to me and had something to do with this, I will personally put a bullet into your skull. Now, please leave my land."

Owen climbed back onto his horse and rode back up the hill and back through the gate, a grin upon his face.

Anna walked up to Henry after the man had disappeared.

"Did you hear any of that?" Henry asked.

"Yes," she said softly and hugged him. "I heard and saw everything from the porch. What are you going to do?"

"I don't know," Henry said. His mind was racing. He was almost sure it was a trap. He was also confident that James would die either way. He had finally found happiness and accepted his new life with the woman he loved. And they had a child on the way.

"You know it's a trap. They'll kill both of you." Tears were flowing down her cheeks.

"It probably is, and that coward Owen probably betrayed me. But it doesn't mean we both have to die."

"The entire navy wants you both dead! You cannot just walk in and rescue James."

"I've spent my whole life figuring ways out of impossible situations. If I do nothing, James will die, and they will come for me. They know where I am, Anna." Henry turned away and cursed under his breath.

"Then we just need to leave now! We can go somewhere else and start over. We have money. They cannot search the entire country. Owen said it was two weeks before they would hang him."

Henry thought deeply as he watched the cattle meander about the lower pasture. "James saved my life. He is the reason we are even here. He wouldn't be facing death if he hadn't agreed to help us. How can I just run off and let him die for saving me?"

Anna cried openly now and covered her face with her hands. "He knew the risks!" she sobbed. "Now, you'll get yourself killed, leave me widowed and your child fatherless, for nothing?"

"If I go, it won't be to go to my death. I won't try to save James unless I think we can both survive. I need to go talk to Je…John. I'll be back in a few hours." He quickly kissed her wet cheek and strode to the barn to get Tempest.

***

John sat at the end of the big table, with a couple of stacks of papers in front of him. Henry guessed he read the look on his face and decided to skip the small talk. "Have a seat and tell me about it."

Henry recounted his encounter with Owen. John shook his head silently when Henry finished. "Not a good situation."

"No. I'm not sure if even the Hawk can get out of this one."

"You're not thinking about trying to rescue him, are you? You know that's what they want you to do."

"I'm sure it's a trap, but I have no doubt they will kill James either way and then come after me. After *us*."

John rubbed his fingers through his thick hair and cursed. "I hadn't thought about that. They could sail a couple of sloops up the river and blast this town to pieces."

"And they will….unless we do something about it," Henry said.

"And just what could we do?"

"Rescue James. Kill Commodore Cord, Captain Smith, Owen, and anyone else in our way. That will disrupt the squadron for a while. In the meantime, we will find another place to settle. They won't find us again."

"Look, I know you have pulled off some daring deeds, but not against the full force of the squadron when they're expecting it," John said bluntly.

Henry stood up and began pacing about his end of the room. A large hand-drawn map of the southern United States and Spanish Main was on the wall beside the table. He walked over to it and studied it thoughtfully. "But what are they expecting?"

"What do you mean?" John stood up and joined Henry.

"Are they expecting me to arrive in New Orleans or attack them en route?" Henry pointed to the map. "They're in Pensacola now, so they'll probably allow time for a three-day voyage. The quickest route is to pass right along in front of this chain of islands and our old hideout, the Rock. I know every inch of those islands and the surrounding water. I'm betting they're not expecting me to have a crew or ship. They'll think I'll just try a daring rescue similar to the one in Port Royal."

John studied the map. "There would be several good places to hit them, especially with you knowing those islands. But how would you get a ship and crew in two weeks?"

"I'd have to get to New Orleans quickly and see if I could find any of my old crew. I would also like to ask if I could recruit you and your men. We could either buy or steal a ship or two."

John shook his head. "I'm afraid me and my men are too old for that. And my men all have families now. Although I'm sure you'll have a great plan, I just don't know if you can round up enough men to take down whatever they're sailing to New Orleans. Chances are, they'll have more than one ship, and all will be fully manned. I'll talk to the men, but I wouldn't count on our help."

"I'm sorry to hear that. But I have no choice. I couldn't live knowing that I sent my brother to the gallows for giving me my freedom. Can you do two things for me?"

"Anything."

"Look after Anna and my child if I don't come back. And I'll need Bart to get me down to Pascagoula."

"Of course, friend. I wish I could be there with you," John said sincerely.

"Me too. Me too."

"But I might be able to help you in other ways. Get your thoughts and plan together and come back to see me." He shook Henry's hand heartily and clapped him on the back as he left.

***

Anna was in bed but awake when he reached the house and sat up as soon as he entered the room. "Tell me you've decided not to go." Her eyes and nose were red from crying.

"Anna, I have to." Henry removed his clothes and climbed

into bed.

"Then take me with you."

"That's absurd!"

"I can shoot a gun nearly as well as you," she protested.

"First, you are pregnant. Second, shooting is only part of it. I will have to get onto James's ship and rescue him. There will be a lot of hand-to-hand fighting, and a petite, pregnant female is not cut out for swordplay."

"Then I'll stay on your ship while you get James. I can handle the helm, too, if you recall. Or put me in the crow's nest."

"Anna, I cannot take you. If something were to happen to me, you and our child would still have your entire lives in front of you. All of us dying would be pointless. They do not want you. You can live anywhere you want. It is just me, James, and Lafitte they want."

"Lafitte?" Anna asked.

Henry realized his slip of the tongue. It was too late now. "I'll tell you the whole story later, but John is really Jean Lafitte."

Growing up in New Orleans, Anna knew much about the infamous Lafitte, and the revelation didn't entirely shock her. It actually explained a lot. "Is Jean going with you at least?"

"It doesn't sound like it."

"Henry, look at me," she said, grabbing his chin and gently turning his head to face her. "Do you think you can save James and yourself too? Or are you planning on dying?"

Henry stared into her beautiful eyes for several moments. Tears welled up in the corners again, and her lips quivered. "I wouldn't go if I didn't think we had a chance."

"And you'll try to come back to me?"

"If any life is left in me, I will always return to you."

CHAPTER XXX

The sloop slid silently into the New Orleans dock three days before James was to be hanged. Hawk grinned as he read the name of the nearby West Indies Squadron schooner: USS *Grampus*. It was the same ship that had nearly foiled his plan to meet James at St. Thomas and had also been involved with the defeat and capture of the last famous pirate captain, Cofresi.

Bart, Levi, and Ferdinand had purchased the sloop a week prior. They had also learned that the *Grampus* spent a lot of time around New Orleans and was captained by Thomas Smith. Smith was the same captain who'd questioned Hawk that night at the Treasure Cove. Hawk finally remembered him as James's first mate in St. Thomas. If he were a betting man, he would say Owen Davis was one of Thomas's officers.

All the men on the sloop departed and dispersed in different directions. There appeared to be a number of sailors aboard the *Grampus*, their voices and laughter heard from the deck, but no one paid attention to the sloop. Hawk headed to an alehouse he had never been to before; he knew he couldn't return to the Treasure Cove. He took his time getting to his destination. He used many extra streets and alleys, frequently stopping to ensure he wasn't being followed. After an hour, he finally entered The Thirsty Pelican.

The tavern was far from Jackson Square and, as a result, wasn't very crowded. Hawk quickly surmised that the patrons were mostly local regulars. No one paid him much attention as he walked to a small round table in the far, dim corner. His chair was close to a man with a wide-brimmed hat pulled low sitting at the table beside him. Hawk could see the white hair sticking out from around the sides.

He waited a few minutes until the serving lady had brought him a pint of ale and checked on the man at the other table before he spoke. "Hello, old friend," he said softly. Both men's eyes were busy watching the rest of the patrons.

"A sight for sore eyes, you are," Jack replied.

Another mission Jean's men had completed was to find Jack. Luckily, he had stayed in the city after the pardon. They gave him a letter from Hawk that instructed him to round up as many men as he could and have them ready to sail on this night. It also set the time and place for this meeting.

"And the crew?" Hawk knew they didn't have time for pleasantries.

"Got Jimmy, Billy, Charles, Edward, and about seventy-five men. Mort was killed a few months back, breaking up a fight. Bones says he's retired for good."

Hawk silently cursed. He had hoped for at least a hundred. "Gonna be tough."

"Always is."

"Where are they?"

"Scattered about the taverns and gamin' houses. I have half a dozen runners stationed about. As soon as we're ready, I'll start 'em spreadin' the word. Can you share your plan?" Jack asked, grinning.

"The first part. If it doesn't go well, we won't have to worry about the second and third parts."

"I ain't goin' to lie; I'm a little bit excited!" Jack said, a little too loud.

Hawk gave him a scowl, then a wink, and revealed the first part of the plan.

***

It was close to midnight when the first man walked down the dock and boarded Hawk's sloop. The docks were still fairly busy this time of night since many of the sailors returned from the gambling houses, taverns, and brothels to sleep on their ships. Most couldn't afford a room for the night. Every few minutes, another person boarded the sloop.

The *Grampus* also had its fair share of returning, mostly drunk, sailors. Freshly promoted to lieutenant, Owen Davis was one of these men—although he was cold sober. He walked with a slow, deliberate stride, his chest puffed out. He wore his new promotion well and wanted to ensure everyone knew he was an officer of the squadron. Captain Smith had asked him to keep an eye on the crew and ship while he and several others stayed at the Treasure Cove. The *Grampus* had been docked at New Orleans with a full crew for the past week, just in case Hawk showed up early for James's execution.

Owen surveyed the dock area for several minutes before boarding his ship. He looked with disdain at the mostly drunken crew strewn about the deck, talking, sleeping, or passed out. Hopefully, they wouldn't be needed for action this night. He did have several sober soldiers, though, who had been forbidden to go into town, keeping watch on the docks. He went below deck to his cabin to get some sleep.

An unusual number of sailors continued to approach the docks, even after a dozen or more had boarded the sloop. The sentries on the *Grampus* took note of the activity but saw nothing to report. Most of the men were spread about the docks in small groups, and some milled around the various ships, likely just talking a bit before they boarded for sleep. It was a little unusual, but not against any laws.

An hour later, had it not been so dark, and had they paid more attention, the sentries would have noticed that a wall of armed men had formed in front of the entrance to the docks. They did notice the small bands starting to converge into one large group in front of their ship. The sentry on the bow leaned over the rail. "You men need to disperse!"

A man stepped out of the crowd and looked up at the sentry. "I need to speak to your captain."

"He is not onboard. You may speak to him in the light of day," the sentry replied. He now had his musket resting on the rail, although not pointing at the speaker yet.

"Then get me whoever is in charge—now."

The sentry wavered for a moment, unsure of the best course of action. He finally called out to one of the few conscious sailors and told him to fetch Owen.

A few minutes later, Owen appeared at the bow. "What is the meaning of this?" he demanded.

"Well, well. Mr. Owen Davis," the man on the docks said. He slid his hand down to the handle of his half-cocked flintlock.

"I am Lieutenant Owen Davis of the USS *Grampus* of the West Indies Squadron. Who are you?" Owen called down, straining to discern the speaker's face. Several other sailors now stood around Owen and the sentry.

"Impressive, Mr. Davis. I'm afraid your career is coming to a tragic end, though."

Owen retrieved a flintlock and leveled it at the speaker. "Who are you? And what is your purpose here?" he demanded, shaking slightly.

"It's Hawk, Owen. I told you a while back that I would put a bullet in your head if you had lied to or betrayed me. Owen, unlike you, I'm a man of my word." Hawk's movement was a blur. He drew his flintlock, fully cocked it, and fired it in less than half a second. A split second later, a hole appeared in Owen's forehead. Before his body had hit the ground, the men behind Hawk opened fire with their muskets on the sentry and other visible sailors.

The sailors sitting and laying across the deck of the *Grampus* suddenly came to life, staggered to their feet, and rushed to find weapons. Then two loud explosions rocked the ship, sending many back down to the deck. The sloop beside them had fired two cannons into the hull of their ship, right below the waterline. Before the sailors had recovered, the throng on the dock, led by Hawk, charged up the gangplank and onto the deck. Cutlasses flashed as they began attacking the stunned sailors.

As most of Hawk's men slaughtered the *Grampus's* crew, others began locking down the hatches that led to the lower decks. Hawk figured at least one hundred sailors were down below. Now they would stay below, with the hold quickly filling with water. As the battle wound down on the *Grampus*, shots erupted from the dock. Hawk looked over the rail to see the pirates blocking the docks firing upon a group rushing toward them. Hawk knew it had to be Captain Smith and his men.

After discharging their muskets and then flintlocks, the pirates fell back onto the docks and retreated to the sloop and the *Grampus*. They had killed a number of Captain Smith's men, but the survivors kept coming. Captain Smith and a half dozen officers stopped on the dock, some twenty yards from the ships, to reload their flintlocks. "You will finally hang, Hawk, and right beside your cowardly brother! Then I'll deal with your wife and Lafitte!" Captain Smith shouted.

Hawk grabbed a musket from the closest pirate. "Unfortunately, you won't be there to see it. Oh, and say hello to Bloodstone and Kragg for me." A flash of fire erupted from the end of the musket barrel. A second later, the ball struck Captain Smith in the chest, just as he had opened his mouth in retort. He fell backward into the men behind him. Before the men could react, two cannons erupted from the starboard side of the sloop, striking the dock right at their feet. The explosions tore through the sailors, sending them and their body parts flying in every direction.

The *Grampus* sailed out first. The sloop followed but not before firing the remaining three port cannons at the navy sloop docked on the other side of the *Grampus*. All three shots hit, close to the waterline. A few muskets fired from that ship and the remaining officers on the dock, but the balls flew harmlessly overhead or struck the water.

Hawk strode over to the first hatch and listened briefly to the shouts and commotion from the lower deck. Finally, he called them, "I'm going to crack the hatch open, and you will pass all your weapons through it. Then you will start pumping water and patching holes. If not, you will be the first to drown."

"And if we do what you ask?" a voice called up.

"I'll set you free on the first island we come to, where you'll most like be picked up soon after. I am the Hawk, and you have my word."

Hawk heard whispering and muffled talking down below for a moment. "OK. Open the hatch," said a sailor. The hatch slowly raised, and the weapons were tossed into a pile on the deck.

"What are you goin' to do with them?" Jack asked as Hawk walked about inspecting the ship and speaking to his old crewmembers.

"Just as I said."

"Set them free? So they can go back to tryin' to kill us?"

"They'll be unarmed. And our fight will be over one way or another before they're rescued. Remember, Jack, this is a one-time voyage. We're not back in the pirating business."

"Aye, Cap'n." Jack spat and walked away.

"Good to see you again, Hawk," Billy said as he and Jimmy came rushing over.

"Same here. You boys been keeping out of trouble?"

"Reasonably so, sir. Now, what's the plan?"

"We'll discuss that a little later. First, we need to get to open sea and make sure this bucket isn't going to sink."

After Hawk was confident both ships were under control, he grabbed Billy and half a dozen men and opened one of the hatches. They descended the stairs with flintlocks in hand. Some fifty sailors were milling about the gun deck. They all stared at Hawk and the pirates, but none made a move to attack. Hawk and his men climbed through another hatch down to the next deck, crowded with another fifty men. A large group was taking turns manning two pumps, switching off to stay fresh. The rest were frantically repairing the two cannon ball holes in the hull. The water was still several inches deep on the deck, and Hawk was sure much deeper in the hold below. The holes were almost patched now, with a mixture of sail canvas, pitch, and boards.

A man dressed like an officer approached Hawk. "You are not going back on your word, are you?" he asked, his face pale and strained.

"Of course not. Just making sure you were living up to yours. I'm Hawk."

"First mate, Andrew Robinson."

"How's the hold?"

"Better. Most of the water was kept out of the magazine, which I assume is what you're asking."

"Good," Hawk nodded. Despite him being a naval officer, he liked Andrew.

"Sir, may I ask you something?" Andrew said, shifting his feet nervously.

"Go ahead."

"Why did you do this?"

"What do you mean?" Hawk asked.

"Why did you return to pirating? Why did you steal this ship?"

"To save my brother, of course."

"Your brother?"

"James Wellington. He is to hang three days from now in New Orleans for helping me escape."

Andrew wrinkled his brows together. "I have heard nothing of this. If Lieutenant Davis knew, he never shared with his crew.

"You weren't stationed there in preparation for the hanging?"

"I do not think so, sir. We were told that the Hawk was alive and might be heading back to New Orleans. That is all."

"What's that mean?" Billy asked Hawk.

"With snakes like Davis and Smith, it's hard to say. Something is amiss, though. Did Owen say anything else about me or James?" Hawk asked Andrew.

"Not that I heard, sir. Just that Hawk was alive and trying to gather up a crew and ship."

"I appreciate your honesty, Andrew. I'll let you know when we've reached a suitable island." Hawk turned and led his men back to the upper deck. His mind was desperately trying to figure out what he was missing with the squadron's plan.

***

A few hours later, the *Grampus* began to slow. Hawk, Jack, Jimmy, and Billy wrapped up their strategy meeting and returned to the main deck. The sky glowed pink in the predawn light, and the sun was soon to rise in front of them. As the ship approached a small island, they all noticed the sails being lowered to half-mast. The island, part of a small chain of islands directly east of New Orleans, was mostly sand with a patch of palm trees and some scrub in the middle. A few minutes later, Jack gave the order to drop anchor. The ship was as close to the shore as possible without risking getting stuck in the sand. A longboat was quickly lowered to the water, with rope ladders thrown over the rail above it.

Hawk flung the closest hatch open. "We're here."

The sailors began climbing up the ladder and moving toward the starboard rail. The pirates had retreated to open the middle of the main deck. Soon, close to a hundred sailors stood crowded on the deck. First mate Andrew moved through the throng to stand before Hawk.

"I appreciate you saving us from sinking," said Hawk. "I have no issue with any of you. Several ships pass these islands daily, so if you build a fire on the beach, you'll be rescued before dark."

The sailors all stood in place, most looking toward their first mate, who was in charge since they had no captain or lieutenant. Andrew finally cleared his throat and spoke. "Captain Hawk, my men and I talked below deck. I told them about your situation. We all know and respect Captain Wellington, and most of us have served with him at one time or another. If he is to be hanged, we are not in agreement with it."

"I thank you, but we need to let you off so we can get to sailing. Time is not a luxury we have right now."

"But you misunderstand me. A number of us have decided we want to sail with you. There is definitely some kind of treachery in the works, and Lieutenant Davis and Captain Smith were a part of it. They have misled and used us without our knowledge and agreement. That is something we cannot tolerate. We would rather sail with you and try to save James than have to return to Commodore Cord. I do not know about all your past deeds, but this campaign is a just one."

Hawk glanced back at Jack and then Billy. Both men shrugged, and Hawk turned back to the sailor. It could all be part of Captain Smith's plan, but Hawk had survived well on his ability to read people. He trusted Andrew. "Any that want to stay are welcome. Just know this mission is treacherous, and many of us won't survive. The ones that do might face the gallows or be forced to disappear forever."

Andrew turned to his crew. "Anyone that wants to leave, leave now." A line of sailors slowly formed and climbed over the rail and down the rope ladders to the boat below. When it was full, the boat was rowed to shore. All climbed out except the rowers, and they returned to the ship. After several trips, about half the crewmembers remained on the *Grampus,* and half were on the island. Hawk grinned. An extra fifty men might just be the break he needed.

***

The two ships sailed uneventfully to the Rock. The trees that used to block and hide the harbor were long gone. The *Grampus* sailed halfway into the lagoon and the sloop a little farther in. Both anchored, and pirates and sailors began setting about the many tasks that had to be done on the ships and the shore. It would be sometime that night or the next day when the Squadron ships passed.

After having the name of the USS *Grampus* painted over and *Anna* painted in its place, Hawk, Billy, Jack, and Andrew walked from the beach onto the arm of land that protected the lagoon from the sea. Behind them, three-dozen pirates struggled to move the two large thirty-two-pounder cannon barrels, their bases, shot, and powder. The narrow strip of land peaked into a high ridge that ran the entire length, protecting the cove from both sight and storms. An old, overgrown trail followed the ridge, where the pirates used to keep lookout for Bloodstone to return from voyages.

"The biggest flaw in my plan is what I don't know," Hawk

said to the group as they worked to widen the trail with their cutlasses. "I don't know whether they'll be in one ship or two or three. I know they'll pass on this side of the island, but I don't know how far out they'll be. I also don't know whether they'll sail through today or tonight."

"I assume you have guesses for each?" Jack asked, panting from the exertion.

"Of course. I think they'll be in two ships, just in case the Hawk attacks. Three is doubtful. They know I won't have had enough time to gather a large crew, so I'll either have a medium size ship or two small ones. I think they'll hug these islands fairly close. They may even want to encourage an attack. Cord is a cocky devil, and I think they'll pass during the day. Night would be too much of an advantage for an attacker."

"How often are your guesses correct?" Andrew asked.

"Have you heard of the Hawk before?" Billy asked, eliciting laughter from the pirates.

Two hours later, the two cannons were set in their mounts on top of the ridge, shooting lanes were cut, and the guns were sighted in at about five hundred yards. The thirty-two-pounders had a longer range than most ships' cannons. A crew of four men stayed behind with each.

CHAPTER XXXI

Captain James Wellington stood on the bow of the frigate USS *Congress*. Beside him stood his old captain, the man who had raised him, Commodore Nathaniel Cord. James's mind had been reeling since they had left Pensacola. He had been preparing to set sail on his ship, the USS *Avenger*, when the commodore boarded and entered his cabin. He told him spies caught wind that Hawk was alive and gathering a crew. Cord said they had to sail immediately toward New Orleans in anticipation that Hawk would steal a ship somewhere between there and Mississippi. Mississippi was where he was rumored to have been hiding out.

The commodore had acted strange to him ever since. He didn't accuse him of letting Hawk go. He just said Hawk must have survived somehow. He also made James ride on his flagship, the *Congress*, explaining that Hawk might come after the *Avenger*, seeking revenge on James. The *Avenger* sailed a few hundred yards behind them. Each ship had a full crew of over three hundred men. Cord said that Captain Smith was on the *Grampus*, watching the docks at New Orleans in case Hawk showed up there. Hopefully, they would catch the pirate somewhere in between.

It wasn't hard for James to act surprised when he heard the news—he was in shock. He couldn't believe Henry would go back on his word, leave the woman he loved, and return to pirating. He refused to believe it. Yet something had to be going on for the commodore to have organized the mission. James had risked his career and life to free his brother. If Henry had gone back to pirating, James would have to personally stop him. More innocent men would not die because of his mistake and his brother's treachery.

Cord and James shared a spyglass and studied the start of the barrier islands off the coast of Mississippi, the first one just coming into sight on the horizon. It was midday on a clear, sunny, beautiful day. They were tacking into the wind, so their speed was slow and steady. On one of the barrier islands some years ago, they had found an old fort that had most likely been used by Bloodstone and Hawk—the infamous Rock. They had destroyed it, but Cord thought Hawk might return to that area while he mobilized a new crew.

"Don't you think we're sailing a little close?" James asked, accepting the spyglass from Cord.

"If he is there, I want him to attack. Per my sources, he has only had two weeks to try to muster a crew and ship. He will be no match for two fully armed and manned frigates. We will sail on to New Orleans if he does not attack."

"A lot of people have died from underestimating Hawk."

"I am not underestimating him. But bravery and cunning can only carry him so far. He will bear the full brunt of the United States Navy. If not today, soon. And this time, he *will* die," Cord said firmly and walked away.

James spotted the sails in the spyglass about the same time the topman in the crow's nest shouted, "Sail ho." He saw only two masts on what he could now discern was a sloop, sailing in their direction with the wind in its sails. It was farther south of them, though.

Cord quickly rejoined him on the bow. James handed him the spyglass, and Cord studied the approaching ship keenly. "What do you make of it?" he asked James.

"Looks like a merchant sloop, maybe ten guns, small crew visible. Not likely to be Hawk."

Cord scanned the horizon and the islands to the starboard. "Not likely to be Hawk but could be part of one of his infamous traps."

James knew both of the squadron ships had fifty cannons

and full crews. A sloop like the one approaching wouldn't last but a few minutes in a cannon duel. But against the Hawk, they had to be prepared for anything.

"Mr. Johnson, have everyone look alive and put the gun crews on standby. Get word to Captain Scott on the *Avenger*," Cord ordered.

First mate, Isaac Johnson, a middle-aged, burly sailor, turned and went about shouting orders to the men on the main deck and to the topman, and then he disappeared through a hatch. The topman turned to the trailing ship and flashed a series of hand gestures to his counterpart on the *Avenger*. James and Cord continued to study the quickly approaching sloop. "Should we hail it?" James asked.

Cord was silent for a few seconds. "No. That would just further play into a trap. Let it make the first move."

The sloop soon sailed past them, and several sailors on its deck waved. Once the sloop had cleared their ship, James and Cord finally turned back around, dismissing it as not a threat. They didn't see it ever so lightly alter its course toward the *Avenger*.

James followed Cord to the ship's starboard side and studied the island they were coming alongside. It was the island they thought had been the infamous Rock. Nothing moved on or around it. James was a little surprised. If Hawk were going to make a move before New Orleans, it would probably be here. The island had a protected harbor that was hard to spot from the sea.

Just when the stern of the *Congress* cleared the Rock and James began scanning farther ahead, cannon fire erupted. He quickly turned back to the island and saw smoke rising from the bushes on a ridge in front of the harbor. Screams and yells sounded in the distance on the *Avenger*. A few seconds later, he saw a flash of fire and heard a second cannon erupt. Smoke billowed from the *Avenger*.

***

Captain Daniel Scott of the *Avenger* had been at the port rail, watching the sloop angle toward them and wondering whether to fire a shot across their bow, when he felt the impact and heard the splintering of wood, screams, and the roar of a cannon. It had come from the starboard side, though. He quickly sprinted across the deck to see the smoke drifting from the trees and bushes on the island they were just coming upon. The shot had hit somewhere below the main deck. Before even issuing an order, he saw the flash of fire and felt another impact low in the hull, followed by the boom. "Return fire!" he yelled. His command was quickly relayed below deck.

About the time he imagined the cannon fuses were lit below on the gun deck, all five cannons on the port side of the sloop fired. One ball tore through the mainsail and broke the main boom in half; an explosion set the sail on fire. Another shot struck the bow, exploding and sending splinters and chunks of wood scattering into nearby sailors. A third shot exploded on the stern, sending bodies flying. The *Avenger's* navigator was one of those seriously injured. A fourth shot sailed harmlessly over the deck. The fifth struck a gunport, blowing a hole in the hull and incapacitating a gun crew.

The starboard cannons of the *Avenger* fired, but the rocking of the ship from the four cannon strikes made them wildly inaccurate. They were also shooting at drifting smoke and not hard targets. The balls hit different parts of the finger of land, some throwing up dirt and sand and others crashing through the trees. Captain Scott wouldn't know if they hit their attackers unless the cannons didn't fire again. He turned to order the port cannons to fire on the sloop, but with the wind and ship's speed, it was already past.

A moment later, he had his answer. The first cannon on the island fired again, once more striking right at the waterline below the gun deck. A few seconds later, the second one fired, striking toward the bow of the gun deck. The balls didn't explode but were large and heavy and did damage.

"They're club hauling!" Scott's first mate, Alexander Nelson, yelled. He now manned the helm for the injured navigator.

The captain rushed back to the stern to see the sloop drop

an anchor and come about hard to port. The sloop turned 180 degrees until its starboard cannons faced the rear quarter of his ship. He knew none of his guns could hit it unless he turned the entire ship. He ordered all available hands to fire at the sloop with their muskets, a mostly ineffective strategy with only a handful of sailors on the main deck of the fast-moving ship. The five sloop cannons roared, raining more explosive and ball and chain shots onto his ship. One shot missed and landed harmlessly in the sea. Two exploded on the main deck, causing more injury and death. One tore through the main mast rigging, further debilitating the vessel. The last shot was the most serious—apparently striking the rudder. Alexander confirmed it a moment later. "I can hardly steer!"

***

"Come about!" Cord yelled, sprinting from the bow of the *Congress* to the helm. "Come about hard!"

James followed quickly after him. By this time, they were well past the Rock and the battle behind. The *Avenger* had apparently suffered damage to her sails, only increasing the distance. They didn't know exactly what was happening on the *Avenger*, but they knew the ship was getting attacked from the shore and apparently from the sloop too. Their large ship would take several minutes to turn completely and start heading back toward the battle.

James and Cord rushed back to the stern as the big ship turned to see what they were sailing into. "Hawk!" Cord shouted.

James quickly spotted the large schooner that had emerged from the harbor, apparently just after they had passed, and was turned leeward, fast approaching the *Avenger*. The *Avenger* had reloaded and fired again at the cannons on the shore. Reloading would take a minute or more, and they didn't have that much time before the new foe reached them. The schooner sailed directly toward the bow of the larger frigate. *Why, Henry?*

***

Captain Scott was quickly overwhelmed. He usually sailed a much smaller ship and had limited combat experience. His few encounters had been against single ships that he clearly outgunned. The commodore had asked him to captain the *Avenger* only a few days before. The plan had been for both ships to attack Hawk, who would most likely be on a much smaller ship. Now he was getting attacked on two fronts. The sloop was small, and apparently, only two cannons were on shore, but Scott was paralyzed. He couldn't steer the ship now, so he couldn't turn to get his cannons aimed at the sloop. And even if he could, he then wouldn't be able to fire at the shore.

"Captain, enemy schooner, coming hard to bow!" Alexander shouted.

Captain Scott shook his head and rushed across the body-littered deck to the bow. He stared in shock at the ship that approached. It appeared like one of the squadron's own schooners. His ship was hardly moving into the wind, with the loss of the rudder and so many sails. On the other hand, the schooner was fully rigged, with the wind in its sails. It was sailing at an angle, preventing Scott from hitting it with any cannons yet. He finally shouted orders to ready the starboard cannons and prepare for a broadside against it. At least with the schooner beside them, the cannons on shore wouldn't be a threat.

***

Hawk stood aboard the bow of the *Anna*, a musket in hand. All his men were either on the running rigging lines or lining the starboard rail, except for Edward, who was at the helm. Hawk could have sailed right beside the big frigate and fired a point-blank broadside. It might have even sunk the ship. But that wasn't the plan. He needed the larger ship to face the *Congress.*

"Fire!" Hawk called as soon as the ship was in range. All the pirates and the newly joined navy sailors fired muskets into the sailors rushing to the bow of the *Avenger*. The musket balls tore through the scrambling sailors, most finding targets. A few of the remaining sailors returned fire, but only one pirate was wounded in the arm. "Strike the sails!" yelled Hawk.

Edward steered directly into the frigate, the two bows

scraping together until the *Anna* ground to a halt against the *Avenger*. "Drop anchor," Hawk shouted. "Grenadoes and grapple!" He lit and tossed his own grenadoe onto the deck of the frigate. It was joined by a couple of dozen more from his crew. Explosions and screams rang out across the deck of the *Avenger*.

No sailors were nearby to stop the grappling hooks from catching the railing. Pirates swung and dropped onto the deck of the *Avenger* as others scampered up the grappling lines and climbed over the railing. The sailors tried to rush forward to repel the attack, but the pirates opened fire with their flintlocks and then charged with their cutlasses.

**

No one was left on the stern of the ship to notice the two dozen pirates, led by Billy, climb from the sloop over the stern rail of the *Avenger*. The sloop had raised anchor, caught the floundering ship, and used grappling lines to board. The pirates spread out and sought out the hatches. Each tossed a stinkpot onto the gun deck below, shut the hatches, and quickly chained them closed. They then fired their flintlocks into the backs of the sailors trying to hold off Hawk and the other pirates.

**

"Take some wind out!" Cord shouted onboard the *Congress*.

James had just watched in horror as the schooner sailed into the *Avenger* and the pirates boarded. He knew that Captain Scott was greatly overmatched. The pirates had killed a fair share of sailors, but probably two hundred were still alive on the ship. The already damaged ship could sink if the *Congress* opened fire with its cannons, killing all aboard. Plus, they couldn't be sure Hawk didn't have any other tricks up his sleeve.

As they drew closer, James recognized Hawk's schooner, the *Anna*. "The *Grampus*!" That probably meant that Captain Smith and Lieutenant Davis were dead, as well as their crew.

"I hate that pirate!" said Cord.

"What's your plan?" James asked, watching in disbelief as Hawk and his men attacked the *Avenger's* crew.

"I think we sail to the port side of the *Avenger* and pick off as many pirates as possible. If we see the pirates are taking the ship or its cannons, we sink it."

"Even with sailors still alive?" James asked in surprise.

"If need be. Hawk will not win or escape today."

***

Hawk fought like a man possessed. As he feared, James and Cord were on the other ship. He knew they had to take the *Avenger* as quickly as possible. He hoped to convince as many of the crew as possible to surrender. That would keep Cord from sinking the ship. He would have to come aboard, try to kill the pirates, and retake it. That's where the plan became murky. The pirates would be significantly outnumbered, and Hawk had no idea where James would be or how to get to him. He thought he might try the same move he did in the first battle with Cord, climbing in through a cannon port, but he was reasonably confident Cord would be ready for it. All he could do now was fight and hope that fate, or God, would give him some assistance.

***

"Commodore, we cannot fire upon our own ship while there are still over a hundred sailors alive onboard," James said as the *Congress* neared the bow of the other frigate. "Word of that would spread straight to the president. I say we fire a few volleys and then board the *Avenger*. We have three hundred men, plus whoever is left over there. It looks like Hawk barely has one hundred."

Cord swore under his breath. "Very well. Bring all hands to the main deck except for two dozen. They'll stay below in case anyone tries to climb in through a gun port. And James, I have a special task for you."

The orders were given for the *Congress* to sail broadside to the *Avenger*, close enough to grapple when the time was right. Sailors began streaming up through the hatches, and soon, the deck was packed by most of the three hundred men, musket's ready. Cord and James watched the battle rage on the other ship for several minutes. The pirates were outnumbered, but they were skilled and vicious fighters. The entire naval crew wasn't on the main deck, however. Something must be keeping the men below deck. They also noticed the sloop moored against the stern of the *Avenger*, apparently now empty.

"There's the coward!" Cord cried out, pointing to the blond-haired pirate currently engaged with Captain Scott. Hawk's blade was a silver blur as it rained down upon the severely overmatched captain. "Give me your musket," Cord demanded of the closest sailor.

James stared at Cord in surprise. Cord had never been a hands-on commander, preferring to stay back and direct the action. Then Cord handed the musket to him.

"When Scott falls, kill Hawk. That is an easy shot for you. Hit him in his cold, black heart. You can redeem yourself for letting him escape last time."

James clutched the musket and stared from it to Hawk and Scott. It would be an easy shot, and he had sworn to himself that he would kill Hawk if he ever returned to pirating. But although Hawk had apparently returned and would send many innocent men to their deaths today, James couldn't bring himself to shoot him. First, Hawk had no chance to defend himself. He deserved better than to be shot unaware from a distance. Second, James still wondered the true reason Hawk had returned. He wanted a chance to talk to his brother face-to-face and hear what he had to say before he issued a death sentence.

"What is the matter, James? You shot him once before, correct?"

"Yes…sir. It's just…I don't like the idea of shooting him like a coward from a distance. Let me board and face him man to man."

"You have tried hand-to-hand before. Obviously, that did not work. Let me put it to you a different way. Shoot and kill your brother, or you will hang for treason for aiding his escape the last time and now for refusing a direct order. And Hawk will still die by one of these other sailor's bullets."

James realized that Cord did suspect he let Hawk go and knew they were brothers. He also surmised that this was probably part of Cord's plan all along—to force him to kill his brother. If he didn't shoot him, he had no doubt he would die, as well as Hawk. Reluctantly, he placed the musket's barrel on the rail and cocked the hammer. He leaned down behind it and put the bead on the front of the barrel onto the back of Scott. Scott's body was blocking all but Hawk's head. But Hawk was wearing Scott down, and it was only a matter of time before he fell. Then Hawk would be an unobstructed target.

James's heart pounded as he watched Hawk leap back to dodge a desperate swing from Scott. As Scott's sword swung harmlessly past, Hawk stepped forward and jabbed his blade forward. The blade's tip momentarily appeared through the back of Scott's blue jacket. The captain looked down at the sword, and then the tip disappeared as Hawk withdrew it. The captain dropped to his knees and slowly toppled forward. Hawk stood over him for a second, bloody sword in hand, presenting a dream shot for any marksman.

"God be with us both," James whispered. He slowly exhaled as he squeezed the trigger. The shot hit Hawk high in his left breast, knocking him back a step. He looked up, and his eyes instantly found James's, despite the throng of sailors surrounding him. Hawk's face was one of total shock. But something made James think it was shock for more than just getting shot. Hawk mouthed something and then collapsed onto the deck.

"Now, was that so hard?" Cord snatched the smoking musket back from a shaken James. "Men, take this traitor and lash him tightly to the main mast," Cord ordered the nearby sailors. He turned back to James. "We will talk later."

James couldn't move or even speak as his cutlass and flintlock were quickly removed, and the rough hands of four nearby sailors half dragged him to the main mast. They quickly tied him to the mast so tightly that he couldn't move his upper body at all. He could only helplessly watch the battle unfold.

CHAPTER XXXII

The remaining pirates and their ally sailors, led by Jack, quickly resumed the battle. Ordinarily, losing their captain could demoralize a pirate crew, especially a captain like the Hawk. But these pirates and sailors knew that defeat would mean their deaths, either by sword or noose. There would be no surrender.

Soon, all four ships—*Anna, Avenger, Congress,* and the sloop, were all lashed together. The sailors on the *Avenger* were still losing the battle with the desperate pirates. It hurt that so many of their companions were trapped below deck. Their captain had been killed, and they would probably have surrendered if not for the *Congress* and its fresh soldiers streaming onboard. Very quickly, sailors packed the deck, and slowly the ebb of the battle changed. The mass of bodies pressed the pirates back toward the rail.

***

No one from either ship noticed yet another sloop approaching fast with the wind. It had rounded the western edge of the Rock about the same time the Congress came alongside the *Avenger*. It lowered its sails and coasted silently alongside the *Congress*. A small group of men quickly threw their grappling lines and climbed over the railing of the larger frigate. A hundred sailors were still on board, but all were pressed around the far rail, either looking for musket shots or waiting their turn to enter the fray.

The men crouched and ran to the main mast. The leader drew his dirk and quickly cut the ropes binding James. James stared at the man in stunned silence. "James Wellington?" the man asked, with a French accent.

"Uh, yes. But who are you?"

"Jean Lafitte, sir. Here to rescue you."

***

Hawk opened his eyes. He halfway expected to find he was in hell, or possibly heaven. But instead, he stared at the feet of his crew, shuffling about the bloodstained deck battling against a horde of sailors. Hawk's chest and shoulder ached and throbbed, and his left arm was probably unusable. He looked down at his blood-soaked shirt. He wasn't sure why he was still alive or how long he would be, but he was. The shot must have hit above his heart. He slowly climbed to his feet, grasping the rail for a moment until the deck quit spinning and the darkness in his eyes retreated.

He reached down and grabbed a cutlass lying on the deck. He realized that the sailors from the *Congress* had apparently boarded the ship. His crew had been decimated, with only a small, bloody, exhausted group left surrounding him, pressed from three sides. He inhaled a deep, painful breath, tried to ignore the pain, and charged into the battle. "The Hawk lives!" he shouted.

The pirates rallied one last impossible time at the sight of their bloodied leader. Hawk's left arm hung uselessly by his side, but the cutlass danced in his right. For a moment, the pirates pushed their attackers back—but only for a moment. The sheer weight of the sailors once again pressed against them. Soon, not more than two dozen pirates remained.

Then, a loud sound rang out over the battle. It was a horn blast. The combatants continued to battle until the horn sounded two more times. Slowly, the swordplay ceased, and both sides sought the source. The navy sailors slowly parted, all the way back to the deck of the *Congress*.

Commodore Cord dropped the horn and strode confidently through the middle of his troops. His lip curled up as he stepped over bodies and pools of blood. His uniform was still pristine, and he appeared more like he was at a formal ball than in the middle of one of the greatest battles in the history of piracy. He casually drew his rapier and headed straight toward the bloodied pirate captain.

The pirates also moved back along both sides of the rail, leaving the two men facing each other. "You seem to have many lives, Mr. Hawk," Commodore Cord said loudly, stopping six feet from the famous pirate captain.

"Never enough, apparently," Hawk replied wearily. He leaned forward with his right fist resting on his right knee, sword still in hand.

"No. Unfortunately for you, this will be the last. I will finish the job your bungling, traitorous brother has failed at—twice. I do propose a deal, though."

"Let's hear it."

"I don't want any more bloodshed. But you and your men know you have no chance to win this battle. You all will definitely die. So, I propose that you and I duel to the death. If I win, your remaining crew, and your brother, James, will stand trial for their crimes. A fair judge will decide their fate."

"And if I win?"

Cord laughed. "If you win, my crew will let you, James, and your remaining men go free. If any of you return to piracy, I'm sure my successor will see you all receive a quick death."

Hawk glanced over at Jack, who stood bloodied from head to toe. Jack stared at him weakly, expressionless. Hawk then looked from Billy to Andrew on the other side. They appeared about the same as Jack and were also too exhausted to respond. Hawk didn't trust Cord, but Cord was right. They couldn't survive much longer. And he had no more "Hawk miracles." He also knew that if Cord had any skill with his rapier, the naval officer would kill him. Hawk only had one good arm and was exhausted. But that was the best chance he could give his crew. Maybe some could claim he had forced them into piracy at their trial, especially the sailors. He thought of Anna and his unborn child for a moment. He silently told Anna he loved her and to take good care of their child. Then he told her goodbye.

"Let's do it," Hawk said to Cord.

***

James stared incredulously at the dead man that had just rescued him. Lafitte and his men were pirates, but he faced certain hanging if he stayed aboard the *Congress.* He let the men escort him to the far rail, and they all climbed back down to the sloop's deck. He saw one pirate high up in the crow's nest and only a handful on the deck. He assumed more were below deck manning the cannons.

"Ready the guns!" Lafitte yelled through the closest open hatch. The grappling lines were quickly removed, and the sloop was pushed away from the frigate.

***

The two combatants circled each other for a moment. The sailors were loud in their cheers for their commodore. The pirates were mostly silent, using the time to catch their breath. Hawk attacked first, suddenly swinging an overhand blow at Cord's head. He hoped Cord would try to block it with his thin blade. But Cord nimbly leaped to the side, flicking his sword out as Hawk's blade swung harmlessly past his other side. The rapier blade pierced Hawk in his good shoulder. The stab was quick and not very deep, but it hurt and drew blood. Hawk tried a quick backhand slash, but with the same result. Cord jumped back and jabbed his blade into Hawk's injured left shoulder, eliciting a grunt from Hawk.

Hawk fought valiantly but ineffectively. The commodore was quick, skilled, and, most importantly, fresh. His blade darted in and out, leaving bloody holes behind. Hawk was soon bleeding from half a dozen wounds, his shirt soaked with blood. Each wound not only hurt but also sapped more strength. He became slower and wilder with his attacks. For the first time in his life, he knew he couldn't win a fight—or even survive it. He faced a death he couldn't escape. The worst part, of course, was never getting to see his beautiful wife again or meet and raise his unborn child. The next worse part was dying at the hand of Cord.

Cord continued to circle Hawk, feinting, jabbing, and inflicting damage. Then, as if sensing Hawk's weakness, he suddenly stepped forward and rained furious blows upon him. Hawk was barely able to keep up with parrying them.

Hawk was slow in bringing his cutlass back from his right side after a parry, and Cord quickly drew back and prepared to plunge his blade through the pirate captain's chest. Then, his shoulder suddenly twisted forward, and a gunshot rang out from somewhere behind him. He screamed as the blade dropped from his hand. Forgetting his foe, he glanced back over his shoulder. The sailors behind him had all turned to look back too.

Hawk saw what Cord and his crew were staring at—another ship on the other side of the *Congress*, mostly blocked by the sails and rigging. A tendril of smoke was still floating in front of the crow's nest on the new ship, barely visible between furled sails. Hawk took advantage of the miraculous distraction and thrust his blade toward Cord. The captain must have realized his mistake and quickly whirled around just as Hawk's blade transfixed him. He looked from the blade up to Hawk's blood-and-sweat-covered face, his mouth open but unable to speak. Hawk pulled his sword free, and Cord collapsed to his knees. A moment later, he fell forward dead onto the deck.

Hawk watched as the sailors were thrown into a state of shock and confusion. Apparently, they had to face a new pirate ship now, their muskets had been left behind on their ship, and their flintlocks had been fired. They had also tied their captain to the mainmast of the *Congress,* and the commodore was dead. Many sailors started rushing back to the *Congress*, while the remainder turned to see what Hawk and the pirates would do.

***

"Fire!" Lafitte yelled as soon as the deck of the *Congress* had filled with returning sailors.

From this angle, James couldn't see who had been shot from the crow's nest. He knew Hawk and Cord had been in a duel and hoped Cord lay dead. The sloop was almost at point-blank range to the frigate when the five cannons fired into its side. The sloop sat much lower in the water, and the cannons were angled down. There was only one way to defeat a ship that big with only five shots and not enough pirates to reload.

As the sailors arrived back on the *Congress*, some went for the muskets, while others poured down through the hatches to prepare the cannons. Suddenly, explosions ripped through the side of their ship as the cannons erupted from the sloop. The sloop had fired explosive shot into the hull from extremely close range. The first four explosions opened up huge holes in the hull and caused powerful blasts in the hold. The fire from those shots, and the water rushing in, might have been enough to sink the ship. But the fifth ball found the magazine. One explosion turned into another, and soon a series of explosions ripped through the ship.

***

Hawk and his crew had resumed the battle with the pirates when he heard the explosions on the *Congress*. The sailors turned in horror to see the fireballs tear through the other ship. They froze and gaped, forgetting about the pirates behind them.

Hawk motioned for everyone to retreat back to the *Anna*. Quickly, they climbed over the rail and slid down the grappling lines back to their ship, Hawk last to arrive. "Push off and hoist the sails!" He shouted hoarsely.

The anchor line and grappling lines were quickly cut, and the sails furled. Only a dozen pirates had made it back to the *Anna*, not enough to load and fire the cannons below. The wind had started to shift during the battle, but the sails still caught enough to start the schooner moving down the length of the frigate. The pirates were too tired to cheer, and all looked shocked to have survived. If they cleared the stern of the *Avenger*, they were free. Hawk wasn't sure who had shot Cord or to whom the other ship belonged, but he would find out soon.

They never cleared the hull of the *Avenger*. Hawk stared in horror as the cannons fired on the ship beside them. The sound was deafening, and the air erupted in a cloud of fire, shrapnel, and debris. He turned and sprinted toward the far rail. Pain exploded in the back of his head just as he left his feet to dive overboard. Blackness took him even before he felt the cold water.

***

James helped lower the longboat from Lafitte's sloop. They had been too close when the magazine on the *Congress* blew, and their ship had nearly capsized and was now ablaze. Flying pieces of wood and debris had killed several pirates and seriously wounded others. They had just enough time for the ones who could still walk to climb into the longboat before the sloop sank. Only seven of them remained now.

They started rowing around the Congress's sinking remains to determine the fate of Hawk and his crew. They had heard the cannons fire from the *Avenger* and had seen it set sail and limp slowly away, so they knew it was not likely to be good news. James studied a thin pirate with a large floppy hat and long, loose cloak. He was the one who'd fired the musket from the crow's nest and the last to climb aboard the longboat.

"Did you kill Cord?"

"No. I hit him in the back of the shoulder but caused him to drop his weapon and turn to look at me. Hawk finished him off."

James's mouth dropped open when he heard the feminine voice of the speaker—a voice he knew. He glanced at Lafitte, who merely grinned and shrugged. The pirate removed the floppy hat, letting her long brown hair fall about her shoulders.

"Anna," said James.

***

Hawk vaguely knew he was floating, and it was dark and silent. He wondered if he was finally dead. He didn't know how long he floated or if he floated in the water, in the air, or somewhere in the heavens above. After some time, he saw a faint, blurry glow. The blur began to clear, and the glow came into focus.

He heard voices, either coming from a great distance or significantly muffled. The glow slowly materialized into a pale face. He blinked a few times and realized it was Anna. She smiled at him—her warm, sweet smile. She spoke, but her words were too muffled to understand. He noticed her clothing in the dim light and realized she was dressed as a pirate. He accepted that this must be death. He tried to tell Anna he loved her one last time but wasn't sure if he actually spoke. Anna's face blurred again, the glow faded, and darkness reclaimed him.

CHAPTER XXXIII

"The end."

"The end?" the young blonde-haired boy asked in dismay. "Did the Hawk live? Did Anna have her baby? What happened to James? And Billy and Jack and Lafitte and the other pirates?"

The man laid the large hardbound book, *The Last Pirate*, on the table beside the rocking chair. He looked down at the six-year-old boy on his lap and laughed. "That, young Peter, is for you and your imagination to decide."

"Awe! I bet they did. I bet the Hawk and Lafitte are still out there capturing ships!"

"Now, Peter, there are no more pirates," a woman said, entering the room from the kitchen.

Peter climbed off the man's lap and ran over to hug her legs. He looked up and flashed a mischievous grin. "Wait till I get big, mother! I'll be Peter the Pirate King!"

"You'll do no such thing! Now go get ready for bed, or you'll be Peter, the red-bottomed young boy!"

Peter put his hands behind his back, covering his bottom, and ran squealing down the hall to his bedroom.

"Do you think he might be a little young for that story?" she asked the seated man, shaking her head and failing to suppress a slight grin at Peter's antics.

"I'm beginning to wonder," the man replied, chuckling. "At least we're in Tennessee and not close to the sea or a ship. He's the spitting image of his father, though. The memories he conjures up...."

"Don't you think he'll get suspicious of our names being in

the book when he gets older?" Anna asked.

"I bet his little head is pondering that right now. If only his father was here to go explain it to him," James replied.

Anna nodded silently.

"Explain what to him?" Henry asked, walking in the front door of the house. He carried a musket over one shoulder and a pair of grouse in the other hand. He held the grouse up in front of him. "A hard day of farming, followed by a successful hunt. Life is good!"

Fact vs. Fiction and Glossary of Terms

Much research went into the creation of *Blood Tides*, and a considerable amount of actual history was woven into the fictional tale. Please visit my website for a Fact vs. Fiction section. I've also included a Glossary of Terms. Some terms didn't make the final version of the manuscript, but you might find them interesting if you enjoyed the story.

http://www.crsturgill.com/

FOR MORE INFORMATION & UPDATES:

Follow on Facebook
https://www.facebook.com/crsturgillauthor/

Visit Website
http://www.crsturgill.com/

Other Books by C.R. Sturgill:

Fantasy World

Dreams from the Heart: Tales of Hope & Love